# DOUGLAS KENNEDY

# Five Days

HUTCHINSON
LONDON

Published by Hutchinson 2013

6 8 10 9 7

Hutchinson
Random House, 20 Vauxhall Bridge Road,
London SW1V 2SA

www.randomhouse.co.uk

Addresses for companies within The Random House Group Limited can be found at:
www.randomhouse.co.uk

The Random House Group Limited Reg. No. 954009

A CIP catalogue record for this book
is available from the British Library

ISBN 9780091795825

The Random House Group Limited supports The Forest Stewardship
Council (FSC®), the leading international forest certification organisation.
Our books carrying the FSC label are printed on FSC® certified paper.
FSC is the only forest certification scheme endorsed by the leading
environmental organisations, including Greenpeace.
Our paper procurement policy can be found at
www.randomhouse.co.uk/environment

Typeset in Adobe Garamond by Palimpsest Book Production Limited,
Falkirk, Stirlingshire
Printed and bound by CPI Group
(UK) Ltd, Croydon, CR0 4YY

For Christine

'Hope is the thing with feathers
That perches in the soul,
And sings the tune without the words,
And never stops at all.'

– Emily Dickinson

# Thursday

*One*


I SAW THE cancer immediately. It was right there in front of me. As always, I found myself taking a sharp intake of breath as the realization hit: I am looking at the beginning of the end.

The cancer was shaped like a dandelion. Sometimes this sort of tumor looks like a cheap Christmas decoration – a five-and-dime star with ragged edges. This specific one was more like a minor-looking flower that had been denuded, stripped down to its seeds, but with an insidious, needle-like design. What radiologists call a 'spiculated structure'.

*Spiculated.* When I heard that word for the first time I had to look it up. Discovered its origins were actually zoological: a spicule being 'a small needle-like structure, in particular any of those making up the skeleton of a sponge' (I'd never realized that sponges have skeletons). But there was an astronomical meaning as well: a short-lived jet of gas in the sun's corona.

This last definition nagged at me for weeks. Because it struck me as so horribly apt. A spiculated cancer – like the one I was looking at right now – might have commenced its existence years, decades earlier. But only once it makes its presence known does it become something akin to the burst of flame that combusts everything in its path, demanding total attention. If the flame hasn't been spotted and extinguished early enough, it will then decide that it isn't a mere fiery jet stream; rather, a mini supernova which, in its final show of pyrotechnic force, will destroy the universe which contains it.

Certainly the spiculated species I was now looking at was well on its way to exploding – and, in doing so, ending the life of the person within whose lung it was now so lethally embedded.

Another horror to add to the ongoing catalog of horrors which are, in so many ways, the primary decor of my nine-to-five life.

And this day was turning out to be a doozy. Because, an hour before the spiculated cancer appeared on the screen in front of me,

I had run a CT scan on a nine-year-old girl named Jessica Ward. According to her chart she'd been having a series of paralyzing headaches. Her physician had sent her to us in order to rule out any 'neurological concerns' . . . which was doctor shorthand for 'brain tumour'. Jessica's dad was named Chuck; a quiet, hangdog man in his mid-thirties, with sad eyes and the sort of yellowing teeth that hint at a serious cigarette habit. He said that he was a welder at the Bath Iron Works.

'Jessie's ma left us two years ago,' he told me as his daughter went into the dressing area we have off the cat scan room to change into a hospital gown.

'She died?' I asked.

'I wish. The bitch – 'scuse my French – ran off with a guy she worked with at the Rite Aid Pharmacy in Brunswick. They're livin' in some trailer down in Bestin. That's on the Florida Panhandle. Know what a friend of mine told me they call that part of the world down there? The Redneck Riviera. Jessie's headaches started after her ma vanished. And she's never once been back to see Jessie. What kind of mother is that?'

'She's obviously lucky to have a dad like you,' I said, trying to somewhat undercut the terrible distress this man was in – and the way he was working so hard to mask his panic.

'She's all I got in the world, ma'am.'

'My name's Laura,' I said.

'And if it turns out that what she has is, like, serious . . . and doctors don't send young girls in for one of these scans if they think it's nothing . . .'

'I'm sure your physician is just trying to rule things out,' I said, hearing my practiced neutral tone.

'You're taught to say stuff like that, aren't you?' he said, his tone displaying the sort of anger that I've so often seen arising to displace a great fear.

'Actually, you're right. We are trained to try to reassure and not say much. Because I'm a technologist, not a diagnostic radiologist.'

'Now you're using big words.'

'I'm the person who operates the machinery, takes the pictures.

The diagnostic radiologist is the doctor who will then look at the scan and see if there is anything there.'

'So when can I talk to him?'

*You can't* was the actual answer – because the diagnostic radiologist is always the behind-the-scenes man, analyzing the scans, the X-rays, the MRIs, the ultrasounds. But he rarely ever meets the patient.

'Dr Harrild will be talking directly to Jessica's primary-care physician – and I'm sure you'll be informed very quickly if there is—'

'Do they also teach you to talk like a robot?'

As soon as this comment was out of his mouth, the man was all contrite.

'Hey, that was kind of wrong of me, wasn't it?'

'Don't worry about it,' I said, maintaining a neutral tone.

'Now you're all hurt.'

'Not at all. Because I know how stressful and worrying this all must be for you.'

'And now you're reading the script again that they taught you to read.'

At that moment Jessica appeared out of the changing room, looking shy, tense, bewildered.

'This gonna hurt?' she asked me.

'You have to get an injection that is going to send an ink into your veins in order for us to be able to see what's going on inside of you. But the ink is harmless.'

'And the injection?' she asked, her face all alarmed.

'Just a little prick in your arm and then it's behind you.'

'You promise?' she asked, trying hard to be brave, yet still so much the child who didn't fully understand why she was here and what these medical procedures were all about.

'You be a real soldier now, Jess,' her father said, 'and we'll get you that Barbie you want on the way home.'

'Now that sounds like a good deal to me,' I said, wondering if I was coming across as too cheerful and also knowing that – even after sixteen years as an RT – I still dreaded all procedures involving children. Because I always feared what I might see before anyone else. And because I so often saw terrible news.

'This is just going to take ten, fifteen minutes, no more,' I told Jessica's father. 'There's a waiting area just down the walkway with coffee, magazines . . .'

'I'm goin' outside for a bit,' he said.

'That's 'cause you want a cigarette,' Jessica said.

Her father suppressed a sheepish smile.

'My daughter knows me too well.'

'I don't want my daddy dead of cancer.'

At that moment her father's face fell – and I could see him desperately trying to control his emotions.

'Let's let your dad get a little air,' I said, steering Jessica further into the scan room, then turning back to her father who had started to cry.

'I know how hard this is,' I said. 'But until there is something to be generally concerned about . . .'

He just shook his head and made for the door, fumbling in his shirt pocket for his cigarettes.

As I turned back inside I saw Jessica looking wide-eyed and afraid in the face of the CT scanner. I could understand Jessica's concern. It was a formidable piece of medical machinery, stark, ominous. There was a large hoop, attached to two science-fiction-style containers of inky fluid. In front of the hoop was a narrow bed that was a bit like a bier (albeit with a pillow). I'd seen adults panic at the sight of the thing. So I wasn't surprised that Jessica was daunted by it all.

'I have to go into that?' she said, eyeing the door as if she wanted to make a run for it.

'It's nothing, really. You lie on the bed there. The machine lifts you up into the hoop. The hoop takes pictures of the things the doctor needs pictures of . . . and that's it. We'll be done in a jiffy.'

'And it won't hurt?'

'Let's get you lying down first,' I said, leading her to the bed.

'I really want my daddy,' she said.

'You'll be with your daddy in just a few minutes.'

6

'You promise?'

'I promise.'

She got herself onto the bed.

I came over, holding a tube attached to the capsule containing all that inky liquid, covering with my hand the intravenous needle still encased in its sterilized packaging. Never show a patient an IV needle. Never.

'All right, Jessica. I'm not going to tell you a big fib and say that getting a needle put into your arm is going to be painless. But it will just last a moment and then it will be behind you. After that, no pain at all.'

'You promise.'

'I promise – though you might feel a little hot for a few minutes.'

'But not like I'm burning up.'

'I can assure you you'll not feel that.'

'I want my daddy . . .'

'The sooner we do this, the sooner you'll be with him. Now here's what I want you to do . . . I want you to close your eyes and think of something really wonderful. You have a pet you love, Jessica?'

'I have a dog.'

'Eyes closed now, please.'

She did as instructed.

'What kind of dog is he?'

'A cocker spaniel. Daddy got him for my birthday.'

I swabbed the crook of her arm with a liquid anesthetic.

'The needle going in yet?' she asked.

'Not yet, but you didn't tell me your dog's name.'

'Tuffy.'

'And what's the silliest thing Tuffy ever did?'

'Ate a bowlful of marshmallows.'

'How did he manage to do that?'

'Daddy had left them out on the kitchen table, 'cause he loves roasting them in the fireplace during Christmas. And then, out of nowhere, Tuffy showed up and . . .'

Jessica started to giggle. That's when I slipped the needle in her arm. She let out a little cry, but I kept her talking about her dog as I used tape to hold it in place. Then, telling her I was going to step out of the room for a few minutes, I asked:

'Is the needle still hurting?'

'Not really, but I can feel it there.'

'That's normal. Now, I want you to lie very still and take some very deep breaths. And keep your eyes closed and keep thinking about something funny like Tuffy eating those marshmallows. Will you do that for me, Jessica?'

She nodded, her eyes firmly closed. I left the scan room as quietly and quickly as I could, moving into what we call the technical room. It's a booth with a bank of computers and a swivel chair and an extended control panel. Having prepped the patient I was now about to engage in what is always the trickiest aspect of any scan: getting the timing absolutely right. As I programed in the data necessary to start the scan I felt the usual moment of tension that, even after all these years, still accompanies each of these procedures: a tension that is built around the fact that, from this moment on, timing is everything. In a moment I will hit a button. It will trigger the high-speed injection system that will shoot 80 milligrams of high-contrast iodine into Jessica's veins. After that I have less than fifty seconds – more like forty-two seconds, given her small size – to start the scan. The timing here is critical. The iodine creates a contrast that allows the scan to present a full, almost circular image of all bone and soft tissue and internal organs. But the iodine first goes to the heart, then enters the pulmonary arteries and the aorta before being disseminated into the rest of the body. Once it is everywhere you have reached the Venus phase of the procedure – when all veins are freshly enhanced with the contrast. Begin the scan a few critical seconds before the Venus phase and you will be scanning ahead of the contrast – which means you will not get the images that the radiologist needs to make a thorough and accurate diagnosis. Scan too late and the contrast might be too great. If I fail to get the timing right the patient will have to go through the entire procedure again twelve hours later (at the very minimum) – and the radiologist will not be pleased. Which is why there is always a moment of tension and doubt that consumes me in these crucial seconds before every scan. Have I prepped everything correctly? Have I judged the relationship between the diffusion of the iodine and the patient's physique? Have I left anything to chance?

I fear mistakes in my work. Because they count. Because they hurt people who are already frightened and dealing with the great unknown that is potential illness.

I especially fear moments when I have a child on that table, that bier. Because if the news is bad, if the images that emerge on the screen in front of me point up something catastrophic . . .

Well, I always absorb it, always assume a mask of professional neutrality. But children . . . children with cancers . . . it still pierces me. Being a mom makes it ten times worse. Because I am always thinking: Say it was Ben or Sally? Even though they are now both in their teens, both beginning to find their way in the world, they will always remain my kids – and, as such, the permanent open wound. That's the curious thing about my work. Though I present to my patients, my colleagues, my family, an image of professional detachment – Sally once telling a friend who'd come over after school: 'My mom looks at tumors all day and always keeps smiling . . . how weird is that?' – recently it has all begun to unsettle me. Whereas in the past I could look at every type of internal calamity on my screens and push aside the terribleness that was about to befall the person on the table, over the past few months I've found it has all started to clog up my head. Just last week I ran a mammogram on a local schoolteacher who works at the same middle school that Sally and Ben attended, and who, I know, finally got married a year ago and told me with great excitement how she'd gotten pregnant at the age of forty-one. When I saw that nodule embedded in her left breast and could tell immediately it was Stage Two (something Dr Harrild confirmed later), I found myself driving after work down to Pemaquid Point and heading out to the empty beach, oblivious to the autumn cold, and crying uncontrollably for a good ten minutes, wondering all the time why it was only now so getting to me.

That night, over dinner with Dan, I mentioned that I had run a mammogram on someone my own age today (this being a small town, I am always absolutely scrupulous about never revealing the names of the patients who I've seen). 'And when I saw the lump on the screen and realized it was cancerous I had to take myself off somewhere because I kind of lost it.'

'What stage?' he asked.

I told him.

'Stage Two isn't Stage Four, right?' Dan said.

'It still might mean a mastectomy, especially the way the tumor is abutting the lymph nodes.'

'You're quite the doctor,' he said, his tone somewhere between complimentary and ironic.

'The thing is, this isn't the first time I've lost it recently. Last week there was this sad little woman who works as a waitress up at some diner on Route 1 and who had this malignancy on her liver. And again I just fell apart.'

'You're being very confessional tonight.'

'What do you mean by that?'

'Nothing, nothing,' he said, but again with a tone that – like much to do with Dan right now – was so hard to read.

Dan is Dan Warren. My husband of twenty-one years. A man who has been out of work for the past twenty-one very long months. And someone whose moods now swing wildly. As in, having just made that somewhat catty comment he followed it up with:

'Hey, even the best fighter pilots lose their nerve from time to time.'

'I'm hardly a fighter pilot.'

'But you're the best RT on the staff. Everyone knows that.'

*Except me.* And certainly not now, positioning myself in front of the bank of computer screens, staring out at Jessica on the table, her eyes tightly shut, a discernible tremor on her lips, her face wet with tears. A big part of me wanted to run in and comfort her.

But I also knew it would just prolong the agony; that it was best to get this behind her. So clicking on the microphone that is connected to a speaker in the scan room, I said:

'Jessica, I know this is all very spooky and strange. But I promise you that the rest of the procedure will be painless – and it will all be over in just a few minutes. OK?'

She nodded, still crying.

'Now shut your eyes and think about Tuffy and . . .'

I hit the button that detonated the automatic injection system. As I did so a timer appeared on one of the screens – and I turned my vision immediately to Jessica, her cheeks suddenly very red as the iodine contrast hit her bloodstream and raised her body temperature by two degrees. The scan program now kicked in, as the bed was mechanically raised upwards. Jessica shuddered as this first vertical movement startled her. I grabbed the microphone:

'Nothing to worry about, Jessica. Just please keep very still.'

To my immense relief she did exactly as instructed. The bed reached a level position with the circular hoop. Twenty-four seconds had elapsed. The bed began to shift backwards into the hoop. Thirty-two seconds when it halted, the hoop encircling her small head.

'OK, Jessica – you're doing great. Just don't move.'

Thirty-six seconds. Thirty-eight. My finger was on the scan button. I noticed it trembling. Forty-one. And . . .

I pressed it. The scan had started. There was no accompanying noise. It was silent, imperceptible to the patient. Instinctually I shut my eyes, then opened them immediately as the first images appeared on the two screens in front of me, showing the left and right spheres of the brain. Again I snapped my eyes shut, unable to bear the shadow, the discoloration, the knotty tubercle that my far too-trained eye would spot immediately and which would tear me apart.

But professionalism trumped fear. My eyes sprang open. And in front of me I saw . . .

Nothing.

Or, at least, that's what my first agitated glance showed me.

Nothing.

I now began to scrutinize the scan with care – my eyes following every contour and hidden crevasse in both cerebral hemispheres, like a cop scouring all corners of a crime scene, looking for some hidden piece of evidence that might change the forensic picture entirely.

Nothing.

I went over the scan a third time, just to cover my tracks, make certain I hadn't overlooked anything, while simultaneously ensuring that the contrast was the correct level and the imaging of the standard that Dr Harrild required.

Nothing.

I exhaled loudly, burying my face in my hand, noticing for the first time just how rapidly my heart was pounding against my chest. The relief that Jessica's brain showed no signs of anything sinister was enormous. But the very fact that my internal stress meter had shot into the deep red zone . . . this troubled me. Because it made me wonder: Is this what happens when, over the years, you've forced yourself to play a role that you privately know runs contrary to your true nature; when the mask you've worn for so long no longer fits and begins to hang lopsidedly, and you fear people are going to finally glimpse the scared part of you that you have so assiduously kept out of view?

Nothing.

I took another steadying breath, telling myself I had things to be getting on with. So I downloaded this first set of scans to Dr Harrild – whose office was just a few steps away from the CT room. I also simultaneously dispatched them into the PACS system – that's the Picture Archiving and Communication System – which is the central technological storage area in Portland for our region of the state (known by its code name, Maine 1). All scans and X-rays must, by law, be kept in a PACS system for future reference and to ensure they are never mixed up, misplaced, assigned to the wrong patient. It also means that if a radiologist or oncologist needs to call up a specific set of patient scans – or compare them with others on file – they can be accessed with the double-click of a mouse.

The images dispatched, I began running a second set of scans to have as back-up, to compare contrast levels, and to double-check that the imaging hadn't missed anything. Usually, if the scans in the first set are clear, I relax about the second go-around. But today I heard a little voice whispering at me: 'Say you got it all wrong the first time . . . say you missed the tumor entirely.'

I grabbed the mike.

'Just a few more minutes, Jessica. And you have been just terrific. So keep lying still and . . .'

The second scan now filled the two screens. I stared ahead, fully expecting to see proof of my corroding professionalism in front of me as a concealed nodule appeared in some ridge of her cerebellum. But again . . .

Nothing.

That's the greatest irony of my work. Good news is all predicated on the discovery of nothing. It must be one of the few jobs in the world where 'nothing' provides satisfaction, relief, the reassertion of the status quo.

A final scan of the scan.

Nothing.

I hit the 'send' button. Off went this second set of scans to Dr Harrild and the PACS storage centre. I picked up the mike again and told Jessica we were done, but she would have to remain very still as the bed was brought back to ground level again.

Ten minutes later, dressed again and sucking on a lollipop, Jessica was reunited with her father. As I brought her into the waiting room, where he sat slumped, anxious, he was immediately on his feet, trying to read me the way a man on trial tries to read the faces of the jurors filing back into court with a verdict already cast in stone. Jessica ran over to him, throwing her arms around him.

'Look, I got four lollipops,' she said, holding up the three untouched ones in her hand and pointing to the one in her mouth.

'You deserve them,' I said, 'because you were such a brave, good patient. You would have been proud of her, sir.'

'I'm always proud of my daughter,' he said, picking her up and putting her on a bench, asking her to sit there for a moment, 'while this nice lady and I have a talk.'

Motioning for me to follow him outside into the brisk autumn morning, he asked me the question I always know is coming after a scan:

'Did you see anything?'

'I'm certain the diagnostic radiologist, Dr Harrild, will be in contact with your primary-care physician this afternoon,' I said, cognizant of the fact that I also sounded like a scripted automaton.

'But you saw the scans, you know—'

'Sir, I am not a trained radiologist – so I cannot offer a professional opinion.'

'And I don't design the ships I work on, but I can tell when something's wrong if I see it in front of me. Because I have years of on-the-job experience. Just like you. So you now know, before anyone, if there is a tumor in my daughter's head.'

'Sir, you need to understand – I can neither legally nor ethically offer my opinion on the scans.'

'Well, there's a first time for everything. Please, ma'am. I'm begging you. I've got to know what you know.'

'Please understand, I am sympathetic . . .'

'I want an answer.'

'And I won't give you one. Because if I tell you good news and it turns out not to be good news . . .'

That startled him.

'Are you telling me there's good news?'

This is a strategy I frequently use when the scans show nothing, but the diagnostic radiologist has yet to study them and give them the all-clear. I cannot say what I think – because I don't have the medical qualifications. Even though my knowledge of such things is quite extensive those are the hierarchical rules and I accept them. But I can, in my own way, try to calm fears when, I sense, there is clinical evidence that they are ungrounded.

'I'm telling you that I cannot give you the all-clear. That is Dr Harrild's job.'

'But you think it's "all-clear".'

I looked at him directly.

'I'm not a doctor. So if I did give you the all-clear I'd be breaking the rules. Do you understand, sir?'

He lowered his head, smiling, yet also fighting back tears.

'I get it . . . and thank you. Thank you so much.'

'I hope the news is good from Dr Harrild.'

Five minutes later I was knocking on Dr Harrild's door.

'Come in,' he shouted.

Patrick Harrild is forty years old. He's tall and lanky and has a fuzzy beard. He always dresses in a flannel shirt from L.L.Bean, chinos, and brown desert boots. When he first arrived here three years ago, some unkind colleagues referred to him as 'the geek' – because he isn't exactly the most imposing or outwardly confident of men. In fact he does veer towards a reserve which many people falsely read as timidity. Before Dr Harrild the resident diagnostic radiologist was an old-school guy named Peter Potholm. He always came across as God the Father, intimidated all underlings, and would happily become unpleasant if he felt his authority was being challenged. I was always ultra-polite and professional with him – while simultaneously letting him play the role of Absolute Monarch in our little world. I got along with Dr Potholm, whereas three of the RTs actually left during his fourteen-year tenure (which ended when age finally forced him to retire). Dr Harrild couldn't have been more different than 'Pope Potholm' (as the hospital staff used to refer to him). Not only is he unfailingly polite and diffident, he also asks opinions of others. But he did quietly engineer a staff member's early retirement when she messed up five scans in a row. He's a very decent and reasonable man, Dr Harrild – and an absolutely first-rate diagnostician. The diffidence and the slight social awkwardness mask reinforced steel.

'Hey, Laura,' Dr Harrild said as I opened his office door. 'Good news on the Jessica Ward front. It looks very all-clear to me.'

'That is good news.'

'Unless, of course, you spotted something I didn't.'

Peter Potholm would have walked barefoot across hot coals

rather than ask the medical opinion of a lowly RT. Whereas Dr Harrild . . .

'I saw nothing worrying or sinister,' I said.

'Glad to hear it.'

'Would you mind talking to Jessica's father now? The poor man . . .'

'Is he in the waiting area?'

I nodded.

'We have Ethel Smythe in next, don't we?' he asked.

'That's right.'

'Judging by the shadow on her lung last time . . .'

He let the sentence hang there. He didn't need to finish it – as we had both looked at the X-ray I'd taken of Ethel Smythe's lungs a few days earlier. And we'd both seen the very sinister shadow that covered a significant corner of the upper left ventricle – a shadow which made Dr Harrild pick up the phone to Ethel Smythe's physician and tell him that a CT scan was urgently required.

'Anyway, I will go give Mr Ward the good news about his daughter.'

Fifteen minutes later I was prepping Ethel Smythe. She was a woman about my age. Divorced, No children. A cafeteria lady in the local high school. Significantly overweight. And a significant smoker, as in twenty a day for the past twenty-three years (it was all there on her chart).

She was also relentlessly chatty – trying to mask her nervousness during the X-ray with an ongoing stream of talk, all of which was about the many details of her life. The house she had up in Waldeboro which was in urgent need of a new roof, but which she couldn't afford. Her seventy-nine-year-old mother who never had a nice word for her. A sister in Michigan who was married to 'the meanest man this side of the Mississippi'. The fact that her physician, Dr Wesley, was 'a dreamboat, always so kind and reassuring', and how he told her he 'just wanted "to rule a few things out", and he said that to me in such a lovely, kind voice . . . well, there can't be anything wrong with me, can there?'

The X-ray said otherwise – and here she was, now changed into

16

the largest hospital gown we had, her eyes wild with fear, talking, talking, talking as she positioned herself on the table, wincing as I inserted the IV needle in her arm, telling me repeatedly:

'Surely it can't be anything. Surely that shadow Dr Wesley told me about was an error, wasn't it?'

'As soon as our diagnostic radiologist has seen the scan we'll be taking today—'

'But you saw the X-ray. And you don't think it's anything bad, do you?'

'I never said that, ma'am.'

'Please call me Ethel. But you would have told me if it had been bad.'

'That's not my role in all this.'

'Why can't you tell me everything is fine? Why?'

Her eyes were wet, her voice belligerent, angry. I put my hand on her shoulder.

'I know how frightening this all is. I know how difficult it is not knowing what is going on – and how being called back for a scan like this—'

'How can you know? How?'

I squeezed her shoulder.

'Ethel, please, let's just get this behind you and then—'

'They always told me it was a stupid habit. Marv – my ex-husband. Dr Wesley. Jackie – that's my sister. Always said I was dancing with death. And now . . .'

A huge sob rose in her throat.

'I want you to shut your eyes, Ethel, and concentrate on your breathing and—'

More sobs.

'I'm going to step away now and get all this underway,' I said. 'Just keep breathing slowly. And the scan will be finished before you—'

'I don't want to die.'

This last statement came out as a whisper. Though I'd heard, over the years, other patients utter this, the sight of this sad, frightened woman had me biting down on my lip and fighting tears . . . and yet again silently appalled at all this new-found vulnerability. Fortunately Ethel had her eyes firmly shut, so she couldn't see my distress. I hurried into the technical room. I reached for the microphone and asked Ethel to remain very still. I set the scan in motion. In the seconds before the first images appeared on the screen I snapped my eyes shut, opening them again to see . . .

Cancer. Spiculated in shape, and from what I could discern, already metastasized into the other lung and the lymphatic system.

Half an hour later Dr Harrild confirmed what I'd seen.

'Stage Four,' he said quietly. We both knew what that meant – especially with this sort of tumor in the lungs. Two to three months at best. As cancer deaths go, this one was never less than horrible.

'Where is she right now?' Dr Harrild asked.

'She insisted on going back to work,' I said, remembering how she'd told me she had to hurry back after the scan because the school lunch she'd be serving started at midday, and 'with all the cutbacks happening now I don't want to give my boss an excuse to fire me'.

Recalling this I felt myself getting shaky again.

'You OK, Laura?' Dr Harrild asked me, clearly studying me with care. Immediately I wiped my eyes and let the facade of steely detachment snap into place again.

'Fine,' I said, hearing the enforced crispness in my voice.

'Well,' he said, 'at least the little girl's news was good.'

'Yes, there's that.'

'All in a day's work, eh?'

'Yes,' I said quietly. 'All in a day's work.'

## *Two*

PEMAQUID POINT. A short stretch of sand – no more than a quarter-mile long – facing the open waters of the Atlantic. The 'point' is more of a cove: rocky, rugged, fringed on either side by vacation homes that are simple, but clearly upscale. Ostentation is never liked in this corner of Maine – so even those 'from away' (as anyone not born in the state is called) know better than to throw up the sort of garish shows of money that seem to be accepted elsewhere.

In Maine so much is kept out of sight.

I had the beach to myself. It was three-eighteen in the afternoon. A perfect October day. A hard blue sky. A hint of impending chill in the air. The light – already beginning to decrease wattage at this hour – still luminous. Maine. I've lived here all my life. Born here. Raised here. Educated here. Married here. All forty-two years I've had to date rooted in this one spot. How did that happen? How did I allow myself to stand so still? And why have so many people I know also talked themselves into limited horizons?

Maine. I come down to this point all the time. It's a refuge for me. Especially as it reminds me of the fact that I am surrounded by a natural beauty that never ceases to humble me. Then there is the sea. When I was in a book group we worked our way through *Moby-Dick* two years ago. A retired navy woman named Krystal Orr wondered out loud why so many writers seemed to be drawn to the sea as a metaphor for so much to do with life. I heard myself saying: 'Maybe it's because, when you're by the sea, life doesn't seem so limited. You're looking out at infinite possibilities.' To which Krystal added: 'And the biggest possibility of them all is the possibility of escape.'

Was that woman reading my mind? Isn't that what I was always thinking as I came out here and faced the Atlantic – the fact that there is a world beyond the one behind me now? When I looked out at the water my back was turned to all that was my life. I could dwell in the illusion of elsewhere.

But then there was the distinct *bing* of my cellphone, bringing me back to the here-and-now, telling me that someone had just sent me a text.

Immediately I was scrambling in my bag for my phone, as I was certain that the text was from my son Ben.

Ben is nineteen; a sophomore at the University of Maine in Farmington. He's majoring in visual art there – a fact that drives my husband Dan just a little crazy. They've never been able to share much. We're all products of the forces that shaped us, aren't we? Dan was raised poor in Aroostook County; the son of a part-time lumberman who drank too much and never really knew how to spell the word r-e-s-p-o-n-s-i-b-i-l-i-t-y. But he also loved his son, even if he often thought nothing of lashing out at him while tanked. Dan grew up both adoring and fearing his dad – and always trying to be the tough outdoorsman that his father considered himself to be. The fact that Dan himself rarely touches alcohol – and looks askance at me if I dare to have a second glass of wine – speaks volumes about the lasting trauma of his dad's considerable drink-fueled furies. He privately knows his own father was a weak, cowardly little man who, like all bullies, used brutality to mask his own self-loathing. As such, I've tried to talk to Dan on many occasions about the fact that he is a much better person than his father – and that he should extend his innate decency to his son, whatever about their polar differences. It's not as if Dan is in any way cruel or hostile towards Ben. He shows only nominal interest in him, and refuses to explain to me why he treats his only son as a stranger.

Only recently, after Ben was written up in the *Portland Phoenix* as a young artist to watch – on the basis of a collage he had exhibited at the Portland Museum of Art, which turned 'the deconstructed remnants' of lobster pots into 'a chilling vision of modern incarceration' (or, at least, that's what the critic in the *Phoenix* called it), Dan asked me if I thought Ben was, in any way, 'disturbed'? I tried to mask my horror at this question, instead asking: 'What on earth makes you think that?'

'Well, just look at that damn collage which all those smarty-pants down in Portland think is so fantastic.'

'People respond to the piece because it is provocative, and uses something indigenous to Maine – a lobster pot – as a way of—'

'*"Indigenous"*,' Dan said with a decided sneer. 'You and your big words again.'

'Why are you being so hurtful?'

'I'm just voicing an opinion. But go on and tell me I'm shooting my mouth off again. And this is the reason I'm still out of work twenty-one months after—'

'Unless you were keeping something from me, you didn't lose your job for saying the sort of inappropriate things you're saying now.'

'So I'm also inappropriate, am I? Unlike our "brilliant" son. Maine's next Picasso.'

Ever since he'd lost his job Dan had begun to increasingly display flashes of unkindness. Though an apology for this last harsh comment was immediately forthcoming ('There I go again, and I really don't know why you put up with me') the effect was, yet again, corrosive. Even if these momentary lapses only arose twice a month, they were coupled with the way Dan was increasingly withdrawing into himself – and refusing to share any of the under-standable anger he felt about being laid off. The result was that things just seemed askew at home. I can't say ours was ever the most romantic or passionate of marriages (not that I had anything since my marriage to compare it to). But we had rubbed along for years in a reasonable, stable way. Until the lay-off that suddenly opened up a dark recess which seemed to grow larger with each ensuing month when Dan was stuck at home, wondering if his career would ever be resuscitated again.

What I sensed most unsettled Dan now about his son was the fact that he was, at the age of nineteen, already getting recognition for his work. To be chosen to exhibit in the Young Maine Artists show at the Portland Museum of Art, to be just one of two college students included in the exhibition, to have a critic call him innovative and a talent to watch . . . All right, I know my maternal pride is talking here. But still it's quite an achievement. And Ben is such a thoughtful, considerate, and wonderfully quirky young

21

man – and one who just wants his father's love and approval. But Dan simply can't see that. Instead, from hints dropped here and there, it's clear that he's quietly uncomfortable with the fact that the boy he always wrote off as different, weird, not the sort of son he expected, is very much coming into his own – and being publicly praised for that. I often tell myself that once Dan finds a good job again, all will be well. Just as I simultaneously think: If only an instant fix could change everything.

*Bing.*

More pips, informing me that this newly arrived text was demanding my attention. I now had the phone in my hand and was squinting at the screen, the sunlight blurring the message. Cupping my hand around it I could make out the following words:

**Please call me now . . . Ben**

Immediately I felt anxiety coursing everywhere within me. The same anxiety that now hits whenever Ben sends me one of these messages. My son is currently in a somewhat dark place. From the outside – if you just look objectively at the facts – it might seem like much ado about a silly romance. Nine months ago Ben met a young woman named Allison Fell. Like him she's studying visual art at Farmington. Her father is a big-deal lawyer in Portland. They live in one of those big houses that hug the coast in Cape Elizabeth – the most exclusive suburb of the city. I gather that her parents were wildly disappointed when she didn't get into a variety of ultra-prestigious colleges ('I was never that into studying,' she told me) and had to 'make do' with U Maine Farmington (which has actually become quite a respected liberal arts college, despite the State U tag). She's relatively pretty and seriously bohemian; the sort of nineteen-year-old who dresses all the time in black, keeps her long nails also painted black, and wears her elbow-length black hair in an elaborate braid. I often think she targeted Ben because he was the most talented of the small group of young visual artists at Farmington and because he was so 'cute and vulnerable'. For Ben, the fact that this very outgoing, very confident, very flamboyant, rather rich young woman wanted him . . . well, considering how in high school he was girlfriend-less

and often considered himself 'something of a freak', he was just completely overwhelmed by Allison's desire for him. Just as I'm pretty sure she also introduced him to the pleasures of sex.

All this started in January of this year – though Ben told me nothing about it until Easter when he was back from college. He asked if we could go out to Moody's Diner for lunch. There, over grilled cheese sandwiches, he informed me, in such a shy, hesitating way, that he'd met someone. His difficulty in articulating this – the way he also said, 'Please don't tell Dad. I don't think he'll like her' – filled my heart with such love and worry for him. Because I could see that he was in an unknown territory and rather deluged by it all.

'What do you feel exactly for Allison?' I asked him at the time.

'I want to marry her,' he blurted out, then blushed a deep red.

'I see,' I said, trying to sound as neutral as possible. 'And does Allison want this?'

'Absolutely. She said I am the love of her life.'

'Well . . . that's lovely. Truly lovely. But . . . you've been together how long?'

'Ninety-one days.'

'I see,' I said again, thinking: *Oh my God, he knows the exact number of days and maybe even the exact number of hours.*

'First love is always so . . . surprising,' I said. 'You really cannot believe it. And while I certainly don't want to rain on your parade . . .'

*Oh God, why did I use that cliché?*

'. . . but . . . all I'm saying to you, is – how wonderful! Just give it all a little time.'

'I love her, Mom . . . and she loves me.'

'Well . . .'

There was so much I wanted to say . . . and so much I realized I couldn't say. Except:

'I'm so happy for you.'

We met Allison once. Poor Ben was so nervous, and Dan asked a lot of leading questions about how much seafrontage her parents had in Cape Elizabeth, and Allison was looking around our rather simple home and smiling to herself. Meanwhile I was trying to will everyone to relax and like each other, even if I knew this was downright impossible. I didn't like the way she was so deliberately tactile with Ben, stroking his thigh with her hand at one point in full view of both Dan and myself, whispering things in his ear (she may think herself a Goth, but she behaves like an adolescent), and playing on his evident neediness. All right, maybe I was being far too maternal/cautious – but what worried me most here was that Ben was so in love with being in love. How could I explain to him that sometimes we project onto others that which our heart so wants. As such, we aren't seeing the other person at all.

Dan told me after the dinner:

'She'll drop him like a hot potato the moment she's decided he's outlived his interest to her.'

'Maybe you should have a talk with him about—'

'About what? The kid never listens to me. And he finds me so damn conservative, so Republican . . .'

'Just talk with him, Dan. He really needs your support.'

To my husband's credit the next time Ben was home for a weekend from college they did spend much of the afternoon raking leaves in our garden and talking. Afterwards Ben said that his father seemed genuinely interested in knowing how he felt about Allison and just how serious it was. 'And he didn't lecture me about anything.'

Then, just six weeks ago, I got a phone call early one morning from the college. Ben had been found by a campus security officer in the middle of the night beneath a tree near his dormitory, oblivious to the pouring rain that had been cascading down for hours. He was brought to the college nurse, diagnosed with a bad chill (thank God it was only the tail end of August) and sent back to his dorm room. After that Ben refused to get out of bed, refused to speak with anyone. When this carried on for two days his roommate did the smart thing and alerted the college authorities. A doctor was called to Ben's bedside. When he didn't respond to the doctor's entreaties to speak or even make eye contact with him Ben was transferred to the psychiatric wing of the local hospital.

That's when Dan and I both rushed up to Farmington. When we reached the infirmary and Ben saw us, he turned away, hiding his head under a pillow, refusing to engage whatsoever with us, despite the nurse on duty asking him to at least acknowledge his parents' presence in the room.

I was doing my best to keep my emotions in check, but Dan actually had to leave the ward he was so upset. I found him outside, smoking one of the three cigarettes he still smokes a day, his eyes welling up with tears, clearly so unsettled by the psychological state of his son. When I put my arms around him he briefly buried his head in my shoulder, then shrugged off my embrace, embarrassed by the outward sign of emotion. Rubbing his eyes, sucking in a deep lungful of smoke, he said:

'I want to kill that little rich bitch.'

I said nothing. Except:

'He'll be OK, he'll get through this.'

The psychiatrist on duty – a large, formidable woman named Dr Claire Allen – told us later that day:

'I suppose you are aware of the fact that Ben's girlfriend took up with someone else just a few days ago. My advice to you is to give him a little space right now. Let him start talking with me over the next few days. Let me help him find his way to an easier place – and then I'm certain he'll want to talk to you both.'

To Dr Allen's credit she phoned me every few days to update me on his progress – though she also informed me that the information she was providing me with was 'very generalized' so as not to breach patient/doctor confidentiality. As such she would never go into anything that was discussed during their sessions. To Dan's credit he was eager to hear all the developments from Farmington and seemed relieved to discover that Ben was talking and 'genuinely wants to get better' (to quote Dr Allen's direct words). He left the hospital after a week. But it was a full three weeks before Ben returned to classes and before Dr Allen gave us the all-clear to see him. On the day in question Dan had a first interview for that job in Augusta, so I went up on my own to the college. I met Dr Allen alone in her office. She pronounced herself pleased with

Ben's progress, telling me that, though still rather vulnerable, he seemed to have come to terms with what had befallen him and was having two sessions a week with her to 'talk through a lot of things'.

'I have to say that, without revealing too much of what Ben told me, he still does have a great deal to work through. I know all about him being chosen for that big exhibition in Portland. But like so many creative people he is also wracked by considerable doubt – especially when it comes to the issue of self-esteem. He has told me he is very close to you.'

'I like to think that,' I said, also noting her professional silence on the subject of his father.

'There's a sister, isn't there?'

'That's right, Sally.'

'They are rather different, aren't they?'

Understatement of the year. If Ben is creative and withdrawn and tentative about himself, yet also given to thinking outside the box, then Sally is his diametric opposite. She is wildly outgoing, wildly confident. Dan adores her, as she adores her dad – though his testiness has been getting to her recently. My own relationship with Sally is a little more complicated. Part of this, I think, has to do with the usual stuff that adolescent girls (she's seventeen) have with their moms. But the other part – the part that troubles me – stems from the fact that we are, in so many ways, such profoundly different people. Sally is Ms Popularity at her high school. She has worked hard at this role, as she truly cares about being liked. She is very all-American girl. Tall, clean-limbed, sandy-haired, always fresh-faced and well scrubbed, with great teeth. Her image means so much to her – to the point where she is already obsessively working out two hours a day and spends at least forty-five minutes every night ensuring that her face is blemish-free. She uses teeth-whitening strips to make certain that her smile is electrifying. No wonder she has half the football team chasing after her, though her current steady, Brad, is the school's baseball star pitcher. He's also something of a politician in the making who, I sense, sees Sally as nothing more than a very good-looking girl to have on his arm. Sally knows this too. When Brad was admitted early decision to Dartmouth a few weeks ago, I found her crying in our living room after school. In a rare moment, she confided in me:

'He'll be in that fancy Ivy League college in New Hampshire and I'll be up in Orono at stupid U Maine.'

'U Maine is where I went.'

'Yeah, but you could have gone anywhere you wanted to.'

'U Maine offered me a full scholarship. My parents didn't have any money and—'

'Well, if I had the grades to get into Dartmouth, would we have the money to—?'

'We would find the money,' I said, sounding a little tetchy on this subject, as Sally will sometimes bemoan the fact that we have to live so carefully right now – though, thankfully, she only targets me for these comments, as she knows it would devastate her father to hear his much-adored daughter going on about the lack of family capital. But she also chooses me to vent her frustration to about most things to do with her life – especially the fact that she wasn't born into a family of Wall Street big shots. For Sally there are always points of comparison. Brad's father made a lot of money opening a small chain of big box hardware stores around the state – but still decided to send his very ambitious youngest son to the local public school (I like that fact). Brad's parents live in a big waterfront house with all sorts of deluxe fittings (a sauna, a jacuzzi, an indoor gym, an outdoor pool, plasma televisions in every room). They now also have a home in 'an exclusive gated development' (Sally's exact words) near Tampa. She spent a week with Brad down at their Florida spread, and went out with Brad and his father on the family cabin cruiser. And Brad already has his very own 'cool' car: a Mini Cooper. And . . .

I truly love my daughter. I admire her optimism, her verve, her forward momentum. But I also wonder often what she's driving towards.

'I know Brad's going to drop me as soon as we graduate next summer and we both head to college. Because he thinks of me as his high-school fun, nothing more. And he's after somebody who can be a future senator's wife.'

'Is that what you want to be – a senator's wife?'

'Do I hear disappointment in your voice, Mom?'

'You never disappoint me, Sally.'

'I wish I could believe that.'

'I don't want you to be anything you don't want to be.'

'But you don't like the fact that I want to marry a man like Brad.'

*As opposed to specifically marrying Brad? Was that the underlying theme here – marrying a guy with money who has firmly planted himself on the career escalator marked 'Up'?*

'Everyone has their own agenda, their own aspirations,' I said.

'And there you go again, putting me down.'

'How is what I said putting you down?'

'Because my aspirations strike you as small. Because I am not going to do anything fantastic with my life . . .'

'You have many gifts, Sally.'

'You consider me shallow and vacuous and someone who, unlike you, never picks up a book.'

'You know that I think the world of you.'

'Ben is your favorite.'

'I consider you and Ben equally wonderful. And the thing is, you honestly have no idea what your life is going to turn out to be. Or where it will land you. Even when you think: "So this is what my life is now," well, things can change in an instant or two.'

'You think that because you look at other people's tumors all day.'

*Ouch.* I smiled tightly.

'Well . . . it does give me an interesting perspective on things.'

'I don't want to be a slave to routine.'

'Then don't be somebody's wife.'

There. I said it. Sally flinched, then shot back with:

'You're somebody's wife.'

'Yes, I am. But—'

'You don't have to complete the sentence, Mom. And I know if I were a really creative type like Ben . . .'

There are certain arguments with children that you simply cannot win.

*'There's a sister, isn't there?'*

*'That's right, Sally.'*

*'And they are rather different, aren't they?'*

I was snapped back into the here-and-now of Dr Allen's office.

'Sally is a rather different person to Ben,' I said, hopefully sounding neutral.

'Ben intimated that to me. Just as he intimated he feels closer to you than to his father.'

'Dan stills loves Ben.'

Dr Allen looked at me with care.

'I'm sure he does, in his own way,' she said. 'But let me ask you something, Laura – do you always feel the need to make things better?'

'Is there anything wrong with that?'

'It can be rather disheartening, can't it? I mean, other people's happiness – it's ultimately their own concern, isn't it? And that also includes your children at this point in their lives. You can't blame yourself for Ben's problems.'

'Easier said than done.'

Half an hour later I met Ben – as arranged by Dr Allen – at a café off campus. He'd lost a noticeable amount of weight – and he was already skinny before all this. His face still looked a little pasty. He let me hug him, but didn't respond in kind. He had difficulty looking at me directly during the half-hour that we spoke. At first, when I told him how well he looked, he said: 'Mom, you've never lied to me about anything . . . so please don't start now.' He then proceeded to ask me how things were going at home, whether his sister was 'still hung up on Mr Jock Republican' (I was very reassured to hear his natural acerbity hadn't vanished), and how he'd actually started a new canvas that was not a collage.

'It's a painting this time. So it doesn't contain body parts or try to replicate a car crash with me behind the wheel of a Porsche.'

'You mean, like James Dean?' I asked.

'My mother the Culturally Aware Technologist.'

'Not that culturally aware.'

'You just read more than anyone I know.'

'That's more of a hobby . . .'

'You should try and write, Mom.'

'What would I have to write about? I've not done anything that interesting or important with my life . . . outside of raising you and Sally.'

'You were under no obligation to add that.'

'But it's the truth.'

Ben reached out briefly to touch my arm.

'Thank you.'

'You look a little tired,' I said.

'I'm finally starting to sleep again without pills. But I'm still on other medication. Pills to keep me happy.'

'There's no real pill for that,' I said.

'Isn't that the truth,' Ben said with just the barest hint of a smile.

'But you seem stronger . . .'

'You're being far too nice again.'

'Would you rather me be far too mean?'

Another half-smile from Ben.

'You'd never pull it off,' he said.

'It's good to see you OK, Ben.'

'I'm sorry if I freaked you out.'

'You didn't freak me out.'

'Yeah, right . . .'

'OK, I was very concerned. So was your father . . .'

'But you're here today.'

'Your dad's got a job interview this morning.'

'That's good news. Because it's all such bad news with him now.'

'That's a little extreme, Ben. He loves you very much.'

'But we're not friends.'

'That will change.'

'Yeah, right.'

'At least *we're* friends,' I said.

Ben nodded.

'You're sure you're not angry at me?' he asked.

'I'm never angry at you.'

Upon returning home that evening from Farmington I wrote my son a text, informing him that, though I was always here for him day and night, I still wouldn't crowd him.

Take your time, know that I am always at the end of the phone – and can be with you in ninety minutes if you need me.

Since then, I've had at least two texts a day from Ben – often funny/ruminative (Do you think the only real broken hearts are in country and western songs?), sometimes troubled (Really bad night's sleep. Session with Dr Allen today), sometimes just a hello. Twice a week there'd always be a phone call. But still no indication that he wanted to spend a weekend at home, or wanted to see me.

Until . . .

*Bing.*

Staring out at the water from Pemaquid Point, my brain awash with so many thoughts, I dug out my cellphone and found myself reading:

Hey Mom. Want to finally get out of Dodge this weekend. Thinking maybe we could meet somewhere like Portland. A couple of good movies in town. We could also catch dinner somewhere. You up for this?

Damn. Damn. Damn. This would have to be the one weekend in literally nine years that I am going out of town. I texted back:

Hey Ben. Would love to do dinner and a movie Saturday . . . but I have that professional conference this weekend in Boston. I could try to get out of it . . .

His immediate reply:

Don't do that for me.

My immediate reply:

It's just a work thing. But you are more important than that.

31

And you never go anywhere – so let's push the night out to next weekend.

Now I'm feeling guilty.

You're always feeling guilty about something, Mom. Go run away for a few days – and try not to feel bad about it.

I stared at this last text long and hard. Thinking of a phrase my poor father invoked time and time again whenever considering the limitations he'd placed on his own life:

Easier said than done.

And considering my own personal condition, Ben's admonition genuinely unsettled me. Because the only response that came to mind was:

Easier said than done.

# Three

*. . . you never go anywhere . . .*

*Ouch.*

Though I know Ben didn't mean that comment to hurt it still did. Because it articulated an uncomfortable truth.

Walking back to my car, putting the key in the ignition, pulling out of the parking lot, the ocean now behind me, I turned left and followed the spindly, narrow road left, knowing it would curve its way past the summer homes now largely empty with autumn edging closer to winter's dark harshness, before veering right again and ascending a gentle hill lined with the homes of the peninsula's full-time residents. Outside the occasional artist or New Age reflexologist, the majority of the houses here are owned by people who teach school or sell insurance or work for the local fire brigade or have retired from the navy or the shipyard in Bath and are trying to get by on a pension and social security. These houses – many of which (like my own) could use several licks of paint – soon give way to open fields and the main route back west towards town. I mention all this because I have driven this stretch of road three, four times a week ever since Dan and I moved here years ago. Bar the two weeks a year when we have been out of town on vacation, the town of Damariscotta, Maine, has been the centre of everything in my life. Just recently the thought struck me: *I don't have a passport.* And the last time I left the country was way back in 1989, my senior year at the University of Maine, when I talked my then-boyfriend Dan to drive with me up to Quebec City for a long weekend. Back then you could still cross into Canada with an American driver's license. It was the Winter Carnival in Quebec City. Snow was everywhere. The streets of the Old City were cobbled. The architecture was gingerbread house. Everyone spoke French. I'd never seen anything so magical and foreign before. Even Dan – who was initially a little unnerved by the different language, the weird accent – became charmed by it all. Though the little hotel in which we spent those four happy days was a bit run-down and had a narrow double bed that creaked loudly every time we made love, it was a sublimely romantic time for us – and, I am pretty certain, the moment when I became pregnant with Ben. But before we knew that we were about to become parents – a discovery that changed the course of everything in our lives – Dan told me that we'd always go back to Quebec City. Just as we'd also visit Paris and London and Rio and . . .

One of the many naive pleasures of being young is telling yourself that life is an open construct; that your possibilities are limitless. Until you conspire to limit them.

*I have rooted myself to one spot.* This thought has been on my mind considerably. But, honestly, there is no anger towards Dan underlying this realization. Whatever about the other problems in our marriage, I don't blame him for the way my life has panned out. After all I was the co-conspirator in all this. It was my choice to marry him. I now see that I made certain huge decisions at a moment when my judgment was, at best, clouded. Is that how life so often works? Can your entire trajectory shift thanks to one hastily made resolution?

I hear these sorts of ruminative regrets frequently from patients. The smokers who are now ruing the day they took their first puff. The morbidly obese who wonder out loud why they have always needed to compulsively eat. Then there are the truly sad souls who are wondering if some chance tumor – with no direct link to what doctors like to refer as 'lifestyle' – is some sort of retribution (divine or otherwise) for bad behavior, accumulated sins, or an inability to find simple happiness in this one and only life that has been granted to them.

There was a time when these scan-room confessions – usually blurted out in moments of mortal terror, shadowed by the great fear of the unknown – were all in a day's work for me. Are they beginning to unnerve me because, in their own direct way, they are now forcing me to reflect on the ever-accelerating passage of time? For here we are again in October. And I am now in my forty-third year and still can't totally figure out how a year has simply vanished. My dad – who taught calculus at a high school in Waterville – once explained this to me with elegant simplicity a few years back, when I mentioned how one of the stranger aspects of impending middle age was the way a year was over in three blinks.

'And when you get to my age . . .' he said.

'*If* I get to your age.' (He was seventy-two back then.)

'Always the pessimist. But I guess it comes with your professional territory. OK, I will rephrase. *If* you get to my age . . . you will discover that a year passes in two blinks. And if I make it to, say, eighty-five, it will be, at best, a blink. And the reason is a simple mathematical formula – which has nothing to do with Euclidian precepts, and more with the law of diminishing returns. Remember when you were four years old and a year appeared huge and so slow . . .'

'Sure. I also remember thinking how, every time Christmas had come and gone, the wait until next year would be endless.'

'Exactly. But the thing was – a year back then was just one quarter of your life. Whereas now . . .'

'One thirty-ninth.'

'Or, in my case, one seventy-second. This means that time shrinks with the accumulation of years. Or, at least, that's the perception. And all perception is, by its own nature, open to individual interpretation. The empirical fact is that time doesn't elongate or shrink. A day will always have twenty-four hours, a week seven days, a year three-hundred and sixty-five days. What does change is our awareness of its speed – and its increasing preciousness as a commodity.'

Dad. He died last year after a slow, cruel descent into the fog that is Alzheimer's. Twelve months earlier he had still been so mentally sharp. As sharp as my mother before the pancreatic cancer that came out of nowhere and killed her just four summers ago. Was it the love story of the past and present century? I can certainly remember moments when I was younger – especially during my adolescence – when there was a decided chill between them. I recall Dad dropping hints that teaching calculus in one of Maine's smaller cities wasn't the career stretch he had envisaged for himself when he was an undergraduate and the star of the U Maine math department. But it was Dad who had elderly parents in Bangor and felt beholden after college to turn down a doctoral scholarship at MIT in favor of one at U Maine in order to be on standby for his aging mother and father. And it was Dad who took the job in Waterville when he couldn't find a college post in-state.

Dad.

I got lucky on the parent front. Despite those few years of quiet, yet perceptible tension – about which neither of them ever really spoke during or afterwards – I grew up in a reasonably stable household. My parents both had careers. They both had outside interests – Dad played the cello in an amateur string quartet. Mom was something of an expert on historical needlework. They both encouraged and loved me. They kept whatever sorrows or misgivings they had about their individual and shared lives out of my earshot (and only when I was a woman in my thirties, coping with all the daily pressures of family life, did I realize how remarkably disciplined they were in this respect). Yes, Dad should have been a chaired professor at some university and the author of several ground-breaking books on binary number theory. Yes, Mom should have seen the world – as she herself once told me was her ambition when younger. Just as I also sensed she often rued the fact that she married a little too young and never really knew a life outside of that with my father. And yes, there was the great sadness that happened two years after my birth, when Mom had an ectopic pregnancy that turned frightening. Not only did she lose the baby, but the complications were so severe that she had to undergo a hysterectomy. I only found this out around the time I was pregnant with Sally and had a bad scare (which turned out to be nothing more than a scare). Mom then told me why I was an only child – something I had asked her about many years earlier, and which was explained simply as: 'We tried, but it never happened again.' Now, looking into the nightmare of a possible ectopic pregnancy, Mom told me the truth – leaving me wondering why she had waited so long to trust me with this tragedy that must have so upended her life at the time and still haunted her. Mom could see the shock in my eyes; a wounding sort of shock, as I struggled to understand why she never could have simply told me what had happened, and why Dad – with whom I thought there was such total transparency – had conspired with her on this huge central piece to the family puzzle. Me being me – and yes, Ben was right, I always want to make things right for those nearest to me – I never once spat out the hurt that coursed through me in the days after this revelation. Me being me I rationalized it as all coming down to their worry about the effect it might have on me, and whether (had they told me when I was much younger) I might have even suffered my own dose of survivor guilt over it. But it still bothered me. And hearing the whole terrible story for the first time when I was twenty-four . . . well, it just seemed to exacerbate the confusion I felt afterwards.

Dan's reaction was direct, to the point. And though I initially considered it just a little brusque, in time I realized he had cut to the heart of the matter when, after musing about it all for a moment or two, he just shrugged and said:

'So now you know that everybody has secrets.'

Cold comfort. Dan never does touchy-feely. But at the outset we did function well as a couple. We had little money. We had a big responsibility as new parents. We coped. Not only that, bills got paid. A house got bought. We managed to hold down two jobs and simultaneously raise two children without any sort of serious childcare (except the occasional babysitter or mother-in-law). We suffered broken nights courtesy of babies with colic and were able to laugh about our four a.m. tetchiness the next day. We were frustrated about our lack of latitude. But even though we both felt a little closed in, a little overwhelmed with children and financial obligations, what I remember most about those years together was the way we fundamentally got along, dodged so many potential areas of conflict, helped each other through rough patches without ever playing the 'I did this for you, now you do that for me' game. We seemed to be a reasonable match.

*A reasonable match.* It sounds so profoundly pragmatic, so down-to-earth, so devoid of passion. Well, ours too has never been the love story of the century. Nor, however, is it one of those marriages where the last time we made love Clinton was president. Sex is still there – but even before Dan lost his job and began to disengage from me, it had lost its basic exuberance or the sense of mutual need that fuelled it for so long. When we met the attraction was (for me anyway) the fact that he was stable, unflappable, together, responsible. Unlike the man who came before him and was . . .

No, I don't want to think about that . . . *him* . . . today. Even though, truth be told, I think of him every day. Even more so over the past two years when the realization was hitting me so constantly that . . .

*Stop.*

I have stood still.

*Stop.*

You lose things and then you choose things.

Didn't I hear someone sing that somewhere? Or as my dad once ruefully noted when he said to me, in passing, during the weekend of his seventieth birthday, 'To live a life is to constantly grapple with regret.'

Is that the price we pay for being here: the ongoing, ever-increasing knowledge that we have so often let ourselves down? And have settled for lives we find just adequate.

*Stop.*

This morning underscored for me what our life together has become. Dan sleepily reached for me when the alarm went off, as always, at six a.m. Though half-awake I was happy to have his arms around me, and to feel him pulling up the long men's shirt I always wear to bed. But then, with no attempt at even a modicum of tenderness, he immediately mounted me, kissing my dry mouth, thrusting in and out of me with rough urgency, and coming with a low groan after just a few moments. Falling off me, he then turned away. When I asked him if he was OK he reached for my hand while still showing me his back.

'Can you tell me what's wrong?' I asked.

'Why should there be anything wrong?' he said, now pulling his hand away.

'You just seem . . . troubled.'

'Is that what you think I am? *Troubled?*'

'You don't have to get angry.'

'"*You seem troubled.*" That's *not* a criticism?'

'Dan, please, this is nuts . . .'

'You see! You see!' he said, storming out of bed and heading to the bathroom. 'You say you don't criticize. Then what the hell do you do? No wonder I can never, *ever* win with you. No wonder I can't . . .'

Then, suddenly, his face fell and he began to sob. A low throttled sob – so choked, so held back. Immediately I was on my feet, moving towards him, my arms open. But instead of accepting my embrace he bolted to the bathroom, slamming the door behind him. I could still hear him crying. But when I knocked on the door and said: 'Please, Dan, let me—' he turned on the sink taps and drowned out the rest of my sentence.

*Let me help you. Let me near you. Let me . . .*

The water kept running. I returned to our bed and sat there for a very long time, thinking, thinking, despair coursing through my veins like the chemical dye I have to shoot every day into people who may be harboring a malignancy.

Is that what I am harboring here? A cancer of sorts. His cancer of unhappiness, caused by his loss of career, and now metastasizing in so many insidious directions that . . .

The water was still running in the bathroom. I stood up and went over to the door, trying to discern if I could hear him still crying over the sound of the open taps. Nothing but cascading water. I checked my watch: 6:18 a.m. Time to wake Sally – unless she happened to hear all the shouting earlier and was already up and concerned. Not that Sally would ever show much outward concern – her one comment after being nearby when Dan railed against me a few weeks ago was a blasé:

'Great to see I come from such a happy family.'

Were we ever a happy family? Do I even know a truly happy family?

I knocked lightly on her door, then opened it an inch to see that she was still very much asleep. Good. I decided to let her have another fifteen minutes in bed and went downstairs to make coffee. Dan showed up a few minutes later, dressed in jeans and a sweatshirt, his gym bag in hand.

'Heading off to work out,' he said, avoiding my line of vision.

'That sounds like a good idea.'

He moved towards the front door.

'See you tonight.'

'I'll be home at the usual time. But you know I have my weekly book talk with Lucy at seven. And tomorrow—'

'Yeah, you'll be heading to Boston at lunchtime.'

'I'll make all your dinners for the weekend tonight.'

'You don't think I can cook?'

'Dan . . .'

'I'll take care of the dinners myself.'

'Are you angry I'm going to Boston?'

'Why should I be angry? It's work, right?'

'That it is.'

'Anyway, if I were you I'd want a break from me.'

'Dan . . .'

'Don't say it.'

'You have me worried.'

He stopped and turned back, still not able to look at me directly. Then, in a half-hushed voice, he said one word:

'Sorry.'

And he was gone.

Now, nearly eleven hours later – turning down my road after having spent much of the working day trying to keep the entire unsettling aftertaste of the morning somewhat at bay – a certain dread hit me. A dread that has been so present since that day twenty-one months ago when Dan walked in from work and said that he'd just been laid off. The economic downturn had meant that annual sales at L.L.Bean had fallen by 14 percent. The people on the executive floor decided that they could shave some excess off the info tech department – which handles all the online sales and marketing for the company – by cutting the two people in charge of ever expanding its sales capabilities. One of these people happened to be my husband. He'd put in twelve years at L.L.Bean – and was floored by such a summary dismissal, just four days after New Year's Day. The look on his face when he came in through the front door that night . . . it was as if he had aged ten years in the ten hours since I'd seen him. Reaching into his back pocket he pulled out a letter. *The letter.* There it was, in hard typography. The notice that he no longer had a job, the regret of the company at ending such a long association, the assurance that a '*generous termination package would be offered*', along with '*the services of our Human Resources department to help you find new employment as quickly as possible*'.

'What a joke,' Dan said. 'The last time they laid off a bunch of people from my department none of them found any work for at least two years . . . and the only people who did find new jobs had to go out of state.'

'I'm so sorry,' I said, reaching for his hand. But he pulled it away before I could touch it. I said nothing, telling myself at the time the man was so understandably floored by what had happened. Even if Dan was never the most tactile or outwardly affectionate of men, he still had never pulled away from me like that before. So I reached out again for his outstretched hand. This time he flinched, as if I was threatening him.

'You trying to make me feel bad?' he said, the anger sudden.

Now it was my turn to flinch. I looked at him with shock and just a little disbelief.

I quickly masked it by changing the subject, asking him about the sort of 'package' they had offered him. As these things go, it wasn't too mean: six months' full salary, full medical insurance for a year, plenty of free career counselling. At least they had the decency to wait until after Christmas before delivering the terrible news – and it wasn't just the IT department that had suffered cuts, as around seventy employees across the board had been shown the door. But as soon as Dan said 'six months' full pay' I could almost hear what I was thinking simultaneously: *We're just a bit screwed.* Only three months earlier we'd taken a $45,000 home-improvement loan to reroof our house and deal with a basement that was riddled with damp. As home upgrades go they were hardly sexy – but absolutely necessary. We took them after much dinner-table discussion and scribbled calculations on the backs of assorted envelopes. Our roof was leaking, our basement was wet. We were filling the space between these two encroaching molds. We had no choice but to borrow the money, even though we knew it would strain our already stretched household budget. Between our $1,200 mortgage per month, the $15,000 it cost to send Ben to U Maine Farmington (and that was a bargain, compared to a private college like Bowdoin), the $250 lease on the car that Dan drove to work (my vehicle was a twelve-year-old Camry with around 133,000 miles on the clock and in urgent need of a new transmission), and the $300 in essential monthly premiums to cover Ben and Sally under my hospital insurance scheme, the idea of burdening ourselves with another $450 per month for ten years was disheartening. Add all these essential outgoings together, and we were already spending close to $3,500 per month. Now Dan earned $43K per year and I earned $51K. After tax we had a combined net income of $61K – or $5, 083 per month. In other words, this left us with just under $1,600 after our main outgoings to pay for all our utilities, all our food, all our clothes, all Ben and Sally's additional needs, and whatever we could squeeze out every year to fund a one-week vacation.

I knew many families around us who were making do on far less. Even though Sally did complain that we always seemed to be counting pennies she finally got wise and started using her weekend babysitting money to buy all the iPods and funky earrings and the butterfly tattoo (don't ask) that she came home with after a day out with some girlfriends in Portland. Ben, on the other hand, never asked us for a penny. He had a part-time job at the college, mixing paints and stretching canvases in the visual arts department. He refused anything more than the room and board we provided for him in addition to his annual tuition.

'I'm living *la vie de bohème* in Farmington,' he said to me once when I tried to press $100 into his hand (I'd done a week's worth of overtime). 'I can live on air. And I don't want you to lose the roof because you slipped me a hundred bucks.'

I laughed and said:

'I doubt that is going to happen.'

Actually we decided to pay off part of the new roof loan with Dan's severance. The basement was now dry. And Dan turned in his leased car and used $1,500 to buy a 1997 Honda Civic that never made it above 60 mph. But at least he had wheels while I was at the hospital. The one-salary situation meant that money was ferociously tight. We were just about making all our bills every month and had absolutely no cash to spare. Dan had knocked on every door possible within the state. Perhaps the most terrible irony of his story was that, around eighteen months after he'd lost his job at Bean's, he discovered that they were readvertising his old post. Naturally he contacted the head of personnel. Naturally the guy spun some yarn about sales upturn allowing them to re-expand the department they had just reduced. Naturally the guy also told Dan he should reapply for the job. Then they went and hired someone else who was (again according to the head of personnel) 'simply more qualified'. Shortly after that Dan also lost what seemed to be that shoo-in position in the State of Maine's IT department in Augusta – and the outbreaks of rage really started, perhaps augmented by the fact that, just two days ago, the head of personnel at Bean's called and said they did have an opening – but it was in the stockroom. Yes, it was an assistant supervisor's position. And yes, after six months he would be back in their health insurance system. Yet it only paid $13 an hour – but, hey, that was almost twice the minimum wage – and just about $15K a year after taxes.

That extra $15K would give us just the necessary breathing room, and avoid debt (which I have been so damn determined to dodge, but which we are careening towards very quickly). It might even allow us to borrow Dan's brother-in-law's condo in Tampa for a week during Christmas and have a proper family vacation in the sun. Of course Dan knew all that. Just as I also so understood he hated the idea of going to work in the stockroom – and for half of what he used to be making within the same organization.

'It's like he's throwing me a bone,' he said to me on the evening it was offered to him. 'A crappy consolation prize – and a way of soothing his conscience about having fired me.'

'It wasn't him who fired you. It was the boys upstairs. It was their decision to make the cutbacks.'

'Yeah, but he carried out their dirty work for them.'

'Unfortunately that's his job.'

'You sticking up for him?'

'Hardly.'

'But you want me to accept his offer.'

'I don't want you to take the job if it is something you absolutely don't want to do.'

'We need the money.'

'Well, yes, we really do. Still, we would find a way to keep things somehow ticking over . . .'

'You want me to take the job.'

'I'm not saying that, Dan. And I have asked the hospital if they would let me do ten extra hours of overtime a week – which would bring in around two hundred and fifty more dollars.'

'And make me feel guilty as hell . . .'

Now, as I was turning this all over in my mind, I headed down my road. It's a country road, around a mile from the center of Damriscotta. A road that loops its way through slightly elevated countryside . . . though the realtor, when he first brought us to see it, referred to the surrounding landscape as 'gently rolling'. When I mentioned this once to Ben (in a discussion we were having about the way salesmen inevitably pretty things up) he just shook his head and said:

'Well, I suppose if you were a rabbit you'd think it was "gently rolling".'

The fact is that, down towards the waterfront, the terrain is elevated, humpy. The town lawyers and doctors live on those wonderful prospects overlooking the Kennebec River. So does one rather successful painter, a reasonably well-known writer of children's books, and two builders who have cornered the market in this part of mid-coast Maine. The houses there are venerable clapboard structures – usually white or deep red – beautifully maintained and landscaped, with recent SUVs in the driveways. Hand on heart I have never had a disagreeable thought about the people who are lucky enough to live in these elegant, refined homes. Hand on heart there is a moment every day when I drive by this stretch of waterfront houses and think: *Wouldn't it be nice if . . .*

If what? If I had married a rich local doctor? Or, more to the point, had become that doctor? Is that a tiny little stab I always feel – and yes, it has been a constant silent prod recently – whenever I pass by this stretch of real estate, before turning upwards towards my far more modest home? Is midlife inevitably marked by the onset of regret? I always put on a positive face in front of my work colleagues, my children, my increasingly detached husband. Dr Harrild once referred to me (at a surprise fortieth birthday party two years ago) as 'the most unflappable and affirmative person on our staff'. Everyone applauded this comment. I smiled shyly while simultaneously thinking: *If only you knew how often I ask myself: 'Is this it?'*

My dad often sang a tune to me about 'accentuating the positive' when I was younger and getting into one of those rather serious moods I used to succumb to during the roller-coaster ride that was adolescence. But considering how often I caught him singing those upbeat words to himself I can't help but think that he was also using the song as a way of bolstering his own lingering sense of regret. Dr Harrild actually heard me humming this once in the staff room and said:

'Now you are about the last person who needs to be telling herself all that.'

Dr Harrild. He too always tries to accentuate the positive – and genuinely be kind. The trip I'm taking this weekend being an example of that. A radiography conference in Boston. OK, Boston's just three hours down the road, so it's not like being sent to somewhere really enviable like Honolulu or San Francisco (two places I so want to visit someday). Still, the last time I was in Boston . . . gosh, it must be two years ago. A Christmas shopping trip. An overnight with Sally and Ben. We even went to a touring production of *The Lion King* and stayed in an OK hotel off Copley Square. The city was under a fresh dusting of snow. The chic lights along Newbury Street looked magical. I was so happy that Ben and Sally were so happy. And I told myself then that I was going to find the money to start travelling a little every year; that life was roaring by and if I wanted to see Paris or Rome or . . .

Then, a few weeks later, Dan was out of a job. And the dream was put on permanent hold.

Still, thank you, Dr Harrild. An all-expenses-paid trip to Boston. Gas money. A hotel for two nights. Even $300 in cash for expenses. And all because he was invited to this radiological convention, but his eldest boy has a football game this Sunday and he wanted the hospital represented at the convention, and when I raised the concern that maybe I wasn't senior enough (i.e. a doctor) to be attending, he brushed that worry away with the statement: 'You probably know more about radiography than most of the senior consultants who will be there. Anyway, you deserve a trip on us, and a break from things for a few days.'

Was that his way of letting me know that he'd heard something about the state of 'things' at home? I had been pretty damn scrupulous about not telling anyone at the hospital or around town about Dan's problems. Still, small hospitals and small towns breed small talk.

Not that Dr Harrild would ever really engage in such gossip. But he was right about me needing a break – even one that would last just under seventy-two hours. A change of scene and all that. But also – and this was a realization which, when it hit me a few days ago, truly shocked me – the first time I had been away on my own since Ben and Sally were born.

*I have let myself stand still.*

But tomorrow I am on the road. Alone. Even if it is a destination I already know – and one that's just a small jump from the place I call home – travel is travel. A temporary escape.

I turned into our driveway. The reclining rays of an unusually bright autumn sun reflected off the new roof of our house. A two-story house, somewhat squat, finished in off-gray clapboard that I would love to darken by two shades if I could ever find the $9,000 our local house painter told me it would cost to redo the entire exterior (and it really needs it). Just as I'd love to landscape the half-acre of land that fronts it, as it has become rather scrubby. Behind us, however, is a wonderful oak tree that, right this moment, is almost peacock-like in its autumnal beauty. Sometimes I think it was the tree that sold me on the house – as we bought it knowing it was a fixer-upper, a starter place from which we'd eventually graduate.

But enough of that (as I tell myself most days). We have raised two children here. It's our home. We worked hard to buy it. We continue to work hard to keep it (though the last mortgage payment falls in seventeen months – hurrah). It is our history. Only now can I honestly say that I've never warmed to the place. Nor has Dan. How I wish we'd talked ourselves out of ever buying it.

Our home.

I thought that as I pulled up our driveway and saw Dan sitting on the bench that covers most of the front porch, a cigarette between his lips. As soon as he spotted my car pulling up he was on his feet like an anxious schoolboy, dumping the cigarette onto the porch deck and then trying to hide the evidence by kicking it into the crabgrass below. Dan has been allegedly off cigarettes for six months – but I know he smokes several every day.

'Hey there,' I said, all smiles as I got out of the car. He looked at me sheepishly.

'It's the first cigarette in over a week,' he said.

'Fine,' I said. 'Good day?'

'I took the job.' He was staring down at his feet as he said this.

At that moment I felt relief and a terrible sense of guilt. Because I knew that the last thing Dan wanted to do was accept that offer in the stockroom. Just as I knew that he knew the breathing space that extra money would bring us. I tried to take his hand. He stiffened and pulled away, putting his hand behind his back, out of reach. I said nothing for a moment, then uttered two words:

'Thank you.'

## Four

MEATLOAF. DAN HAD prepared a meatloaf. He'd used his mother's recipe – covering the loaf in Heinz's tomato sauce and flavoring the beef with three cloves of crushed garlic (a recipe, he'd told me on several occasions, that was somewhat radical for Bangor, Maine, in the 1970s . . . when garlic was considered nothing less than foreign). He'd also made baked potatoes and a fresh spinach salad to accompany the meatloaf. And he'd bought a bottle of Australian red wine – Jacob's Creek – which he told me that 'the guy at the supermaket said was "very drinkable"'.

'That's high praise from a guy at a supermarket,' I said. 'I really appreciate you going to all this trouble . . .'

'Thought we should celebrate me landing the job.'

'Yes, I think that's worth celebrating.'

'And I know you've got your book thing with Lucy at seven.'

'That still gives us an hour – as long as the meatloaf is ready by—'

'It will be done in fifteen minutes.'

'Wonderful. Shall we open the wine?'

He reached for the bottle and screwed off the cap, pouring wine into two glasses. He handed me one and we touched them.

'To your new job,' I said.

'I never thought I'd be toasting a job in a stockroom.'

'It's a supervisor's job . . .'

'Assistant supervisor.'

'Still, it's a *management* position.'

'In a stockroom.'

'Dan . . .'

'I know, I know. It will ease up so much for us.'

'And it will also lead to other things for you. I'm certain it's just a temporary—'

'Please stop trying to make me feel better.'

'Should I try to make you feel rotten?'

He smiled. I came over and put my arms around him and kissed him straight on the mouth and whispered:

'I love you.'

Instead of kissing me back, he hung his head.

'That's nice to hear,' he finally said.

I put my finger under his chin and tried to raise his head. But he shrugged me off.

'I need to check the potatoes,' he said.

I stood there, feeling numb. *Maybe I'm sending out the wrong signals. Maybe I'm telling him things subconsciously which he is interpreting as belittling or critical or . . .*

'Have I done something to upset you?' I heard myself asking out loud. Dan closed the oven door, stood up and regarded me with bemusement.

'Did I say that?' he asked.

'Do you feel I am not supportive enough or am conveying some sort of negative—'

'Why are you bringing this up?'

'Because . . . because . . .'

The words were catching in my throat, as they were being intertwined with a sob.

'Because . . . I'm lost.'

What he said next was . . . well, 'unbelievable' was the only word that came to mind.

'That's not my fault.'

Now the sobs were no longer trapped in my throat. Now I was sitting down in a kitchen chair, crying. All that I had been repressing for weeks, months, suddenly cascaded out in heaving sobs.

Then Sally wandered in.

'Another happy night at home,' she said.

'I'm fine, I'm fine,' I said, forcing myself to stop sobbing.

'Sure you are. And Dad's fine too. And we all love each other. And everything is just great. And, by the way, I'm skipping dinner.'

'But your father's prepared a wonderful meatloaf.'

'Since when was meatloaf ever "wonderful"? Anyway, just got a call from Brad. His parents have decided to eat at Solo Bistro down in Bath tonight and asked if I wanted to come along.'

'It's a little late for that,' Dan said.

'And why?' Sally asked.

'Because your dinner is in the oven.'

'I'll eat the leftovers tomorrow.'

'Sorry,' Dan said, 'but I'm not allowing it.'

'That's unfair,' Sally said.

'Too bad you think that.'

'Come on, Dad – Solo Bistro is a great restaurant . . .'

'Can't say I've ever eaten there.'

'That's because you've been out of work and miserable for the last year and a half.'

'Sally . . .' I said.

'Well, it's the truth – and you know it, Mom.'

Silence.

Dan slowly bent down and put the potatoes back in the oven. Then, standing up again, he turned away from his daughter as he said:

'You want to eat with those people, off you go.'

Sally looked at me for confirmation. I nodded and she ran off out the door.

I heard a car pull up outside – and glanced out the window to see Sally heading towards Brad's silver Mini convertible. He got out to greet her and give her a very full kiss right on the lips. She didn't hold back either. At that moment I was absolutely certain that they were sleeping together. Not that this had come as a shock, as I was pretty sure this had been going on for a year. Just as I also knew that she had asked for an appointment with my gynecologist six months ago and just said it was 'routine stuff'. Did that mean my daughter was on the pill or had been fitted for a diaphragm? Either way I suppose it was better than getting pregnant. Gazing at Brad – so tall, so lean, so deeply preppy in a town where preppy wasn't a common look – all I could think was: *He is going to break her heart.*

I watched the car zoom away, and saw Sally put her arm

around Brad as they headed off into the actual sunset. Immediately I thought back to the time when I was seventeen, on the cusp of everything, so determined to succeed. I reached for the wine bottle and splashed a little more in my glass. In the wake of Sally driving off Dan had stepped outside and lit up another cigarette. The joylessness in his eyes was palpable. Seeing him staring out at the world beyond I felt a desperate stab of empathy for him, for us. Coupled with the realization: *He is now a stranger to me.*

I set the table. I took out the meatloaf and the potatoes. I ladled sour cream into a bowl. I rapped on the glass of the kitchen window. When Dan swivelled his head I motioned for him to come inside. Once back in the kitchen he looked at the dinner ready to be eaten and said:

'You should have let me do all that. I was making dinner. I didn't want you to have to do anything tonight.'

'It was no trouble at all. Anyway, I thought you might need a little time out.'

'I'm sorry,' he said. 'I'm so sorry.'

He came over and put his arms around me. As he buried his head in my shoulder I felt a momentary shudder come over him and thought he was about to cry. But he kept himself in check, while simultaneously holding me tightly. I returned the embrace, then took his face in my hands and said:

'You know I am on your side, Dan.'

His body stiffened. Had I said the wrong thing again – even though I meant the comment to be reassuring, loving? Could I ever say the right thing anymore?

We sat down to eat. For a few moments silence reigned. I finally broke it.

'This is wonderful meatloaf.'

'Thank you,' Dan said tonelessly.

And the silence enveloped us again.

\* \* \*

'For me, it really is one of the great modern novels about loneliness,' Lucy said, motioning to the waitress that she should bring us two more glasses of chardonnay. 'And what I loved about the novel was how it so brilliantly captured forty years of American life in such an economic way. I mean, I couldn't get over the fact that the novel's only two hundred and fifty pages long . . .'

'That really intrigued me as well,' I said. 'How he was able to say so much about these two sisters and the times they passed through in such a compressed way, and with such descriptive precision.'

'This is one of those rare instances when you can actually say there's not a wasted word in the novel, along with this absolute clear sightedness about the way people talk themselves into lives they so don't want.'

'And by the end, we really feel we know these two women so desperately well. Because their lives and choices are a reflection of so many of our own wrong choices, and the way despair and disappointment color all our lives.'

'I'll drink to that,' Lucy said as our two glasses of wine arrived.

Lucy and I were sitting in a booth in the Newcastle Publick House – a rather decent local tavern, where the din was never so overwhelming that you couldn't have a conversation – engaged in our weekly book talk. Actually 'book talk' makes this weekly get-together sound formal, rule-bound. The truth is, though we have been having this Thursday get-together for over a year, the only principle that we follow is that the first part of the conversation is all about the novel we have agreed to read that week. That's right – we try to read a different novel every week, though when we tackled *The Brothers Karamazov* a few months ago we gave ourselves a month to work through that mammoth enterprise. The only other rule we have is that we take turns choosing the book under discussion and never raise objections if it is out of what Lucy once dubbed 'our respective literary comfort zones'. The truth is, we both share a similar sensibility when it comes to novels. No fantasy. No science fiction (though we did, at my suggestion, read Ray Bradbury's *The Martian Chronicles* – which we both agreed had more to do with things mid-century American than actual extraterrestrial matters). And no treacly romantic stuff. Having discovered early on that we both read to find windows into our own dilemmas, our choices (outside of *The Brothers Karamazov* – my idea – and *Gravity's Rainbow* – Lucy's suggestion, and a book which we spent four evenings trying to understand) have largely centered around books which reflect the difficulties inherent in day-to-day life. So we've veered towards novels about family complexities (*Dombey and Son*), money complexities (*The Way We Live Now*), state-of-the-nation complexities (*An American Tragedy, Babbitt*), and (no surprise here) marital complexities (*The War Between the Tates, Couples, Madame Bovary*). We always spend around ninety minutes each week talking animatedly about the novel under discussion – though these Thursday rendezvous (which inevitably stretch to three hours) are also an opportunity for us to catch up with what Lucy once elegantly called 'our ongoing weather systems'; the stuff that has seemed to constantly circle around our respective lives.

Lucy is a year my senior. She is about the smartest person I know. She went to Smith, joined the Peace Corps, taught in difficult places like The Gambia and Burkina Faso (I had to check out a map to see where that was), then traveled the world for a year. Upon returning to her native Boston she promptly fell in love with a PhD candidate at Harvard named Harry Ricks. Harry landed a job teaching American history at Colby just after he got his doctorate. Lucy retrained in library science and also found a job at the college. Then she lost two pregnancies back to back – the first at three months, the second (even more heartbreakingly) at eight months. Then her newly tenured husband ran off with a colleague (a dance instructor). Then she was badly advised legally and came away from the marriage with virtually nothing. Then she decided that staying at Colby was emotionally impossible – for all sorts of obvious reasons. So she packed up her decade-old Toyota with her worldly goods and headed down to Damariscotta after landing a job at the local high school, running their library.

She was thirty-six when she got here – and I met her during one of her weekend 'extra money' shifts at the library in the center of town. We became fast friends. She is the one and only person in the world with whom I confide – and she also knows she can talk with me about virtually anything. Dan has always been pleasant and reasonably welcoming towards Lucy – especially as she usually spends part of Christmas Day with us (she has no direct family of her own). But he is also a little suspicious of her, as he knows she is my ally. Just as he senses what I know Lucy thinks, but has never articulated: that Dan and I are a mismatch. That's been one of the unwritten rules of our friendship: we tell ourselves everything that we want to share. We ask advice and give it reciprocally. But we each stop short of saying what we really feel about the other's stuff. Lucy, for example, had a two-year relationship with a wildly inappropriate man named David Robby – a would-be writer who'd fled a bad marriage and a failed career in advertising, and was one of those guys who had just enough of a trust fund to ruin him. Coastal Maine is full of metropolitan refugees like David – whose personal or professional life (or both) have flat-lined and who have come to our corner of the northeast to reinvent themselves. The problem is: Maine is quiet. And underworked. And largely underpaid. Its visual pleasures – the ravishing, primary sweep of its seascape, the verdancy of its terrain, its sense of space and isolation and extremity (especially in winter) – are counterbalanced by the fact that life here throws you back on your own devices, on yourself. And David – an outwardly charming, but clearly unsettled man – was about the last thing my friend needed in her life back then. Still, between the divorce and the lost babies, and the knowledge that her dream of motherhood might be finished, David was, for a time, something of a recompense (even though I found him creepy). But I never said a word against him. Just as Lucy never made any comments about Dan. Was this wrong – a personal confederacy based on being there to hear each other out, but not to ram home certain self-evident verities? I think we trusted each other because we didn't blitzkrieg each other with lacerating observations – because we both understood our different fragilities and were best keeping ourselves buoyed.

But the book under discussion tonight – Richard Yates's *The*

*Easter Parade* – was one of those profoundly disquieting novels that hit you with the most lacerating (and unsettlingly accurate) observations about the human condition.

'I read somewhere that Richard Yates wasn't just a serious alcoholic, but a manic depressive as well,' Lucy said.

'Wasn't there that well-reviewed biography of him a few years back,' I said, 'which talked about how, even when he was on a binge – which was most of the time – he somehow managed to grind out two hundred words a day?'

'Words were obviously a refuge for him from all of life's harder realities.'

'Or maybe the way he tried to make sense of all the craziness he observed within himself and others. Do you know what the biography was called? *A Terrible Honesty.*'

'Well, that is, without question, the defining strength of *The Easter Parade*. It pulls no punches when it comes to examining why Sara and Emily Grimes lived such unhappy lives.'

'And the genius of the book,' I said, 'is that even though Emily becomes a desperate alcoholic, she's never painted as sad or pathetic. Yet Yates also makes it so clear that the two sisters have nobody but themselves to blame for their disappointments.'

'His psychological clarity and his humanity are everywhere. As you said, we all know these women because they are, more or less, reflections of ourselves. It's what Emily says to her niece's husband at the end of the book, "I'm almost fifty years old and I've never understood anything in my whole life." That's the hard truth at the center of the novel. There are no solutions when it comes to life. There's only mess and muddle.'

'But we all want answers, don't we?'

'You're talking to a Unitarian,' Lucy said. 'We pray "to whom it may concern".'

'And the one thing I liked most about being an Episcopalian – besides all that good Anglican choral music – was that it always preached a gospel of thinking about faith in a personal and non-doctrinal way. No real directives from on high. No Old Testament God who kicked butt if you didn't believe he was the

Man in Charge. Still, the one problem with being part of a thinking religion is that there is absolutely no certainty whatsoever.'

'Does that truly bother you?'

'Sometimes, honestly, yes, it does unsettle me – the idea that this is it, that there is nothing beyond this except mystery. God knows I've tried to believe in a hereafter – that is a component of Episcopalianism. But it's always held out as more of a poetic idea – a fantasia, so to speak – than an absolute divine truth. As such I doubt I am ever going to run into anyone I know in the afterlife either. But if there is no hereafter, then how do we make sense of this very flawed business called life?'

'Now there's a question that will never have a definitive answer. But I do have a question about a completely unrelated, but nonetheless important matter – did Dan take the job?'

I nodded.

'That's good news, I guess,' Lucy said.

'Not for him. But I didn't coerce him or force his hand . . . though he acts as if I did.'

'That's because he feels guilty about being out of work for so long, as he also hates the fact that he has no choice but to take this job.'

I stared into my glass of wine.

'I wish it was as simple as that. I just feel that we're kind of lost together. And that's an oxymoron, isn't it? If you are together you're not supposed to be lost. Then again . . .'

'So many of us are lost together. Have you suggested counseling?'

'Of course. To Dan the idea of talking about our problems in front of a third party . . . it's anathema to him. Anyway, I only know one marriage that was saved by counseling—'

'And that's because they had a suicide pact.'

I found myself laughing. Loudly.

'You're terrible,' I said.

'I think it's called being a realist.'

'I don't want the marriage to end.'

'But you don't want it to continue as it is.'

'No. But . . . how can I put this? I don't know of a way out. If I leave, then what?'

'You'll be like me. A woman in her early forties on her own in small-town Maine. Were I the devious type I'd encourage you to leave him – so you'd end up where I am now. Alone. Wondering what the future holds. Thinking: *Maybe I should try my luck in a bigger place – Boston or Chicago or somewhere in the Sun Belt, not that I could stand the politics down there.* But then what? You cart your baggage with you wherever you go. So, I suppose the real question is—'

'I know what the question is,' I said.

'The thing is – do you have an answer?'

Again I looked down into my wine.

'I have many answers and no answers,' I finally said.

'Join the club.'

* * *

Outside the tavern Lucy said:

'So tomorrow's the big day.'

'A trip to a radiography conference in suburban Boston is hardly a trip to Paris.'

'Still, you get to play hooky for a couple of days.'

'And if you tell me that the time away will make things seem clearer . . .'

'Fear not. If anything you'll just come back feeling even more conflicted because you've stepped away from it all for a couple of days. Such is life.'

She leaned forward and gave me a hug.

'You know what I want more than anything?' she said. 'Surprise. A surprise or two would be nice.'

'Don't you have to be on the lookout for surprises in order to find one?'

'You're a philosopher, Laura.'

'No, I am a wife and mother and radiographic technician who works nine to five forty-nine weeks a year. My life.'

'And if I were to tell you: "It could be worse . . . "'

'I'd hate you and agree with you at the same time.'

* * *

On my drive home my cellphone began to emit the *bing* sound indicating that I'd just received a text. It had to be Ben. No one else texted me at this hour. I didn't reach for it until I was parked in our driveway, simultaneously noting that all the lights in the house were off, except for the one in the downstairs hallway that we always leave on to indicate someone is home – and, more recently, to welcome back children arriving home late. On which note, I had received a text earlier tonight from Sally:

Sleeping over at Brad's. Will come by early tomorrow for my school stuff.

'Sleeping over'. What a clever use of an innocent, pre-college euphemism. No doubt Brad's parents knew that my daughter would be sharing his bed tonight and that they wouldn't be doing so as 'just friends'. Then again, Sally turns eighteen in nine months. I was sleeping with my boyfriend when I was her age. So I can't exactly reproach her for 'sleeping over' at Brad's. But this is the first time she has been direct and open about the fact that she is sexually active – and I can't help but figure that she decided, after all that went down tonight with her father, to be finally direct about her relationship with Brad. Or, at least, direct with me – as I doubted she texted Dan the same information. Like so many fathers he's rather queasy about the idea that she is no longer the innocent daddy's girl . . . not that she has been a daddy's girl for some time. I texted Sally back:

Leaving about nine for Boston, so will still be here to see you. Love – Mom.

Pressing 'send' I watched it disappear. Then I turned my attention to Ben's message:

Am wondering if true love really exists? Answers on a postcard to my new website: thesorrowsofyoungwertherinmaine.com. Trying to paint. Not having much luck. Don't call tonight

– going to sit in my studio all night and force myself to do something with a brush. B xxx

Ben citing Goethe. I smiled and tapped out a reply:

Hope all goes well in the studio tonight. If not will go right eventually. Important thing is to go easy on yourself – I know easier said than done, but also absolutely crucial. You have been through a difficult time. Don't expect too much of yourself right now.

Immediately I deleted those last two sentences. *'I know I've been through a difficult time,'* I could hear him saying, *'and I always have – and always will – expect a lot of myself . . . so don't tell me to short-change myself.'* It's one of the most complex aspects of parenting – knowing when *not* to say something or when to sidestep the sort of advice that sounds like a bromide or a band-aid applied to a major wound. And even if, in time, Ben may look upon the loss of his first love as a necessary rite of passage, the fact is that he still remains raw and fragile in its aftermath. To tell him that, five years from now, he might consider it all much ado about nothing would be so counterproductive. So I rephrased the end of the text to read:

Do know I am always here for you whenever you need me. Love – Mom

I wanted to add something about me hoping that he could still come home next week, but again applied the brakes, thinking that he doesn't want to feel pushed into anything right now. If I say nothing he'll probably show up.

I checked my watch. It was almost ten p.m. – and I needed to be on the road by seven tomorrow. I went inside. Dan had cleared away the dinner plates and turned on the dishwasher and left everything tidy. I shut off the hall light and went upstairs, hoping that Dan was already asleep and wouldn't question our daughter's whereabouts. I too needed rest. Today had been a particularly complex day. But aren't all days complex? Don't they all throw something in your path that upends the momentum of things, or simply reminds you that life never goes the way you want it?

Then again, what is it that any of us truly want out of life?

When asked about this rather large, frequently troubling question people often talk in headlines: happiness, someone to love, a life without fear, money, sex, freedom, nothing terrible to happen to my family, recognition for what I am . . . All reasonable requests. Yet show me a life where anyone really ends up getting what they want. I see this all the time with the patients awaiting results from scans. The terror and hope etched in their eyes. The sense that fate may have just short-changed them. The need to believe that there is a way out of what might be a terminal situation . . .

*Enough.*

Opening the bedroom door I saw that my husband was very much asleep – his arms clutching the pillow so tightly I couldn't help but wonder if it wasn't some sort of nocturnal life preserver keeping him afloat. Dan suddenly groaned, then let out a sharp cry – as if something had startled him. I rushed over to comfort him. But by the time I reached the bed he had turned over and was back in the unconscious world. I sat and stroked his head and thought: *In the best of all possible worlds he'd sit up and take me in his arms and tell me that we were golden.* No wonder we all love the fairy tales that don't end with the princess getting eaten by the dragon . . . or (worse yet) finding herself sad and alone.

I get a taste of the great outdoors tomorrow. A few days away from all this. A brief flirtation with escape.

But I don't want escape. I want . . .

Yet another question for which I don't have an answer.

Dan groaned again, seizing the pillow even tighter. I suddenly felt very tired.

Lights out now. Close the door on the day. Close it tight.

# Friday

## One

THE ROAD. HOW I love the road. Or, at least, the idea of the road. The summer before our senior year at the University of Maine, Dan and I piled into the ancient (but still very serviceable) Chevy that he had throughout college and headed west. The car could do seventy-five miles an hour at a push. There was no air conditioning – and we were trailed by ninety-degree temperatures (at best) everywhere. We didn't care. We had $2,000 and three months before we were due back east for the start of classes. We stayed in cheap motels. We ate largely in diners. We left highways all the time to explore two-lane blacktops. We spent four days in Rapid City, South Dakota, because we simply liked that crazy Wild West town. We broke down on a stretch of Route 111 in the Wyoming badlands and (this being the days before the cellphone) had to wait three hours until a car showed up. It was a guy in a pickup with a gun rack. We hailed him down and he brought us the forty miles to the next outpost of civilization, and the mechanic there was around seventy and never without a Lucky Strike between his teeth. He insisted on putting us up in a room over his garage for the two days it took him to perform a valve job on the engine: a huge piece of work that should have cost over $1,000, but for which he only charged us $500. Through a lot of crazy budgeting – and the fact that gas back then was just over a dollar a gallon – we were able to carry on west to San Francisco, then head back east through the desert to Santa Fe, which we both fell for.

'Let's move here after I finish med school,' I said, seeing us living in some adobe house (with a swimming pool) out in the mesa that surrounded the city, me having a thriving pediatrics practice in town, my patients the children of artists and New Age types who ate macrobiotically and wrote music for the gamelan and drank green tea with Georgia O'Keeffe and . . .

'As long as you don't make me drink green tea or only eat lentils,' Dan said.

'No – we'd be the weirdos out here. Meat-eaters, smokers –'
(Dan was a two-pack a day man back then) 'and decidedly not
into crystals or the zodiac. But I bet we'd meet a lot of young
types like us. Santa Fe strikes me as one of those places that attracts
refugees from everywhere else in the country – people who want
to escape from all the pressures of big-city life, big-city success.
We could live really well here – and, hey, it's the West. Wide open
spaces. Big skies. No traffic.'

Of course Dan agreed with me. Of course, within twelve months,
all these pipe-dreamy plans were finished. And that big wonderful
coast-to-coast drive – in which I truly fell in love with the scope
and possibility and sheer insane vastness of my country – was to
be our one and only romance of the road.

The road.

We all have our little patch of earth, don't we? Especially those
of us who do the nine-to-five thing and rarely venture further than
our home and our place of work. And this morning, on the way
south, I was passing through my usual parameters.

Main Street Damariscotta. Tourists come here in the summer.
An archetypal Maine fishing town. Lots of white clapboard. Austere
historic churches. A few decent restaurants (we don't do fancy
around here). A couple of places where you can buy three types
of goat's cheese and the sort of fancy English biscuits that are way
out of my budget. And small-town lawyers and insurers and doctors
and our hospital and three schools and six houses of worship and
one supermarket and a decent bookshop and a funky little cinema
where they show the live relays from the Metropolitan Opera once
a month (I always go with Lucy – even if it is $25 a ticket) and
water everywhere you look. Then there's that ingrained Maine
sense of independence that pervades so much of our life here, an
attitude which can best be described as: 'You stay out of my business, I stay out of yours, and we'll treat each other with courtesy
and unspoken respect, and we won't pass judgment out loud.'
What I like about life here is that, though we all know so much
about each other, we still maintain the veneer of outward disin-
terest. It's the curious Maine dichotomy: we're as nosy about other

people's mess as anyone else, but we also pride ourselves on keeping our own counsel.

From Damariscotta through the township of Newcastle then onto Route 1 and into Wiscasset. I hate that damn sign they put at their southern boundary: *Wiscasset: The Prettiest Village in Maine.* I suppose what annoys me most about it – once you sidestep the smugness of that claim – is the fact that it *is* the prettiest village in Maine. A virtually intact throwback to the colonial past, grouped around a sweeping Atlantic cove, the town's white clapboard angularity is so authentic, so visually striking – especially as the water too is everywhere. Outside the absurd vacation traffic that backs up the town every weekend during July and August, this is coastal Maine at its most ravishing. Yet like everything else to do with the state, Wiscasset is so low-key about its wondrousness . . . outside, that is, of that damn sign.

South of Wiscasset there are a couple of depressing strip malls and a supermarket and the requisite McDonald's which they only opened around a year ago. Then woods which eventually give way to encroaching water and the bridge into Bath. That bridge – across the wide expanse of the Kennebec River – always strikes me as spectacular. I must make two round-trips across it every week (that's over two thousand single trips in the last decade – have I ever considered that huge number before now?). Heading south, if you look to the left you see the shipyard of Bath Iron Works – one of the last true industrial centers in the state – with at least two half-finished battleships for the US Navy always under construction. But it only takes up a small lip of a shoreline otherwise pristine and expansive. Besides being such a key economic force in our region, I love the fact that ships are still built in our corner of the state. Just as I love looking right while crossing the bridge and seeing the sweep of the Kennebec, especially at this time of the year, the aptly named fall, when the foliage is a hallucinatory palette of crimsons and golds.

Were I a cartographer of the fifteenth century, the map of my flat earth would terminate at the town of Brunswick, as I so rarely venture beyond its boundaries. Brunswick is a college town.

Bowdoin is there. It was also, until recently, the home of a naval air station. There used to be a paper mill on the banks of its river. It's now long closed. But as a kid passing through the town I can always remember the strange toxic whiff of glue that seemed to permeate the place. We were in Brunswick two or three times a year, as Dad's closest childhood friend – Arnold Soule – was a professor of mathematics at Bowdoin. Dad and Arnold grew up in the same small town and bonded at school over advanced calculus. But whereas Dad chose U Maine and a high-school teaching career, Soule got a full scholarship to MIT and followed that with a doctorate from Harvard. He was a tenured professor at Bowdoin by the time he was twenty-eight and wrote wildly theoretical books about binary number theory (his specialty) that, according to Dad, were hugely acclaimed 'in the theoretical mathematics community'. Arnold also happened to be gay – something he confided to my father when they were much younger, and at a time when such a revelation could have destroyed his life. Dad, for his part, kept Arnold's secret just that – something that Arnold told me many years later when I was supposed to be coming down to the college with Lucy to hear a chamber music concert. When Lucy was flattened with flu and had to cancel at the last minute I called this great family friend and asked him if he'd like to join me. That was just over five years ago. Arnold had finally come out in the early nineties and was living with a graphics designer twenty years his junior named Andrew. When we met up that night Arnold was seventy and had just retired. He was a little rueful about giving up teaching, even though he was engaged in a massive ten-year writing project that was (as he told me) an accessible history of mathematical theory from Euclid onwards. I always liked Arnold, always felt that he was the interesting, understanding uncle I never had (I had rather judgmental aunts on both sides of the family). That evening five years ago – when we talked over a dinner in an Italian restaurant on Maine Street before hearing a visiting pianist from New York play a sublime program of Scarlatti, Ravel and Brahms at the college recital hall – he asked me a direct question:

'Happy with your life, Laura?'

The question immediately unsettled me. Arnold saw that.

'My life is fine,' I said, hearing the defensiveness behind my response.

'Then why did you flinch when I posed the question?'

'Because it took me by surprise, that's all.'

'Your father tells me you're highly regarded in your field.'

'My father is being far too kind. As you know I run scanning machinery in a small local hospital. It's hardly a great accomplishment.'

'But it's very important, skilled work. The thing is – and I say this as someone who has known you since you first arrived in this world of ours – I've always wondered why you seem to short-change yourself. And maybe it's absolutely none of my business. But I'll say it anyway, because you're still a young woman with possibilities—'

'I have two children and a husband and a mortgage and far too many bills. So my actual possibilities are few and far between.'

'So you say. The truth is, we all have greater possibilities than we ever realize or want to accept. Look at me – I always wanted to live in Paris, teach absurdly abstruse calculus at the École Normale Supérieure, master the language, and take up with a marvellous French chap whose family just happened to own a château in the Loire. And yes, I know that all sounds so clichéd – a gay mathematician's picture-postcard reverie. But here I am, at seventy, and except for a week in the City of Light every summer with Andrew – to whom I've never revealed the French lover fantasy – have I ever used a sabbatical break or even the three months we get off every summer to live there? Hell, no. Know what I think? I think part of me still believes I don't deserve Paris. Isn't that terrible? And Andrew – who I also didn't think I deserved when I first met him, but thankfully he thought otherwise – is now insisting that next summer, when he can take some leave from his job, we spend six months there. He's already apartment hunting for us. And I am finally giving in to the idea.'

'Good for you,' I said, noticing that I was simultaneously strangling the napkin in my lap.

'Yes, it's only taken me fifty years of adult life to finally come to the conclusion that I deserve happiness. Which, in turn, leads me to ask: when are you going to start thinking you deserve happiness?'

'I'm not unhappy, Arnold.'

'You remind me so much of your father. He could have had the full ticket to Harvard or Chicago or Stanford or any other major university – because, on many levels, he was even cleverer than me. Just as I know you got accepted here at Bowdoin, but chose U Maine.'

'You know why I chose U Maine. They offered me a full scholarship. Here it was only fifty per cent – and I would have had to take out a loan . . .'

'Which – had you gone to medical school – you would have paid back five years after getting your MD degree. And having just said that, I know I've overstepped . . .'

'Perhaps you have,' I said. Thinking: *You cannot begin to imagine how many times over the years I have privately reproached myself for this piece of late-adolescent bad judgment.*

'I'm truly sorry,' Arnold said. 'But I just want you to not make the mistakes I made.'

'I'm afraid it's too late for that. And I really think I'd like to get off this subject now . . .'

'Of course, of course.'

The remainder of the meal was rather forced, our conversation stilted, guarded, overshadowed by the uncomfortable exchange that had just occurred. Then we listened to the concert – but I didn't hear a note, as everything Arnold told me kept churning around my head. Because it was, sadly, all so true, so right on the money. Afterward, my father's friend walked me to my car, his head lowered, clearly distressed.

'Will you forgive a foolish old man his foolhardy attempt to give out advice?'

'Of course I forgive you,' I said, embracing him lightly.

'OK,' he said quietly, realizing the landscape between us had changed. 'Don't be a stranger, eh?'

'And don't you find a way of *not* going to Paris.'

'I'll try not to.'

I never heard from Arnold again. Two months later he woke up one morning with chest pains – and died of a coronary occlusion less than an hour later. Life is like that. You're here, in the midst of things. Then, out of nowhere, something shows up and snuffs your existence out. It's always so dreadful, a sudden death like that. Always so profoundly unfair. And so distressingly common.

Brunswick. The border beyond which I rarely cross. My world: the thirty miles from Damariscotta to Brunswick.

And now . . .

Portland.

Our one proper city in Maine. An actual functioning port. A place of business. A foodie paradise – and a town which, if I was twenty-five and wanted to start out in a city away from the big metropolitan ambitions and pressures of a New York, a Los Angeles, a Chicago, I'd certainly think about considering. Ben especially likes what he calls 'the Portland vibe – urban Maine bohemia'. I think he envisages himself in the future in some warehouse space near the docks, living simply, but having a huge studio space and doing well enough as an artist to meet his bills and fund his work. 'I don't really want to go to New York or Berlin,' he told me recently. 'I just want to stay in Maine and paint.' As this comment came in the wake of that terrible period of his life I didn't want to say that, quite honestly, the best thing that could happen for him as an artist was to get out of Maine for a few years.

Still, if he ends up in Portland . . . well, of course, I'll love the fact that he's just an hour down the road. And it will give me an excuse to drop down here more often – because this is a city I should be using frequently. And maybe now that Dan is bringing in a salary again . . .

No, let's not think about any of that this weekend. Let's call a moratorium on all domestic thoughts for the next forty-eight hours.

As if.

Kennebunkport. Summer home of the Bush family. I voted for Bush Senior, but couldn't give my support to Junior – as he reminded me of a richer, more vindictive version of the frat boys I always seemed to dodge at college. I've always loved the beach at Kennebunkport – a curiously rugged stretch of the Atlantic and a wondrously savage contrast to the well-heeled, upscale community that fronts it. I would love to somehow, sometime, live directly by the sea. Just to be able to wake up every day and immediately look out at the water. No matter what was going on around me there would be the immense consolation of water.

I glanced at my watch. I was making good time, listening to a Mozart symphony on Maine Public Radio. The 36th, subtitled the Linz. The announcer explained how Mozart showed up, in 1781, on a Monday at the home of the Count of Linz, wife in tow, and the Count, knowing Mozart's habit of running up debts, offered him a nice sum of money if he could write a symphony for the court orchestra by Friday. Four days to write and orchestrate a symphony! And one that is still being played over two centuries later. Is genius, among other things, the appearance of effortless-ness when it comes to great work? Or is there some sort of mystique hovering around the notion that all truly serious art must have a long gestation period; that it must be the result of a profound and torturous struggle? Even as the reception began to crackle, once I crossed the bridge that links Maine to New Hampshire, I couldn't help but be carried along by the immense lyricism of the symphony – and the way Mozart seemed able to reflect the lightness and darkness lurking behind all things in the course of a single musical phrase.

New Hampshire – just a stretch of highway here on this corner of I-95. Then Massachusetts – and suburban Boston announced itself with billboards and shopping malls and fast food and strip bars and places to buy lawn furniture and endless car dealerships and cheap motels. The conference was being held in a Fairfield Inn along Route 1, just a few miles from Logan Airport. I'd Googled the place in advance – so I knew it was a large airport hotel with a conference centre attached to it. Up close it was a concrete block. Inconsequential. Uninteresting. A place you would never notice unless you were stopping by. But I didn't care if it was big and squat and all reinforced concrete and this side of ugly. It was an escape hatch for a couple of days. Even the unappealing can look pretty good when it represents a break from routine.

*Two*

FLORAL CARPET. FLUORESCENT lights. Concrete walls painted industrial cream. And a big reception desk made from cheaply veneered wood, over which were clocks that showed the time in London, Chicago, San Francisco and (of course) here in Boston. This was the reception area of the Fairfield Inn, Logan Airport. It did not look promising, especially since there was already a huge line in front of the desk.

'Must be all the X-ray people,' said the man who had just joined behind me.

I smiled.

'Yes, must be,' I said.

'"X-ray people",' the man said again, shaking his head at this comment. 'Makes it sound like 1950s sci-fi. Not that you were around in the 1950s . . .'

'Glad you think so.'

'I would say you were born in 1980.'

'Now that is flattery.'

'You mean, I got it wrong?' he asked.

'By about eleven years, yes.'

'I'm disappointed.'

'By my age?'

'By my inability to guess your age,' he said.

'That's a major personal fault?'

'In my game it is.'

'And your game is . . .?'

'Nothing terribly interesting.'

'That's quite an admission,' I said.

'It's the truth.'

'And the truth is . . .?'

'I sell insurance.'

I now stepped back and got a proper look at this insurance man.

72

Mid-height – maybe five foot nine. Reasonably trim figure – with the slightest hint of a paunch around his stomach. Graying hair, but not thinning hair. Steel-rimmed glasses in a rectangular frame. A dark blue suit – not particularly expensive, not particularly cheap. A mid-blue dress shirt. A rep tie. A wedding ring on his left index finger. He had a Samsonite roll-on bag in one hand, and a very large black briefcase on the floor next to it – no doubt filled with policy forms just waiting to be filled in as soon as he landed the necessary clients. I judged him to be somewhere in his mid-fifties. Not particularly handsome. Outside of the gray hair, not looking bloated or too weathered by life.

'Insurance is one of life's necessities,' I said.

'You should write my sales pitch.'

'I'm certain you've got a better one than that.'

'Now it's you who's flattering me.'

'And where do you sell insurance?'

'Maine.'

I brightened.

'My home state,' I said.

Now he brightened.

'Born and bred?' he asked.

'Absolutely. Heard of Damariscotta?'

'I live about twenty miles away in Bath . . .'

I then told him where I'd grown up, also mentioning my years at U Maine.

'I'm a U Maine grad as well,' he said – and we quickly discovered which dorms we lived in during our respective freshman years and that he was a business studies major at the college.

'I did biology and chemistry,' I said.

'Far more brainy than me. So you're a doctor?'

'What makes you guess that?'

'The two science majors, and the fact that there is a radiography convention this weekend at this hotel – and all you X-ray people are delaying my check-in.'

That last comment came out with a smile. But I took his point, as there were fifteen people ahead of us and only two receptionists at work. We were going to be here awhile.

'So you've decided I'm an X-ray person,' I said.

'That's just deduction.'

'You mean, I don't look like an X-ray person?'

'Well, I know I look like the sort of man who sells insurance.'

I said nothing.

'See,' he said, 'guilty as charged.'

'Do you like selling insurance?'

'It has its moments. Do you like being a radiographer?'

'I'm just a technologist, nothing more.'

'If you're a radiographic technologist, that's a pretty important job.'

I just shrugged. The man smiled at me again.

'Which hospital?'

'Maine Regional.'

'No kidding. Were you working there when Dr Potholm ran the department?'

'Dr Potholm hired me.'

The man smiled and stuck out his hand.

'I'm Richard Copeland.' He simultaneously handed me his business card.

I took his hand. A firm grip. A salesman's grip. I pocketed the card. I told him my name.

'My first grade teacher was named Laura,' he said, 'though we called her Miss Wigglesworth.'

'Well, my mother told me that, after much debate, the name choice came down to Laura or Sandra. My father preferred the latter, but my mother was certain I'd end up being called Sandy.'

'Sandy's a little bit Californian, isn't it?'

Now it was my turn to giggle. Richard Copeland certainly had an easy conversational style. But he was also somewhat cautious with his body language, as if he was always fighting a certain physical shyness. I could see him looking me over and then trying to mask the fact that he was looking me over. The banter between us was simultaneously breezy and guarded. I characterized him as a flirt who was not totally at ease with being a flirt. But this was, without question, a flirtation – of the sort that two strangers have when caught together in a long line and they know that, in fifteen minutes, they'll never be seeing each other again.

'Funny you say that. When I was thirteen my dad mentioned to me that I almost ended up with another first name, but "Mother hated the name Sandra". And when I asked her why she was so against that name, Mom said that Sandy would have made me sound like "a surfer girl".'

'Spoken like a true Maine mother.'

'Oh, Mom would have been very much at home in the Massachusetts Bay Colony.'

He looked a little surprised by that last comment – almost flinching a bit.

'Have I said the wrong thing?' I asked.

'Hardly,' he said. 'It's just that it's not every day you hear someone make reference to the Massachusetts Bay Colony.'

'Most of us read *The Scarlet Letter* at some point in school.'

'And most of us have forgotten all about it.'

'Well, I can't say I've downloaded it onto my Kindle . . . not that I have one.'

'You prefer paper?'

'I prefer real books. And you?'

'I'm afraid I've crossed over to the dark side.'

'It's not a mortal sin.'

'I do have twenty books in my in-box right now.'

'And what are you reading right now?'

'You wouldn't believe me if I told you.'

'Let me decide that. What's the book?'

I could see him blush. And stare down at his well-polished black cordovans.

'Nathaniel Hawthorne's *The Scarlet Letter*.'

'That *is* a coincidence,' I said.

'But the truth.'

'I'm sure.'

'I could show you my Kindle if you don't believe me . . .'

'No need, no need.'

'Now I'm sure you think I'm weird.'

'Or just weirdly literate. Anyway, *The Scarlet Letter*. Hester Prynne and all that.'

'It remains a great novel.'

'And rather prescient, given the current wave of religiosity sweeping the country.'

'"*Prescient*",' he said, phonetically sounding it out as if it was the first time he'd ever spoken it. 'Nice word.'

'That it is.'

'And even if I don't agree with a lot of what the Christian Right bangs on about, don't you think there are certain things about which they have a point?'

Oh, no. A serious Republican.

'Such as?' I asked.

'Well, such as the need to maintain family values.'

'Most people with families believe in family values.'

'I wouldn't totally agree with that. I mean, look at the divorce rate—'

'But look at the time before divorce, when people were trapped in marriages they loathed, when there was absolutely no latitude for anyone, when women were expected to give up careers the moment they got pregnant, when if you dared turn your back on a husband and children you were considered a social outcast.'

I realized I had raised my voice a decibel or so. Just as I also saw Richard Copeland a little taken aback by the vehemence with which I had rendered that homily.

'I didn't mean to upset you,' he said.

'I'm not usually so fierce.'

'That wasn't fierce. That was impressive. Even if I disagree with much of what you said.'

He delivered that last line with his chin pointed down at his tie, as if to dodge the heated exchange he was nonetheless courting. I didn't like this. It struck me as timid-arrogant. Say the controversial thing – but do it in such a way where you don't bury its import by speaking it into your damn shirt.

'Well, I'm hardly surprised to hear that,' I said.

'What I meant to say was—'

'You know what? I think this is a good moment to draw a line in the sand and simply say: Have a nice weekend.'

'Now I feel bad. I really didn't mean—'

'I'm sure you'll get over it.'

At the reception desk there was a young woman in a maroon suit with a yellow shirt and a name tag that let it be known she was called Laura.

'Hey, Laura, say hello to Laura,' she said after perusing my driver's license.

'Hi, Laura,' I said, hoping I didn't sound too dry.

'And how's your day been so far?'

'Curious.'

This caught her by surprise.

'I guess curious is better than boring, right?'

'That is a very good point.'

'Let me see if I can turn your "curious" day into a better day – by offering you a complimentary upgrade. Top floor, king bed, view of the pool. How does that sound?'

'Just fine,' I said. 'Thank you.'

The pool view was only possible if you opened the window, stuck your head out and engaged in some serious vertigo as you looked straight down onto the cinder-block patio below. The problem was, when you opened the window you were hit with an interesting amalgamation of traffic noise and traffic fumes – and this was clearly the quiet side of the hotel with the preferred view. So after a quick look down and into the near distance – more gas stations and parking lots – I closed the window, shutting out the outside world.

I sat down on the bed and wondered why I was feeling so cheerless just now. Maybe it was something to do with the less than inviting nature of this room, with decor that hadn't been updated in over twenty years. A floral carpet with faded coffee stains. A floral bedspread and matching floral drapes that all looked like they belonged in a home for the aged. The bathroom had a tub in molded plastic and a shower curtain that had begun to mildew. Oh, well, you're only sleeping here this weekend – and it is just for two nights. But these were the only two nights I would be away from home this year. Had I the money I would have checked myself out of this sad place immediately, grabbed a taxi into Boston, and checked myself into something nice overlooking the common. But that was so out of my financial league, so beyond anything I could afford. *Make the best of it . . . enjoy the freedom of being away from everything for a few days.*

And, of course, before I heeded that advice (could I heed that advice?) I popped open my phone and began to text my son:

Sorry we didn't connect last night. In Boston now. Please send update on life and art when you have a moment. Or if you feel like calling, even when I am in conference about lymphatic dyes (yes, there is one!) my cell will buzz silently. Will also do me a huge favor by getting me out of 'The Case for Fewer Colonoscopies' . . . not that I will be at that one! Miss you. Love – Mom

Then I sent a fast text to Sally:

I know things can get difficult between you and your father. Just as sometimes we get up each other's noses (excuse the metaphor!). Please know I am always here for you, always in your corner. If you need me this weekend just pick up the phone day or night. Love you – Mom

Once the text was sent, I had two more duties. The first was a call to Dan – but I got his voicemail, making me think he might have headed to the gym or the beach. He started work again at four a.m. Monday morning – and though I was certain he was already dreading the job I hoped that, at least, he was finding a way of relaxing for these three final days before he was back in the workaday world. I also hoped that he was taking a long view when it came to the job and saw it as a way back into the company which had tossed him away like an ill-fitting shoe twenty-one months earlier; a stepping stone to better things.

*You really do try to see the best in everything, don't you?*

But is there anything truly wrong with that? What else can any of us do except travel hopefully?

'Hi, hon,' I said, speaking after the beep commanded me to leave him a message. 'In Boston. The hotel could be better. And it would be lovely if you were here to share the city with me. I hope to go there sometime tomorrow. Anyway, just wanted to say hi, hope you're having a lovely day. Miss you . . .'

As I clicked the phone shut it struck me that I hadn't said: 'Love you.' Did I still love Dan? Did he still love me?

No. Not now. Not this weekend.

The endless refrain.

I stood up. I checked my watch. I glanced down at the convention welcome pack on the bed. I saw that the talk on 'CT Scanning and Inoperable Stage Three Lung Cancer' was beginning in ten minutes. Better than loitering in here, thinking, thinking. Imagine using a seminar like that the way most of us use a movie we know isn't going to be very good – as a form of pure escapism. Still, anything is better than this room.

I grabbed my convention badge, attached to a red ribbon. I dropped it over my neck and gave myself a fast glance in the mirror, thinking: *God, I'm looking older.* Then I headed downstairs, thinking over that curious conversation I had with the insurance man from Bath – and how I had enjoyed the banter, the harmless flirtation, before he began to sound like a knee-jerk Republican.

*No, that's not fair. He was literate (who makes a reference to Nathaniel Hawthorne these days?) and clearly well-informed and, like me, nervously enjoying this exchange. And you overreacted when he said something that you took the wrong way.*

Was I overreacting because I was flirting with him? Was my petulance bound up in the sense that I was doing something I shouldn't have been doing . . . that I can never recall having done before during all the years of my marriage?

*Oh, please. It was conversational give-and-take, nothing more. The guy was as awkward as you are – so it was clearly something he didn't engage in very often either. But he was also far more intelligent than any insurance man you've ever encountered . . . not that you've exactly encountered vast numbers of men selling you indemnity against life's possible horrors.*

Still, I shouldn't have snapped at him like that.

In the elevator going down to the main lobby there was a woman who stood about five foot four. Slight to the point of being petite, yet with eyes that seemed so animated. She was wearing a plain mid-brown pants suit. Her gray hair was cut simply. She was a woman so unimposing that you would pass her on the street without noticing her. Until you caught sight of her smile. A smile which hinted that she was one of those rare souls who have a sanguine way of looking at the world. I glanced at her conference badge: *Ellen Wilkinson / Regional Memorial Hospital / Muncie, Indiana.* Standing next to her (with her back to me) was a tall, spindly woman, also in her mid-fifties. As the elevator door closed behind me I heard Ellen Wilkinson tell this lofty woman:

'. . . what can I say? I come home after a day full of horror in the scanning room. And Donald is there. And after thirty-eight years together I still look at the guy and think: *Lucky me.* And from the way he always smiles at me – even if he too has had a terrible day – I know he's thinking the same thing. *Lucky us.*'

Out of nowhere I found myself lowering my head as my eyes filled up with tears. I turned away, not wanting these two women to see my distress; a distress that had caught me so unawares. But Ellen Wilkinson of Muncie, Indiana, clearly caught sight of my upset, as she put her hand on my shoulder and asked:

'Are you all right, dear?'

To which I could only quietly reply:

'Lucky you indeed.'

Then the elevator door opened and I walked straight into the seminar about 'CT Scanning and Inoperable Stage Three Lung Cancer'.

# Three

SOMEWHERE DURING THE third seminar of the late afternoon – no, it was now early evening – the thought struck me: *I've not absorbed a word of anything I've heard.* Deep technical discussions about the new MRI techniques for uncovering cerebral arterial sclerosis. A long, badly delivered, but still important (I suppose) paper from a research fellow at the Rockefeller Institute about the complexities of coronary valve imaging. Two radiographic technologists from St Louis doing a double act on a pioneering technique they developed for early ultrasound detection of ectopic pregnancies (I was cheered by my fellow technologists being saluted for a breakthrough that research scientists usually handle – and which they discovered through sheer application of all their years of technical knowledge). And a talk about advances in intravenous radiographic dyes and their heightened efficacy.

Yes, I did listen to everything being said in these back-to-back sessions. Yes, my brain occasionally did register interest in what was being discussed. But, for the most part of the long afternoon I spent in that large, overheated conference room, I was elsewhere. It was all due to that overheard conversation in the elevator. A declaration of long-term marital love that I'd never heard expressed in such a direct and simple and touching way. And behind my distress was a certain envy. How I so wanted to look at the man who shares my life and think: *Lucky us.* But that was simply not our story. And that made me cry. In public. A fact which so unnerved me. Because, yet again, tears arrived without warning, and I had let my guard down. The same heavily guarded self which had enabled me, for all these years, to never hint to anyone (outside of Lucy) that I come home to unhappiness night after night. Then again, I was brought up with the idea that complaining was a shabby thing to do. My mother couldn't tolerate anyone who moaned about how difficult things were in their life. 'You can complain all you want when you're dead – and then not be able to do a damn thing about it. But while you're alive and kicking, you just keep working. Complaining is lashing out against things over which you largely have no control . . . like the smallness of other people.'

Mom said all that to me on a Saturday afternoon four years ago when I went up to see her at her home. She had just completed her last chemotherapy session and was rail thin with little hair.

'The oncologist is making all sorts of noises about him being the General Patton of cancer doctors, and leading an onslaught against all those crazy T-cells that have landed me in this mess. But I'm not convinced.'

'Oncologists rarely say positive things until they believe they can deliver good results,' I said.

'Well, this guy would tell a man already half-eaten by a shark: "Hang in there, there's still a way out of this." But I know my body better than anyone. And my body is telling me: *This is a battle we're going to lose.* I am resigned to that. Just as I am resigned to the fact that I should have done more with the time I had . . .'

'Mom, you've done loads . . .'

'Now you are talking nonsense. I've had a rather small, little life. Outside of your father, yourself and a few friends, my passing will be noted by no one. I am not being excessively morbid, just honest. I have spent my whole life in one corner of Maine. I have worked in a library. I have been married to the same curious man for forty-four years and have raised a daughter – who is a much more accomplished person than she gives herself credit for. And that's about the sum total of it all . . . besides the fact that I should have made more of things over the years.'

That last sentence came back to haunt me many times after her death. Just as it returned yet again today as I sat through the final session of the early evening, listening to a 'radiology fellow' at the Rockefeller Institute engaging in a long, wildly technical discourse on future possibilities of imaging early-stage cancer. Might a next-generation MRI system actually trope malignant cellular activity? Had it been functioning three years ago would it have helped detect the pancreatic cancer early enough to save my mother? Then again, pancreatic cancer is a largely silent disease; 'the Trojan Horse of cancers', as my mother's oncologist described it, and almost always a death sentence. The problem with life-taking illnesses is: you can never completely control them. You can zap them, tame them, try to get them to disintegrate or take another course. Even when subdued or even temporarily vanquished they so often reassemble their forces for another toxic push for control. In this sense you can't truly control their strange logic any more than you can control the actions of someone whose behavior you want to change . . . or, worse yet, whom you want to love you.

But can we ever know the truth about another person? How can we ever really understand the inner workings of someone else if we so barely grasp all that is transpiring in ourselves?

Why is everything, everyone, such a damn mystery? And why did I allow that woman's happiness to so devastate me?

When the last session finished I drifted out into the lobby. It was after six p.m. and I needed to eat. There was a restaurant in the hotel, but it looked just a little greasy and depressing. Why give myself an additional dose of grimness tonight? So I headed up to my room, checked my phone for messages en route (there were none), then grabbed my raincoat against the evening chill and returned downstairs to the parking lot and my car. Twenty minutes later I found myself in Cambridge and got lucky, finding a parking spot on a side street right off Harvard Square. I wandered into a diner that I remembered once eating in around twenty years ago – when I came down with Dan from U Maine for a weekend. We were both seniors. We had no money, and we had just made several big decisions about our joint future together which I was already beginning to rue (correction: I had rued it from the start). Still, it had been a peerless late spring day in Cambridge, we'd found a cheap hotel near Harvard (they still existed back then) and had just spent the morning at the Museum of Fine Arts in Boston (my choice – there was a big Matisse show on at the time), then sat in the upper deck at Fenway Park, watching the Red Sox beat the Yankees in ten innings (Dan's choice – though I actually rather like baseball). Then we came back to Cambridge and had

83

grilled cheese sandwiches in this diner opposite the university. Though we were the same age and generation as all the students in the place, between us there was that unspoken discomfort of being around all these representatives of academic privilege and prestige – and how they would have an easier entree into the adult world with their Harvard degrees.

Then one of the undergraduates at a nearby booth – clearly drunk and preppy with an entitlement complex – began to berate the Latino waiter taking his order. The guy's Harvard cohorts egged him on. The waiter was very distressed by the way they were chiding him for his bad English. Dan and I listened to this in tense silence. When the preppy ringleader began to tell the guy that he 'should really get the next bus back to Tijuana', Dan suddenly stood up and told him to stop the trash talk. The preppy stood up, towering over Dan, and told my boyfriend to mind his own damn business. Dan stood his ground and said: 'If you say another racist thing to this man, I'm getting the cops. And then you can explain to the police – and the Harvard administration – why you like to bully people and make cracks about their background.'

The preppy got even more belligerent.

'You think I'm scared of some hayseed nobody like you?' he asked Dan.

To which my boyfriend replied:

'Actually, yeah, I do think you're scared. Because you're wasted and breaking the law. And if I call the police, you're going to get expelled . . . or force your rich daddy to build a new science center at Harvard to keep you from being thrown out . . .'

'Fuck you,' the preppy said.

'Have it your way,' Dan said, and headed towards the front door. But when the preppy grabbed hold of his jacket his Harvard friends were on their feet, restraining him, and quickly apologized.

'Fine then,' Dan said. 'I presume there will be no more trouble.'

As he slid down opposite me in the booth I looked at him wide-eyed with admiration.

'Wow,' I whispered. 'That was amazing.'

He just shrugged and said:

'I hate bullying . . . almost as much as I hate preppies.'

That was the moment when I thought I really did want to marry Dan – because who doesn't swoon when someone stands up to unfairness and shows himself to be so chivalrous? Though part of me was still dubious about our future together, another part of me reasoned after this incident: *He is that rare thing, a decent, honest guy who would be there for me.*

Such are the ways futures are made – out of an incident in a coffee shop and a need for certainty at a moment after everything had been so profoundly painful.

I wandered into that diner off Harvard Square. Everything else about this area had changed. The big revival-house cinema that faced the square was long gone. So too the countless number of used bookshops that once seemed to be an intrinsic part of Cambridge life. In their place were fashion boutiques, upmarket chain stores, cosmetic emporiums, places to buy exotic teas, and yes, the one constant from that time twenty years ago, the Harvard Coop. And, of course, this coffee shop.

I went inside. It was just after seven; that quiet time before the arrival of all the students who would roll in much later on, fresh from whatever the evening had brought them. The waitress told me to take any booth I wanted. On the way in I'd passed by an on-the-street red box and picked up a copy of the *Boston Phoenix*, remembering when it cost a dollar. I liked paying for it (rather than getting it free now), as it felt as if you were funding a little corner of the counterculture. I ordered, for old times' sake, a grilled cheese sandwich and a chocolate milkshake (promising myself an hour on the cross-trainer in the hotel gym tomorrow to atone for all the comfort-food indulgence). Then opening the *Phoenix* and going directly to the arts pages, I considered taking in the eight p.m. show at the Brattle Cinema. It was the last remaining revival-house movie theater in the Boston area. They were showing *The Searchers*. When was the last time I saw a classic old western on a big screen? And God knows, I didn't need to be running back to that grim hotel in a hurry, as the first seminar of the morning began at ten and I'm certain I could get an hour in at the gym beforehand, and . . .

I suddenly wanted to speak to Dan, to tell him where I was. So I dug out my cellphone and hit the autodial button marked 'Home'. He answered on the second ring.

'You will not believe where I am sitting right now,' I told him.

When I informed him of the location his response was muted: 'That was a long time ago.'

'But I still remember how you stood up to those Harvard guys.'

'I can't really recall much about it.'

'Well, I certainly can. In fact, all of the details came rushing back just now.'

'By which you mean happier times?'

He didn't pose that comment in the form of a question; rather as a statement of fact, and one so bluntly delivered that it took me a little aback.

'By which I mean,' I said carefully, 'I was just recalling how wonderful you were . . .'

'During my one unrepeated "profile in courage"?' he said.

'Dan . . .'

'If you remember I start work Monday morning at four in the morning – which means I am trying to adjust to this new brutal schedule by getting to bed every night by eight. It's now nearly nine-fifteen and you woke me up with this call, which is why I am sounding grumpy. Because you should have thought about that before phoning. So if you'll excuse me . . .'

'Sorry for waking you,' I said.

With a click, he was gone.

The grilled cheese sandwich and the milkshake arrived moments after I put my cellphone down. I suddenly had no appetite. But I couldn't let the food go to waste. I ate the sandwich and drank the shake and settled the check. Then I wandered down the street to The Brattle. There were only a handful of people standing outside the box office. I bought a ticket and went upstairs. What a little gem this place turned out to be: maybe three hundred seats, including a balcony, in a room that looked like it was once a small chapel, but which had been outfitted as the perfect place to watch old movies. The seats were very 1950s. The screen was stretched across a small stage, and the lights were just bright enough to squint at the program of forthcoming films. There couldn't have been more than ten of us in the cinema. Just as the lights came down a man came rushing in, dropping into the row in front of me. He looked a little out of breath, as if he was truly high-tailing it in here to make it just before the film started. I noticed immediately the blue suit, the graying hair, the tan raincoat – all of which seemed out of place among this largely student crowd. As this businessman stood up again to take off his raincoat his gaze happened upon me. At which moment he smiled and said:

'Well, hello there! Didn't know you liked westerns.'

It was the insurance man from the hotel. The insurance man from Maine. It was Richard Copeland.

Before I could reply – not that I knew how I should reply to this greeting – the cinema went dark and the screen burst into technicolor life. I spent the next two hours watching John Wayne riding across the empty spaces of the American West, struggling with his demons as he tried to find his way back to a place he might just call home.

I RARELY CRY in the movies. But there I was, sobbing over a western I'd never seen before. It centered around a man who carries so many griefs and furies with him – such anger at the world – that he spends years trying to track down his young niece who was kidnapped by the Apaches when she was just a girl. When he finally discovers her as a young woman – and now one of the wives of the chieftain who had slaughtered her family – his initial instinct is to kill her. Until a profound sense of personal connection kicks in and he saves her, returning her to her remaining relatives. As they welcome her back with open arms, the man who has endured so much while searching for her watches as she disappears inside their home. Then, as the door closes behind her, he turns and heads off into the vast nowhere of the American West.

It was in this final scene of the film that I found myself crying – and being surprised by the fact that I was crying. Was the reason due to the fact that, like the John Wayne character in the movie, I so *wanted* to go home? But was that 'home' I so longed for just an idealized construct, with no bearing on reality? Do we all long for homes that have no bearing on those we have built for ourselves?

All these thoughts came cascading out in the last minute or so of the film – along with the tears that once more arrived out of nowhere and made me so uncomfortable.

The lights were now coming up – and I was racing around my handbag for a Kleenex, trying to dry my eyes in case that man decided to engage me in further chat. I really was hoping he'd do the easier thing, maybe nod to me goodnight, then be on his way.

I dabbed my eyes. I stood up, along with the other ten or so people who were seated in the downstairs part of the cinema, and deliberately walked the other way out of the theater to avoid running into Richard Copeland. But when I reached the exit door and turned back I saw that he was still in his seat, lost in some sort of reverie. Immediately I felt a little ashamed about wanting to get away from a man who was simply trying to be nice to me in the few moments we'd spoken together, and who had been as touched by the film as I'd been. So, without thinking too much about what I was doing, I lingered for a moment or so in the lobby until he came out. Up close I could see that his eyes were red from crying. Just as he was registering the fact that mine were red too.

'Quite a film,' I said.

'I never cry in movies,' he said.

'Nor do I.'

'Evidently.'

I laughed. An awkward pause followed, as neither of us knew what to say next. He broke the silence.

'You get talking with a guy standing in line for the hotel reception, next thing you know he's at the same movie theater as you.'

'Quite a coincidence.'

'I'd just had dinner with a client of mine who runs a machine tool company in Brockton. Not a particularly interesting town – in fact, it's the wrong side of grim – and not the most interesting guy in the world either. Still, he's been a loyal client for eleven years – and we knew each other back in high school in Bath. And I've no darn idea why I'm telling you this, bending your ear. But would a glass of wine interest you now?'

I hesitated – as I was somewhat thrown by the invite, even if I was not displeased by it either.

'Sorry, sorry,' he said in the wake of my silence. 'I completely understand if . . .'

'Is there somewhere nice around here? Because the hotel bar . . .'

'Agreed, agreed. It's pretty damn awful. I think there's a place next door.'

Again I hesitated – and simultaneously glanced at my watch.

'Listen,' he said, 'if it's far too late . . .'

'Well, it is just after ten o'clock. But it's not a school night, right?'

'Right.'

'OK – let's go next door, Richard.'

'You remembered my name.'

'You did give me your card, Mr Copeland.'

'I hope that wasn't too forward of me.'

'I just thought you might be trying to sell me some insurance.'

'Not tonight, Laura.'

I smiled. He smiled back.

'So you remembered my name,' I said.

'And without a calling card as well. Then again, salesmen always remember names.'

'Is that what you consider yourself, a salesman?'

'Yes, unfortunately.'

'I had a grandfather who ran a hardware shop in Waterville – and he never stopped telling me that everybody's always selling something. At least you sell something of value to people.'

'You are being too kind,' he said. 'And I'm probably now keeping you from something.'

'But I just said I was happy to have a glass of wine with you.'

'You sure about that?'

'I won't be if you ask me that question again.'

'Sorry, sorry. A bad habit of mine.'

'We all have bad habits,' I said as we walked out of the cinema and into the street.

'Are you always so kind?' he asked.

'I wasn't kind to you this afternoon.'

'Oh, that . . . I really didn't think . . .'

'I was bitchy. I'm sorry I was bitchy. And if you tell me I wasn't bitchy—'

'OK, you were bitchy. Totally bitchy.'

He said this with a small, somewhat mischievous smile crossing his lips. I smiled back.

'Good!' I said. 'Now that we've gotten all that out of the way . . .'

The café into which he steered us was called Casablanca and had been done up to very much resemble the joint that Humphrey Bogart managed in the film. The bartenders all wore white tuxedo jackets, the waiters gendarme uniforms.

'You think we'll run into Peter Lorre tonight?' I asked Richard.

'Well, as he got shot in the third reel . . .'

'You know your movies.'

'Not really – though, like everyone, I do love *Casablanca*.'

The maitre d' asked us if we were here to eat, drink or enquire about letters of transit out of Casablanca.

'Drinks only,' Richard said.

'Very good, *monsieur*,' the waiter said in what could only be described as a Peter Sellers French accent. As soon as we were installed in a booth Richard rolled his eyes and said:

'Sorry. If I'd known this place was a theme bar . . .'

'There are worse themes than *Casablanca*. At least you didn't bring me to a Hooters.'

'Not exactly my style.'

'Glad to hear it.'

'But if you'd rather go elsewhere . . .'

'And miss the charms of Morocco in Cambridge?'

'I've never been to North Africa. In fact, never outside of the US or Canada.'

'Me neither. And the thing is, I always told myself, when I was much younger, that I was going to travel, going to spend an important part of my life on the road.'

'I told myself that too.'

'Looking around here . . . it's funny, but I remember when I was around fourteen and going through the usual adolescent nonsense – and having a really bad time of it with my mother – I announced to her one day: "I'm joining the French Foreign Legion," because I'd seen some old Laurel and Hardy movie on TV where they ended up in the Foreign Legion . . .'

'*Sons of the Desert*.'

'And you say you know nothing about movies.'

'Just useless bits of information, like that one.'

'Anyway, I did that thing kids do when they're furious with their parents: I got a bag out of the closet, counted up all the allowance money I'd saved over the past months, thought about which bus I'd take to New York, and would I have enough cash to buy myself a ticket to wherever it was these days that the French Foreign Legion hang out.'

'Probably Djibouti,' he said.

'Where's Djibouti?'

'Somewhere in the Sahara.'

'And how do you know the Foreign Legion are there these days?'

'Read an article in *National Geographic*. Had a subscription since I was a kid. My dreams of travel started there, with that magazine. All those interesting color features about the Himalayas and the Brazilian rainforests and the Outer Hebrides and—'

'Favorite desert hangouts of the French Foreign Legion?'

He smiled again.

'Exactly,' he said. 'And that's why I know where Djibouti is.'

'Do you think Laurel and Hardy shot their movie there?' I asked.

'You're quick, did you know that?'

'Actually, I've never thought myself that.'

'You mean, nobody ever told you that you were clever?'

'Oh, a teacher, a professor, from time to time. Otherwise . . .'

'Well, you are clever.'

'Now you're trying to flatter me.'

'You don't like being flattered?' he asked.

'Of course I like being flattered. It's just . . . I don't think I merit it.'

'Why's that?'

'Aren't we getting a little personal here?'

His shoulders suddenly hunched, and he was back again, looking away, looking guilty. Much to my surprise I no longer found this disconcerting. Rather I felt a certain compassion for him – a compassion rooted in the fact that I so understood what it was like to be self-conscious and just a little ill at ease with my place in the larger scheme of things.

'Sorry, sorry,' he said. 'There I go again, talking before thinking.'

'And there you go again, being self-deprecating . . .'

'Even though my self-deprecation was due to your self-deprecation?'

'Touché.'

'I wasn't trying to score a point.'

'I know that. I also know that what we sometimes criticize in others is something that we find wanting in ourselves.'

'I didn't think you were criticizing me.'

'Well, I thought that.'

'Are you always so self-critical . . . speaking as someone who shares the same habit?'

'So I noticed. And now I'm dodging the question, right?'

Richard smiled at me. I smiled back – and simultaneously found myself disarmed by the fact that it was surprisingly easy to talk to this man, that we seemed to riff off each other. The waiter arrived. We both ordered a glass of red wine – and I liked the fact that when asked whether he preferred a merlot or a cabernet sauvignon or a pinot noir, Richard told the waiter that he knew very little about wine, and said that he'd follow his advice.

'A light or robust red?' the waiter then asked.

'Something in between maybe,' Richard said.

'Pinot noir will do the job then. Same for the lady?'

'Why not,' I said.

The waiter disappeared.

'So you're not afraid to admit you don't know something,' I said.

'I don't know many things.'

'Nor do I. But most people would never dream of revealing that little fact.'

'My dad always told me that the three most important words in life were: "I don't know".'

'He has a point.'

'*Had* a point. He's no longer with us.'

'Sorry.'

'No need to be,' he said. 'A rather complex man, my dad. Someone who always gave advice he couldn't himself follow. Like ever admitting that he didn't know things.'

'What did he do?'

'Fifteen years in the Marine Corps. Worked his way up to the

93

post of colonel. Then got married and returned to Maine – he was a Bath boy – and started a family. He also opened a little insurance company.'

He said this last line quietly, his gaze averted from mine, his need to state this and get it out of the way underscored by his discomfort in admitting this.

'I see,' I said.

'Yep. Followed Dad right into the family firm.'

'Is it a big firm?' I asked.

'Just me and my receptionist/bookkeeper . . . who also happens to be my wife.'

'So it's a real family firm.'

'Two people are hardly a firm,' he said, and again looked away – clearly not wanting to talk about this anymore. So I asked if he had children.

'A son. Billy.'

'How old?'

'He turns twenty-six next month.'

Which must make Richard around fifty-five or so.

'And where's he now?'

'For the moment he's living at home. Billy's kind of between things right now.'

The way he stated this I could tell he wanted to get off this subject as well.

'I too have a child living at home.'

I could see him exhale as he got me talking about my kids and my husband. He told me he knew all about that downsizing period at L.L.Bean. Three friends of his also got the axe around the same time as Dan. But wasn't it a great thing that my husband had been re-hired by the company, especially given how tough times are right now. How long had I been married? Twenty-one years? Well, he beat me on that score – 'twenty-nine years and counting' – and wasn't it rare and wonderful to be the last couple standing, so to speak, given how so many marriages fall apart these days?

He said this all with an air of bonhomie which I found curious.

A look of skepticism must have crossed my face, as he suddenly asked:

'Am I laying it on a little thick?'

'Not at all. Many people do have happy marriages. Then again, many people say they have happy marriages because they can't say that theirs is difficult. But I'm glad yours is happy.'

'Sorry, sorry . . .'

'For what? You don't have to keep apologizing.'

'For coming across like a salesman. All slick patter, all "Everyone's happy, right!"'

'Was your father like that?'

'I was always the salesman, Dad the numbers cruncher.'

'But he must have been something of a salesman to have started the firm.'

'He initially had a business partner – Jack Jones. A fellow Marine. Unlike my father Jack actually liked people. Don't know what he was doing in business with my father, as Jack was a genuinely happy-go-lucky guy and Dad was kind of dyspeptic about life.'

'I like that word, dyspeptic.'

'"Bilious" would be a good descriptive word as well. "Liverish" might also fit the bill.'

'How about "disputative"?'

'A little too legal, I think. Dad was a misanthrope, but never litigious.'

I looked at him with new interest.

'You like words,' I said.

'You're looking at the Kennebec County Spelling Bee Champion of 1974, which is kind of the Middle Ages now, right? But once you get hooked on words you don't really ever lose the habit.'

'But that's a most aspirational habit.'

We shared another smile. I saw him looking at me with new-found ease, as we were now on interesting common ground.

'"Aspirational",' he said. 'Upward mobility, Horatio Alger and all that. Very American.'

'I think aspirational is not simply an American construct.'

'"Construct",' he said, repeating the word to himself, taking evident pleasure in its sound. 'Even though it has two syllables it has a certain musicality, doesn't it?'

'If used constructively.'

'Or affirmatively?'

'That's too Boy Scout.'

'OK, I give you that. How about "abrogatory"?'

'Now you're getting far too fancy. "Approbative"?'

'That's not fancy? Sounds downright florid to me.'

'Florid isn't "aureate".'

'Or "churrigueresque"?' he asked.

'Oh, please! You are beyond flamboyant, baroque or, indeed, churrigueresque.'

'And I am wildly bedazzled by your vocabulary. Were you in the spelling bee racket as well?'

'Actually I sidestepped all that, even though I had an English teacher in junior high who was really trying to get me to join the spelling club after school. The thing is, I always had my nose in a thesaurus . . .'

'Just like me.'

'A geeky habit, as everyone else at school was happy to remind me. But though the teacher who ran the spelling team actually thought I could be the captain . . .'

'So he thought you were that good?'

Before I could reflect on that question I heard myself saying:

'I've never thought myself that good.'

'At anything?'

Now it was my turn to look away.

'I suppose so,' I finally said.

'Why's that?'

'You ask a lot of questions, sir.'

'My name is Richard, and the reason I ask a lot of questions is part professional habit, part personal interest.'

'Why should you be interested in me?'

'Because I am.'

I felt myself blushing. Richard immediately saw that, and it was his turn to get all embarrassed, saying:

'That really wasn't supposed to sound so forward. And if it did . . .'

'It didn't. You were just being nice to me.'

'Was I?'

'Oh, please . . .'

The drinks arrived. Richard raised his glass. And said:

'Here's to Roget, and Webster, and Funk and Wagnalls, and the *OED* and . . .'

'*The Synonym Finder* . . . which was my bedtime companion throughout most of high school.'

'Well, I suppose your parents didn't object to that.'

'My father was a mathematician, and one who really preferred the abstract to the concrete. So he largely stayed charming and affectionate and rather disinterested – in a thoroughly nice way – when it came to anything to do with my life, including my first boyfriend.'

'And who was the first boyfriend?'

'Surely that's not a question you ask on the life insurance form?'

'I wasn't aware that we were filling in a policy questionnaire.'

'The wine is good. Pinot noir. I have to remember that.'

'Is that a way of telling me you're not going to say anything about your first boyfriend?'

'Exactly.'

'Well, then I certainly won't push the point. But when it comes to your love affair with *The Synonym Finder* . . .'

'I actually saved up two weeks' babysitting money when I was fourteen to buy it. It was about twenty dollars, a small fortune at the time, but worth every penny.'

'What made it so valuable?'

'The fact that I could lose myself in it. Have you ever seen *The Synonym Finder*?'

'I actually own two.'

'You *are* a fellow geek.'

'Absolutely. But you are not a geek.'

'Actually I am. But getting back to *The Synonym Finder* – you know that the great pleasure of that book is that it's not as

97

formalized or rigid as a normal thesaurus; that it has real depth and breath when it comes to equivalent words, and that it really is geared towards semantical junkies.'

'"Semantical junkies". I like it.'

'Well, that's me. In fact, it's always been me.'

'Even though the sciences were your real métier?'

'Are sciences a "métier"?'

'Isn't everything a métier?' he asked.

Again I found myself looking at this man with care – because it was so rare to run into somebody who could utter such an eloquent phrase in the midst of normal conversation. Richard saw me considering him differently, and reacted with a shy smile, then a quick bowing of the head to avoid my gaze. This immediately made me think: *Oh God, were you projecting interest or – worse yet – infatuation?* I felt myself blushing again. And then – now this was really compounding things – I registered the fact that he was registering the fact that I was blushing. So I tried to mitigate things by saying:

'You have a nice turn of phrase . . .'

'And I seem to have embarrassed you . . .'

'No, it's me who's embarrassed me.'

'But why?'

'Because . . .'

I couldn't say what I was thinking: *Because you're clearly smart and I find that attractive and I shouldn't be finding you attractive for about ten obvious reasons.*

'Well, nobody has ever told me that before,' Richard said.

'Told you what?'

'That I have a nice turn of phrase.'

'Surely your wife has . . .'

As soon as those words were out of my mouth I regretted them. Because I realized I had overstepped a boundary.

'Sorry, sorry,' I said immediately. 'I shouldn't have implied that . . .'

'You implied nothing. It's a reasonable question. I love words. I love using words. I love painting with words – even though I don't get much of a chance to do so in my normal day-to-day work. And yes, it would be lovely if my partner in life, my wife, appreciated the way I use words. But when does your spouse ever really appreciate you the way you think you should be appreciated? I mean, that's asking a little much, isn't it?'

He said this with such lightness, such high irony, that I found myself giggling.

'I don't think it is asking much,' I said. 'Still, my father used to say that one of the problems of being smart at something is that you unintentionally show the other person up. It really gets under their skin, the fact that you have an ability, a talent, a way of looking at the world, that they so clearly believe they lack.'

'Having a thing about words is hardly a talent. It's more of a hobby. Like collecting model trains or stamps or old fountain pens.'

'It's a little more cerebral than any of those talents.'

'So you consider yourself cerebral?'

'Hardly.'

'See! We're cut from exactly the same Maine cloth. We might love things semantical. We might have both spent long involving hours exploring the world of synonyms. We might both have this love affair with language. But that doesn't make either of us intelligent, now does it?'

Again I found myself smiling and nodding my head.

'Bull's-eye,' I said, raising my glass. He picked his up and clinked it against mine.

'Here's to low self-esteem,' I said.

'Better known as – the insidious art of undervaluing yourself.'

'Do you write?'

Richard seemed taken aback by that question.

'Why do you ask that?'

'Just a hunch. The way you use language, love language.'

'I'm hardly a published writer . . .'

'But you have written, do write . . .?'

Richard lifted his glass and downed the remaining wine.

'I had a story published four years ago in a little magazine in Portland.'

'But that's great. What was the magazine?'

'Kind of a lifestyle mag. Chic places to eat and shop. Designer apartments. Hotels in which to spend a romantic weekend. That sort of thing.'

'And was your story about chic places to eat and designer apartments, with a romantic weekend in a coastal bed and breakfast thrown in?'

Richard smiled. 'I walked into that, didn't I?'

'You were apologizing for being in a lifestyle magazine.'

'Well, it's not exactly the *New Yorker.*'

'That might happen one day.'

'Wishful thinking.'

'Positive thinking,' I said.

'Very Norman Vincent Peale.'

'You've lost me.'

'*The Power of Positive Thinking* by Rev. Norman Vincent Peale. Probably the first American self-help book.'

'By a man of God.'

'A 1950s man of God – who now seems positively secular compared to the Bible thumpers out there right now.'

'But I thought you supported their "family values" sentiments.'

'You have quite a memory,' he said.

'Well, at least you didn't quote the Book of Revelations to me.'

'I'm hardly religious.'

'Then what's with the support for the born-agains?'

'I just don't like knee-jerk liberal dismissal of all things Christian.'

'Now speaking as a liberal – albeit a sensible one – I think what worries even the more sensible Republicans I know is the fact that the charismatic Christians have a political agenda that runs up against basic American ideas about separation of church and state, about basic human rights like a woman's right to control her own body or a gay couple's civil rights when it comes to having the legal protection afforded by marriage.'

'You know I'm not against anything you just said.'

'And I know I sound like I'm on a soapbox.'

'That's fine with me. You're a sensible liberal, I'm a sensible Republican . . . though some people nowadays might think that a tautology.'

He flashed a mischievous little grin at me. I couldn't help but think: *He's smart. And he can argue smart, and can use language so incisively, and in such a quick-witted way.*

'So tell me about your story,' I asked, changing the subject.

'You mean, you no longer want to hear my views about the Almighty?'

'A personal friend of yours?'

'Hey. I sold him a Full Life Policy last year which pays out five percent above the deductible.'

I laughed.

'So God lives in Maine?' I asked.

'Well, there is a reason why they call it "Vacationland". As such, He doesn't answer prayers very often.'

'Have you asked Him for a favour?'

'Haven't we all?'

'But I thought you were a non-believer.'

'I'm reserving judgment,' he said. 'Raised Presbyterian – but that was a family heritage thing. And I think my father approved of Presbyterianism because it was so dour, so austere.'

'And your mother?'

'She went along with everything my father said. Then again, his authority was never to be challenged.'

'Did you try?'

'Of course.'

'And?'

A pause – in which Richard looked down into his empty glass. Then:

'I'm running his company.'

'But you're still writing.'

'He couldn't stop me from doing that.'

'And if you asked God to get you into the *New Yorker* . . .?'

'Even He doesn't have that kind of pull.'

Again I laughed.

'But you believe in . . .'

He looked up and met my gaze straight on.

'I believe in wanting to believe in *something*.'

Silence – as that statement hung in the air between us. Ambiguous. Perhaps charged with meaning. Perhaps not. But the way he was looking at me right now . . .

A voice behind me curtailed the moment.

'How you folks doing?'

It was the waiter.

'Now I wouldn't want to speak for the two of us,' Richard said, 'but I think – just fine.'

'I concur,' I said.

A smile crossed between us.

'So are you ready for a second glass of wine?' the waiter asked.

'Well . . .' I said, thinking of at least five excuses I could give for an early night.

'If it's too late or you've got stuff to do in the morning . . .' Richard said.

I knew the simplest way to end the evening would be to say something along the lines of: 'Alas, the first group conference – Advanced Bone Marrow MRI Techniques – is scheduled for ten . . . and the radiologist back at my hospital will want to know all about it.' (Not true at all – we always send bone marrow cases to Portland.) And yes, fretting about a second glass of wine while driving would be a good exit strategy. Because I was finding this interesting conversation a little *too* interesting. And because, moments earlier, when Richard looked up at me and said: 'I believe in wanting to believe in *something*,' I couldn't help but think that his hesitancy was due to the fact that he stopped himself from saying 'someone'. And also because, as his eyes met mine when he uttered that sentence, I actually found myself disconcerted by the fact that the insurance salesman I first saw as gray and just a little drab was now holding my interest.

So yes, there were sensible reasons why I was about to tell Richard: 'You know, I really think it's getting a little late for me.'

But instead, something else – something hitherto unknown to cautious little me – kicked in. And I heard myself saying:

'I'm up for the second glass of wine if you are.'

Richard looked momentarily taken aback by this – as if he too would have found it easier if I had called it quits and let us both go our separate ways back to the hotel. But instead his moment of disconcertion was replaced with a smile. And five surprising words:

'If you're in, I'm in.'

*Five*

THE SECOND GLASS of wine lasted two hours. I didn't realize that so much time had evaporated until someone else informed us that it was indeed late. All right, I am being a little fast and loose with the truth. Once or twice I did ponder the fact that we were talking, talking, talking – and the conversation was so surprisingly spirited, so free-flowing and smart (I feel like such an egoist noting that), that, though a voice in the back of my mind occasionally annoyed me with a reminder that it was getting late, I chose to ignore it. Just as I carefully nursed that second glass of wine, worried that if it was drained too quickly it might spark a nervous exchange about perhaps ending the evening there and then, especially as we were both driving and both had things to do tomorrow morning.

But I'm getting ahead of myself here. We agreed on a second glass of wine. When it arrived Richard let the waiter know that he shouldn't trouble us again by simply stating: 'We're good now.'

The waiter nodded acknowledgment, then left us alone. As soon as he was out of earshot Richard said:

'I bet he's an MIT PhD candidate in astrophysics who really wishes he didn't have to get dressed up four nights a week in that gendarme uniform and work for tips.'

'At least he knows that, all going well, he'll be in some high-powered research or academic post in a couple of years and will be able to use his year as a part-time waiter at the Cambridge Casablanca as a sort of party piece.'

'If astrophysicists actually have party pieces.'

'Doesn't everybody?' I asked.

'OK then, what's yours?'

'I doubt I have one.'

'But you just said . . .'

'That's the problem with a witty retort. It always lands you in trouble.'

'All right, let me put it this way, if I asked you to sing something . . .'

'I have a terrible voice,' I said.

'Play something?'

'Never learning an instrument remains one of my great regrets.'

'Recite something?'

I felt myself momentarily clench – and, in the process, foolishly give the game away.

'So you do recite things?' Richard asked, all smiles.

'What makes you think that?'

'The way you're blushing right now.'

'Oh God . . .'

'Why get embarrassed?' he asked.

'I don't know. Maybe it's because . . .'

'Yes?'

'Poetry,' I said, sounding very direct – as if I was spitting out a confession. 'I recite poetry.'

'Impressive.'

'How would you know? You've never heard me recite anything.'

'Do so now.'

'No way.'

'Why not?'

'Because . . . I don't know you.'

As soon as I said that I had a fit of the giggles.

'Sorry, sorry,' I said, 'that sounded ridiculous.'

'Or rather wonderfully old-fashioned – "I never recite poetry on a first date."'

I felt myself clench again.

'This is not a first date,' I said, sounding rather terse.

Now it was Richard's turn to express embarrassment.

'That might be the stupidest thing I've ever said. And totally presumptuous.'

'Just needed to get that clear.'

'It was clear already. I just sometimes let my mouth work before my brain. And not for a moment did I think—'

'Emily Dickinson,' I heard myself saying.

'What?'

'The stuff I recite to myself. It's frequently Emily Dickinson.'

'That's impressive.'

'Or weird.'

'Why is it weird? I mean, if you told me it was Edgar Allan Poe or, worst yet, H. P. Lovecraft . . .'

'He didn't write poetry.'

'And he might be the most overrated writer this country ever produced – but I've never gone for High Gothic. I suppose the sort of writing I like most deals with the heart of the matter, the everyday stuff of life . . .'

'As Emily Dickinson did.'

'Or Robert Frost.'

'He's very underrated now, Robert Frost,' I said. 'Everyone always characterizes him as the old Yankee, the grandfatherly poet. And yes, there is "the woods are lovely, dark and deep, and I have promises to keep, and miles to go before I sleep" . . . which is always held up as American Pastoral and the sort of poem that even truck drivers can appreciate.'

'Unlike Wallace Stevens.'

'Well, he did sell insurance. In fact, he remained in Hartford – insurance capital of America.'

'That's some claim to fame.'

'Ouch.'

'Sorry – that was catty of me.'

'But you're right. Hartford has little to recommend it.'

'Mark Twain lived there for a while . . . while he was selling insurance.'

Richard paused for a moment, clearly taking me in.

'Did I say something wrong?' I asked.

'On the contrary, I was just allowing myself to be impressed by all that you know.'

'But I don't know that much.'

'Even though you can talk about the early non-literary career of Mark Twain and cite Wallace Stevens.'

'I wasn't citing Wallace Stevens. I was talking about Robert Frost.'

'And your favorite Frost poem?' he asked.

'It's probably the least traditional and the most disquieting of all his poems . . .'

'"Fire and Ice"?'

Now it was my turn to look at Richard with care.

'You really know your stuff,' I said.

This time there was no shy smile, no turning away from my field of vision. This time he looked directly at me and said:

'But the only reason I am talking about these things is because *you* know your stuff.'

'And the only reason why I'm telling you all this is because *you* know your stuff. You know "Fire and Ice".'

'But I can't recite it.'

'I bet you can.'

I took a large steadying sip of my wine. Lowering my head I gathered my thoughts, my memory flipping me back to senior year in high school, that day in assembly when I had been asked by my English teacher, Mr Adams, to stand up in front of the school and recite . . .

*No, no, don't replay that again. Don't remember how you . . .*

Why do we always seem to hark back to the bad stuff? The moments when we were embarrassed, mortified, mocked. When the very thought now of reciting something and being rewarded for it tosses up the most anguished remembrances of things past. When . . .

> *'Some say the world will end in fire*
> *Some say in ice.*
> *From what I've tasted of desire*
> *I hold with those who favor fire*
> *But if it had to perish twice*
> *I think I know enough of hate*
> *To say that for destruction ice*
> *Is also great*
> *And would suffice.'*

Silence. Richard's gaze – which he held from the moment I looked up at him and began to recite the poem – didn't waver from me. But having finished the recitation I found myself almost looking at him for validation. Then realizing that I was staring at him like a schoolgirl wanting to be told she had pleased the teacher, I turned away. Richard saw this and ever so briefly touched his hand against my left arm as he said:

'That was impressive. Very impressive.'

I felt myself flinch as he touched me – even if the gesture was in no way redolent of anything but gentle reassurance.

'Again you're being far too kind,' I said.

'No, just accurate. Why do you know that poem?'

'Doesn't everyone know that poem?'

'You're being disingenuous.'

*Disingenuous.* He actually used that word. I smiled. He smiled back. And for the first time in this conversation I let down all the self-editing barriers and found myself telling him a story I had always kept to myself.

'I read the Frost poem during my first semester of senior year. I had an English teacher, Mr Adams, who actually rated me – even though I was a science geek. He was this man in his fifties – very patrician New England, very erudite, very much a bachelor about whom nobody knew a thing. Anyway, Mr Adams worked out early on that, though I was very much drawn to chemistry and biology, words played such an important role in my life. Mr Adams gave a seminar on "Great Writing" for seniors. It was an elective, and there were only five of us in the class. "Book geeks" is what the cheerleader brigade called us. And, of course, they were right. Mr Adams called us his "literate brigade" – and over the course of that final year, he had us reading everything from Joyce's *Portrait of the Artist* or Henry James's *The Wings of the Dove* to Chekhov's *The Cherry Orchard* . . . which I particularly loved because it so dealt with self-delusion and the way we all resist looking at the reality around us. But he also made us read American poetry. Dickinson. Whitman. Stevens. Frost. I remember the first time he introduced us to "Fire and Ice" – and I couldn't believe this was the Robert Frost whom everyone looked upon as the kindly grand-father. This was a poet who had a libido, who felt desire and anger and rage. All the things I was feeling in my own messed-up, "no one gets me, why am I so alone?" teenage way. We spent two whole classes talking about the poem – and how, in just a few short lines, it pointed up the fact that, within all of us, there is this capacity for love, for grace, and for all the dark stuff we don't want to acknowledge.

'Anyway, the poem became a real benchmark for me. At the end of the semester – right before Christmas – I actually signed up for a speech competition that was to be held at an assembly in front of the entire school the day before we broke up for the holidays. My speech teacher, Mrs Flack, encouraged me to go in for the competition – the first prize for the winner being that year's edition of the Webster dictionary . . . which, for a word junkie like me, was something I really wanted to win. And Mrs Flack – who once told me she tried being an actress for around ten minutes in New York during the late sixties – really thought the poem was an amazingly original choice for the competition. She worked with me for a couple of hours on my presentation. It involved all the lights in the hall blacking out and me being discovered in a single white spot and then reciting the poem in a highly controlled, quiet way, with me staring out at the audience at the end, and the light snapping off. When I think about it now, maybe it was all too Greenwich Village circa 1965 for Waterville High in 1986. But I thought it really edgy and out there.

'Then backstage on the day of the competition, right before going on, I had the biggest case of nerves imaginable. Completely seized. Terrified of getting out there in front of the whole school and looking like an idiot. Don't know where this came from. Never had it before. When they called me – told me it was my time to go on – I refused to move. Mrs Flack was backstage. She coaxed me onstage. The light blacked out. I moved quickly to the assigned spot. The spotlight snapped on. There I was, alone, staring out into blackness, knowing I just had to say the words as I had rehearsed them, and all would be over in less than a minute, and

I could retreat again into my private little life. But, standing there, that spotlight glaring down on me, feeling absolutely naked, exposed, absurd, my mouth couldn't open. I was frozen, immobile, ridiculous. After a half a minute like this, the giggles started. Even though I could hear some of the teachers hushing the other students, slow hand-clapping started, and a few whistles, and then a girl – whom someone told me later was Janet Brody, the captain of the cheerleading team – yelled: "Loser." Everybody laughed. The spotlight snapped off. Mrs Flack hurried out and got me off the stage. And I remember, once we were in the wings, putting my head on her shoulder, crying uncontrollably, and Mrs Flack having to call my mother to come collect me. Mom – who was never the most touchy-feely of people, and who hated any kind of personal weakness – drove me home, shaking her head, telling me I would spend the rest of my senior year trying to live down what had just happened, and "Why on earth did you set yourself up to fail like this?" I said nothing, but those words slammed into me like an out-of-control car. Because they were so accurate. I'd set myself up. I'd allowed myself to be publicly shamed. I'd short-changed myself. Just as I did so often afterwards as well . . .

'And I never recited "Fire and Ice" again.'

'Until now,' Richard said.

Silence. I hung my head.

'I'm sorry,' I finally said.

'Sorry for what?'

'Sorry for boring you with an adolescent embarrassment I should have gotten over years ago. And something I shouldn't have shared with you.'

'But I'm glad you shared it.'

'I've hardly shared it with anybody before.'

'I see,' Richard said.

'There's nothing to "see" here. There's just the fact that there are moments in life you find so mortifying . . .'

I let the sentence die before finishing it. I suddenly wanted to be anywhere but here. Suddenly felt as vulnerable and awkward and lost as I felt that moment on that high school stage with that white-hot spotlight on me. I fingered my glass.

'I should go,' I said.

'Just because you told me that story?'

'Something like that, yes.'

'Your mother . . . was she always so brutal with you?'

' "Brutal" is perhaps too brutal a word. She was very much pull-no-punches. All tough love. No real warmth. Why do you ask?'

'My dad. He was brutal. Physically brutal – as in hitting us with a belt when we stepped out of line. Once my brother and I were beyond the spanking stage – though being whacked on the thighs with a belt is not exactly spanking – he then started working on us in different ways. Like the time I won the short story competition at the University of Maine. A story about a lobster man who takes his teenage son out to teach him the basics of his trade, and the boat capsizes and the son drowns. The prize was two hundred and fifty dollars and the story not only got printed in the college literary magazine, but also in the weekend supplement of the *Bangor Daily News*. It turns out half my father's clients Down East saw the story. He called me up at college and tore a strip or two off of me, telling me that I had caused him all sorts of professional problems, as he had insured a whole bunch of lobster men, and my depiction of the lives of these men, and – most of all – a terrible tragedy happening owing to one man's negligence . . . well, it was just outrageous. Especially as I didn't know a damn thing about their world, me being a guy who was anything but hearty, and who had the audacity to think of himself as a writer when I was just turning out "mediocre drivel". Those were his exact words.'

Silence. Then I said:

'And you're telling me this to make me feel better?'

'Absolutely. Because I know what it means to have any sort of confidence zapped out of you through the unkindness of others.'

'My unkindness was towards myself – which is far worse. Because we all short-change ourselves.'

'Not you.'

'You're sugaring the pill.'

'Well then, how have you short-changed yourself?'

'That's another conversation.'

The smallest smile formed on Richard's lips as I uttered that.

'OK,' he said.

'If there is another conversation.'

'I'd like that.'

'My weekend's really busy.'

'All those radiology conferences?'

'All those radiology conferences.'

'That's a shame,' he said. 'Except for another morning meeting tomorrow in Brockton, I have the day free.'

'Well, I don't.'

My tone was sharp, dismissive, so stupidly defensive. I turned away – but from the corner of my eye I could see that Richard had been unsettled by the hint of anger underlying my reply. Again I had just slammed shut a door . . . out of fear. Fear of what? The fact that this man was suggesting we spend the afternoon together? The fear that I had just told him a story that I could never bring myself to tell my husband – perhaps out of the knowledge that his reaction would have been the roll-of-the-eyes, *poor silly Laura* look that I saw Dan give me on so many occasions.

'I've obviously uttered the wrong thing again,' Richard said, simultaneously motioning to the waiter for the check.

'No, it's me who's been the impolite one here.'

'I shouldn't have been so personal, asking you how you've short-changed yourself.'

'That wasn't the reason I got tetchy. The reason was . . .'

I broke off, not wanting to say anything more.

'You don't have to explain anything,' Richard said.

'Thank you,' I whispered, suddenly wanting a hole in the floor to open up and suck me out of this embarrassed place.

The check arrived and Richard insisted on paying it. He then asked me if I could get email on my cellphone.

'I could,' I said, 'but it's too expensive to run on a monthly basis. So I rely on texting.'

'Well then, I am going to put the ball completely in your court. Here again is my card. My cell number is the one at the bottom. I am free tomorrow as of twelve noon – and I would love to spend the day with you. If you don't contact me, no hard feelings whatsoever. It's been lovely sharing this time with you. And I truly wish you well. Because – if I may say so – you deserve good things.'

Silence.

'Thank you,' I finally said. 'Thank you so much.'

We stood up. I found myself wanting to say: *Shall we meet somewhere downtown around one p.m.?* But again I held back.

'Can I walk you to your car?' he asked.

'No need. I got lucky and found a spot right outside the movie house.'

'That still requires a few steps.'

We left the bar and said nothing as we walked less than half a block to my elderly vehicle. If Richard noticed its decrepitude he was very good at not showing it.

'Well then . . .' I said.

'Well then.'

Another silence.

'I'm sorry tomorrow won't work out,' I said, thinking: *Now the door has been slammed twice.*

'You have my number.'

'That I do.'

'And that cheerleader – the one who heckled you – I bet she regrets all that now.'

'I tend to doubt it. But do you want to hear one of the great supreme ironies of my life? My daughter's a cheerleader. Not a mean one, I hope. But very much a cheerleader. And very much desperate to be popular at all costs.'

'So she's lonely.'

And I heard myself say:

'Aren't we all?'

As soon as those words were out of my mouth, I whispered a fast goodbye and climbed into the car, unnerved by the fact that

I had just told a stranger the one central thing that had been unsettling me for days, months, years: the fact that I've felt so terribly alone.

And having made that huge admission, what did I do? I slammed the door and drove right off into the night.

*Six*

WHEN I GOT back to the hotel it was almost one a.m. When was the last time I had stayed up so late, talking, talking, talking?

I felt a stab of self-reproach. Especially as I saw a text from my husband.

**I was out of line before. Sorry. Dan**

So there it was. An apology of sorts. Terse. Telegraphic. Devoid of emotion. Devoid of love.

And how did I react to this detached expression of regret? Without a pause for reflection I texted back:

**No problem. We all have our off moments. Love you. Laura**

Once contempt is finally articulated in a marriage, it never really stops. And though Dan's anger of late had been so quietly contemptuous, his surliness tonight was, in part, due to the stress he'd been under, and the fact that he'd been roused out of sleep by my ill-timed call.

Why was I excusing his very bad behavior right now? Because part of me was feeling just a little guilty about having those two glasses of wine with Richard . . . and so enjoying myself. Just as I was also simultaneously castigating myself for turning my blurted-out admission of loneliness into a reason to dash off into the night. No doubt he now considered me highly strung and profoundly uptight. Except for that one innocent aside about this being something akin to a first date – an aside which I absurdly jumped on – Richard did absolutely nothing to indicate that he was in any way cruising me. Nor did he signal whatsoever that he was unhappily married or so frustrated with his personal situation that he wanted to . . .

But the way we talked about words, the way he got me to recite that poem by Frost, the way this man – who struck me initially as rather gray and fusty – suddenly came alive when we got discussing matters literary. He really seemed to get me on a level that . . .

*Oh, will you listen to yourself. 'He got you?' Now you sound like an adolescent who's met the fellow class geek and is dazzled by the fact that he seems genuinely interested in what you yourself so value.*

And what is so wrong with meeting someone who actually thinks there is worth in language spoken and written? And why the hell are you classifying yourself and Richard as geeks?

*Because I married a man who told me once he feared his son had 'inherited the geek gene from his mom'.*

Of course, I never said anything about this remark (made just before Ben had his breakdown and was already displaying signs of fragility). Of course, when Dan saw my shocked expression in the wake of this comment, he then backpedaled, telling me he was just jesting, ha-ha. Me being me I let it drop. But it has nagged at me since. Because it struck me as so unkind. And because, before that, Dan had never done unkind.

And now . . .

*Once contempt is finally articulated in a marriage, it never really stops.*

*Bing.*

Another text on my phone.

**Hey Mom – weird thing happened today. Out of nowhere Allison dropped by my studio.**

Oh God. Why do manipulative heartbreakers always come back to wreak more havoc? I read on.

**She was being all-friendly. Saying what a brilliant artist I am. Making really complimentary noises about the new painting I'm working on. Dropping all these hints that she really missed me. I know you're going to say not to go near her. But the thing is, I want to. Even if I get burnt again. Maybe will be a bit more flame-resistant this time. No lectures, please, but would like to know your thoughts. B xxx**

Oh God. Allison the Arch Manipulator. Having aided and abetted my son's breakdown she now has probably sniffed out the fact that he's gotten over her and is back painting. So, naturally, she has to see if she can inflict more damage on him. But, reading through Ben's text around five more times, what intrigued and

116

pleased me most was the hint that he knew she might do her best to hurt him, but he could handle it. Part of me wanted to tell him: *Slam the door in that vixen's face.* But I knew that Ben would interpret this as far too maternal, edging perhaps into the puritanical. Ben saw himself as a bohemian – and one who reacted badly when lectured on morality or the need to 'be responsible' or act like 'some dull asshole who sells insurance'.

I thought about phoning Ben right back – he never got to bed before three on most nights – but also knew that this was not a wise idea. When Ben wanted to talk he'd phone me. When he wanted to limit the communication to the written word he'd email. When he wanted an immediate response – without direct conversation – he'd text. So I resisted the temptation to dial his number. Instead I punched out the following message:

Ben – all cliches are true, especially: leopards don't change their spots. I think she's toxic. But I am not you. If you feel you can get involved again – and not get hurt – then by all means enjoy the sex, but don't think it's romance, let alone love. Those are my words of wisdom for Friday night. Call me whenever you want to talk. I love you – Mom

As always I read through the text several times before sending it, making certain it didn't sound too cloying. I hit the 'send' button, then sent a text to Sally:

Hi hon – in Boston. Hotel isn't much, but nice having a little time away. Hope you're having a chilled weekend. You deserve some serious downtime. Around if you need me. Otherwise see you Sunday night. Love – Mom

Again I scrutinized the message carefully before sending it, taking out the word 'chilled', as that was an expression Sally used all the time (as in: 'I so wish I could chill' – something she genuinely found hard to do). Coming from me it would sound a hollow note, as if I was trying to use her generation's argot and could stand accused of trying to be 'with it' (to use *my* generation's argot). Just as I know that Sally certainly didn't need some 'serious downtime'. She needed seriousness.

Children: the ongoing open wound. And the two people without whom life would be unimaginable. As I once told Sally when she went into a 'I know you'd prefer a brainier daughter' routine:

'I have never – and would never – think that. You are my daughter – and I love you without condition.'

'Love always has conditions.'

'Who told you that?'

'I just know it.'

'Well, between a parent and a child . . .'

'You mean, your mother loved you unconditionally?'

*Ouch.* Though I hadn't talked much with Sally about my mother's pronounced chilliness, I did drop some hints to her that our relationship was less than a close one (even though I remained a dutiful daughter until the end of her life). Yet Sally had far more emotional insight than she gave herself credit for.

'My mother was my mother,' I replied to her rather tart (and painfully acute) question. 'But I am not my mother – and I do love you unconditionally.'

'I'll quote that back to you when you find me smoking crack.'

'That will never happen.'

'How can you be so sure?' she asked.

'Because if given the choice between five hundred dollars a week on drugs and spending the same amount of money on clothes . . .'

'I'm going with the clothes.'

We both laughed.

'You know, Mom, sometimes you can actually "do" cool.'

High praise from my daughter.

The text scoured for any possible tricky phrases, I hit the 'send' button, then tossed my cellphone on the bed, kicked off my shoes, and collapsed backwards against the synthetic floral bedspread. I closed my eyes.

*Bing.* A text. From Ben.

Mom – never thought my mother would say have sex with someone and dump her at first sign of trouble. Know if I start I might get smitten again. That's the thing about love, right? You have to take risks. Which invites possibility of hurt. So – is it potential for pain, or caution, hesitation, no risk? Am sleeping on it. B xxx

My son the philosopher. Reading through his text again I couldn't help but marvel (maternal pride talking once more) at the way Ben could get to the heart of the matter when it came to the nature of choice. Especially the choice that sends you onto a little island of safety that becomes sterile and confining.

*'Yep. Followed Dad right into the family firm.'*

Out of nowhere that comment popped into my head. But when is anything 'out of nowhere'? Especially as Richard had been there, seated opposite me, much of the evening. Ever since then, he'd been clouding my thoughts.

You have to take risks.

My son the purveyor of uncomfortable, ever-so-evident truths.

I sat up. I reached into my pocket and dug out the card that Richard had given me – the card with his cellphone number. I picked up my phone. I sent a text.

Sorry about hasty exit tonight. Not my best moment. As contrition, how about lunch in Boston tomorrow? Should be able to meet around 1 p.m. Any thoughts? Best – Laura

I hesitated for a moment before hitting 'send'. But less than a minute after it was dispatched, *bing* – a reply:

Laura – no need to apologize. I had a lovely evening. And am happy to meet you for lunch tomorrow. I'm buying. Will make a reservation and text details anon. So – can I say this?– it's a date. Best – Richard

I smiled. After all my objections before when he had dropped that word, now . . .

I texted back.

Yes. It's official. It's a date.

Saturday

*One*


'THE MULTIX SELECT DR is a cost-efficient digital radiography system particularly designed to provide doctors in private practice and smaller hospitals entry into the world of digital radiography. And with Mobilett Mira, Siemens launches a mobile, digital X-ray system with a wireless detector and a more flexible swivel arm to increase ease of use for the clinical staff.'

The gentleman pitching this machine to the fifty or so of us had great teeth. And a real slick salesman's delivery which still didn't do much for the turgid copy he was clearly reading from a prepared script. I tried to focus on what he was saying. I failed. And decided that ducking out of this conference early wasn't going to make me miss much – especially as Dr Harrild had already hinted that he wasn't likely to pick my brains too much about what, if anything, I'd gleaned from the conference. A light *bing* on my phone indicated the arrival of a text. I glanced down at the screen. I read:

Cleaning out the garage today. Hope the conference is interesting. D xxx

Part of me was touched by this text. Cleaning out the garage – which has been hopelessly stockpiled with all his home improvement equipment, car mechanic equipment, and the home gym stuff that he never uses – has been a request I've been making of my husband for the past eighteen months. I've not nagged him about it. I hate nagging – though in any long-term relationship there are always domestic details that seem to cause friction – like one person's inability to make the bed, or do a load of laundry or, indeed, divest the garage of all his accumulated junk, so we can actually park our two cars there when the snow falls. The few times I have mentioned these ongoing annoyances to Dan, they have been met with gruffness or sheer silence. Which, in turn, has meant that I have quietly gone on making the beds, doing the laundry and parking my car outside of our overfilled junk-shop garage (and I am now really sounding just a little too put-upon here). The fact that he has just announced that he is now finally clearing it out . . . well, that too was his way of saying sorry for last night. But I don't want acts of contrition. I just want a husband who desires me, who actually seems to want to be with me.

Reaching my room I texted back:

**Thanks for doing that. It's really appreciated. Love you – Laura**

A text straight back from Dan:

**Tell me if you want anything else done around the house.**

He really is feeling guilty. Though I don't want to say 'good', there is a part of me that was pleased he was finally conscious of the fact that his behavior frequently did undermine things between us . . . and actually hurt me. Just as I could only hope that this desire to do something to please me was the start of something more reasonable between us.

*Something more reasonable between us.*

Just playing those words over in my head saddened me. Because it underscored how distant and flat things had gotten between us; the continental drift that had become our marriage.

**Cleaning out the garage will be more than sufficient. I am missing you. L xxx**

I hit 'send'. And moments later: *Bing.*

**OK, on the job now.**

Reading this I found myself taking a sharp intake of breath. My husband was tone deaf when it came to my gentle entreaties for affection. He couldn't respond to a comment like 'I am missing you' with even the slightest hint of reciprocal fondness. He had to null and void it all. In doing so he made me feel small . . . and very isolated.

*Bing.* Another text. This one from Sally.

**Hi Mom – any chance I could borrow fifty dollars from your secret stash?**

Some time ago, I let Sally in on the fact that I was the proud owner of an old tin tobacco box, bought at a yard sale for $3 because I liked the 1920s Lucky Strike design on its battered cover.

I keep the box on a shelf in my closet and always try to have about $100 in it as emergency, *just-in-case* funds. I told Sally about this box; I wanted to ensure that she had access to cash when she needed it, but also insisted that she would never dip into it without first asking me. Was this a little schoolmarmish on my part? Perhaps – but as Sally was something of a spendthrift, money remained an ongoing drama for her. Though she did regularly ask me for supplements to the $30 allowance she received from me per week – and the babysitting money she accrued – to her credit she never once reached into the money stash without first calling me. She knows that I know that she still owes me $320 (she reminded me of this recently when she did put $40 back in the box after a weekend of waiting shifts in Moody's Diner up in Waldoboro). I haven't pressed her for it. Just as I worry that this need to buy stuff all the time is a reflection of a larger despair – and one which I don't seem to be able to help her shake.

What's the fifty bucks for? I texted Sally back.

*Bing.* Her instant reply:

Cocaine and ecstasy and a tattoo of a Hell's Angel I thought would look really good on my right arm. You cool with that?

I found myself smiling. Sally as Ms Irreverent was so far preferable to Sally as Miss Popularity.

I could live with the Hell's Angel, I texted right back. The question is: could you?

*Bing.* Her instant reply.

Thanks for maternal words of wisdom. Jenny has last minute ticket for gig in Portland. All heading down there tonight. Need $15 for ticket, then dinner and stuff. Dad said I've been spending too much recently.

I texted back.

Did he say you couldn't go?

Hasn't grounded me or anything – but giving me no money is his way of keeping me home.

Well, at least he didn't forbid her from going out – as I had never contradicted him when he gave a directive to one of our children.

Who's driving?

Jenny's sister Brenda.

That was reassuring, as Brenda was twenty-three and working as a receptionist at Bath Iron Works. The few times I met her Brenda always struck me as reasonably grounded. Very grounded, as she weighed around three hundred pounds and was trying to lose weight to realize her dream of joining the US Navy. From what I'd heard from Sally since then, she'd gained twenty pounds in the last few months. But even if she couldn't get her girth together she was an absolute teetotaler (as Sally reported she was always lecturing her sister on the dangers of alcohol). So I was reassured that she'd be the designated driver tonight.

If it's Brenda behind the wheel I'm OK with that. Will text your dad and get his OK.

He's cool with all that.

Then let him tell me himself. And I immediately sent Dan a text, explaining that Sally wanted to go out and—

*Bing.* A text back from Dan.

I told her she couldn't go. Why are you over-ruling me here?

Oh God. It never stops. Sally was, as usual, playing us off against each other.

I would never dream of undermining your authority. But is it really a big deal if she goes out tonight? She has money from me, and I see no reason why she should stay at home.

*Bing.*

She's staying at home because I told her she's staying at home.

I felt myself clench again. Until recently Dan had doted on his daughter – and was, at times, a little too lenient with her. But recently his wide-ranging dyspepsia has also clouded his relationship with Sally – to the point where she recently said to him: 'When did you start resenting my existence?' (This was after he grounded her for a weekend when she ignored his directive to clean up her catastrophe of a room.) Though I did try to play the diplomat then – even getting Sally to actually do a major tidy – Dan still wouldn't budge.

'You're still grounded,' he told her after inspecting her now squared-away room. 'Because you need to be taught a lesson now and then.'

No, you're wrong there, I should have informed Dan at the time – none of us need to be 'taught' lessons. We need to be shown love. But worried about being seen to undermine his paterfamilias stance I said nothing.

This time, however . . .

I texted:

This is an unwise move. Sally really wants to go out with her friends. Why be punitive here? You're doing yourself no favors. You tell her that she is again grounded and you deal with the fallout.

And I hit 'send' before even reading it through.

*Bing.*

Dan's angry reply, no doubt.

But actually it was a text from Richard.

Just out of meeting. Booked a table at the bistro in Beacon Street Hotel – on Beacon Street (no surprise there). See you in an hour? Richard. PS Had a boring morning. How was yours?

I texted back:

An hour it is. Looking forward . . .

After sending the text I decided that there was no further reason to stay put and listen to any more of this radiographic sales pitch. So I headed up to my room. Once there I changed my clothes, putting on a pair of jeans, a black turtleneck and the black trench-coat that I'd had for around ten years – and which Ben had always complimented me on, saying that it made me look 'Parisian'. Applying a little makeup to my face I paid particular attention to the area under my eyes. I seriously don't like the ever-darkening crescent moons that now exist there. No amount of generic anti-aging serum (I can hardly afford the absurdly expensive stuff) or sleep seems to lighten them. With all those fine lines hovering nearby – lines that would ever deepen in the coming years – all I could feel (as I so often do whenever I have to face myself in a mirror) is that this middle passage of life is so much about damage limitation. But applying a slightly bolder shade of lipstick than I ever wear at work I also reminded myself of something my mother said in one of her few ruminative moments when she knew time was something she no longer had much of:

'Until they bury you, you're still young.'

I checked my lipstick again, thinking Mom wouldn't approve of this shade. A little too rougey for her. A little too showy. Would Richard think the same?

Oh please. It's hardly Electric Red. Just a shade up from what I usually wear. There you go again, endlessly examining the motivations behind a simple decision like choosing a shade of . . .

I re-rouged my lips, deepening the color. There. An act of defiance against that part of me which always acts like a permanent restraining order on myself.

Then, turning up the collar of my black raincoat (Mata Hari in an airport hotel?), I headed out. I didn't get far, as my cellphone binged again.

**Dad just gave me fifty bucks himself and said he'd be asleep when I got back and please not to wake him. Don't know what you did to make him change his mind . . . but, hey, I'm not complaining. S xxx. PS Thanks.**

So Dan had a volte-face after all. He was obviously trying to make amends.

*Bing.*

This time it was from Dan.

**All agreed with Sally. I hope you're happy.**

*Yes, I'm pleased. But are you happy?*

I texted back:

**Glad it all got resolved. Thank you.**

No terms of endearment this time. No entreaties for affection. Because what I so wanted to hear I knew would not be forthcoming.

There was a shuttle bus from the hotel to the airport T-stop. I was the sole passenger. For the first time today I was outside and cognizant of the fact that it was a peerless autumn afternoon. Getting into the shuttle bus outside the hotel I chose not to look at the big long-term parking lot across the street, or the series of gas stations that lined the road in all directions. Rather I turned my gaze up towards the hard azure sky, all the while blinking into the high-intensity sun. When the bus reached the T-stop a mere $2 whisked me away from all the concrete realities of Route 1. Ten minutes later it deposited me in front of the first public park ever erected in this once New World.

The rural girl in me – who's always dreamed of living in a city – loves the idea of subways. The notion of criss-crossing a city subterraneanly. Of plunging through tunnels to a new destination. Of the noise and sense of possibility and sheer urbanity that comes from the rush of an underground train.

But as the subway charged towards central Boston, I found myself looking at four exhausted Latino women who had also gotten on with me at the airport stop. They were all dressed in maid's uniforms. They all must have been working since four that morning, as they were now clearly going home. From the way they were slumped across their respective seats, so enervated and fatigued by that early Saturday shift, I'm certain they found this daily ride to and from the airport less than an uplifting experience. Especially with the drunk crashed out opposite them, his scrubby beard flecked with food and drool.

Still, when I got off at Park Street and came right up the escalator, the first sounds I heard were a couple of street guitarists singing that great Kurt Cobain number, 'Moist Vagina'. Yes, I was a fan of Nirvana back in the 1990s. I remember one particularly happy moment just after we met when Dan and I were driving some- where, a Nirvana cassette in the deck of his twenty-year-old Chevy, and he was crooning that tune at the top of his lungs. Back then Dan had frequent moments of sheer irreverence. He actually believed in the idea of fun.

Songs do that to us, don't they? They bring us back to a moment in our respective stories. Because we seem to benchmark so much of our adolescence and early adulthood with music, a certain song will always trigger, later in life, an instant flashback to a time when, perhaps, life seemed so less serious, so less cluttered.

The two guys singing this Kurt Cobain classic (well, I think it a classic) were both very much carrying on the grunge look that he pioneered. Neither of them could have been more than twenty, and despite appearing just a little strung out, their musicianship and vocal harmonies were just sublime. The area around this entrance to the Common was bustling. Tourists in guided groups. Locals on bicycles or jogging or pushing baby chairs. Couples everywhere. The newly in-love ones with their arms entwined around each other's waists. A few teenagers kissing a little too passionately on park benches, and one duo courting arrest up against a tree. A few evident first-date types, all caution and nervousness. The new parents with their babies in strollers, all so sleep-deprived, the domestic strain so apparent. The middle-aged couples – some distant with each other, some affable. And an elderly man and woman, sitting on a bench at the entrance to the park, both reading sections of that morning's *Globe*, holding hands.

Naturally I was envious of that couple, and wanted to know their story. Were they childhood sweethearts who had met sixty years ago and had been in love ever since (a very *Reader's Digest* version of marriage)? Or had they gotten together much later in life, after being widowed, divorced, profoundly lonely? Was theirs one of those marriages that had gone through huge upheavals and periods of true disaffection, only to find an equilibrium as it edged into twilight? Had they stuck together out of fear, or resistance to seismic upheaval or the pursuit of something better . . . and now were two old people on a park bench, holding each other's hand, resigned to the fact that life held no further possibilities beyond this other person, whom they should have jettisoned years ago?

Of course I so wanted to believe the first scenario – the devoted couple for over sixty years. Of course I knew that this was the stuff of fantasy – that no relationship of such calendric magnitude could have been one long love song from the outset. But how we so want to buy into that fairy tale and how we always wonder if conjugal happiness is just outside our reach.

I checked my watch: 1:18. I was now three minutes late – and Beacon Street was . . . where, exactly? I asked someone for directions. He pointed me towards the State House on a raised piece of land just above the Common, and told me to turn left when I reached it.

'Beacon Street is the first big one you come to,' he said. 'You can't miss it. And I'm sure whoever is waiting for you will wait for you.'

I couldn't help but smile – but I was still late, and I really didn't want to have Richard thinking: *So she's the sort of woman who plays games by keeping a guy waiting.*

But would he really think that? And why was *I* thinking that?

I reached the Beacon Street Hotel at 1:27, twelve minutes late. The bistro was on the street level. It looked stylish, chic. Richard was already there, seated in a booth in a far corner. I could see he was dressed in his idea of casual: a blue button-down shirt, a zip-up navy blue jacket, khakis. I suddenly felt silly about my Parisian boho look. He was hunched over his BlackBerry, tapping out a message with ferocious concentration. From the expression on his face, he was clearly disconcerted by something.

'I'm so sorry,' I said as I reached the booth. Instantly Richard stood up, trying to put a smile on his face. 'I misjudged the travel time and—'

'No need to apologize,' he said, motioning me to sit down. 'In fact it's me who should be apologizing. I might have to cut this lunch short.'

'Oh,' I said, trying to mask my disappointment. 'Has something come up?'

I could see his lips tightening. He hit the off button on his BlackBerry and shoved it away from him, as if it was the harbinger of bad things.

'Yeah, something kind of—'

But he cut himself off, forcing himself to look cheery.

'Not worth ruining lunch over. I don't know about you, but I could truly use a bloody mary.'

'I wouldn't say no to one.'

'I wouldn't say no to two.'

He motioned to the waiter – and put in the order for the drinks.

When the waiter was gone I could see that Richard had already reached for the napkin on the table and was twisting it between his hands – something I repeatedly did whenever I was feeling unsettled.

'Something's happened, hasn't it?' I asked.

'Am I that obvious?'

'You're that distressed.'

'Distressed, discomposed, disconcerted . . .'

'Vexed. And now I know you too are a walking thesaurus.'

A small, sad smile from Richard.

'I'm sorry,' he said. 'I really didn't want to even talk about . . .'

I reached over and lightly touched his arm. It was a gesture that couldn't have lasted for more than a moment. But from the way he took a deep intake of breath when my fingers landed on his jacket . . . well, I couldn't help but wonder when anyone had last touched him in such a reassuring way.

'Tell me, Richard.'

He lowered his gaze from me, staring down at the varnished wood tabletop between us. Then, without looking back up in my direction, he said:

'I lied to you about something.'

'OK,' I said, trying to maintain a neutral tone, and stopping myself from feeling *distressed, discomposed, disconcerted*. After all, this was a man I had spent all of two and a half hours with before now. A passing acquaintance. Nothing more. So why was he admitting that he'd already fabricated something?

'My son, Billy,' he finally said, still keeping his gaze downward.

'Has something happened to him?'

He nodded.

'Something serious?' I asked.

He nodded again. Then:

'When I told you he was living at home I wasn't telling you the truth. Billy's been in the psychiatric wing of the state prison for just under two years. I just found out they've put him in solitary confinement because he tried to stab a fellow inmate last night. It's the third time he's been in solitary in the past eighteen months.

And as the prison psychiatrist just told me: "I can't see him being let out of solitary for the foreseeable future." '

Silence. I placed my hand again on Richard's arm.

'I don't know what to say except, that is truly terrible.'

'That it is,' he said. 'The end of hope.'

'Don't say that. There's always hope.'

Now he looked up at me directly.

'Do you really believe that?'

It was my turn to look away.

'No,' I finally said.

## Two

'He was diagnosed as bipolar when he was nineteen.'

The bloody marys had just arrived. Though Richard had been, after the initial revelation, reluctant to say anything more about his son ('I don't want to bore you with my troubles'), I gently insisted that he tell me all. A sip of his drink. Another long, tense stare at the tabletop, during which I could see him weighing up whether he could spill this story. I squeezed his arm tighter. He covered my hand with his for a moment, then reached for his drink and (in doing so) pulled his arm gently away. A second long sip, and I could see the slightest of twitches as the vodka worked its way into his system. Then:

'We knew, from an early age, that Billy was not a normal kid. Withdrawn. Always keeping to himself. Secretive – or, at least, that's how I saw it. Then there were the moments when everything came right with him – when, out of nowhere, he would suddenly become hyper-animated and wildly outgoing. A little too outgoing, if you ask my opinion. But after the episodes of sullenness, of being so shut off, so *solipsistic* . . .'

*Lovely word,* I thought. As if reading my thoughts, Richard raised his eyebrows for a moment after he uttered it. I smiled back. Richard continued on:

'We were both so happy when he had these periods of apparent high spirits. Especially as he spent so much of his adolescence keeping to himself. At the local high school in Bath, he was always regarded as the class weirdo. The school psychologist ran tests on him and felt that he had some "issues". And he sent him to a therapist for a while, though Muriel – that's my wife – was against it all.'

'Why was that?'

'Muriel is very much someone who believes that "mind stuff" – as she calls it – is a sign of weakness. I guess that kind of comes with her childhood territory. She was raised down in Dorchester, where her dad was the ultimate in tough-guy Irish American cops. A drinker, of course – and someone who regularly used his wife as a punchbag. Eventually Muriel's mom could take no more. As she herself was raised in Lewiston, back she and Muriel and her two brothers went to the family home when Muriel was just twelve. She never saw her father again. He decided that, by following their mother back to Maine, all the children had rejected him. So he shut them out of his life until the bottle finally killed his liver five years later . . . and that's all far too much detail, isn't it?'

'It's interesting detail,' I said.

'You're not saying that to be nice, are you?'

'I'm saying that because I want to hear the story. *Your* story. How did you meet Muriel?'

'My dad hired her as his secretary.'

'When was that?'

'Late 1981. She'd been to secretarial school in Portland and had been married briefly to a cop . . .'

'History repeats itself.'

'Especially Freudian history. But that's another story, me and Muriel.'

'Just the one child?'

'She'd had around three miscarriages before Billy. So we both considered him our great gift, our recompense for all the grief that the three failed pregnancies had caused. But when Billy finally arrived, Muriel was thirty-six, which is not an old age now for a first-time mother, but in those days was regarded as pretty darn late. From the outset, though Muriel did all the right things when it came to looking after Billy, I always had the sense that she hadn't ever bonded really with the boy, that there was a part of her that always sensed he was so different from the start.'

'Did he hit all the usual developmental marks?'

'Absolutely. And when he had some of those early aptitude tests he was shown to be off-the-scales bright. Especially when it came to math. That was always his great saving grace throughout school – the fact that, when it came to all things mathematical, he was a wizard. I remember getting a call from his tenth grade calculus teacher – I think his name was Mr Pawling – asking me to come in, and him telling me that Billy had the most gifted theoretical mind he'd encountered in twenty-five years of teaching, and would I agree to extra tutoring after school, and enrollment that summer in an intensive math camp that was held at MIT, of all places. Muriel felt it was all too much – '*What's he going to do at a math camp except become more withdrawn?*' was how she saw things. But I argued that his was a great gift that we needed to encourage, and that math really could be a way out of the isolation and loneliness that had categorized his life so far. The way I figured it, once he got to that math camp at MIT he'd be with like-minded kids – what Billy himself called "us numbers geeks", and of which there were none at Bath High School. Muriel also complained about the cost of it all – almost three thousand dollars, which was a stretch for us back then, despite the good times. Still, I prevailed. Billy went to MIT Math Camp. For the first two weeks he seemed so incredibly happy. Loved the professors. Loved his fellow math whizzes. I even dropped in on him after ten days. I had never seen him so focussed, so at ease with himself and his surroundings. And this professor who was teaching Lambda Calculus – I had to look up what that meant – took me aside and told me that he was going to put a word in with the admissions department about getting Billy fast-tracked for entry into MIT the following autumn.

'I drove back to Bath elated. My son the math genius. My son the future math professor at MIT or Harvard or Chicago. My son the Nobel Laureate. And yes, I know this was all the stuff of pipe dreams. But what this professor was saying to me really made it seem like Billy could do it all.

'And then, five days later, we got a phone call from MIT. Billy had tried to set fire to the sheets and mattress in his dorm room. Fortunately there was a fast-thinking proctor down the hall. He smelled smoke. He got a fire extinguisher and put the flames out. But Billy had caused several thousand dollars' worth of damage. When he admitted that he'd started the fire himself he was expelled on the spot.

'Of course I was devastated by what had happened. What

devastated me more was the fact that, when I came to pick Billy up, he wouldn't talk about what happened.

'"Guess I just wanted to screw up,"' was all he said.

'When he repeated that statement to his mother she wanted him committed to the nearest insane asylum. Then again they hadn't been getting along for years. Billy knew that his mother considered him nothing less than strange and different. Muriel has never been comfortable with anything or anyone outside of her comfort zone. She hates to travel. She's only been out of Maine twice in the last five years – and that was owing to family funerals in Massachusetts. And she can't really cope with her brilliantly gifted, but truly eccentric son. I've tried repeatedly to talk with her about all that – and tried to get her to show some empathy towards the boy. But when Muriel has decided that somebody is bad news, that's that.'

He broke off the sentence, reaching again for the bloody mary. I too took a long sip of my drink, my mind now endeavoring to work out the complex contours of Richard's marriage. From the way he was reporting things, Muriel sounded cold, judgmental, emotionally detached. But was I thinking that because I could see the immense distress that her husband was embroiled in right now?

'We all have our private griefs, don't we?' he said. 'And I certainly didn't want to go upending our lunch with—'

'Do not apologize. What has happened to your son is so evidently huge and terrible . . .'

'*What has happened to my son?*' he said, his voice just above a whisper. 'You make it sound as if all this was visited upon him. Whereas the truth is . . . he visited it all upon himself.'

'But you said he was bipolar. And if you are bipolar—'

'I know, I know. And you're right. *Father, forgive them, for they know not what they do.* Muriel threw that line from Luke at me when I tried to explain away Billy's behavior after getting expelled from the MIT Math Camp. "Making excuses for him as usual. You should march him down to the nearest Marine Corps recruiting office and get him signed up. Three months of basic training at Parris Island will knock all that craziness out of him."

'Now I know that all makes Muriel sound rather extreme. But the truth is, when I brought Billy home from MIT and he refused to talk with her, I woke around three in the morning to find Muriel sitting in a chair by the window in our bedroom, crying uncontrollably. When I tried to comfort her she told me that she blamed herself for so much that had befallen Billy. "I know I've been a bad mother. I know I've never given him the love he needs." And it was wonderful hearing that. Because she had articulated a certain truth that I was always afraid of discussing with her.'

*But why were you afraid?* I stopped myself from posing that question. Because I knew just how much of a long, difficult marriage is often based around sidestepping so many painfully evident truths, and how we all are afraid of opening up the sort of conversations that can lead us into the darker, distressed recesses of the lives we have created for ourselves.

'I've always hated myself for not confronting her about the antipathy that she felt towards our son. And the way she was incapable of showing any nurturing affection.'

'Towards him *and* towards you?' I asked.

I could see Richard tense, and silently cursed myself for over-stepping a mark.

'Sorry, sorry, that was an inappropriate question,' I said.

He took another sip of his drink.

'Actually, it was a perfectly appropriate question. And one which I think you already know the answer to.'

Silence. I broke it.

'So after the MIT Math Camp . . . did he get help?'

'Naturally I got the school therapist immediately involved. She was a very nice woman, if something of a lightweight who talked all this touchy-feely stuff, but was very out of her depth when it came to dealing with the clinical reasons why Billy had done something so destructive, so calamitous. She did send him to a psychiatrist. The psychiatrist diagnosed depression and put him on Valium. A reasonable year followed. He saw the psychiatrist once a week. The medication seemed to be working. Billy finished his senior year in high school. He scored high on his SATs

138

– including a 750 in math. The incident at MIT was in the past. I paid the four thousand dollars in damages. They never pressed charges, so there was no record against Billy. Several colleges were seriously interested in him – including Chicago and Cornell. Another great triumph happened when CalTech came through with a complete four-year scholarship. CalTech! Billy was thrilled. I was thrilled. Even his mother was truly chuffed that her boy got into one of the world's great science and math schools. The thing was, Billy was going out with a girl from his class. Mary Tracey. Lovely young woman. Quite the chemistry whizz. And she seemed to really understand our quirky son. She'd even gotten accepted on full scholarship to Stanford. It all looked so good.

'Then, around three weeks before his high school graduation, he disappeared. Vanished completely. The local and state police were involved. His photo was in all the papers and on all Maine news bulletins. The fact that he had taken Muriel's car and stolen her ATM card – he knew her PIN number because she'd asked him to get money out on occasion – well, naturally, this was serious stuff. The bank informed us that he'd only made one withdrawal of three hundred dollars on the day of his disappearance. We didn't stop the card because, as the police advised us, they'd be able to easily track his whereabouts. But after that first withdrawal, nothing. No sign of him anywhere. The trail had gone cold. And I couldn't help but fear the worst: that he'd taken his own life.

'But then, eight days after he'd disappeared – eight days during which I had maybe slept three hours a night – we got a phone call at around four in the morning from our local police captain, Dwight Petrie. Bath's a small town. Dwight and I had gone to high school together. His father had been in the police force. My dad had insured their family house and cars. Dwight came to me for all that when he got married and started a family. He was the only friend I confided in about the business at MIT. He was one of the few people I could trust to keep a secret. The fact is, the MIT business was kept pretty hush-hush. Billy's disappearance, on the other hand, was big local news – and somehow word got out about Billy's MIT business. I'm pretty damn certain it was a parent of one of Billy's classmates. Her son was also at the same math camp, but he'd been passed over by CalTech and everywhere for scholarship. This woman – her name was Margaret Mallon – went around telling everybody that it was absurd that "that little freak Billy Copeland gets all the scholarships" and her boy got nothing. It was Dwight Petrie who told me she'd been overheard saying that. Being a police captain, Dwight never repeats anything incriminating unless he's received it from impeccable sources. Next thing we know that too got into the newspapers. And the world being so linked now by Google and Yahoo, naturally someone in the admissions office at CalTech flagged it. The college guidance counselor at Bath High then got a call from the director of admissions at CalTech, demanding to know why the school had concealed Billy's expulsion. The Bath college guidance counselor told him this was the first he had heard of it. Which meant that Muriel and I were asked to come into the principal's office and were essentially carpeted for concealing this "felony", as the principal put it. I tried to explain that, since the matter wasn't reported to the police and it was all privately settled between ourselves and MIT, we didn't feel it essential to "share" this information with the school. I knew this sounded lame – and that we were essentially guilty of a cover-up.'

'What makes you think that?' I asked.

'The school should have been informed.'

'Did MIT know the name of Billy's high school?'

'Of course. They had all his details.'

'But they chose not to inform Bath High that he had been expelled. The very fact that MIT didn't think it necessary to inform Bath High School of this unfortunate incident—'

'It wasn't an "incident". It was an offense.'

'Your son is bipolar . . .'

'That diagnosis came later. And arson is hardly a petty crime.'

'Still, MIT decided the *infraction* was not so severe as to ruin the future of a hugely gifted young man.'

'I lost around a half-dozen clients. And they all said the same thing – they didn't want to do business with someone who played fast and loose with the truth.'

'That's awful and pretty damn judgmental, if you ask me,' I said.

'You're being far too kind.'

'Are you saying that because you're not used to kindness?'

Silence. Richard closed his eyes for a moment. From the way his lips tightened I could only wonder if I had crossed a forbidden frontier, and if he might just stand up and end our lunch before it had ever really begun.

'I'm sorry,' I heard myself saying.

Richard opened his eyes.

'For what?'

'For prying into something that I had no business—'

'But you're right.'

Silence. I chose my next words with prudence.

'How am I right?'

'About me not being used to kindness.'

Silence. Now we both reached for our drinks. Then:

'I know a thing or two about that as well,' I said.

'Your husband?'

I nodded.

Silence. The waiter broke it, arriving at our booth, all smiles.

'How are you guys doing. Ready for another mary? And just to remind you of our brunch specials—'

'Why don't you do that in around fifteen minutes?' Richard said.

'No problem, no rush,' the waiter said, getting the message.

'Thank you.' Then, when the waiter was out of earshot, he said:

'So . . . your husband . . .'

'We'll get to that. Anyway, my point was—'

'What's his name?'

'Dan.'

'And he got laid off at L.L.Bean and starts again in the stockroom on Monday?'

'Good memory.'

'Salesmen remember everything.'

'But outside of the insurance business, you don't strike me as someone who's always selling, always trying to close.'

'Maybe that's because, when I'm selling, I'm playing a role. And outside of that—'

'Aren't we all playing a role?' I asked.

'That's a point of view.'

'But one with a certain veracity to it. I mean, we all construct an identity, don't we? The problem is, do we like the identity we have made for ourselves?'

'You don't expect me to answer that, do you?'

I laughed, and Richard favored me with a sly smile.

'OK – cards on the table,' I said. 'I look at my life and frequently wonder how I have ended up with this existence, this identity, this daily role to play.'

'Well, we all do that, don't we?'

'So what role would you play, if you could?'

'That's easy,' he said. 'I'd be a writer.'

'No doubt, living in a house by the water up in Maine . . . or maybe you do that already.'

'Hardly. We live in town in Bath. And the house, though nice, is pretty modest.'

'So's mine.'

'Anyway, if I was a writer I would be living here, in Boston. City life and all that.'

'Then why not New York or Paris?'

'I'm a Maine boy – which means Boston is my idea of a city. Small, compact, historic, in the East. And then there's the Red Sox . . .'

'So you *are* tribal.'

'Aren't all Red Sox fans?'

'Most everyone is tribal. Especially when it comes to their own flesh and blood. Look at that woman, Margaret what's-her-name, who ensured that your son's incident at MIT went public. Why did she do that? Because her own son wasn't as talented or gifted as Billy. So she turned tribal and decided to wreak havoc. From where I sit, that's five times worse than you and your wife saying nothing about Billy's math camp problem. You were simply trying to protect your son. She was being deliberately malicious – and, in the process, damaging a young man. She ought to be ashamed of herself.'

'Trust me, she isn't.'

'What happened after CalTech found out about Billy's problems?'

'The inevitable happened. They withdrew their offer of admission and, with it, the full scholarship. What made this even more terrible was that this transpired while Billy was still missing. Next thing I knew I had reporters on me from all the local and regional papers, even a TV team from the NBC affiliate in Portland, parked outside my house, wanting a statement from me about why I covered up for my son. I'm surprised you weren't aware of it all, Maine being such a small place.'

'I rarely watch TV. And I tend to get my news from the *New York Times* online. Dan always says that, for a Maine lifer, I have little interest in local stuff. Maybe because it's often nothing more than local gossip. Other people's small-town miseries and tragedies. I'm sure if I asked some of my colleagues at the hospital about the incident they'd remember it all. But, trust me, I'm not going to do that.'

'Thank you.'

'Did you release a statement to the press?'

'I had my lawyer do it. A short statement saying that, as Billy was still missing – and we were genuinely fearful about whether or not he was still alive – we asked to be left in peace "during this very difficult time" and all that. To Dwight Petrie's credit he came out on our side, declaring that since MIT had decided it was a private matter, he felt we were right to say nothing to the school – and he was appalled that "some very bad citizen felt it necessary to inflict more damage on a clearly troubled young man by leaking it to the press". Dwight also made it clear that we had been friends for forty years – and under the circumstances he would have done what I had done. But the terrible fact was, Billy's chances of getting into any college were null and void. And all thanks to the maliciousness of one little woman.

'Meanwhile, the trail had gone cold in the search for Billy. Those eight days . . . they were beyond terrible.'

'And how did your wife take it?'

'She did what she often does when things get on top of her – she voted with her feet. Went to stay with her sister in Auburn. Called me once a day for an update. Otherwise she was elsewhere.'

'And it didn't get to you?'

Silence. His eyes snapped shut again for a moment – something I noticed that frequently happened whenever the conversation strayed into difficult territory. Yet he never tried to dodge the tough stuff. Instead, opening his eyes again he said:

'I thought I would go out of my mind.'

'Was there any specific reason why he'd vanished?'

'His girlfriend told him it was over between them. Just like that. Out of the blue. I only found this out around seventy-two hours after Billy went missing. Early one morning – it must have been around six – someone started banging loudly on my front door. I staggered downstairs and found Billy's girlfriend, Mary, standing there, tears running down her face. Once inside my kitchen, the whole story came out – how Billy had become over the past few months so remote, so difficult and unsettling, that she finally had no choice but to tell him that it was over. As she filled me in on all this, I felt a desperate sense of shame, especially when she asked me: "Did you notice him acting stranger than usual?" The truth was, I hadn't noticed anything different about him, yet here was my son coming undone due to this break-up with the first woman who had ever loved him.'

As if reading my thoughts – or maybe the expression on my face told all – he looked at me and said:

'That's right. Billy never knew much in the way of maternal love. But in Muriel's defense, I suppose she did her best.'

'Do you really believe that?'

'No.'

He met my gaze straight on as he said that – and I felt the strangest shudder run through me. Because from the way he was meeting my gaze I felt what he felt: that this was a moment of shared complicity. And a silent frontier had just been traversed.

'So where did they finally find Billy?' I asked.

'Way up north in the County,' Richard said, using the Maine verbal shorthand for Aroostook County: the most isolated, under-populated, and largely unexplored corner of the state, defined by its vast forests and intricate network of logging roads that never appeared on any official map of the state.

'How bad a shape was he in?'

'Very bad. He told the state trooper who found him that he'd driven up to Presque Isle, went into a Walmart there, bought a garden hose and some thick electrical tape, and was planning to drive deep into the woods, tape the hose to the exhaust pipe, feed it in through the car window, use the tape to mask the crack in the window, then turn on the engine and leave this life.

'But he also bought a week's worth of food at the same time and a sleeping bag and a portable stove. So I can't help but think that part of him still wanted to live. Then, once he had all these supplies, he started driving deep into the woods, crossing eventually onto those logging roads that are off-limits to anyone not working for one of those big paper companies up there. He drove and drove and drove until the car hit a ditch on one of those unpaved tracks. It broke an axle. There he was, in late April, snow still on the ground up there, the temperatures still well below freezing after dark, stranded in real wilderness. He had all the equipment necessary to take his life. But instead he simply lived in his car. Keeping the heater on at night until his gas finally ran out. Using the woods as a toilet. Eating meals made on the portable stove. All alone in the forest. And – as he told me some months afterwards – happy for the first time in his life. "Because I didn't have to confront the fact that I was this freak of nature who couldn't fit in anywhere. And because being alone is, Dad, the best place for me." His exact words.

'Then he got lucky. A logger came upon him at dawn. At this point, Billy had completely run out of food, and besides being starved and suffering from exposure, he was also delirious. He had locked all the car doors, and wouldn't open them when the logger kept slamming his fist against the window, trying to get Billy to allow himself to be rescued. But Billy was so out of it that he refused to open the door. That's when the logger drove off and returned around four hours later – that's how isolated the spot was – with the state police. Again they tried to convince Billy to open the door and let them help him. This time, seeing the men in uniform, he became irrational. Refused to unlock the door. Started screaming abuse at the officers. When they finally had to jimmy open the door with a crowbar, he turned violent. So violent that they had to subdue him. After they'd handcuffed him, he still went crazy in the back of the squad car, and they drove him to the nearest doctor, who administered such a strong tranquilizer that Billy was under for over twenty-four hours.

'When he awoke he found himself in the big state psychiatric hospital in Bangor. Dwight had gotten the call from the state police up in Aroostook County. Great friend that he is, he insisted on driving me up there. When we arrived at the hospital – a big Victorian place, somewhat modernized inside, but still pretty damn formidable and unnerving – Billy was in the secure wing. In an isolated cell. I was able to visit him. He looked so emaciated and rough from all those days freezing in that car. Unwilling to talk to me, though at one point crying wildly when I told him how much I loved him. But when I attempted to comfort him by putting my arms around him he went ballistic, throwing a punch at me – which I fortunately dodged – then hurling himself against a wall before barricading himself in the little bathroom. Four staff members – big, tough guys – came rushing in and ordered me and Dwight out while they subdued my son. Now Dwight – besides being my oldest friend – is also the king of plain talkers. After that incident in Billy's room he marched me over to the nearest bar, insisted I have a double Jack Daniel's to settle my nerves, then gave it to me straight: "Your son is in a very bad place – and after what's happened there's no way the state is going to let him out onto the street for a very long time."'

'Where was his mother at this moment?'

'At her sister's in Auburn, awaiting my call.'

'Why didn't she accompany you to Bangor?'

'When I told her over the phone what had happened she started to cry like I never heard her cry before. I said that it was probably best for all concerned if I went alone with Dwight up to the psychiatric hospital. She didn't disagree with me.'

'But she did eventually see him?'

'You don't think much of her, do you?'

This comment caught me unawares – especially as its tone was so defensive.

'I am just responding to what you've reported to me about her.'

'She's not that bad.'

'I believe you.'

'Even though I've painted her as a bad mother?'

'Richard . . . your marriage is your business. And I would never dream of making a value judgment about—'

'I didn't mean to snap at you like that.'

'That was hardly snapping. Your story is a terrible one.'

'It's not my story, it's *his* story.'

'But you are his father.'

'I know, I know. As you can imagine, life's never been the same since all this happened. Muriel went to see him with me around a week after that first incident at the psychiatric hospital. We first had a meeting with his psycho-pharmacologist. He told us that he had switched Billy onto Paxil – it's a form of Prozac – and though it was early days, he seemed to be responding to the new medication. When we saw him that afternoon – it was in very controlled circumstances, with two burly male nurses in attendance, just in case things got out of hand – he seemed really animated and upbeat and happy to see us both. Promising us that he was going to "beat this thing" and would be entering CalTech as planned that autumn. We had both agreed in advance that we'd say nothing to him about the rescinded admissions offer or the fact that his disappearance had been a two-week media event. But poor Muriel almost broke down at that point. When we got back to the car she buried her head in my shoulder and cried for a good ten minutes. Later, on the drive south, her composure regained, she turned to me, all glacial, and said: "That boy's lost to us now."

'Of course I didn't believe that. I told myself: *Look at how he's rebounded since they put him on the new medication.* I started scheming of ways to get him into a good college come autumn. I didn't give up on him.

'Then, forty-eight hours later, there was another call from the state hospital. Billy had gone berserk the previous night. Out of nowhere he'd gotten violent. Punched and bitten one of the guards. Tried to slam his head through a window. Had to be tranquilized and subdued – and was now in their version of solitary confinement. I wanted to run back up to Bangor immediately, but Dwight counseled me to stay put.

'Days went by. The director of the psychiatric hospital then called me. All very concerned. All very *mea culpa*. It turned out the psycho-pharmacologist had completely misdiagnosed Billy, as it was now clear that he was bipolar. I discovered by asking around, if you put someone who is bipolar on Paxil they light up like a Christmas tree. No wonder the poor boy had those manic episodes.'

'So they switched his medication?'

'Yes – and put him on Lithium. The thing is, because of his attack on the state police officer, and because of his explosions at the hospital, the state decided to press for ongoing incarceration. I asked my lawyer to see if we could make a case against the hospital for misdiagnosis and putting him on the sort of medication that turned him psychotic. The lawyer got me in touch with a criminal attorney down in Portland. The guy charged nearly four hundred dollars an hour. He told me that if I was willing to spend twenty grand, they could mount a case against the state. But he felt the state would win out in the end, as Billy was already violent and unstable before he'd been wrongly put on Paxil. I took out a loan against my house – something Muriel truly objected to – and we mounted the case. And we lost. Even on Lithium, Billy was still showing signs of serious mental disturbance. The state had all the cards. The state was granted the right to lock Billy away in that hospital until such a time as they considered him fit for reintegration into society.'

*Is there any chance of that happening?* I felt like asking, though I already knew the answer. Again clearly reading my thoughts Richard said:

'But that will not happen anytime soon. Because in addition to his bipolar diagnosis, he was subsequently classified as a dangerous schizophrenic. And now – *now* – there's that phone call from the state hospital an hour ago. For the first time in four months he was allowed back in the common living area that is shared by the other male patients on his ward. A fight broke out and he stabbed someone in the throat with a pencil.'

'Is the man all right?'

'The wound was a superficial one, according to the psychiatric head of the unit where Billy is kept. But this means that my son is back in solitary confinement. And the chances of him being let out again in the foreseeable future . . .'

He broke off and put his face in his hands. I reached over and put my hand again on his arm. This time he did not pull away.

'Of course I called his mother as soon as I heard the news from the hospital. And I told you her response. "He's lost now forever."'

'Do you believe that?' I asked.

'I don't want to believe that. But . . .'

Silence.

'If you have to run up to the hospital now . . .' I said.

'My son is back in solitary confinement. Which means no visitors. The resident psychiatrist told me that they would be keeping him isolated until they felt he was stabilized. The last time this happened, it was eight weeks before we could see him. The only reason I told you earlier I had to run was because I didn't think I could face recounting all this to you. And you've been so kind, so patient, so . . .'

The waiter was back at the table, all smiles. Richard withdrew his arm from my grasp.

'So . . . any thoughts about brunch?' the waiter asked.

'We still need a few minutes,' I said, and the waiter headed elsewhere. As soon as he was out of earshot I whispered to Richard:

'Please go if you need to.'

'Where would I go to? *Where?*' he asked. 'But if, after hearing all this, you want to run off . . .'

'Now why would I want to do that?'

'You sure about that?'

'I'm sure about that.'

'Thank you.'

'No, thank you.'

'For what?'

'For telling me about your son.'

'Even though it's a terrible story?'

'Especially because it's a terrible story.'

Silence. Then Richard said:

'There are moments in life when one really needs a second drink.'

To which I could only reply:

'Good idea.'

*Three*

We drank the second round of bloody marys. We ate the omelets that we ordered. We didn't mention the subject of Richard's son again during the course of the brunch. I would have continued the conversation about Billy, as there was so much I wanted to ask Richard about – especially when it came to finding a legal way through this nightmare story. Surely there's a way of exploring other forms of treatment for him. Though he'd had violent episodes, he had not actually broken any laws – which had to mean there was some way for him to be in a form of managed care that was not state-sanctioned incarceration. And (this was the mother in me talking) surely heaven and earth could still be moved to rescue this boy from such an ongoing horror show.

But Richard had spent serious money on a lawyer. Unlike his wife he was not giving up hope. Though Muriel really did sound unable to cope with Billy's monstrous illness, I knew it was wrong to judge her reportedly distanced reaction to her son's mental collapse. That's the thing about other people's tragedies. You can stand on the sidelines and make all sorts of pronouncements about how they should be handled. But in doing so you forget an essential truth: there is no appropriate way to react to the worst that life can throw at you. To attempt to impose your own so-called 'game plan' on a nightmare that you yourself aren't living is the height of heinous arrogance. That's why we find other people's tragedies so compulsive: because they so terrify us; because we all privately live with the knowledge that, at any moment, the entire trajectory of our lives can be upended by the most terrible and unforeseen forces.

But getting us off the subject of his son and onto my own children, he now got me talking about Sally and her considerable adolescent heartaches.

'Maybe this Brad guy dumping her will make her consider looking beyond status when it comes to choosing the next

151

boyfriend,' he said. 'But let me ask you something. Is Brad's father Ted Bingham, the lawyer fellow?'

'Sometimes the world is just too small.'

'Especially when it comes to Maine.'

'And yes, his dad is indeed Damariscotta's big-cheese lawyer – though I might have just uttered an oxymoron.'

Richard smiled, then added:

'Of course, had you said, "Damariscotta's big-headed lawyer", you might have stood accused of uttering a tautology.'

'Well, Ted Bingham has the reputation of being both big-headed and very *grand fromage*. Don't tell me you insure him?'

'Hardly. He works with Phil Malloy, who has basically cornered the Damariscotta insurance market.'

'Tell me about it. Phil insures our home and cars.'

'That's Maine. And the reason I know Ted Bingham is because his wife was at school with Muriel in Lewiston.'

'That's Maine again – and, of course, I've met the famous Julie Bingham.'

'Hard to believe she ever grew up—'

'—somewhere other than Palm Beach,' I said.

'Or the Hamptons.'

'Or Park Avenue.'

'Still, that big place they have on the coast by Pemaquid Point—'

'—is my dream location,' I said. 'And I now feel so tacky for being so catty about Julie.'

'But she is one of those people who invites cattiness.'

'I'm afraid I know all about that. Sally actually once heard Julie on the phone with a friend, telling her: "Now I think Brad's girlfriend is a cutey . . . but it's a shame her parents are struggling."'

'And you worry about being catty about her. Sometimes people deserve cattiness. Especially when they look down their long noses at everyone else. And I'm certain that your daughter saw right through Julie's *noblesse oblige* act.'

'If only Sally understood what *noblesse oblige* was. She's so bright and so intuitively smart. But she underestimates her own intelligence, and is so bound up in the superficial . . . even though I'm sure that, privately, she sees that this pursuit of the shallow is an empty one.'

'Then she'll hopefully move away from it all once Young Mr Bingham goes off to his Ivy League college.'

'That is my great hope. But as you well know, when it comes to children, you can never really shield them from danger or themselves.'

'That still doesn't lessen the sense of guilt that accompanies being a parent . . .'

'True. But even if I keep telling you that Billy's bipolar condition has no connection whatsoever to anything you've done as a father – and, in fact, from what you've reported, you've been the parent who has always been there for him . . .'

'Yes, I will still feel guilty about this until the day he's allowed out of that hell hole. Even then I'll still remain guilty about the horror he's been through.'

'Does parental guilt ever cease?'

'Do you really want me to answer that question?'

'Hardly. Because after all that happened with my son Ben . . .'

That's when I told him about my son's amazing promise as a painter, the subsequent breakdown after that spoiled little rich girl dropped him, and how he'd already been in one major exhibition and . . .

'So Ben's going to be the next Cy Twombly.'

Again I found myself looking at Richard with considerable surprise.

'You know your modern painters,' I said.

'I saw that big 2009 retrospective of his at the Art Institute of Chicago. Actually invented a reason to go to Chicago on business in order to catch the exhibition. Funny thing is – my dad, conservative ex-Marine that he was – still had a thing about art. Only his taste ran towards Winslow Homer and John Singer Sargent, which is still pretty good taste. Dad always had a secret hankering to be a painter. Had a little studio in his garage. Tried his hand at seascapes. He wasn't bad. Gave a few away to some family members. Even had a gallery in Boston take a few of the Maine coastal studies he did. But they never sold. Dad being Dad he decided that this was a sign they were no damn good. Even though my mother – who was some class of a saint – and his brother Roy told him otherwise. One night, after another of his big bouts of drinking – the guy could really put away cheap Scotch – he staggered out to the garage and burned all his paintings. Just like that. Dumped around two dozen canvases outside on the lawn, doused them with kerosene, lit a match. *Whoosh*. My mother found him sitting by the fire, looking sloshed, tears running down his face, so sad and furious with the world . . . but especially with himself. Because he knew he was burning all sense of hope and possibility, and a life beyond the one he had created for himself. There I was – a child of fourteen – watching this all from my bedroom window, telling myself I'd never live a life I disliked . . .'

'And your father never painted again?'

Richard shook his head.

'And yet he then ripped several strips off you when you dared to publish a short story.'

'Well, the guy was such a total hard case.'

'Or just jealous. My dad had a father like that. He saw that his son was a brilliant mathematician – and had teachers and college guidance counselors encouraging him to apply to everywhere from Harvard to MIT, just like your Billy. Only my dad's father was not a good father like you. Instead he was quietly enraged by his son's brilliance and worked assiduously at subverting his progress. Insisted he turn down a full scholarship at MIT because he needed him to work in the family hardware store every weekend. Dad went along with this – agreeing to U Maine and returning every weekend to Waterville to put in a full Saturday at my grandfather's shop. Can you imagine forcing a gifted young man to do that . . .'

'Actually I can.'

'Oh God, listen to me talking before thinking. I am so, so sorry.'

'Don't be. The truth doesn't hurt anymore. It's just *there*. Right in my face. And the thing is, even though my father also played undermining games with me – and I was no way as brilliant as your father . . .'

'Don't say that.'

'Why not? It's the truth.'

'But that short story . . .'

'*A* short story, written thirty years ago . . .'

'And one published a few months ago.'

'You remembered that?'

'Well, you did tell me about it yesterday.'

'It's just a small thing . . .'

'I actually Googled it this morning. And read it. And guess what? It's very good.'

'Seriously?'

'A man looks back on a childhood friend who was allegedly swept off the rocks at Prout's Neck . . . but who the friend knows was being investigated for fraud at the accountancy firm where he's a partner. Very Anthony Trollope.'

'Now you're being far too extravagant.'

'But you must have read *The Way We Live Now* – because the whole theme of personal and social corruption is—'

'I am hardly an Anthony Trollope. And a small Portland accountancy firm isn't exactly a great City brokerage house in London.'

'Does that matter?'

'Trollope was looking at the way money is the ongoing human obsession. And the fact that he used the grand canvas of London at the height of Victorian power—'

'And you use a small New England city in the middle of a recession to highlight the same concerns about the way we all are in thrall to money, and how, like it or not, it always defines us.'

Richard looked at me with something approaching bemusement – and clearly found himself incapable of articulating anything.

'You seem speechless,' I said.

'Well, it's not every day I get compared to one of the great masters of the nineteenth-century novel. And though I'm flattered . . .'

'I know, I know – you don't deserve it. It's just a two-thousand-word scribble in a minor magazine. And your father was right about your writing all along. Happy now?'

He reached for his drink and finished it.

'No one has ever been so encouraging about my writing before.'

'Did your wife read the story?'

'She said it was "readable, but depressing".'

'Well, the story really grabs you from the outset. But the apparent suicide at the end is incredibly disturbing. Still, I loved the moral ambiguity behind all that. It's like that line from Eliot's "The Hollow Men" – "Between the motion and the act . . ."'

'". . . falls the shadow".'

As he finished my sentence, finished the quote that I was quoting, I found myself looking up at Richard and thinking: *This man is full of surprises.* Perhaps the most surprising thing is the fact that I find him so . . . 'compelling' is the right word. And when he took those rather shapeless steel-rimmed spectacles off for a moment to rub his eyes I suddenly saw that, if you took away the dull golfing clothes and the actuarial inspector eyewear, there was a not unattractive man seated opposite me, and one whose initial grayness had now shaded into something warmer. I could also see, as he finished that T.S. Eliot quote, that he was regarding me in a different way now; that he too had discerned that the landscape between us was changing. Part of me was trying to tell myself: *This is a pleasant, interesting lunch, no more.* The other part of me – the person who always wondered why she imposed so many frontiers on her life – knew otherwise.

'Have you always worn glasses?' I asked.

'They're pretty damn awful, aren't they?' he asked.

'I didn't say that.'

'I'm saying that. I let Muriel choose them for me around eight years ago. I knew from the outset they were a mistake. She told me they looked businesslike, serious. Which are synonyms for dull.'

'Why did you buy them then?'

'Good question.'

'Maybe a little too direct,' I said, noting his discomfort. 'Didn't mean to be so blunt. Sorry.'

'Don't be. I've often asked myself the same thing. I suppose I was raised in a family where the women always chose the clothes for the men, and where I wasn't interested in style or things like that.'

'But the truth is, you do have a sense of style . . .'

He tugged at his zip-up jacket.

'This is hardly "style". I don't even play golf.'

'But you certainly understand visual style, citing Cy Twombly and John Singer Sargent. And when it comes to the world of books, of language . . .'

'I often tell myself I dress like an insurance man.'

'Then stop. Change.'

'*Change*. One of the most loaded words in the language.'

'And one of the easiest, if one can only accept the tenets of change. "*I don't like the eyeglasses I'm wearing, so I'll change them.*"'

'But that might cause some eyebrows to be raised.'

'And are those disapproving eyebrows that important to you?'

'They have been. *Change*. A tricky business.'

'Especially when it comes to eyeglasses.'

'I promised myself a leather jacket last year.'

'What happened?'

'Tried one on in one of those outlets down in Freeport. Muriel said I looked like a middle-aged man having an identity crisis.'

'Is she often so warm and praising?'

'You really *are* direct.'

'Not normally.'

'Then why now?'

'I just feel like being direct.'

'Do you buy your husband his clothes?'

'Do I dress him? The answer is, no. I've tried to encourage him to think about clothes, but he's just not interested.'

'So he dresses like . . .'

'A man who doesn't care how he dresses. You will be amused to hear, however, that I did buy him a leather jacket last year for his birthday. One of those reproduction aviator jackets. He approved.'

'Well, you clearly have taste. And you clearly know how to dress. As soon as you walked in, I thought, you really belong in Paris. Not that I know much about Paris, except for what I've read and seen.'

'Maybe you should find a way to get there.'

'Have you ever been?'

'Quebec City is the closest I've ever come to France.'

'Yeah, I did one trip to New Brunswick to see a client who had some business in Maine. That was thirteen years ago, before you had to have a passport to travel to Canada. Strange, isn't it, not having a passport?'

'Get one then.'

'Do you have one?'

'Oh, yes. And it sits in a desk drawer at home, ignored, unused, unloved.'

'Use it then.'

'I'd like to. But . . .'

'I know – *life*.'

The waiter showed up, asking us if we'd like coffee. I glanced at my watch. It was a bit after two-thirty.

'Am I keeping you?' I asked.

'Not at all. And you?'

'No plans whatsoever.'

'Coffee then?'

'Fine.'

The waiter disappeared.

'I wish ninety minutes would always evaporate so quickly,' I said.

'So do I. But in your work, boredom can't be a big problem. Every day a new set of patients. A new set of potential personal dramas, hopes, fears, all that big stuff.'

'You make the radiography unit of a small Maine hospital sound like a Russian novel.'

'Isn't it? Like you said about my "small" story, the universal problems are always universal, no matter how minor the setting. And you must run into distressing stories all the time.'

'What I see are dark masses and irregular-shaped growths and ominous shadows. It's the radiographer who decides what they all mean.'

'But you must know immediately if . . .'

'If it's the beginning of the end? Yes, I'm afraid that's one of the clinical fringe benefits of my trade – the ability, after almost two decades of looking at the bad stuff, to visually ascertain far too quickly whether it's Stage One, Two, Three or Four. As such I'm usually privy to this news before the radiologist. Thankfully there are very strict rules about technologists never informing a patient whether the prognosis is bad or not – though, if pressed and the news is good, I've developed a code which most patients understand and which gives them a sense that there is no cause for concern. And our radiologist, Dr Harrild, will only talk to a patient if he has discerned that the all-clear can be sounded.'

'So if a radiologist doesn't come to talk with you after a scan or an X-ray . . .'

'It all depends on the hospital. In a big hospital, like the place down the street, Mass General, I'm certain that there's an enforced protocol about never speaking to the patient. But we're not a world-renowned hospital. As you know we're completely local. So we bend the rules a bit when it comes to Dr Harrild meeting with the patient if the news isn't sinister.'

'Which means if he doesn't meet with you . . .'

'That's right. It's probably pretty damn dire.'

'I'll remember that.'

'Hopefully you'll never get a diagnosis like that,' I said.

'The truth is, we're all going to eventually get a diagnosis like that. Because my work is, in part, all about risk assessment. So I too am looking – in a wholly different way – at the frailty of others. Trying to ascertain whether they are the type whose heart will explode before they're fifty-five due to lifestyle and the usual self-destructive habits. Or perhaps a family predisposition to cancer. Or the fact that, to my trained eye, they just look so beaten down and defeated by life that they are simply not a good bet.'

'So you too have a trained eye.'

'Well, if someone walks into my office carrying three hundred pounds in weight and looking like they have had trouble getting up the stairs to meet me . . . no, I am not going to agree to a one-million-dollar life policy.'

'Then again, they might live well into their eighties, despite all that weight. Generic roulette, right? And there's one empirical fact that none of us can dodge – the price of admission for being given life is having it eventually taken away from you. Anyone who says they don't think about it all the time—'

'I think about it all the time.'

'So do I. That, for me, is an ongoing preoccupation since stumbling into middle age – the realization that time is such an increasingly precious commodity. And if we don't use it properly . . .'

'Does anyone really use it properly?' he asked.

'Surely there are people out there who think themselves fortunate and fulfilled in their lives.'

'But the truth is, no matter how successful or happy you may consider yourself to be there is always a part of your life that is problematic, or deficient, or a let-down in some way.'

'That's all a bit actuarial, don't you think?'

'Or just completely realistic. Unless you think otherwise?'

Before I could pause and appear to think this through I heard myself say:

'No, I'm afraid you're absolutely right. There is always something not working in your life. Then again, the great hope is . . .'

I stopped myself from finishing that sentence, and was relieved when the waiter arrived with our coffees. I added milk to mine and stirred it many times, hoping Richard would not ask me to complete the thought. But, of course, he said:

'Go on, finish the sentence.'

'No need.'

'Why "no need"?'

'Because . . .'

Oh God, I want to say this and I so don't want to say this . . .

'Because the great hope in life is being with someone with whom you can weather all the bad stuff that life will inevitably toss into your path. But that's perhaps the biggest fairy tale imaginable. The idea of—'

The check arrived, allowing me not to finish the sentence, which was a relief. I suggested we split it.

'Absolutely not,' he said.

'Thank you for such an excellent lunch.'

'Thank you for being here. It's been . . . well, wonderful is the word that pops to mind.'

'And what are you planning to do next?'

'As in tomorrow, the day after, the week after, the month . . .?'

'Very funny.'

'I have no plans for the rest of the day.'

'Nor do I.'

'Shall we invent some plans?'

'Absolutely.'

Another smile from Richard.

'Right then,' he said. 'Can I show you where I plan to live?'

'You're moving to Boston?'

'I'm moving just down the street to the corner of Beacon Street and the Common.'

'And when are you doing that?'

Without taking his eyes off me he said:

'In the next life.'

I MAY NOT know the world beyond the eastern corridor of the United States, but I can't imagine I will ever encounter anything more perfect than the inherent perfection of a perfect autumn day in New England. Specifically, this day, this afternoon. The sun still radiant, but bathing the Common in coppery late-afternoon incandescence. The sky pure unadulterated blue. A light breeze, the mercury still hovering somewhere between the vanished summer and the impending dark chill of winter. And the foliage festooning the Common in its autumnal eruption of primary colors. The reds and golds of the oaks and elms electric in their intensity.

'Can foliage festoon a park?' I asked Richard as we crossed Beacon Street and entered the Public Gardens. Had I asked Dan such a question he would have rolled his eyes and accused me of one-upmanship for showing off my love of 'big words'. Richard just smiled and said:

' "Festoon" works. And it's more poetic than "embellish" or "adorn" or "decorate".'

' "Decorate" is a synonym I would definitely sidestep.'

'It depends how it is used. For example, "Back then, the Common was decorated with the corpses of the condemned, dangling from trees." '

'My God, where did that come from?'

'Once upon a time, in the early moments of our country, this Common – our first public park in the then-colonies – was also the public hanging grounds. Being Puritans with a rather bleak view of human nature, they believed that public executions set a fine example for the community.'

'And do you know where exactly the executions took place?' I asked. 'Is there a three-hundred-and-eighty-year-old tree in the Common with a plaque on it, informing all visitors that this was the spiritual home of the death penalty in America?'

'I tend to doubt that the Boston tourist board would want to promote such a thing.'

'But up in Salem you can see where all the witches were tried and, no doubt, burned.'

'They actually hanged a witch here on the Common, Ann Hibbens, in 1656.'

'How do you know that?'

'History is a pastime of mine. Especially colonial American history. And the reason why the folks up in Salem have cashed in on the witchcraft trials is because they understand that they can make a tourist dollar or two by playing to that aspect of American Gothic which everyone embraces. It's the Edgar Allan Poe part of our nature. Our love of the *Grand Guignol,* of the freakish and unsettling. The belief – and this is the big one which all the evangelical Christians embrace – that the apocalypse is coming, that we are in "the end of days" and it's only a matter of time before the Four Horsemen of the Apocalypse show up to announce that Jesus is returning to re-establish his dominion on earth, and all the born-agains will get shuffled off to heaven, leaving the rest of us heathens here to live out our lives of eternal damnation.'

'But, yesterday, you were defending the family values that all those evangelicals trumpet all the time – and sounding very Republican.'

'How do you know I'm a Republican?'

'Are you denying it?'

'I have voted Independent on a few occasions.'

'But never Democrat?'

'Once or twice. But they're just not what I am about. Then again, neither is the new Republican Party – which has turned so extreme and mean.'

'So where does that politically put you then?'

'Confused – and unable to figure out where I belong anymore.'

'I feel that all the time.'

'About politics?'

'About everything.'

'"No direction home".'

'Exactly – and that's Dylan, isn't it?'

'It certainly is.'

'You like Dylan?'

'Clearly – and that surprises you, doesn't it?'

'Did I sound surprised?'

'Yes.'

'Pleasantly surprised.'

'Because I'm such a gray middle-aged man who dresses like a weekend golfer.'

'If you don't like how you dress—'

'I know. The C-word. Change.'

Then, looking into the distance, he said:

'A truly perfect day.'

'I was just thinking that a moment ago.'

'I wonder if the British were as entranced by the New England autumn back when this Common was used as a camp by the forces of the Crown during the Revolutionary War?'

'You know your Massachusetts Bay Colony history, Mr Copeland.'

'Anytime I start spouting off about such things my wife tells me I am showing off.'

'That's sad – and sadly not unusual. My husband does the same thing whenever my vocabulary obsessions get articulated.'

'But doesn't he see that this curiosity, this need to learn, is an expression of . . .'

Now it was his turn to terminate the sentence before it was finished.

'Go on,' I said. 'Finish the sentence.'

'I can only speak for myself. But . . . the reason I read so much, the reason my head has always been in a book . . . well, it's an antidote to loneliness, right?'

'I think so.'

We then fell silent for a few moments, continuing to stroll towards the Public Gardens. Richard broke the silence.

'Now, as I was saying, the Brits used the Common as an encampment. And the hanging continued up until 1817. Oh, and there was a major riot here in 1713 when a big mob reacted against food shortages in the city. And do you know the Puritans actually hanged a woman here in the 1660s for preaching Quakerism, that's how doctrinally extreme they were. And . . . oh God, will you listen to me, spouting on as if I'm on one of those quiz shows where you have a minute to show off everything you know about something so trivial as the history of Boston Common.'

'But I actually find what you're telling me interesting. And impressive. And when did you read up about it all?'

Without breaking stride, and with his gaze still very much on a distanced corner of this public park, he said:

'Just last night, online back in the hotel. I wanted to sound erudite when I saw you today.'

I found myself smiling again.

'Well, you succeeded. And I find it rather touching that you would go to the trouble of finding out so much about the Common for my benefit.'

We turned north towards the Public Gardens.

'So, go on,' I said, 'tell me everything you know about this place.'

'You sure you want to hear the prepared spiel . . .'

'No, I'm just saying that to show off my masochistic tendencies.'

Richard laughed.

'You are a toughie.'

'Hardly . . . though if I make a somewhat sarcastic comment like that one to my husband, Dan takes umbrage. Whereas you laughed.'

'Familiarity always breeds . . . complexity.'

'Why didn't you say "contempt"?'

'Because . . . I wish it didn't breed contempt. But it does.'

'In every marriage, every long-term domestic relationship?'

'I can't say I'm that knowledgeable about other people's marriages – which are usually something of a mystery to those on the outside, let alone those actually in the middle of them. But from the ones I do know – and I don't have that many friends who share stuff like that with me – I can't say that I know a great number of people who are genuinely happy. Do you know many happy couples?'

'No. And like you, I can't say that I have many friends.'

'That surprises me. You strike me as someone who—'

'Outside of my family and my best friend Lucy I largely keep to myself. I was this way in school, in college. One or two close friends. Cordial working relationships with those around me, and always this tendency to be standoffish a bit. Certainly not towards my children. Outside of murder and mayhem, I would literally do just about anything for them. And, once upon a time, Dan and I were close.'

'But now?'

'I don't really want to talk about all that.'

'Understood.'

'Now you are being too nice,' I said.

'Why's that?'

'Because you told me a great deal about your son and your wife. And I'm hedging my bets, as usual.'

'You shouldn't feel in any way obliged to tell me . . .'

I stopped in front of a park bench and suddenly sat down, no longer wanting to have this conversation while perambulating. Taking my cue, Richard joined me on the bench, sitting at the far end of it, giving me the distance that he cleverly understood that I needed.

'Dan is a man I don't know anymore. Though I've talked a little about this with my one great friend Lucy, the fact is, I've kept much of it to myself. Because he's been through a major personal crisis with the loss of his job. And because I always felt that I needed to be loyal to Dan. God knows, I wanted things to somehow revert to that time before he was laid off when we had a reasonable and reasonably easy relationship with each other. Now I'm not saying that ours was ever the most romantic of stories.'

'So who was the love of your life?'

The question – so unexpected, so deeply direct – threw me. But without pausing for a moment to reflect about the wisdom of even going there, I heard myself saying:

'Eric. His name was Eric.'

I looked up to see my use of the past tense register on Richard's face. Immediately I regretted letting this small piece of information out. Immediately I was so grateful to Richard for not bringing it up, though again I heard myself say something unexpected:

'That is the first time I've mentioned his name in around fifteen years.'

I held my breath for a moment, hoping that Richard would not follow this revelation with a question. To his immense credit he said absolutely nothing, letting a silence hang between us as I scrambled to think what I should say next. Which turned out to be:

'And now I'm dropping the subject.'

'No problem,' Richard said.

I stood up. Richard followed suit.

'Shall we continue walking?' I asked.

'Absolutely. Where to?'

'You told me you wanted to show me where you'd live in "the next life". So show me.'

'It's not far.'

We headed further on through the Gardens, past a small pond and flower beds still festooned – that word again! – with the final vestiges of that summer's flowers.

'Let me guess,' Richard said. 'Does "festooned" work here?'

I laughed.

'That's impressive.'

The Gardens ended and we found ourselves facing a long avenue, fronted by venerable nineteenth-century residences, a central barrier of greenery stretching all the way north. Directly in front of us was a church clearly dating back to the colonial era, and an apartment building that looked like it belonged in some jazz-age Scott Fitzgerald story.

'So is that where you want to live in the next life?' I said, pointing upwards to the penthouse.

'In my dreams. That used to be the Ritz. Now it's apartments for the super-rich. Even in reserved, button-down Boston – where

ostentation and flashing the cash are still considered bad taste –
there is, like everywhere else these days, truly serious money floating
about. Especially with the density of mutual funds and bio/info
tech people concentrated here.'

'Those mutual fund folk get two-to-three-million-dollar bonuses
every year.'

'Minimum two-to-three-million. If you're at the top of that
financial food chain, it's probably somewhere over ten million.
Unreal, isn't it?'

'What makes it even more unreal is that everyone who is not
a member of that wealth club – by which I mean anyone who
doesn't make over a couple hundred thousand a year – is struggling. I speak from experience. The last eighteen months, with
Dan out of work, have been very tight. As much as he hates the
stockroom job he starts on Monday, the fact that we'll have an
extra three hundred dollars a week . . . well, there will finally be
a little breathing space. Not exactly "take the family skiing in
Aspen" breathing space. Just "we can now meet our basic bills"
breathing space. God knows I don't begrudge anyone their success
or wealth. I chose my profession, my career. I also chose to stay
in Maine where I knew that the salary would be small. And I am
also someone who hates to complain.'

'There you go again, making apologies for yourself, instead of
just speaking the truth. Which is, in America nowadays, you either
have big bucks or you just about get by. And I speak as a Republican
– yet one who was raised with the idea that the middle class could
actually have a very good life; that if you were a teacher, a nurse,
a cop, an ambulance driver, a soldier, you could still have the
house, the two cars in the garage, the two weeks by the lake
somewhere every summer, put your kids through college without
having to take out crippling loans, cover your family's monthly
health insurance bill without worry, even heat your home
throughout the winter without fear. Now, the amount of clients
I see who, even in full-time jobs, find the cost of living impossible
. . . well, it's a good thing that your husband took that job.'

'Even if it's going to make him even more miserable.'

'Better to be miserable earning a salary than be miserable earning nothing. I wish I could say something upbeat and Horatio Alger-esque like, "If he hates the job so much, he can always find another." But in this market . . .'

'Tell me about it. I keep thinking, maybe we should change our lives once Sally is off at college next year. But . . .'

I didn't complete the thought. Because I didn't know how to complete the thought.

'*Change*,' Richard said. 'That ferociously loaded word.'

We started walking up Commonwealth Avenue. I'd been along this boulevard several times before, and had always admired it in a half-fleeting touristic way. Today, however, I began to closely regard the townhouses and apartment buildings and mansions that lined the avenue, and seemed part of a Boston more rooted in Henry James than any contemporary realities. Maybe it was the way the venerable stone and brickwork interplayed with the late-afternoon sun. Maybe it was the matchless autumnal palette of the trees interspersed with the nineteenth-century streetlights. Maybe it was Richard's animated commentary about the history of this avenue and the way he seemed to have a story about every residence we passed . . . and from the immense knowledge he displayed it was clear to me that he hadn't gleaned all this off the Internet late last night; that, in fact, he had made quite the study of this historic thoroughfare, as he knew it with an intimacy and verve that bespoke of serious erudition.

This led me to imagine him in his home in Bath – a modest house, he told me, on one of those streets near the Iron Works. I'm certain it had an attic room he had converted into a home office: a simple desk, an old armchair, a computer that was (like my own at home) a few years out of date – because Richard didn't strike me as someone who spent a lot of money on himself. This office was his escape hatch: the place he could quietly shut the door on a marriage that had evidently flat-lined and was so devoid of comfort, and away from the ongoing sadness that was his son Billy. Here Richard could lose himself in his considerable curiosity. Whether it be the *OED* (and I was pretty certain he had the full multi-volumed Oxford dictionary, that was one indulgence he would have treated himself to), or one of those Norton editions of American poetry, or the vast research possibilities of the Internet – once in that room Richard could vanish into the realm of language and historical detail. And envisage perhaps (as we all do) a life beyond the one that we have constructed for ourselves.

*Change.* The great ongoing desire that underscores all feelings of entrapment. *Change.* Richard was right: it was such a ferociously loaded word.

'Now I don't know who the architect was here,' Richard said as we passed a mansion that he identified as being 'so close to the American Regency style that Edith Wharton wrote about in novels like *The House of Mirth* and *The Age of Innocence* . . . even though most Bostonians would say that New York copied them when it came to mid-nineteenth-century grand houses.'

'You know this avenue so well.'

'I told you, I plan to live here in the next life.'

'Where exactly?'

'Next street up from here. Southwest corner of Dartmouth and Comm Ave.'

'Nice to know what's planned for oneself in the afterlife.'

'"The next life" doesn't mean the hereafter,' he said.

'So when does the next life commence?'

'That's the eternal question.'

'Or not eternal, as life is so profoundly temporal,' I said.

'Do you believe in the notion of "time to come"?'

'I know that faith is the antithesis of proof. Which means that all belief – especially religious belief – is bound up in the acceptance of a storyline which, though comforting, is rather hard to get your head around. Then again, if I was told tomorrow that I had Stage Four cancer, would I be tempted to ask Jesus to be my Lord and Savior? As much as I'd truly like to think there is something beyond all this, the leap of faith that is required is simply beyond me. It saddens me thinking that. But I have wrestled with it a bit – and my conclusion quite simply is, this is it. And you?'

'I'd like to say I'm a hedger of bets. I know several very committed

Christians who are absolutely convinced that they will be handed
a locker room key and a towel from St Peter when they leave this
life. I am certainly not against anyone believing all that – the
primary function of religion being the lessening of fear about
death. But . . . well, I read that when Steve Jobs was dying of
cancer, he told one close friend that, though he was very much
fascinated by all sorts of mystical and spiritual notions of the life
to come, a great part of him couldn't help but think that death
was like the switch on all his computers that shuts everything
down. Death – the ultimate *off* switch.'

'Bizarrely, there is some comfort in that, isn't there? The end of
consciousness. The computer goes blank. Forever.'

'The problem is, we are the only species with a proper consciousness, who can feel guilt, regret. And say you reach the end of your
life . . .'

'. . . with the knowledge that you hadn't really lived your life?'

We were on the corner of Commonwealth and Dartmouth,
in front of a brownstone that had four floors, and whose brickwork was sooty brown, but which still looked (from the state of
the door and the shutters on its windows) well-maintained.
Compared to the other more lavish mansions and apartment
buildings on the street this one was a little more modest but still
utterly charming. There was a *For Sale* sign attached to the iron
railings that fronted the street – the smaller print stating that
the apartment seeking a buyer was a one-bedroom '*with great
Old World charm*'.

'So this is the place?' I asked.

'Third floor, those three windows facing the street.'

The windows were large ones, indicating high ceilings.

'Nice,' I said.

'I actually sneaked down to Boston around two weeks ago
to see the place myself. Really airy space. Great parquet floors.
A living room that stretches the whole length of the building. A
good-sized bedroom. An alcove off the living room that would be
a perfect little office. The bathroom and the kitchen are a bit out
of date. But the realtor told me that the asking price of three

hundred and five thousand was negotiable; that the sellers had a deal which fell through last year, and they really want a fast closing, and if I could pay two sixty-five cash it was mine.'

'Can you pay that?'

'Actually I can. I've been one of those assiduous savers who've set aside twenty percent of his net income every year. I've got about four hundred thousand in the bank. A lawyer I consulted down in Portland – Bath is too small to be talking divorce with anyone – told me that if I was to give Muriel the house in Bath, she'd have no claim on any of that money. And I have another client down here, a builder in Dorchester, who told me he could get a spiffy new bathroom and kitchen installed, repaint the walls, strip and re-stain all the floorboards, all for around thirty-five grand. After taxes and the like, I'd come out with a paid-off Commonwealth Avenue apartment and about seventy-five thousand still left in the bank.'

'Most of all, you'd be living here – where you've always wanted to live.'

'That's right. I know I could even run much of my business down here, and probably hire someone to take over Muriel's administrative job at the agency – though knowing Muriel she'd probably insist on staying on, taking a salary, keeping busy, which would be fine by me. She is very competent.'

'So when are you moving?'

I could see Richard's shoulders tense, his lips tighten.

'Life is never that straightforward, is it?' he said.

'I suppose not. Still, if you have it all worked out . . .'

'Does anyone ever have it "all worked out"?'

I smiled.

'You're far too right about all that. But this time I really do want to make the move . . . as messy and unpleasant as it might all be.'

'Everyone I know who's divorced has always said it's the anticipation of the end of a marriage that is the most devastating. In the end, once they had finally moved out, they were always baffled as to why they hadn't done it years earlier. But now I really *am* speaking far too bluntly.'

'Or maybe revealing a thought that had also crossed your mind as well?' he asked.

Now it was my turn to clench my shoulders and purse my lips.

'Life is never straightforward, is it . . . as you yourself said.'

'And maybe I've crossed a frontier I shouldn't have.'

'Then we're even. And the truth is, I wish I was in your position.'

'I feel a little stupid about regaling you with all the financial details of the sale.'

'But the reason you are telling me this is because you're still trying to see if you can go through with it . . . and are understandably struggling with it, as I certainly would too.'

'You're half right, But the other reason I told you all that is because nobody, not even my closest friend the police captain, knows about this. And because I can actually talk to you. And . . . well . . . a woman I can talk to . . . not something I've had much experience of.'

I reached out and touched his arm.

'Thank you for telling me that.'

He covered my hand with his.

'It's me who should be thanking you.'

'It's also me who should be thanking you.'

'For what?'

'For getting me to let down my guard for a change. It's something everyone at work always says about me. I am perfectly professional and pleasant, but completely guarded. Dan has often told me the same thing – I have this taciturn side.'

'That's news to me,' he said, his hand still covering mine.

'You don't know me yet.'

'You can know a great deal about someone in just a few hours.'

'Just like I now know that you are going to buy this apartment.'

Richard glanced back up at the top of the brownstone, his hand leaving mine. And in a voice just a decibel or so above a whisper he said:

'I hope that's the outcome.'

*Why shouldn't it be?* I wanted to ask him. But instead I held back, simply saying:

'I hope so too.'

Richard's gaze returned to me.

'So . . . any thoughts about what we should do now? If, that is, you want to . . .'

'. . . continue the afternoon? No, I want to flee the elegance of Commonwealth Avenue to return to that God-awful hotel and attend the five p.m. conference on advanced colonoscopy techniques . . . not that I do colonoscopies.'

'But it sounds so romantic.'

I laughed. Then said:

'If you're agreeable, what I'd like to find now is a museum or art gallery, because that's something I can't walk to back home. And I'd prefer something I'm not going to see in Maine. Heard of the ICA?'

'That new place on the harbor front?'

'Exactly. I read an article about it in some magazine. The Institute of Contemporary Art. Modern, edgy, out there. And with a water view.'

'And, no doubt, filled with people wearing black and looking modern, edgy, out there.'

'So . . . we can gawk at all the urban boho types.'

'The way you're dressed you'll fit right in.'

'And you think you won't?'

'The way I'm dressed I will look like the most boring—'

'Then change,' I said, again my mouth working ahead of my usual cautious thought processes.

'What?' he said, staring at me with confusion.

'*Change* – that treacherous verb. As in, if you don't like the way you're dressed now, change your clothes.'

'And how will I do that?'

'How do you think?'

He considered this for a moment. Then:

'That's a crazy idea.'

'But you're not totally against it, are you?'
He considered this for another moment.
'Well . . . "change" does rhyme with "strange". And strange is . . .'
'Maybe not as strange as you think.'

*Five*

SYNONYMS FOR 'RANDOM': 'unselected', 'irregular', 'chance', 'by hazard', 'happenstantial'.

Happenstantial. As in happenstance. As in, the business of stumbling into something new, unforeseen, unpredictable. Like the happenstantial way I met Richard. And met him again at that movie theater. And agreed to lunch. And the happenstantial way we drifted into the trajectory of this afternoon – which, like all events predicated on randomness, had no *foreseen* trajectory to it; the fact that we had proceeded from Commonwealth Ave and Newbury Street was predicated on a wholly aleatorical set of circumstances . . . though aleatorical almost implies chance by design, which perhaps makes it the right synonym to be used to describe all this. Because behind the random lies choice. Which, in turn, means that subtext always lurks behind the happenstantial – except that the subtext is something that only arises courtesy of the pinball-like way an event begets an event, which, in turn, begets the fact that we are now on that exceptionally elegant and luxe stretch of Boston real estate known as Newbury Street, and have just stepped into a boutique (because this is certainly not 'a shop') that sells eyeglasses.

'So do we call this place an opticians, an ophthalmologist, an eyeglass store, or a spectacle emporium?' I asked.

'Spectacles – *specs* – is still, I think, parlance in England. And as we are in New England . . .'

'Well, the place *is* called Specs.'

'Don't think this is the place for me,' Richard said. 'I mean, look at the guy behind the counter.'

The fellow he was speaking about had a shaved head and a pair of high-modern pince-nez glasses hugging his nose. He also had large black circular earrings implanted in both earlobes.

'He looks reasonably friendly,' I said.

'For someone who belongs in 1920s Berlin. This guy is going to look at me—'

'And see a potential customer. Now stop all the fretting and just—'

I opened the door and all but pushed him into the shop. Rather than being all cold and 'too cool for school', the fellow behind the counter was charm itself.

'Now I surmise from the way your wife had to shove you in here,' he said, 'you are just a little reluctant to try a change of style.'

Richard did not correct him about the 'your wife' comment. Nor did he seem to blanch when the guy accurately read his unease. Instead he said:

'That's right. I'm a style-free zone.'

The guy, who had a name-plate on the counter in front of him – '*Gary: Spectician*' (is there such a word?) – reassured Richard that he was 'among friends here'. He then proceeded to expertly take charge. Within half an hour – having put Richard at ease – he talked him through various frame styles, quickly discerning that, when it came to wanting a particular look, Richard hadn't a clue what he really was after. So Gary showed him all sorts of permutations. After talking about how – given his coloring and his oval face – highly geometric frames 'might be just a tad too severe . . . and I really don't think we want the harshness of metal again, now do we?' he convinced Richard to choose a brownish, slightly oval frame: highly stylish, but simultaneously not a radical statement. Nonetheless, seeing them on him, it was clear that they changed his look. Rather than appearing angular and actuarial Richard now came across as somewhat hip, professorial. Bookish. Thoughtful.

'You think they work?' Richard asked, clearly approving of the image reflecting back to him in Gary's mirror, but also needing my sanction.

'They're a great fit,' I said.

'As long as your optician in Bath can give me your prescription over the phone, I'll have them ready for you in about an hour.'

Luck was on our side. The optician in Bath was able to scan Richard's prescription down to Gary – and we headed back out to Newbury Street.

'Now let's find you a leather jacket,' I said.

'I feel strange,' Richard said.

'Because I'm being bossy?'

'You're hardly bossy. But you are persuasive.'

'But, as a salesman, surely you know the thing about persuasiveness is that you can only persuade someone if they truly want to be persuaded.'

'And I clearly want to be persuaded?'

'I'm not going to answer that question.'

'Four hundred dollars for a pair of glasses. I never thought . . .'

'What?'

'That I could be so self-indulgent.'

'Glasses are hardly indulgent.'

'Designer glasses are.'

'And let me guess – you had a father who told you that . . .'

'A father and a mother who counted every penny. And, wouldn't you know it, I married a woman who also thinks that thrift is one of the more profound virtues. And since she is my bookkeeper and sees all my credit card statements . . .'

*She's not your mother* I suddenly wanted to tell him, simultaneously wondering why so many men turn their wives into mothers, and why so many women seemed more than willing to play that emasculating role. And this thought connected to another one: how Dan himself had, in his ongoing resentful moments, talked to me as if I was the actual disapproving woman who had raised him and who had always let him know he was a disappointment to her. Knowing so well the pain that he had carried with him from childhood, I had always tried to tack away from the criticism that so haunted him. And yet, ever since all went wrong with his career, he'd cast me in that mother role. A role I certainly didn't want.

'When she sees the designer glasses,' I said, 'tell her—'

' "I needed new glasses . . . and, by the way, I'm moving to Boston." '

'That's pretty definitive,' I said.

'So where do we find a leather jacket around here?'

We wandered up several blocks, all lined with the big designer label boutiques. Stopping in Burberry, there was an amazing black leather jacket in the window which looked like something a modern Byronic figure would wear . . . and with a list price of over $2,000.

'Even if I had that sort of money I don't think I could carry that jacket off,' Richard said. 'Too Errol Flynn for me.'

A few shops later he also passed on something that – as he interestingly put it – 'looks a little too Lou Reed for me'.

'You know Lou Reed?' I asked.

'Personally? Can't say that he ever bought a policy from me. But *Transformer*? Great album. Can't say I've kept up on his career since *New York*. And Muriel's always been more Neil Diamond than the Velvet Underground . . .'

Richard Copeland: secret Manhattan demimonde wannabe! Or maybe just a fan. No wonder he wanted to get rid of those golfing clothes he had worn assiduously for all those years. Like the suit I first saw him in at the hotel check-in. The same flat style that his father had undoubtedly worn. The uniform of the strait-laced American businessman. Clothes are a language. So often we don't like the language that we've forced ourselves to speak. Look at me. At the hospital, my white lab coat is my daily uniform. Around the house and in downtown Damariscotta I have always dressed soberly. But in my closet there are a few items that hint at another me – like my leather jacket and this black, very Continental rain-coat I'm currently wearing, and even a wonderful fedora that I found in a vintage clothing store during a trip to Burlington. But these clothes – including a pair of black suede cowboy boots that I stumbled upon at a yard sale in Rockland (they fit me perfectly and only cost $15) – stay largely out of sight. Were I to walk around town dressed as I am now, nobody would say anything. That's the Maine way. But everyone would notice. Comments would be passed when I was out of sight. So this somewhat Left Bank wardrobe stays locked away unless I'm heading down to Portland for something cultural. And when I recently put on the leather jacket and the suede boots to hear a jazz concert with Lucy, my daughter caught sight of me getting ready. Surveying my sartorial choices for the evening she said:

'Are you going to a costume party, dressed as a hipster?'

I wanted to tell her that, quite frankly, this is the way I would prefer to dress most of the time – but felt constrained by small-townness and my own innate sense of decorum (which, in uncharitable moments, I thought was also a form of cowardice). Now seeing Richard trying to mask his tenseness as we went into another high-priced boutique in search of the leather jacket he was so fearful of wearing, I couldn't help thinking: *He too is someone who has kept so much of what he's wanted to express under wraps.* And when he eyed, in a shop that sold hip military-surplus-style clothing, a reproduction 1940s Air Force jacket in a dark, somewhat distressed brown (it really was rather stylish) I could see that he was weighing up whether he could get away with wearing it.

'That's the jacket,' I said.

'People will look at me strangely back home.'

'And I never wear this outfit around Damariscotta – because I fear the same thing. Anyway, Boston is going to be home soon.'

Richard tried on the jacket. It was a great fit – but his pale blue, very button-down shirt clearly didn't work with it. So I walked over to a display table where a pile of stylish work shirts were stacked. I figured he would take a large and chose one in black with small steel buttons on its pockets.

'Black?' Richard said when I proffered the shirt. 'Isn't that a bit extreme?'

'It will work so well with the jacket, especially if you match it up with black jeans.'

'I've never worn black in my life.'

'But I bet you've wanted to. Lou Reed and all that.'

'I'm a little gray and boring to entertain such—'

'You're the most interesting man I've met in—'

*When was the last time I met such an interesting man?*

'You're being too kind again,' he said.

'Just accurate. Now . . . what's your waist and inseam size?'

'I'll get the jeans.'

'No – I'm choosing them. And you can veto them if you disagree.'

'Thirty-four waist, I hate to say . . .'

'Dan is thirty-six. And the inseam?'

'Thirty-two. But do you really think black jeans with the black shirt will—'

'What? Make you look "too cool for school"?'

'Or ridiculous.'

'Try it all on and then tell me if you think it's ridiculous.'

I found a wall of shelved jeans and chose a pair of black Levi's in the appropriate size. Then I handed them to Richard and pointed him in the direction of the changing rooms. As he headed off I asked him his shoe size.

'Ten and a half. But really, I feel as if—'

'If you don't like the look you don't have to wear the look. But at least try the look, OK?'

In another corner of this emporium, which was decorated with vintage World War I and II recruitment posters, there was one pair of black lace-up boots – ankle-high, the leather grained, stylish, but not flamboyant – in Richard's size. I brought them over to the changing rooms, knocked on the door of the cubicle where Richard was getting into his assorted new clothes, and slid them under the large gap between the door frame and the floor, saying:

'These might work.'

'More black,' came the voice from within.

'And what's wrong with that? Give me a shout when you're ready.'

A minute later out stepped a very different man. Richard had taken off his soon-to-be-replaced glasses. The effect – coupled with the new clothes – was more than striking. The jeans, the black work shirt, and the black boots all fit him perfectly. And the leather jacket worked wonderfully with the rest of this outfit, though the detachable fur collar was a bit too overblown, reeking of some 1940s war movie set on the Russian front. But that little detail aside, what stood out most was how the clothes so absolutely suited him, and took about ten years off him immediately. Freed from the cost accountant outfit, his face no longer dominated by the dull metallic oval of his glasses, he suddenly assumed a different outward identity. He now looked like a somewhat hip English professor who was at ease with his age. Sidling up next to Richard and looking at ourselves in the mirror – dressed up like a rather stylish metropolitan couple – all I could think was: Why had I spent years dressing myself in such a sober, restrained way? And the most disquieting aspect to this question was the realization that the only person making me conform was . . . myself.

'Well . . .' Richard said, eyeing us in the mirror.

'What do you think?'

'Not bad.'

'Understatement will get you nowhere.'

'OK, the truth – I love the look. Even if it also scares me.'

'Just as I love my look – and would never dream of walking down Main Street, Damariscotta, like this.'

'Well, if you think I could get away with this in Bath . . .'

'I'm sure you could. Just as I'm sure that your clients and your neighbors would accept the new style.'

'If that's the case then why don't you dress the way you want to when you're home?'

'I was just asking myself the same question. Maybe I will do just that . . . if I can get up the courage.'

'Same here.'

'You look like a very different man now.'

'And you look even more beautiful than yesterday.'

I felt myself blush. Yet I simultaneously found myself reaching for his hand and threading my fingers through his. We didn't turn to look at each other. Truth be told our shared nervousness was clearly palpable, as his hand was as damp as mine. Yet he did not pull away. Rather his grip tightened. Staring straight into the mirror we saw ourselves holding hands, looking so profoundly different than we were just twenty-four hours ago.

'Hey, you guys look cool.'

It was one of the shop assistants – her tone somewhat spacey, an amused smile on her face, as if the subtext behind what she was saying was: *Hey, you guys look cool . . . but I'm really humoring you because you're my parents.* Immediately we let go of each other, like a pair of guilty teenagers caught in a compromising position. The girl also saw this and added, rather dryly:

'Sorry if I interrupted anything.'

'You interrupted nothing,' Richard said, his tone corrective. Reaching for my hand again he told her: 'I want to wear all this out.'

'No problem,' she said. 'When you're ready I'll just cut all the tags off. There's a theft device in the coat that's got to be removed.'

She left us alone.

'That shut her up,' I said with a smile.

'I have my occasional assertive moments. And just to make an assertive point, I'm going to take all my old clothes and dump them in the first Goodwill charity box I find.'

It was my turn to squeeze his hand back.

'That's a good call.'

Now we did turn towards each other.

But then . . .

*Bing.*

My cellphone interrupted the moment; that telltale prompt letting me know that a text was awaiting me. Again, the guilt impulse took over. I let go of Richard's hand, but hesitated about reaching for the phone. Richard read this immediately. Not wanting to put me in an awkward position he said:

'I'll get the girl to deal with all the tags. See you up front.'

Richard headed off in search of the shop assistant. I dug out the phone and read:

**Garage all cleared. Love – Dan**

I shouldn't have looked at the damn phone, as a stab of remorse caught me. Becoming very friendly with a man I just met yesterday. Shopping for clothes for him. Holding hands with him . . .

Oh Lord, I sound like a twelve-year-old.

Yes, I could see that Dan's text was a further attempt to make amends. That made me feel somewhat guilty. But . . . but . . . that was the first time he had used the word 'love' in a text to me since . . . well, I couldn't remember the last time he'd said or written anything of the sort. And even the fact that he didn't say, 'Love you' . . . Just writing 'Love' – good friends use that at the end of emails. Whereas had he come out and made a direct declaration of love . . .

In that very instant, as I read his five-word text again, something within me shifted. It's curious, isn't it, how a small detail – the fact that my husband left off a pronoun after a somewhat charged word – can suddenly change everything. And the sad thing was: he was trying to be loving. Yet what he had done was underscore, once again, just how thwarted he was; how he could never really engage with me, let alone be talked into changing his clothes.

**Glad the garage is cleared. Thank you. Up to my eyes in mind-numbing conferences. Hope you'll get some rest tonight. See you tomorrow. L xxx**

Initially I wrote 'Love you' before my initial and the multiple vacuous xxx's. But then I deleted it. I no longer felt like articulating something I actually did not feel.

As soon as the text was sent I did something I'd never done before. I turned off the phone. If Ben and Sally were to text me – and this being a Saturday night, the chance of that happening was up there with a meteor shower directly above Boston Common – it could wait until tomorrow. If there was an emergency Dan knew the phone number of the hotel where the conference was being held, and a message would be awaiting me upon my return. But when had I ever received an urgent message from Dan or Sally? Even when Ben had his crisis, his breakdown (to give it its proper word), the information about all that only came a few days after he'd been found.

*No. No. Let's not revisit that. Because what you are doing, in fact, is trying to crowd this wondrous afternoon, the hugely unexpected moment, with all sorts of unnecessary freight. Because you are feeling no longer guilty but still rather tentative about holding that man's hand.*

*Correction: about bumping into a man who's literate and thoughtful and curious, who takes me seriously and seems genuinely interested in my view of the world.*

*And who, in turn, I actually find rather attractive.*

*He called me beautiful. When has anybody called me beautiful?*

By the time I put my phone away Richard was back at the changing rooms.

'So she's de-tagged me,' he said. 'And I've told her that she can give all my old clothes to charity. She's promised me to put them in a Goodwill bin on her way home.'

'I'd be a little dubious about that. I mean, she's hardly a Girl Scout.'

'Well, it's now her conscience she'll have to talk to if she simply dumps them in a garbage can out the back.'

Leaving the shop without bags – Richard's old glasses back on ('I can't see further than four feet without them') – we walked the two blocks south to the eyewear emporium. Newbury Street was abuzz. This perfect autumn day on this perfect Victorian New England street had brought out the crowds. What struck me immediately was the sense of pleasure on most people's faces we passed by. Yes, I did see one couple – early thirties, with a young baby in a stroller – arguing fiercely as they negotiated their child through the crowds. And there was a woman around my age who came hurrying past us, her face awash in tears, making me want to know immediately what it was that was causing her so much grief. Richard noticed her as well, saying:

'As my misanthropic father used to say, you walk down a street, you bump into unhappiness everywhere.'

'Even on the most glorious of days.'

'Especially on the most glorious of days.'

'So if I were to say to you, *But look at how happy everyone else appears to be*, you'd reply . . .?'

'Bless your positive view of the human condition.'

'But if we all don't travel hopefully . . .' I said.

'Hey, I just let you talk me into . . .'

With a downward sweep of his right hand he motioned towards the new clothes he was now wearing, then said:

'So surely this is traveling hopefully?'

He laced his fingers into mine. At that very moment I so wanted him to pull me towards him and kiss me. From the way his grip tightened on me I sensed that he too wanted to do that. Just as I also knew that part of me would have been unnerved and panicky had he embraced me right there, amidst the stream of people on Newbury Street. Just as I also knew that such a kiss would mean the traversing of a frontier I had never considered crossing, Correction: of course I had imagined, at particularly difficult moments, a life without Dan. Of course there were instances when I saw a photograph in some book review of a particularly handsome, clearly intelligent novelist in his mid-thirties and contemplated a night of passion with him. But . . . *between the motion and the act falls the shadow.* This is an afternoon of make-believe, with nothing to anchor it to actual reality.

But then I felt my fingers tighten around Richard's hand. We exchanged a fast, telling look that said everything, but behind which I could also clearly glimpse his own sense of hesitancy, of apprehension. Yet his hand remained in mine until we reached the eyeglass boutique.

'Well, look at you, sir,' Gary the 'spectician' said as Richard approached the counter. 'Clothes make the man – and you are evidently in re-fit mode this afternoon. Bravo.'

Richard accepted this comment with a nervous smile.

'And to complete the new you . . .'

Now Richard's discomfort was manifest again as he looked down at the tray on which his new glasses were displayed. I put my hand on his shoulder.

'You OK?' I asked.

'Fine, fine,' he said, not succeeding at masking his unease. Gary noted this as well.

'If I may, sir,' he said, reaching out to remove Richard's old frames. Richard initially took a step backwards, as if he was trying to dodge the idea of giving up this last vestige of his old look. But Gary – almost anticipating this – put a steadying hand on his shoulder and quickly pulled the frames off. Then he proffered the tray to him.

'Try them on, sir.'

Richard reached for the new glasses, then slowly raised them onto his face. Was his anxiety due to the fact that, with these glasses, his outward transformation would be complete? Or because, like me, he too felt we were veering far too close to a frontier he had never been within the proximity of during all the years of his own sad marriage?

*Sad marriage.* Now I could stand guilty of presumptuousness. Just as I knew I was talking about the domestic life I'd been leading for so many years.

Glasses on, he didn't look at the mirror in front of him. Rather he turned directly towards me. As before – when he first tried these frames – I couldn't help but think just how perfectly they suited him, giving him a canny, worldly, academic mien. Seen now with his leather jacket, his black jeans and black work shirt . . .

'You look amazing,' I said.

'Really?' Richard said.

'Madame is speaking the truth,' Gary said. With a gentle hand on his shoulder he turned Richard around to face the floor-length mirror nearby. Watching Richard now take himself in I couldn't help but remind myself of the way I stared at myself in the hotel mirror this morning: the fear of casting off my everyday image; the unspoken pleasure in seeing myself transformed into the person I always imagined myself being. Richard was engaged in the same process right now. The old identity, the new identity. I knew just how painful and arduous it was to actually shake off everything you have told yourself you have to be. You can dress up differently. You can change all the externals. But there are still all those ties that bind.

Richard must have regarded himself for a good minute in the mirror – and I instinctually knew it was best not to say anything right now. Gary also was astute here – as he too was watching Richard talk himself out of the anxiety that had overtaken him again as soon as we stepped back into the boutique. And during that very long sixty seconds, I watched as his face divested itself of its dread, his shoulders lost their taut hunch, and a small smile crossed his lips.

'Thank you,' he finally said to me.

At that moment I caught Gary out of the corner of my eye. I could register him working out that we were, in no way, husband and wife, and that what had just transpired was, in its own unspoken personal way, rather huge. His only comment was a most appropriate one:

'Congratulations, sir.'

A few minutes later we were back on Newbury Street.

'Ready to blend in with the fellow hipsters at the ICA?' I asked.

'I feel somewhere between an imposter and—'

'Trust me, you're far smarter and more learned than the hip brigade.'

A smile between us.

'It's a bit of a walk from here, I think,' he said.

'Down in South Boston on the bay. And it probably closes at six.'

We both glanced at our watches. It was now almost four-thirty.

'A taxi then.'

As luck would have it one was cruising right by. Richard hailed it. Within moments we were being driven down Boylston Street, passing by several upscale hotels, and a long cliff of tall nineteenth-century office buildings and a theater that Richard said now all belonged to a performing arts college. He started explaining how, just down the street twenty years ago, the remnants of Boston's red light district – better known as 'the Combat Zone' – was still in full 'drug-dealing, porno-cinema, working-girls-on-the-street splendor'. Now it was just a cleaned-up theater district. Though it was a more pleasant environment, 'there's part of me that thinks we've sanitized everything nowadays, to the point where cities have lost an essential raffishness . . . not that I am the biggest expert on things metropolitan'.

'Still,' I said, 'you have a point. I made a couple of trips during college to New York with my then-boyfriend. Even in the late 1980s, Forty-second Street and Hell's Kitchen and the East Village were still the wrong side of sleazy, and we loved it. Because it was so not what we knew in Maine. Then, the one time I've been back since . . . well, Forty-second Street now looked like an outdoor shopping mall in any major city in the country. And the city – though still amazing – struck me as having lost an essential edgy vitality. But hey, having never lived there, having never lived anywhere but Maine . . .'

'That door isn't shut, is it?'

'As you said earlier, you have to travel hopefully. And believe that you can reinvent yourself anew.'

'Isn't that the real American dream? The illusion of liberty. Hitting the road and all that? If it doesn't work out for you in Maine, get in your car, burn up the highway for a couple of nights, find yourself in New Orleans, start all over again.'

'You ever do anything like that?' I asked.

'In my dreams. And you?'

'A cross-country trip once with Dan. And before that I did end up in Central America for a few weeks with someone.'

'Was that somebody Eric?'

'And here we are in Chinatown,' I said, changing the subject quickly, while also thinking of a moment years ago in a restaurant somewhere near here when Eric told me he loved me, that he was mine forever. A summer night it was. The mercury nearly hitting three figures. The restaurant wonderfully dingy and very authentic and badly air-conditioned. And the two of us holding hands so tightly, as if we were each other's ballast. Though we were kids at the time, we just knew . . .

'You OK?' Richard asked.

'Fine, fine,' I lied.

Richard touched my arm in a reassuring way, but I shrugged him off. Not forcibly, but with enough clarity to let it be known that I had just decided not to initiate any further contact with him. I'd go around the gallery with him, maybe agree to a coffee in the café there, then make my excuses and head back to the hotel. Why was I suddenly walling myself up? Because he had mentioned Eric. And because any mention of Eric threw into sharp silhouette all that my life had not been since those extraordinary two years towards the end of the eighties. And because I had padlocked that part of my past so thoroughly that even the slightest reference to it threw me into freefall.

*Will you listen to yourself, trying to push this man away.*

I just can't cope with the jumble of things that are playing havoc with my psyche right now.

*You want directness? Here's directness: you can't cope with the fact that he is so right for you. And you are so right for him.*

And I am married. And I have made a commitment. And I cannot . . .

*Change.*

I put my face in my hands. I stifled a sob. Richard put his hand on my shoulder. I shrugged him off. But as soon as that happened the sobs started again. This time, I turned and buried my head in his shoulder. He held me tight until I brought the sobs under control. When they subsided he did something very smart. He said nothing except:

'Want a drink?' To which I immediately replied:

'That sounds like a very good idea.'

*Six*

RICHARD WORKED HIS phone and discovered two salient pieces of local information: the gallery was open until nine o'clock this evening (if we did want to head there eventually), and there was a cocktail bar in the same vicinity with the straightforward name of Drink.

'Sounds like it will do the job,' I said, impressed with Richard's ability to glean all this information in under a minute on his phone. I am still such a Luddite when it comes to most things technological. Just as I so appreciated the way he said nothing about my crying fit and didn't even gently enquire why I had broken down. And when, in the wake of him telling me about the late museum hours, I said: 'You know, I might head back to the hotel after a drink,' he worked hard at disguising his disappointment, telling me:

'Whatever works best for you, Laura. There's no pressure whatsoever.'

Again I found myself thinking: *He is such a truly gentle man. And so much in the 'kindred spirit' realm. No wonder you're pushing him away.*

Drink turned out to be an uber-stylish lounge, filled with uber-stylish types drinking uber-stylish cocktails.

'Glad I changed my clothes,' Richard said as the hostess on the door seated us in a rear booth.

'You fit in perfectly here. But the thing is, even if you were dressed as before it wouldn't have mattered one bit to me.'

'Even though I bet you initially characterized me as a gray little man.'

'All right, truth be told, I did consider you, when I first saw you at the hotel, somewhat *traditional.*'

'Which is a euphemism for "dull".'

'You are anything but dull.'

He touched my arm with his hand.

'Thank you,' he said. 'The thing is, I have deliberately allowed myself to be perceived as dull. Outside of Dwight – who actually is quite the reader – I never allowed myself to appear too informed or interesting in public. When I'd tried that as a younger man – with my writing, my editorship of the U Maine literary magazine—'

'You edited *The Open Field*?'

'You remember its name!'

'Of course I remember its name. I was on the editorial staff during my time in Orono.'

'Doing what exactly?'

'The poetry editor.'

'That's extraordinary.'

'Not as extraordinary as being the editor-in-chief, especially as I presume you weren't an English major.'

'Wanted to do English, but my dad put his foot down. So it was economics and business administration. But I still managed to end up as the first non-English major to edit *The Open Field*. That was a real source of pride for me. I spent my first three years at the college working my way up the editorial ranks. Of course, when Dad also found out that I had been named editor-in-chief – and he gleaned that little detail when it accompanied the short biographical note that appeared alongside the short story in the *Bangor Daily News* – he was even more livid. Told me I had to resign the editorship immediately.'

'Did you?'

'I did.'

'That's terrible.'

'Indeed it is. The thing is, though I always hated him for making me give it up – and I only had one more issue to put to bed – the person I really hated was myself. Because I had given in to his limiting meanness. Because I allowed myself to be intimidated by him. Because I was always so desperate to please a father who could not be pleased. And how did we get on this subject?'

'It's all right to be on this subject,' I said. 'That man—'

'—was a bastard. Excuse my language. But it's the only word to describe him. Small, mean, petty, angry at the world, and

192

determined to keep me confined to the limited horizons within which his own life had been lived. The truth of the matter is that I accepted those limitations. I resigned the editorship of the magazine. I followed him into the family business. I never wrote a word again for almost thirty years. I married a woman who matched him for coldness and thrift. On his deathbed, when we were alone together in his hospital room and the colon cancer that was killing him had spread everywhere, and he had maybe forty-eight hours to live, he took my hand and told me: "You were always something of a disappointment to me."'

I reached over and threaded my hand into his.

'I hope you told him what a monster he was.'

'That would have been the good Eugene O'Neill ending, wouldn't it? "May you go to your grave knowing your only son despises you . . . and he's now selling off your nasty little insurance company and is setting sail for the Far East as a crewman on a tramp steamer."'

'Did that thought cross your mind?'

'Variations on that theme.'

'Like me with the French Foreign Legion when I was a teenager.'

'Even though their all-male rule might have put a dent in your plans?'

'Like you, it was all about dreams of leaving. But even my rather cool, distant mother at her chilliest couldn't match your father. He was clearly beyond contemptible.'

The waiter arrived, asking us what we'd like to drink.

'I'm not too knowledgeable about cocktails,' I told Richard, 'but I remember once drinking a very good manhattan on my one visit to New York.'

'Then two manhattans,' he said.

The waiter asked us if we preferred ours with bourbon or rye. We both professed ignorance. The waiter recommended Sazerac rye – 'for a manhattan with a slightly more syrupy texture, but with a complex smoothness'. I could see Richard trying to keep a straight face.

'"Complex smoothness" sounds fine to me,' he said.

'Me too,' I added.

As soon as the waiter was out of earshot, Richard said:

'It's one of the more curious things about modern life: the amount of choice on offer. Back twenty years ago, rye was that cheap Canadian Club stuff my dad used to drink. Now there are probably two dozen different ryes on offer. Just as Scotch was always J&B, and wine was Gallo red or white. We don't just live in a consumerist culture. We live in a *wildly* consumerist culture.'

'But there are benefits to all that – like the fact that good coffee is a given just about everywhere . . .'

'Even in Lewiston?'

'Poor Lewiston – the butt of all in-state Maine jokes. But I'm sure you can still find a decent cappuccino even there.'

'And a decent rye manhattan?'

'That might be a stretch. Maybe I'll give up radiography to open a cocktail bar in Lewiston.'

'And I know a good bankruptcy lawyer you can talk to when it all goes south.'

'"O ye of little faith."'

'Matthew eight, twenty-six.'

'That's impressive,' I said.

'Another legacy from my father. A real Presbyterian. Scots-Irish – the most dour Celtic combination imaginable. No *joie de vivre*. A real Hobbesian view of the human condition.'

'And I bet this is the first time that Thomas Hobbes was ever mentioned in this cocktail lounge.'

'Let alone Matthew eight, twenty-six.'

'Well, there's a first for everything.'

'And thanks to dear old Dad – who made me go to Sunday school for fifteen years – my brain is crammed with far too many scriptural references.'

'Can you do *The Book of Mormon* as well?'

'That's a little beyond my realm of knowledge.'

I found myself laughing – and quietly realized that Richard, in his own canny, quiet way, had just managed to talk me out of the sadness that had overcome me in the taxi, simply by being smart and funny and interesting. And by sharing all that terrible stuff about his father.

'I am so sorry for blubbering like that earlier,' I said.

'Never be sorry for that. *Never.*'

'But I am. Because I was brought up by a mother who thought crying was something akin to a profound character flaw, and a dad who spent much of his life dodging any direct emotion whatsoever. So to cry, openly . . . I've managed to sidestep that one for most of my life. Until recently.'

'And what changed recently?'

'Good question,' I said as the drinks arrived.

'Hope you approve,' the waiter said as he put the two cocktail glasses before us.

'Here's to . . . complex smoothness?' Richard asked, raising his glass.

Hoisting mine I said:

'How about . . . to us.'

Richard smiled. And touched his glass against mine.

'I like that,' I said. 'To us.'

'To us.'

I sipped the manhattan.

'My word,' I said, 'dense libidinous fluency.'

'Or . . . libational eloquence.'

'Or . . . spiritous volubility.'

'Or . . . no, I can't top that,' Richard said.

'I bet you can.'

'You're wonderful, did you know that?'

'Until this afternoon . . . no, I didn't know that. And you're wonderful, did you know that?'

'Until this afternoon . . .'

I raised my glass again to his.

'To us.'

'To us.'

'And yes,' I said, 'I do find myself crying frequently these days. Half the time I think it's about all the usual unsettling thoughts that arrive with middle age. But maybe it's also about my husband. And about my children and all the stuff that seems to be blindsiding both of them all the time. Maybe also about the fact that my work now seems to impact on me in a way that it never used to. That's what unnerves me the most – the loss of professional detachment.'

'But surely that's linked with all the stuff at home.'

'When Ben had his breakdown . . .'

Over the next half an hour or so, Richard got me talking in more detail about all that had befallen Ben; how his depression had only widened the gulf between him and his father, and the way he was inching his way back to some sort of stability.

The first manhattan cocktail was drained. And so was I.

'I've talked far too much,' I said.

'Not at all.'

'I've bent your ear.'

'But I wanted my ear bent. And after having told you all about Billy this afternoon . . .'

'I'm not usually comfortable talking about personal stuff.'

'But it's about you. And I want to know everything about you.'

'Can we ever know *everything* about another person?'

'*Everything?* As in, the whole, the aggregate, the entirety?'

'Or to be colloquial, all but the kitchen sink, the whole megillah.'

'No, we can hardly know the corpus, the lot,' he said, while motioning to the waiter to bring us two more drinks. 'But if you are drawn to someone, surely you want to know about—'

'Eric,' I heard myself saying. As I said it, it struck me that, outside of this afternoon, when I mentioned his name, the word 'Eric' had been banished from my vocabulary. Outside of Lucy – to whom I told the story early on in our friendship – no one else knew about his existence. No one except Dan and my parents. But Mom and Dad never raised the subject of Eric – largely because they both knew it was something I didn't want to talk about, let alone consider. And Dan dodged it completely – for all sorts of self-evident reasons. Even Lucy – having heard the tale – never made reference to it. She understood it was so off-limits. The forbidden topic.

But now . . .

'Eric Lachtmann,' I said. 'A New Yorker. From Long Island. German-Jewish background. His grandfather was a jeweler in the Diamond District of Manhattan, his dad a CPA, his mom classic frustrated housewife territory. Two older brothers, both heading into business careers. And Eric – who had decided at the age of fifteen that he was going to be a Great American Novelist – also spent much of high school pursuing arty pursuits and not caring very much about class work, with the result that his college choices were not exactly prestigious ones. A couple of the better state universities in New York wanted him. He was wait-listed at Wisconsin. But – as he told me later – something about being "way up in the Maine sticks" really appealed to him. If I remember correctly, he told me that his decision was partially based on the fact that, during his senior year in high school, he'd been reading all those early Hemingway stories set up in northern Michigan – and had this romantic notion that landing himself into the boondocks was an essential part of his "writerly training". Of course he was also planning to live in Paris, and travel overland to Patagonia, and get his first novel published by the time he was twenty-five, and marry me and bring me everywhere.

'That was so Eric. Big talk. Big plans. Big brain. Probably the smartest person I'd ever met. But the thing about him was, though he talked in a grandiose way, there was always real substance behind the talk. Even at eighteen he put his money where his mouth was. And he was already, by the time I met him, living a writerly life.

'He was quite the character at U Maine. You remember how conservative the school was, how State U, how the student body was largely rural and backwater. And how few out-of-staters there were. Here was Eric – this "Manhattanite in waiting" as he called himself – dashing around the campus in a black trenchcoat, sporting a fedora, with these ultra-smelly French cigarettes on the go all the time. He'd found a place in Orono where he could actually buy Gitanes – those cigarettes he so adored – and a daily copy of the *New York Times*, at a time when that newspaper was something of a cargo cult up in Maine. And he was always talking books, books, books. And foreign movies. Within his first semester at Orono, not only had he taken over the college Film Society and was programming an Ingmar Bergman retrospective, but he was also fiction editor of *The Open Field*. Which is where I met him. I had talked my way onto the editorial committee of the magazine, even though I was pre-med and clearly not the type the magazine attracted. As you no doubt remember from your own time up there, Orono did boast a small bohemian coterie within their student body – who, like Eric, had ended up there after less-than-brilliant high school careers, but still were very determined to act as if they were all up at Columbia during the era of Ginsberg and Kerouac.'

'And was that your story?' Richard asked. 'Did you end up there because you hadn't been as rigorous as you should have been during high school?'

'No – I ended up there courtesy of my own profound need to self-sabotage.'

And I told him all about being accepted at Bowdoin on a partial scholarship, and turning it down because I could go to U Maine for nothing.

'So that is still a source of immense regret?'

'Of course it is. Because – and I only realize this now – it was the start of a process in which I began to deliberately sell myself short. Clip my wings. Limit my latitude. Still, had I gone to Bowdoin I would never have met Eric. And had I not met Eric . . .'

The second round of drinks arrived. We touched glasses. I took a long sip of the manhattan, part of me telling myself that I should stop talking now.

But the other part of me – fueled, no doubt, by the alcohol, by the low lighting and subdued intimacy of the lounge, and (most of all) by the profound need and desire I felt to impart this story to Richard – forced myself to keep talking.

'So I walked into an editorial meeting of the magazine, having heard word around campus about this smart-assed New York guy who talked a mile a minute and seemed bent on refashioning everything arts-wise at the university to his own liking. Here I was this bookish, science-oriented girl from a middling Maine town, still a virgin –' (God, the manhattans really were playing havoc with my sense of propriety) 'and someone who always felt herself plain, unattractive, especially when compared to all the so-called "popular" girls at school. As I walked into the magazine's office, Eric looked up at me. In that very instant . . . well, I just knew. Just as Eric knew. Or so he told me three days later, after we slept together for the first time. That's right – even though I was just eighteen and completely inexperienced, and Eric, as it turned out, had only had one serious girlfriend before me, and that was just a summer fling – we became lovers in a matter of days. Immediately after that editorial meeting where we first met, he invited me to a local bar – remember when you could drink in Maine at eighteen? – and we must have spent the next six hours there, nursing beers, talking, talking, talking. By the time he walked me home to my dorm that night, I knew I was madly in love. We saw each other the next evening – talking, talking, talking until around three in the morning. Even though we were in his dorm room, he made no move, put me under no pressure whatsoever. Instead he walked me home, kissed me lightly on the lips and told me that I was "nothing less than extraordinary". No one had ever said that to me before. No one after Eric ever did either . . . until you said something very similar just a little while ago. The next night – it was a Saturday – when we found ourselves still talking in my room at two, and he wondered out loud if he should go home, I told him I wanted him to stay. It was my choice, my call. When we awoke the next morning, he told me, quite simply, that he loved me – and that we were now inseparable. And I told him I loved him, and would never love anyone else.

'Saying all that now, part of me thinks, how wondrously naive, how innocent. But the truth is – and this is the middle-aged woman talking – the love I felt, the love given, the love shared . . . it was nothing less than matchless. Yes, we were kids. Yes, we were living in that bubble which was college. And yes, we knew nothing of the larger world and its infernal compromises. But here was a man

199

I could talk to about anything. Here was a man who was so original, so curious, so thoughtful, so vital . . . and who made me feel capable of everything. After the first semester we shocked everybody by finding an apartment off campus and moving in together. When my parents met Eric they were completely charmed. Of course they both found him a little over the top. But they also saw his love for me – and the way he was, in his own determined way, pushing me to do my very best. And Eric's parents – very formal, very stiff, very much in despair over what they saw to be their wayward son – simply adored me. Because I was the small-town Maine girl who clearly loved their son and also seemed to keep him grounded, within the earth's gravity.

'It was love. Absolute extraordinary love. We were both so profoundly happy. Because it was also so easy together. My grades that first year skyrocketed. I made Dean's List. I was asked to join the Honors Program. Eric, meanwhile, was establishing his hegemony – yes, that *is* the correct word – over the literary magazine, the film society, and even managed to talk his way into staging a radical reworking of *Twelfth Night* set in a suburban high school. The guy was just bursting with talent. Hearing me say all this now . . . I know it all sounds so romanticized, so quixotic, too good to be true. I know it was all twenty-two years ago, and time has a habit of soft-focussing so much, especially when it comes to first love. But . . . *but* . . . I think I see life with a certain clarity. My work forces me to do that all the time – because being a radiographic technologist is all about being able to view the most elemental cellular forces within us with absolute pellucidity. But one's emotional life is always more murky, isn't it? There's no clarity when it comes to matters of the heart. Except one thing about which I am still absolutely clear – Eric Lachtmann was the love of my life. I had never been happier, more productive, more fulfilled. Everyone who knew us back then saw that we were, in a word, golden.

'Of course we had plans. So many plans. The summer after our freshman year we both got teaching jobs at a rich kids' prep school in New Hampshire, tutoring the far too well off and stupid who weren't going to get into college if they didn't bump up their grades. The money was pretty good. Good enough for us to head to Costa Rica on the cheap for the last two weeks of the summer vacation. Eric had an artist friend of the family there with a place on the Pacific coast. Even though it was the rainy season, the sun still came out six hours of the day and, hey, we were in Central America, how cool was that? While in Costa Rica we agreed to go to Paris for our junior year, and spend the next twelve months doing intensive French. Eric was pretty certain there was an exchange program for pre-med students at the *Fac du Médecine* at the Sorbonne. There was, and I got in.

'But then a small bit of drama landed in our laps when I discovered I was pregnant. I knew how and why it had happened. While in Costa Rica, I forgot to take the pill two days in a row. Bingo. Back in our apartment in Orono I started getting sick every morning for five straight days. I told Eric my suspicions and how guilty I felt about missing those two doses of the pill, though he already knew that because I told him immediately about it when I realized that all the mezcal we'd drunk one weekend with that crazed artist friend of the family – a real Bukowski type – had led me to slip up on the contraception front. Eric and I had that kind of relationship where we promised to tell each other everything. And did. So when one of those home pregnancy tests confirmed what was readily apparent – I was going to have a baby – Eric being Eric he told me: "Hey, we'll keep it. Bring him or her to Paris. Raise this baby to be the coolest citizen imaginable and just carry on with our lives." His exact words. That also was pure Eric – the art of the possible. Nothing too arduous that couldn't be countered with wild enthusiasm and work. Of course the guy had his dark moments like anyone – and could get into these occasional black funks where he sometimes refused to get out of bed for two days. But that's what came with living life at such a manic, exalted level. Those episodes . . . they were maybe a quarterly event. He always pulled himself out of them. And he always joked afterwards that it was his body's way of telling him to stop trying to be endlessly brilliant – as the guy was a straight A student in English and philosophy, on top of everything else. But outside of those occasional moments it was always "the art of the possible". And part of the "everything is possible" was this baby. Our baby.

'As upbeat and persuasive as Eric was it was me who said: 'Not now.' I was still very young, after all. Even though I was living with a man, and very much in love, and knew that Eric was the person I would travel through life with, I was also very cognizant of what having a child would mean. How it was a non-stop responsibility. How it would limit so much at a time in our lives when we should really be unencumbered. And how Paris would not be *Paris* with a baby.

'So, very rationally and with, I must admit, little guilt whatsoever, I told Eric that it was best for us if we waited a few years – frankly, after I finished medical school – before starting a family. He was cool with that. I sense he was privately relieved – but also would have gone along with it all had I insisted on keeping it. Eric being Eric he took charge of everything. Found me a really lovely, sympathetic clinic in Boston where the termination took place. Booked us into a nice hotel for the weekend, so I could recover after the procedure. Was so supportive and loving throughout. Honestly, I got through that all so easily because, of course, Eric and I loved each other, and we were going to be together for all the decades to come. So, of course, I'd be pregnant again in a few years with Eric's baby. Only this time the moment would be right.

'Just thinking about that – *only this time the moment would be right* – when you're young you are never really conscious of the way time will later on accelerate at such a ferocious speed. Just as you also think that you are invulnerable to that terrible underside of life which is dictated by the random, the happenstantial.

'Anyway, the pregnancy was terminated in mid-September. Our sophomore year was another golden period – where we both continued to surpass ourselves academically, where Eric became fiction editor of *The Open Field* and I was promoted to poetry editor, where we both got into the Sorbonne on that junior year exchange program for the following September, and both did accelerated French to the point where we agreed to spend two hours a day talking with each other *dans la langue de Molière* – one of the few phrases I remember from back then.

'Life was, in a word, splendid. Yes, Eric still had those "black dog" moments – and they had started creeping up on him every other week. But he always shook them off. Always kept going. Always amazed me with his resilience and his ability to constantly embrace life with both hands.

'That Easter we were thinking of heading down to see some friends in Cambridge. At the last minute I got a bad stomach bug, and was up sick the night before we were due to leave. So we stayed put at our place in Orono. I started getting ill again and Eric said he'd run up to the pharmacy and get me something to curb the vomiting. We both had bicycles. Eric took his. Before he left he gave me a kiss and told me he loved me. Then he headed out – and never came back. After an hour I was panicked, but was so weak from being sick that I couldn't get out of bed and go searching for him. Around two that afternoon the police came to my door. A woman social worker was with them. That's when I knew. They told me that Eric had run a red light on his bicycle a block away from the pharmacy and had been knocked down by an oncoming truck. He'd been thrown clear of his bicycle and slammed into a lamppost. Death, they told me, was instantaneous. He probably felt and knew nothing. That's when I started to collapse, to weep uncontrollably. Eric dead. It was beyond unthinkable. It was as if my entire future – all possibility of happiness – had just been permanently decimated.

'The next eighteen months were a depressed blur. My father was never good at emotional ballast. And my mother – though initially sympathetic – essentially told me to snap out of it, that I was young and had my whole life ahead of me, and what I needed to do now was look forward. My college friends were nice. I did talk for a bit to a psychologist on campus. But he wasn't making me feel better, so I stopped the sessions, which I now realize was a bad idea. Back then, I didn't want to feel better. I was so consumed with grief. So profoundly devastated. Everything just started to come asunder. Though my professors were, at first, kind to me, my grades really started to slip, as I no longer cared whether I did well or not. I cancelled the year abroad in Paris because I thought it would be unbearable without Eric. I kept largely to myself. I did middling class work, and my straight A average slipped into the Cs. But so what? I no longer had a purpose. The love of my life had been snatched from me. Though several professors and friends really did try to get me to start some serious therapy I refused. I was wildly depressed, but still functional enough to get through the day, to keep my apartment clean, to do just enough course work to pass my exams and not flunk out. What I realize now is that I was on a self-destructive kick – and really needed to punish myself. I went about it with profound determination.

'Somehow I made it through junior year. My mother looked at my grades and shook her head and said: "There goes your medical career." I didn't care. My dad – when I had his attention – told me I should really think about doing something outside the box for a couple of years, like maybe joining the Peace Corps. But when I started to cry and ask him where and when I would meet another Eric, he just put a hand on my shoulder and told me that life would go on and – if I allowed it – it would get better.

'Actually that was smart advice – especially about joining the Peace Corps and taking myself off to some extreme Third World country where I could maybe get a great deal of distance and emotional perspective. But did I follow it? I was so bent on hurting myself – something that I only understood rather recently – that, in the final trimester of my junior year, I managed to allow myself to be asked out by a guy named Dan Warren. A computer science major from way up north in Aroostook County. A nice enough fellow – whom I met when I got talked into joining an outdoor club by a friend who thought that getting me hiking might improve my mental state. Dan came from a different planet than Eric. Though intelligent he wasn't an intellectual, had no imaginative flights of fancy, preferred the concrete to the realm of ideas, and his basic philosophy could be summed up as: *Feet firmly on the ground is the only way to travel.* Still, he was kind. And he really seemed to get me and couldn't have been more sympathetic and canny when it came to dealing with all the deep, residual grief I still felt for Eric. We were friends for a month before we became romantically involved. Though there was none of the passion I felt for Eric it was an antidote to the past months of agony. Dan himself couldn't have been more thrilled. He thought I was a catch. My friends found him *"nice"*, *"straightforward"*, *"uncomplicated"* – all those euphemisms for dull and less than animated. My parents met him. *"Decent enough guy"* was my dad's rather flat verdict. Mom was more direct. "I hope he gets you out of your dark wood and then you move on to someone with a little more depth in the outfield."

'Still, that summer before our senior year, he took me cross-country on a road trip, which was kind of wonderful. Even if I did frequently wonder what I was doing with this guy. But it was comfortable and easy. So on it went. Then, another small disaster. We'd always used condoms as birth control, as I'd gone off the pill after Eric's death and it really didn't agree with me. One night – around two weeks before our graduation – a condom that Dan was wearing broke while we were making love. At the time it was difficult, but still possible to get the morning-after pill. It required a drive down to that clinic in Boston where I had my termination. I had a biology final on Monday and I was frightened of failing it – that's how much I had let myself slip, even after hooking up with Dan – who, truth be told, wasn't much of a student when it came to chasing high grades. And I was due to have my period in seven days. And . . .

'Oh, the excuses I invented. I think now, deep down, I couldn't bear the idea of terminating another pregnancy, even though the morning-after pill – despite what the born-again lobby thinks – is a far cry from a termination. There was another part of me that, ever since Eric's death, had been carrying a huge amount of guilt about not doing what Eric suggested and having our baby. You can't believe the amount of times I've told myself, if only we'd had the baby Eric would still be here today. If only I had listened to him, and hadn't pushed for an abortion. If only . . .'

Richard reached out and took my hand.

'You can't think that. You did absolutely nothing wrong. *Nothing*.'

'I would have had his baby. That part of him would still be here . . .'

'Had Eric not run that red light at the time—'

'The only reason he ran that light is because I'd gotten sick. Had we gone to Boston despite my stomach flu—'

'Laura, please, *stop*. You had no hand in what happened to Eric. It was the music of chance, nothing more.'

'But afterwards I did have a choice – and what did I do? I walled myself into a life I didn't want. My mother – who never knew about the first abortion – firmly told me that she would "take care of everything" if I wanted to terminate the pregnancy. Even Dan was OK with the idea of ending it. But no. The guilt I felt was so rampant, so unexamined, so self-punitive that I insisted on keeping the child. And to keep Dan's very conservative, very Baptist parents happy we were married that same summer. Even a week before the wedding Mom tried to talk me out of it. Saying I was making the mistake of my life. But . . .'

I reached for my drink and drained it, gripping Richard's hand even tighter as the alcohol provided momentary balm against all I had refused to confront for years, decades. Then:

'Every day I give thanks for the fact that I have my two wondrous children. When I think how, had I terminated that second pregnancy, Ben would not be here now – my brilliant, extraordinarily talented son – that nullifies all the other regrets. Just as Sally – whom I so adore, and who I see is in the midst of a gigantic struggle right now – would also not be here had I not chosen to stay with Dan. So, there are huge recompenses for a life otherwise—'

I broke off, feeling my eyes welling up, a sob in my throat. But I managed to stifle it and say:

'And here's the question with which I keep torturing myself

– had Eric never set off on that bicycle, would the entire course of my life have been different? Would I be a doctor somewhere now? Would my brilliant husband still tell me how extraordinary I am? Would I feel loved? Would I be happy?'

## Seven

'WOULD I FEEL *loved? Would I be happy?*'

Those words lingered for a very long moment after they were uttered. They filled the silence that followed them. A silence during which Richard took my other hand and fixed his gaze directly on me. Then he said:

'But you are loved.'

This statement landed with such quiet force that I felt myself involuntarily tense. Having avoided Richard's gaze while telling him that very long and terrible story, now I could not take my eyes off him. Though I wanted to say exactly the same thing – '*But you too are loved*' – an innate fear kicked in. I was now in a terra incognita that I hadn't known since I was eighteen. But when I fell so madly for Eric, I knew nothing of life's larger intricacies and the disenchantments that begin to pile up within you. Having decided in recent years that there was little future prospect of intimacy, passion, ardor, yet alone the possibility of actual love . . .

No, this was all too strange, all too fast, all too perplexing. I was terrified of being even somewhat adjacent to all that I was feeling right now, to all that I wanted to blurt out in a mad romantic rush . . . and which I knew I couldn't bring myself to do. Because that would mean taking my foot off the emotional brakes for the first time in more than twenty years.

I withdrew my hands from Richard's grasp.

'Have I said the wrong thing?' he asked.

I took my eyes off him, using the swizzle stick from my cocktail glass to draw invisible circles on the paper coaster in front of me.

'No,' I finally said. 'You said a wonderful thing. But one which I can't . . .'

Synonyms came rushing to mind: accept, acknowledge, concur with, mirror, embrace, agree with, acquiesce to . . .

I didn't finish the sentence. My swizzle stick kept making manic circles on the paper coaster. I told myself: *You are being absurd. You are closing down the possibility of something for which you've longed since . . .*

Soon after Eric's funeral, I drove myself in his Volvo to a river not far from our apartment. It was a perfect late-spring afternoon – the sun at full wattage, not a cloud up above, the water unruffled, becalmed. I couldn't help but think: *This is an immaculate day that I can see, but Eric can't.* Just as the realization hit that I would never hear his voice again, never feel his touch, never have him deep inside me, whispering how much he loved me as our passion rose. My grief that afternoon was so new, so raw, so overwhelming and acute that I felt as if the very act of breathing was an affront to Eric's memory. I so remember being so numb, so spent, that I could no longer cry – having spent the past week crying nonstop. Staring at the river, considering that I had lost the man of my life, I told myself that I would never, ever encounter such love again – that there was nothing but emotional sterility ahead. And yes, I do know how wildly melodramatic and bereavement-laden all that sounds now. But in light of what Richard just told me – and my timorous backing away from it – another uneasy rumination clouded my mind. By deciding all those years ago that I would never know such love again, had I actually set myself up to ensure that this prophesy came true? Was that the reason I married Dan – because I knew he could never be the man that Eric was? As such, our relationship – so lacking the zeal and heat of my time with Eric – would ensure that my sense of loss would never dim?

Out of nowhere, I reached for Richard's hands again.

'The truth of the matter is,' I said, 'I'm scared.'

'Me too.'

'And when did—?'

I stopped myself just before the pronoun 'you' came forth.

'When did I know?' he asked. 'From that moment yesterday when you recited that poem.'

'As bleak as it was?'

'It was hardly bleak. It let me know what I had sensed from

the start – the fact that, like me, you have been lonely. Lonely for years.'

My hands tightened within his.

'You got that one right,' I said.

'And that story you just told – the story of Eric – the fact that you perceive yourself to have walled yourself into a life you don't want . . .'

'I know that's your story too.'

'Just as I know you are everything I've hoped, dreamed, of finding . . .'

'But how can you know after just a few hours?'

'Because when it is right you can know after five minutes.'

'And have you ever known . . .?'

'Certainty like this? Never.'

'And real love?'

'Like what you had with Eric?'

'Yes, love as profound as that.'

'Once. When I was twenty-three. A woman named Sarah. A librarian in Brunswick. At the college library there. And—'

He broke off for a moment, then said:

'This is not a story I want to tell.'

'And why is that?'

'Because it's a story I've never told.'

'Because . . .?'

'Because she was married at the time. Because I made a huge mistake. Because I've regretted that mistake ever since. Because . . .'

Now it was his turn to withdraw his hands from mine, and to drum his fingers anxiously on the table, something my ex-smoker father used to do when he was trying to push away that desperate craving for a cigarette.

'Go on,' I said quietly.

More finger-drumming on the table. I could discern the tension coursing within him. A secret lived with for years – never discussed, never re-examined in front of another sentient being – is the most private form of sorrow. Especially if it is the confidential mirror you hold up to everything that has happened in your life since then. From the way that Richard was resisting divulging anything further than her name, the fact that it was an affair, and (to his mind) an error . . .

'Sarah Radley,' he said, avoiding my eyes. 'Her full name. Sarah Makepiece Radley. As you can gather, just a little WASP. In fact, ultra-WASP. A big Boston family that had fallen on its uppers, as they say in a certain kind of Victorian novel. She'd gone to Radcliffe back when it was still called Radcliffe. She'd had a brief career in magazine journalism in New York. She met a doctoral candidate at Columbia. They'd had a fling. She got pregnant. She convinced herself it was love, whereas she privately knew there were manifold problems, the most prominent of which being that she suspected Calvin – his name – of being a rather closeted gay man. Still, the upright Boston WASP in her decided she had to do the right thing when she found herself "with child" – and Calvin was hugely bright and intellectually agile. So when he got an assistant professorship at Bowdoin she married him and off they went to Brunswick. This was the mid-1970s – a time when Maine was still rather isolated and less than metropolitan. But Sarah liked the college, liked the smart people she met on the faculty, and got a job in the cataloging division of the library. She also gave birth to a little boy, Chester – yes, she and her husband went for truly nineteenth-century WASP names. Seven months after he was born she came into the nursery one morning to find her son lying in his crib, lifeless. One of those crib deaths you sometimes read about, and which are so devastating because they are so out of nowhere, so random, so profoundly cruel.

'Sarah, however, surprised everyone in Brunswick with her fortitude, her need to keep the immense grief she was feeling so clearly out of sight, to propel herself forward with what can only be described as a steely dignity. When I first met her – she needed to get her house reinsured and someone had recommended our company to her – it was eight months after her son's death. Though I'd heard about it all before she came into my office, what surprised me most was how she didn't betray the horror of what she had been living with. You know, from your own work, that there are many people among us who, at the drop of a dime, unload their entire life story onto you. Just as there are others who, with a little coaxing, also begin to recount the heartbreak that has been their life. When Sarah came into my office she was business itself. At some point, when we were filling out the policy forms, she said that, though married, there were no dependants, then added: "But you must know that already." I was just a little thrown and impressed by her directness. Just as I was also immediately taken with her elegance and intelligence. Sarah wasn't a beautiful woman like you. In fact, there was something rather plain about her. But the plainness had the sort of formal poise that you see in those sharp-featured, but still curiously sensual wives of Dutch burghers that kept Vermeer's bank account topped up over the years. From the outset it was also clear that hers was a mind of great agility. She also happened to be – until I bumped into you – the best-read person I'd ever met. When I found out she worked in the Bowdoin library I asked her if she could, perhaps, locate a book for me.'

'What was the book?'

'I was looking for Pepys's *Diaries* – which I could have probably ordered at the time from one of the antiquarian booksellers around the state, but which I really didn't have the money to afford. The Bath Public Library's only copy had recently fallen apart. No matter how often I asked the librarian to order it for me, she seemed resistant to the idea of dropping forty dollars of taxpayers' money – a lot of money back then – on a volume that nobody, except for me, was ever going to borrow. So I asked Sarah if she might be able to loan me a copy. This large smile crossed her face as she said: "You are the first man I've ever met who has shown the remotest interest in one of my benchmark writers." Her exact words. *Benchmark writers.* I think I was in love with her as soon as she uttered that phrase. And I think she saw that immediately as well.

'She invited me to lunch. No woman had ever invited me to lunch before. Though she was only seven years older than me – she was thirty when we met – she immediately struck me as so worldly, so cosmopolitan. She brought me to a really nice place in Brunswick and insisted we share a bottle of wine – it was a Saint-Emilion, I always remember that – over lunch. My dad was still very much running the agency – and monitored all my working-hour moves like the Marine drill sergeant he once was. I was also still living at home, as Dad saw no reason for me to be wasting money on an apartment, though he did buy me a second-hand Chevy Impala as a gift when I left college and "joined the firm", as he called our two-person business. So I was still living at home – albeit in a basement apartment that gave me a certain amount of autonomy in the evenings, though Dad would often chide me if he discovered I was up late reading. Dad was something of an insomniac – and even though he was in bed most nights by nine-thirty, he'd always be up around midnight, stepping outside for a few minutes for a walk, but really checking on whether I had the lights on in my place. Why I didn't move out, why I was so cowed by him into joining the firm, instead of forging my own life . . . it remains perhaps the biggest regret of my life to date.

'Anyway, some of this came out at that first lunch with Sarah. She was quite the polite interrogator. She got out of me the fact that I wanted to be a writer, that I had published a story, and that I had an impossibly dictatorial father. She also had me talking about my literary tastes, and ascertained that, outside of a brief, inconsequential four-month thing with a graduate student named Florence during my U Maine years, I was largely inexperienced when it came to the world of women. Sarah, in turn, volunteered several things about herself.

'You know I lost a child,' she told me. 'I doubt I'll ever get over that – though to the outside world I will always maintain a certain decorum. And you possibly know that my husband, of whom I am inordinately fond, has fallen in love with a professor at Harvard named Elliot . . . but for the sake of "decorum" we are maintaining a proper public front for the time being. We live together during the week as he teaches at the college. Calvin goes to see Elliot at the weekends. My husband remains my great friend. We will never have children again – which is my choice, because were I to become a mother again the specter of possible tragedy and appalling loss would always be there, and I know I could never support the fear that would haunt me every day. I am very accepting of that decision, as painful as it is. Just as I am very accepting of Calvin's new life – as I knew, more or less, all this about him from the moment we met in New York eight years ago. As far as Calvin is concerned I have carte blanche when it comes to my own personal life and how I choose to conduct it. Which is why, when we finish lunch, I suggest we return to my house – Calvin is away today – and go to bed."

'She said it just like that. No hemming or hawing. No "Let's get to know each other". No apprehension or fear. She chose me. I certainly wanted to be chosen. And in the seven months that I was Sarah's lover she taught me so much. Both in and out of the bedroom. And God, that must be the second manhattan talking.'

'You're telling me this because you want to tell me this,' I said. 'Keep going.'

'Was it love? I certainly think so. We saw each other three times a week. We managed to sneak off for a weekend to Boston, and to Quebec City . . .'

*Quebec City. The adjacent Paris for entrapped Mainers.*

'. . . and Sarah told me, around four months into our relationship, that what I needed to do, as a matter of urgency, was walk out of my father's "firm" and apply for a top MFA program in writing at Iowa or Michigan or Brown. She was sure I would get in somewhere good. And she would come with me – because she could always find interesting work in a college town. And because she knew I had talent.

' "I may have a talent for life," she told me. "I may know how to make a wonderful *coq au vin* –" that was no lie – "and what wine to pair with it, and which new emerging Polish surrealist poet I should be reading –" she was always glued to literary magazines – "but I don't have any real creative spark in me when it comes to words or music or paints. You, on the other hand, have the possibility of a proper literary career, if you can only shake off your King Lear father. He has been determined to break you of your talent from the moment he read that short story of yours in print."

'Of course she had hit the bull's-eye – as unsettling as it was to hear such truths being articulated. We were sprawled across her bed at the time. And that was the afternoon she told me that she loved me, that we were kindred spirits, that together everything was possible . . . and Sarah was never the most emotionally effusive of people. I told her that I too loved her, that she had changed my life, that, yes, I would start to apply for MFA programs and quit my job at the end of the summer and . . .

'All these amazing plans. All within the realm of possibility. Because love – at its truest – allows all the impediments to fall away. You see a vision of the life you want to lead. A happy life. A fulfilled life. With someone who wants to share everything with you, who so completely gets you, as you get her. A love also based on deep mutual desire. And passion. And a shared curiosity about everything in life. That was my life with Sarah – the whole fairy tale we tell ourselves we so want, and then do everything in our power to subvert.'

He fell silent. I reached out and took his hand.

'Did your father find out?' I finally asked.

'Your interpretative powers are impressive. I applied to about a half-dozen MFA programs. Though I didn't get into Iowa – which is the most prestigious and competitive – I did get accepted to Michigan, Wisconsin, Virginia, Berkeley. An amazing choice of schools. Sarah and I agreed that Michigan was the best option. It was ranked second in the country as an MFA writing program, and Ann Arbor is a great college town. Sarah even had a friend who was a senior librarian there, and who told her there was an opening in the cataloging department. It was all so serendipitous. Here was our immediate future. Here was the life ahead together. I'd even started writing again. A new short story about a man who cannot force himself to leave a bad marriage – even though he knows that the marriage is killing him. It was, at heart, the story of my dad and my mother, but also about my father's anger at me, at the world in general, all fueled by the fact that my mother was such a dry, cold woman. The only good thing I can say about her is that, as she knew my dad was doing the heavy guilt reinforcement on me, she didn't criticize me the way that Dad did. She was just cold and distant.

'Anyway, Sarah and I used her address in Brunswick for all the MFA applications. After I accepted Michigan – which came with a partial scholarship, by the way – they needed my official mailing address. So I put on the form my address in Bath, but also enclosed a note stating that all correspondence should continue to be sent to the Brunswick address I'd been using. Of course, my father discovered it. But being the truly manipulative man he was he kept this knowledge from me for weeks. Then, one evening, as I was about to head down to Brunswick and a weekend with Sarah, he asked if I could step into his office for a moment. Once seated in the chair opposite his desk, he began to talk in this ultra-low voice that he switched into whenever he was angry, whenever he wanted to be ruthless and menacing.

'"I know everything," he told me. "I know about your plans to go to Michigan and pursue a useless degree *in writing*. I know about your relationship with that married harpy down in Brunswick. I know all about the fact that she is planning to move to Ann Arbor with you. I know all about her pederast husband. I know the name of his boyfriend at Harvard. And I know if word of all this got around the community it would profoundly harm our family name and that of our family firm."

'I said nothing during all this – though I started to feel that dewy chill which accompanies fear. I couldn't help but wonder if Dad's friend, the cop, hadn't done a little detective work himself on my father's behalf. The fact that he knew so much about Sarah slammed home the point that he had quite a dossier put together. And remember – in the late 1970s homosexuality was still somewhat closeted. As Dad put it:

'"Bowdoin's the sort of liberal-minded place that doesn't care about such things. But the man is still untenured. Think what will happen if word gets around about his wife and her very young twenty-three-year-old lover, and the fact that the professor is living most weekends with another man . . . well, it might not deny him tenure, but it will certainly be great newspaper copy, won't it? And if you think the college wants that kind of publicity . . ."

'At that point I stood up and told my father he was a bastard. He just smiled and said that if I walked out of the door now I would never be allowed back, that I was effectively dead to him and to my mother. My reply? "So be it." I walked out his door, my father raising his voice just a bit to tell me: "You'll be back here, begging my forgiveness, in a week."

'My mother, as it turned out, was standing outside his office door – having clearly been primed by my father to be there, and to hear everything. She had tears in her eyes – my mom, who never showed an iota of emotion. And she clearly was very thrown by all that she had just heard.

' "Don't do this to us," she hissed at me, choking back this terrible sob. "You are being ensnared by a man-eater. You will destroy yourself."

'But I pushed by her and kept walking.

' "This will kill me," she cried as I headed out the front door. I was now on autopilot. I remember getting into my car and driving at high speed to Brunswick. And falling, punch-drunk, into Sarah's house. And telling her everything that happened. And Sarah stopping me at one point to give me a glass of Scotch. And listening to the whole terrible emotional blackmail story in silence. And then coming over to me and putting her arms around me and saying: "Your real life begins now. Because you have finally walked away from that third rate tyrant."

'I didn't sleep that night. I was wracked by the worst sort of guilt. I also worried enormously that my father would make good on his threat and expose us all. Sarah reassured me, telling me she would be talking to her husband the next day and that there would be a very robust fight-back should my father make good on his promise of trying to destroy the two of them.

'That *did* reassure me. But in the days that followed this rupture I felt something close to deep depression. The exhilaration of standing up to that repellent man was overshadowed by the realization that I had essentially cut the bridge between myself and my parents, that I was now an orphan. Sarah saw the effect this was having on me – and suggested that I might want to speak to someone professionally about all this. *Copeland Men don't go spilling their guts to some therapist,* is what I remember thinking at the time – and how absurd was that? I was resolute about moving forward. I was completely frightened. Even though I now had time on my hands – as I no longer had any gainful employment and it was another four months before we headed to Michigan – I found myself unable to do what I should have been doing during this difficult interregnum, which was writing. I was blocked. The words wouldn't come. Total creative impotence. It was as if the old man had put a curse on me, willing me to be unable to do the one thing that I knew would get me away from his tentacles. Truth be told, a creative block comes from within. Some writers have worked through the most appalling stuff. Me – a rank beginner? I allowed myself to be cowed into a block of major proportions.

'Then came the coup de grâce. My mother made good on her threat. No, she didn't die. But she did suffer a major stroke. So major that she lost the capacity to speak and was catatonic for over three weeks. It was my father who called me with the news. He was crying, and the bastard never cried. He told me to hurry to Maine Medical, as she might die that night, that he needed me there, that *he needed me*. I felt something akin to horror. I'd caused this. I'd killed her. Sarah kept telling me this was a distortion – that strokes are not caused by emotional distress, and anyway, wasn't it my damn father who had caused all this distress? So to now be running back to him . . .

'Of course she wasn't trying to stop me from seeing my mother. She was just warning me of what was going to befall me if I accepted my father's embrace. "He'll weep on your shoulder and tell you he loves you and that he was wrong to cast you out. Then he'll beg you to come back 'just for a little while', to put graduate school on hold for a year. Once you're back you'll never be free of his clutches again. He'll see to that – and you will tragically go

along with all this, even though you know it's self-entombing –
even though one of the terrible results of this decision will be that
you'll lose me."

'As always Sarah said all this in the most preternaturally calm
voice. But I was so overwhelmed by the terrible blow dealt to my
mother – and still convinced that I had pulled the cerebral trigger
which had leveled her – that I raced down to Maine Medical and
fell into my father's outstretched arms.

'Being such a profoundly well-read woman, Sarah had a huge
understanding of subtext. Especially the sort of subtext which is
anchored to the worst sort of emotional blackmail. Everything she
predicted came true. Within a week I was back at the firm. Within
two weeks I had written to Michigan, asking for a twelve-month
deferment owing to my mother's illness. Within three weeks Sarah
wrote me a letter. She was very much someone who didn't like
melodramatic finales and preferred the nineteenth-century epistol-
ary approach to the end of a love affair. And I remember her exact
words: "*This is the beginning of a great grief for both of us. Because
this was love. And because this was an opportunity that would have
changed everything. Trust me, you will rue this decision for the rest
of your life.*"'

Silence. I reached out and took his other free hand. But he
pulled away from me.

'Now you feel sorry for me,' he said.

'Of course I do. But I also understand.'

'What? That I was a coward? That I allowed myself to be black-
mailed into a life I didn't want by a man who always needed to
hobble me? That not a day goes by when I don't think about Sarah
and what should have been? That only now, all these years after
the event, I'm finally getting back to writing, and only because
my damnable father finally died a year ago? That I feel I've wasted
so much of this opportunity that is life? Especially as, four years
after Sarah, a young, quiet woman named Muriel came to work
for us in the firm. I knew from the start that she was somewhat
reserved and certainly didn't share much of my bookish interests.
But still she was relatively attractive and seemingly kind and

genuinely interested in me. "Good wife material," as my father put it. I think I married Muriel to please the bastard. But there was never any way I could actually please the bastard. The tragedy is, I secretly knew this truth about my father from the age of thirteen onwards. And now listen to me, sounding like a self-pitying—'

'You are hardly self-pitying. You just made choices that were fueled by guilt and a sense of obligation. Just as I did.'

He looked directly at me.

'I don't have a marriage,' he said. 'I haven't had one for years.'

He didn't have to tell me more – or to underscore the subtext of that comment. I too was so conversant with this territory: the slow, quiet death of passion; the complete loss of urgency and desire; the sense of distance that accompanied occasional moments of intimacy; the intense loneliness that had installed itself on my side of the bed . . . and, no doubt, on his as well.

'I know all about that,' I heard myself telling Richard, realizing that another forbidden frontier had just been traversed.

Silence.

'May I ask you something?' I said.

'Anything.'

'Sarah. What happened to her?'

'Within a week of me receiving that letter from her she was gone out of Brunswick. Off to Ann Arbor – as her friend did find her a job in the university library there. Divorced her husband who did get tenure at the college and is still with – in fact, married to – the Harvard professor. Around two years after she left I got a letter from her – formal, polite, somewhat friendly – telling me that she had met an academic at Michigan. He was a doctoral candidate in astrophysics, of all things. And she was seven months' pregnant. So she did decide to take the risk again. As desperate as this news made me feel, another part of me was genuinely pleased for her. I didn't hear from her again for another five years – when her first volume of published poetry arrived in the mail. No letter this time. Just the book from her publishers – New Directions, a very reputable house. On the dust jacket there was a biographical blurb, saying she lived in Ann Arbor with her husband and two children. So she'd become a mother twice over again.

'Since then . . . we've dropped out of each other's lives. But that's not totally the truth, as I have bought her five subsequent books of poetry. I also know that she has had a professorship in the English department at Michigan for the past twenty years, and that her last volume was a finalist for the Pulitzer. She's done remarkably well.'

Silence.

'And she *did* love you,' I said, ensuring that this statement didn't sound like a question.

'Yes, she did.'

I touched his hand, threading my fingers in his.

'You're loved now,' I said.

Silence. He finally looked back up at me.

'Let's get out of here,' he said.

## *Eight*

NIGHT HAD SERIOUSLY fallen. It was cold outside. Cold and dark, with a low mist coming in off the nearby bay. As we stepped out onto the street I felt another jolt of doubt course through me: that reproaching voice telling me I was entering a true danger zone. *Make that move and all will change. Change utterly.*

What melodrama. What a good child I had always been. What a responsible young woman, an intensely responsible adult. Faithful, loyal, always there. And though I doubt that Dan has ever cheated on me, I'd come to see his isolation as a form of betrayal.

*Will you listen to yourself. The ongoing endless, sad negotiation you conduct all the time. The blockades you are putting up now in the nanoseconds after you've just declared love for this man. A man who also knows a thing or two about lost love and self-entrapment. A man who is telling you what you are telling him: we are so right for each other. There is a chance here, if only we can both keep our nerve and . . .*

'Shall we head over to the water?' he asked me. 'Unless you want to try for the gallery?'

'I want—' I said.

In an instant we were in each other's arms. Kissing passionately, wildly, grasping each other with such desire, such need. It was as if there had been, between us, a mutual detonation. A sudden eradication of all those years of longing and inhibition and frustration and emotional washout. How wonderful to feel a man's hands on me again; a man who so clearly wanted me. As I so wanted him.

He broke away from our mad embrace for a moment, took my face in his hands, and whispered:

'I've found you. I've *actually* found you.'

I felt myself tighten. But this tightness wasn't due to any reticence or fear or some sort of 'I wish he hadn't said that' reaction to what he had told me. On the contrary, that moment of internal tautness was just a direct, instantaneous confirmation of everything I was sensing; everything that was overwhelming me right now.

'And I've found you,' I whispered back, and we began to kiss again like a couple who'd been separated for an age – and had been envisaging this moment of passionate reunion for weeks, months, years.

'We should go somewhere,' I finally whispered.

'Let's get a room.'

'Not the rooms we have at that hideous hotel.'

'My thought entirely.'

'Glad you're a fellow romantic.'

'A fellow romantic who has looked for you his entire life.'

Another long, wild kiss.

Then:

'A cab is necessary, I think,' he said.

Still holding me tightly with one arm he put up his hand and a taxi stopped. We climbed in the back.

'Ninety Tremont,' Richard told the driver. As soon as the cab took off we were kissing again wildly.

Richard's hand had slid up the back of my turtleneck. His skin against my bare skin. I stifled a little groan of pleasure; the same pleasure that shot through me as I felt his hardness against my thigh, and the way he was grasping me with such barely controlled ardor. I wanted him in a way I had wanted nobody since . . .

The taxi pulled up in front of an entrance to a hotel. Within moments we were in a lobby. Chic. Modernist. Executive. Cool. My hand in his, Richard led me to the front desk. The clerk was a woman in her twenties – and studiously blasé.

'We'd like a room,' Richard said.

She gave us the once-over and I saw her take in the wedding rings on both our hands. Just as the way we were holding hands – and the way we had arrived off the street, without baggage, clearly in a hurry to get upstairs and slam the door on the world – must have told her: *They may be married, but not to each other.*

'Do you have a reservation?' she asked, all disinterested.

'Nope,' Richard said.

'Then I'm afraid the only thing I can offer you is our King Executive Suite. But it's seven hundred and ninety-nine dollars per night.'

I could see Richard try not to blanch at the price. Certainly I was appalled at the cost. It was almost one week's salary for me.

'We can go elsewhere . . . or even back to the airport hotel,' I whispered in his ear.

Richard just kissed me, then reached into his pocket and brought out his wallet.

'We'll take the suite,' he told the clerk, slapping his credit card down on the countertop.

Two minutes later we were in an elevator, heading to the top floor. My hand was still in his, our gazes firmly locked. But we had both fallen silent. Desire and fear: that's what was so engulfing me. But the longing, the immense carnal need, was shoving whatever dread I was feeling away. I wanted him. I wanted him now.

The elevator arrived on the top floor. We followed a hallway down to a large set of double doors. Richard used the key card. There was a telltale click. He pulled me towards him. We fell into the room.

I took in very little of my immediate surroundings, except for the fact that the suite was capacious, the bed was in an adjoining room, the lights were preset low. From the moment the door shut behind us we were locked in an unrestrained embrace, and falling backwards into the bedroom, and pulling each other's clothes off, and kissing wildly, and tumbling together headlong into the sort of unbridled passion that, if you are lucky, you have experienced once or twice in your life – and which might just be the closest thing to raw love imaginable.

Time meant nothing now. All that mattered was the two of us together on this bed, submerged in each other, silently overwhelmed by the magnitude of it all.

And then, in a moment of quietude afterwards, he took my face in my hands and whispered:

'Everything has changed. *Everything.*'

Sometimes the truth is a wondrous thing.

Sunday

*One*

LOVE.

I woke with the dawn. The room was dark, festooned with shadow. Early-morning light creased in from the drawn curtains. Though I had only been asleep for a few incidental hours – sleep finally overtaking us in the wee small hours of the morning after hours of making extraordinary love – I felt wildly, profoundly awake. And wildly, profoundly in love.

Is this what's meant by a *coup de foudre*? That huge overwhelming realization that you have finally met the man of your life, that individual for whom you were destined? Years ago, I thought that man was Eric. But one thing had struck me so forcibly over the past twenty-four hours: the Eric I so cherished and adored was, like me, such a kid when we came together. What did we really know about ourselves or each other? Everyone is, I suppose, a work in progress up until the day they are no longer part of the world. But when you're nineteen you are still so unformed. Still so deeply naive (even though you do your absolute best to convince yourself otherwise). But you really know very little about life's larger profundities. And even if you have – as I did – experienced the worst sort of loss at such an early stage of adulthood, your deeper existential understanding of loss won't gain purchase until you have reached the halfway point of your temporal existence. It is then that you start to reflect on everything still not achieved, everything that underwhelms, everything that gives your life the undercurrent of an ongoing letdown. And it all congeals to remind you that time is now a diminishing commodity, that standing still (though the easier option) had rendered you static. And you quietly tell yourself: *Life must be grabbed.*

But then you throw up manifold excuses for staying put, accepting the cards dealt, telling yourself: *Things could be far worse.*

Until, out of nowhere – at a moment for which you are not prepared, in a situation which is so *not* designed to be conducive

227

to such things – you meet a man who changes everything for you. And within twenty-four hours . . .

Love.

And the man in question . . .

I think it was the moment we started trading synonyms that I began to fall for him. And the way he told the story of his son without an ounce of self-pity. Then showing me the place he wanted to buy on Commonwealth Avenue. That's when I knew. Standing in front of his future place, his new life, I understood the subtext behind this side trip. And just a few hours ago – when we were finally thinking about getting up after the evening in bed, entwined with each other, sharing the sort of intimacy that I never considered possible in my life – he took my face in his hands and said those extraordinary words:

'Everything has changed. *Everything.*'

After I remarked that the truth was occasionally rather extraordinary he then said:

'When I showed you the apartment today this crazy idea was rattling around my head: *Laura and I will move here together.* Of course I didn't dare articulate such a thought at the time. Because I had no idea then if you were feeling what I was feeling. And because—'

'I'll move to Boston with you tomorrow,' I heard myself saying. As soon as that statement was out of my mouth I didn't have a stab of regret. Or a moment thereafter when I thought: *Are you insane, uttering such a drastic, life-altering comment like that . . . especially as you have only known this man a little more than twenty-four hours?*

But the truth was, I now possessed the sort of certainty that I had never thought possible. This certainty was as bemusing as it was absolute. Just as the rational side of my brain was telling me: *You are convincing yourself of a future after just a day together.* But this ultra-cautious voice was trumped by an equally logical voice, reminding me: *What Richard said is veracity itself – everything has changed.*

*I'll move to Boston with you tomorrow.*

That wasn't wishful thinking. That was a declaration.

Love.

We were both so apprehensive at first. Once in bed, desire was initially checkmated by fear. Richard was so apologetic, clearly mortified. I didn't mouth all the usual clichés – *It happens to all men at some juncture . . . the less you think about it the more likely it will happen.* I just kissed him deeply and told him I loved him. And he told me he loved me. And we talked, in hushed voices, lying face to face, about how lonely life had been for both of us and how what we both wanted was a chance. A chance at love. Real love. It might not be the answer to all of life's complexities, all the struggles within. But it would be . . . a chance. And what I have so longed for, what Richard said he has so yearned to find. That prospect of possibility. Of a happier life.

Then we began to kiss even more deeply and passionately. Within moments he was inside me, fear having been banished. The sense of completeness was so immense. I had only slept with two men prior to Richard. I so remember the initial virginal awkwardness with Eric, and the way Dan and myself were, at first, clumsy – and how our sex life settled into a pleasant routine, but largely devoid of anything approaching real passion, real intimacy. But once Richard had entered me, once we began to move together – our bodies immediately, instinctively, attuned to what became, at once, a shared rhythm – the delirious sensuality of it all was heightened by an even more overwhelming sense of fusion.

Love.

I buried my face in his shoulder the first time I climaxed. And was astounded when I climaxed again just a few minutes later. Richard was determined not to rush things (this too was new for me) – and held off for such a long time. And when he came the shudder that ran through him, through us, was accompanied by another declaration of love.

Love.

When we finally got out of bed, slipping into the hotel bathrobes, it was late. Dinner was needed. We ordered room service. Richard also asked for a bottle of champagne. Part of me wanted to say,

'Isn't this all costing a small fortune?' Almost reading my mind, Richard tempered this with the comment:

'You have to toast a new life with champagne.'

Over dinner we couldn't stop talking. About how we had both thought such happiness was beyond our reach, outside of the lives we were living.

'We are all so absurd, aren't we?' I told Richard. 'Always slouching towards some sort of Bethlehem where we hope to find a measure of peace within which we can act out our lives.'

'"Slouching towards Bethlehem". My dream was to fall in love with a woman who could quote Yeats. My dream came true.'

'And you have fulfilled every dream imaginable for me.'

'Even if you have no idea how I live my life? As in, I could be a complete slob.'

'And so could I.'

'I tend to doubt that,' he said.

'You're right about that. And I would be very surprised to learn that you are all over the place when it comes to things domestic.'

'Would that be a deal breaker for you?'

'Nothing would change my love for you.'

'That's a dangerous statement. I mean, say I was part of some strange religious cult? Or if I was an amateur taxidermist?'

'Your imaginative flair is impressive. But even if you were stuffing gerbils in your spare time—'

'Gerbils?' I said, laughing. 'Why gerbils?'

'They've always struck me as a profoundly useless rodent.'

'And therefore worthy of taxidermy?'

'So you do have a flair for the absurd.'

'Like you, sir. Just like you.'

And he leaned over and kissed me.

We ate the dinner. We drank the champagne. We talked, talked, talked. I learned all about his childhood. How his father insisted on him joining the Boy Scouts and forced him to attend a military boarding school for two years – a hateful experience – and how he had a nervous breakdown after a few months and was sent home.

'This is something I never discussed with anyone – and even never told Muriel about it . . . I was so ashamed of it all. But that place – it was like a prison camp. I begged my mother to talk Dad out of sending me there – that is, after my father refused to entertain my pleas that I was not military school material. But my mother never went against Dad's rule of law. "You'll just have to get through it," was her statement to me. But I knew I simply *wouldn't* get through it. Before Christmas rolled around, the endless drill formations and six a.m. reveries and the hazing and mean-spiritedness of the place finally did my head in. I was found by one of my fellow cadets, crying uncontrollably in a bathroom. Instead of getting help he ran off and got six other cadets. They gathered around me and began to taunt me. Calling me a sissy, a baby, all that wonderful macho American stuff which idiots in packs perpetrate against anyone who is perceived to be different or weak.'

'You're hardly a weak man,' I said.

'The truth is, I have always been weak when it has come to the voice of authority. Had I not been weak I would have stayed with Sarah. Had I not been weak I would have quit my father's business years ago. Had I not been weak I would have left Muriel . . .'

'But you're leaving her now. And you were leaving her even before I came into your life. Just as you started writing again – and you got the first new story you wrote in years published. All that sounds anything but weak to me.'

'But I hate the fact that I was so compliant for years.'

'You don't think I hate myself for being equally acquiescing – especially when it came to making decisions that were counter-intuitive? Trust me, I am the poster girl for weakness and self-sabotage.'

'But look at how you got your son through his breakdown. God knows I wish I'd had a parent like you when I went under.'

'How did you get yourself out of it?'

'I had no choice but to somehow shake it off. My father threatened me with a psychiatric hospital if I didn't, as he put it, "snap out of it". But we were talking about your strength. And you conveniently changed the subject.'

'I still don't think myself strong, forceful.'

'You've never trusted yourself, right?'

'What makes you say that?' I asked, a little unnerved by the accuracy of this observation.

'It takes a self-doubter to know a self-doubter. And I have wasted so much energy, so many years, thanks to my own profound lack of self-assurance, of any belief whatsoever in my ability. Just like you.'

'But, hang on, at least you have a creative talent. Whereas I have nothing like that. I can shoot pictures of people's insides, and that's about it.'

'And now I really do think you are engaging in the worst form of self-deprecation. You have hinted how all the radiologists you work with so rate you. And how you can usually work out a diagnosis at first sight of a pattern or shadow on a scan or X-ray.'

'That's just a certain technical know-how.'

'No, sorry, that's a talent. And it's a talent that very few people possess. And one which you should salute yourself for having.'

'It's hardly creative.'

'Define "creative".'

'Inventive, imaginative, visionary, inspired, talented, accomplished, artistic . . .'

'And how about original, ingenious, resourceful, clever, adept, adroit, skilled? You don't think yourself adept, adroit, skilled?'

I just shrugged.

'I'll take that as a "yes",' he said. 'You are creative at your work.'

'I've not always been adept, adroit, skilled.'

'I'm also sure you've never been told enough just how extraordinary you are.'

'There's a reason I'm in this room with you. There's a reason I did something tonight I never thought I could actually do – sleep with another man while still married. The fact that I have fallen in love with you . . . that is to do with you, not my husband. But had there been a marriage still there – a sense of shared destiny, of love and support, of proper intimacy, everything you mentioned before – I would not be here. But I am so happy to be here.

Because I never thought this possible for me. Because you too *are* extraordinary.'

'Extraordinary? Me?' He shook his head. 'I am *vin ordinaire*. All right, I know a thing or two about words. I have written two published works of very short fiction. And I still like to lose myself in the Republic of Letters. But beyond that . . . I am a fifty-five-year-old man who sells insurance.'

'And you accuse me of self-abasement? You are an amazing conversationalist. You have a fantastic take on what can be broadly described as life and art. You have passion – which, trust me, is something you don't bump into every day. And that passion . . . well, the biggest surprise was . . .'

Restraint and modesty suddenly took charge of my vocal cords. But, to my surprise, I shook them off and said, in a near-whisper:

'I have never made love like that before.'

Richard reached for my hand, entwining his fingers within mine.

'Nor have I,' he said. 'Never.'

'Pure love.'

'Yes. Pure love.'

'And making love when you are madly in love . . .'

'. . . is sublime.'

'Kiss me.'

Moments later we were back in bed. This time the passion built so slowly, so acutely, that the final release had me blindsided by its intensity and its immense amorousness. Pure love. With a magnitude and a benevolence that was so intoxicating, so potent, so enabling. As we were clinging to each other afterward Richard whispered:

'I'm never letting you go. Never.'

'I'll hold you to that. Because – and this is another first for me – I actually think everything is possible now.'

'It is. Absolutely, totally possible.'

'But when you've lived for years without that belief . . .'

'That's behind us now.'

And we talked on about how we had both, in our own distinct

ways, given up on the notion of change; how romantic hope was a concept we had both dismissed as outside the possibility of future experience; and how now . . .

Everything is possible. Everything.

We finally succumbed to sleep around two in the morning, his arm enfolded around me, the aura of security, of safety, of invulnerability so pronounced. When I woke before dawn and sat up and reached out and stroked the head of my beloved, all the miraculous discombobulation of the last twenty-four hours was overshadowed by one simple, overmastering observation: my life had irrevocably changed.

Richard stirred awake.

'Hello, my love,' he whispered.

'Hello, my love,' I whispered back.

And he was deep within me moments later.

Afterward we both nodded off again, waking sometime after nine. I stood up, fetched a bathrobe, found a coffee maker in the living room of this vast suite – and returned some minutes later to the bedroom with two cups of freshly brewed Java. Richard was up, having just opened the curtains.

'I don't know how you take your coffee,' I said.

'Black works.'

'Great minds think alike . . . and prefer black coffee.'

We kissed. I handed Richard a cup and we both slid back under the covers. The coffee was surprisingly good. Sun was streaming through the window.

'It looks to be another perfect day,' I said.

'And I'm not returning to Maine tonight.'

'Nor am I,' I said, immediately considering my work schedule tomorrow – and how there were, as of Thursday, only two scans scheduled for Monday morning. Which meant if I could call my colleague Gertie this afternoon she could probably cover for me in the morning. And as for having to explain to Dan why I wouldn't be home tonight . . .

No, I didn't want to consider all that just now. I wanted to think about something I never thought I would be considering two days ago: a future in which happiness played a central role. And Richard – again uncannily reading my thoughts – took my hand in his and said:

'Let's talk about how and when we'll move to Boston.'

A future. The future. Our future.

Love. An actual concrete reality.

*Two*

PLANS. WE NOW had plans.

Over breakfast, we could not stop talking about the project that was our life together. The more we discussed – throwing out ideas about how this huge change would be put into motion, the practical details, the larger overreaching personal concerns – I couldn't help but marvel at the way we so easily bounced ideas off each other; the sheer inventive energy that existed between us; the way we were so much on the same emotional page.

*Inventive energy.* That was what was lacking within me for years. I was diligent at work, diligent at home, always engaged with my children, always trying to put a brave face on things with Dan, and using the world of books as my imaginative escape hatch from the humdrum. But there was never a sense of passionate engagement with life's larger possibilities.

And now . . .

Plans. We now had definitive plans.

'Say I call the realtor in around fifteen minutes?' Richard asked me.

'Ten o'clock on a Sunday morning? Won't he mind?'

'Like all salesmen, he always needs to be closing. The apartment is currently vacant. I know I can get my builder guy in Dorchester to do a structural survey on it this week. All going well we can close on the apartment in about three weeks. A new kitchen, bathroom, paint job, and the stripping and re-staining of the floors . . . that should take about two months tops. So we could probably move in sometime in January, or February at the outside.'

'Well, I will get onto this medical employment service group I heard about here in Boston,' I said. 'They seem to be able to usually find placements for radiographic technicians in the area. Once I have secured something I'll probably have to give at minimum one month's notice at the hospital in Damariscotta. They won't be happy – because there is actually a shortage of technologists in Maine. Still, they've had eighteen years of my life. I will be due around five months' salary when I leave, as I haven't taken enough vacation time over the years. Imagine that. I only allowed myself two of the three weeks' vacation I was granted every year. What was I thinking?'

'We feel guilty about vacations in this country. Something to do with our Puritan roots – and our fear that, while we're away, someone will come along and replace us. Or, in my case, that the business will go elsewhere.'

'Well, I am determined in the future to actually take proper vacations and go to interesting places with you. Just as I'd like to propose that I use half of that five months' back pay from the hospital to buy furniture for our apartment . . .'

'*Our* apartment. I like that. But I can certainly cover the furniture. Anyway, you'll still have Ben's college tuition to pay, then Sally will also be starting college next year . . .'

He was right, of course – especially since Dan would now be having to get by on his salary alone, which, at $15K per year after taxes, would barely cover his daily living expenses. At least the house was virtually paid off. If I could get around $85K per year in Boston – that's the usual salary for technologists at big city hospitals – I could cover Ben and Sally's day-to-day needs, with their tuitions being covered (as Ben's was now) by financial aid from the U Maine system. Once I found a job at a Boston area hospital I was pretty sure I could negotiate a four/three working week deal – in which I put in four ten-hour days in a row, then took the next three off. I'd move out of the family home and probably ask Lucy if I could take over the apartment she has over her garage – which she usually rents out, but which is conveniently empty right now, and which she would probably let me have for a reasonable sum from now until next August. Then what I'd propose to Dan would be – Sally spends four days per week with him, then three days with me. Lucy's apartment has two bedrooms. If Sally was insistent about returning to her room at the family home every night I'd still be around Damariscotta half the week for her.

I mentioned all this to Richard – and also noted that, per usual, my head was focussed on practicalities.

'But a momentous change like this involves vast numbers of practicalities,' he said. 'And naturally you are going to have to be back and forth to Maine for Sally and to see Ben. Just as I will need to find an apartment in Bath. I'll have to be there for business a few days a week. In fact, if Sally decides she doesn't want to spend half the time at your apartment, you can stay in my new place in Bath.'

'But then where would I see Sally?' I said, knowing that Dan would not want me around the house after I moved out to live with another man.

'You're right. You'll still need a place of your own in Damariscotta until she goes to college. My hope is that I can find a buyer in the next year for my insurance company, sell up, and try to write full-time. I also know of a guy who teaches business at Babson College here in Boston, and who told me they're always on the lookout for adjunct professors. I might throw my résumé his way. Maybe they'll need someone to teach actuarial science. It could bring in a little extra income, though I think I can get a good price for my company. And if I give Muriel the house outright I think she'll have a hard time demanding a share of the company.'

'How will she take you leaving her?' I asked, knowing that I was venturing into complex territory.

'I think she'll be shocked, furious. But she knows that the marriage has been moribund for years, that we have been living very separate lives. Still, that's been the status quo. I am about to change all that. And she will not be happy. But I'll be happy.'

I reached for his hand.

'And I'll be happy,' I said. 'Beyond happy.'

'And your husband will be . . .?'

'Shocked, furious, etc. But we too have been adrift for years. He'll probably tell me that he'll change. But it's too late for all that now. My life is, from this point on, with you.'

His fingers tightened around mine.

'Life can be amazing,' he said.

'If you meet the right person at the right moment. Timing is everything. I was only asked to go to this conference ten days ago. Had I not said yes . . .'

'And I was due to see some clients in New Hampshire on Friday afternoon. The fact that they cancelled, the fact that I got to the hotel precisely when you did . . .'

'The fact that you started up a conversation with me while we were in line . . .'

'The fact that we both ended up at that movie house in Cambridge . . .'

'And I only decided to see that film when I saw an ad in the *Boston Phoenix*, and happened to be around the corner from the movie house at the time . . .'

'The fact that I didn't show up until a few minutes later, when the lights were already dark . . .'

'Life is so predicated on the convergence of so many small details that land us in a certain place at a certain time. But happenstance doesn't transform into anything unless choices are made, decisions rendered. Such as the fact that my initial private reaction to your offer of a drink after the movie was: *No way*. Not because I didn't want to, but because I simply had never, in all my married years, gone out with a man I'd just met for a drink.'

'And until last night I've always, like you, been faithful.'

'That's admirable.'

'On a certain level, perhaps. But fidelity only works if there's love. Muriel and I haven't been in love for . . . well, knowing what I felt all those years ago with Sarah and, most tellingly, knowing what I feel now with you, I must ask myself if Muriel and I were ever really in love?'

'It's the same question I've been asking myself since yesterday about me and Dan. The thing is, we're hardly unique. You scratch most marriages, you discover that people chose their spouse for all sorts of highly compromised reasons, and that they projected onto that other person what they believed they needed – or, worse yet, *deserved* – at a given moment.'

'Which is what makes this, *us*, so singular, so extraordinary. I

239

still find myself asking myself if this really happened. Can I really have met the woman of my life?'

My fingers tightened around his again.

'The man of my life.'

'It's astonishing,' he said.

'And just a little crazy.'

'Nothing wrong with some long-overdue romantic madness.'

'And so say all of us. But I know that, back in Damariscotta, people will talk. Especially when word gets around, people will accuse me of being irresponsible, immature, having a whopper-sized midlife crisis. And Sally's classmates – having heard my news from their parents – will, no doubt, say the usual hateful things that teenage girls sling at each other. I will have to talk to Sally about all this – and what she might expect to encounter in school after my news is public.'

'And what will you tell her?'

'That life never operates according to plan. That love is the most longed for, yet most mysterious, of emotions. That I met you and, within twenty-four hours, knew that I loved you profoundly. That she knows her father and I have been rudderless for years. That I have a chance here – a real chance at happiness. And I am taking it. But that she will not, in the process, lose me. That I will still always be there for her.'

'How do you think she'll react to all that?'

'Horribly. Especially since her first concern will be that over-riding adolescent girl worry – *I'm going to be made to look stupid. I am going to be the subject of public ridicule thanks to my love-gooey Mom.* I can hear her already telling me how I have ruined her life. Not because I am leaving her father – but because she's going to be taunted and tormented by her fellow cheerleaders. But Sally will survive this. Dan will survive this.'

'And Ben?'

'My wonderfully quirky and original son will probably say something ironic and knowing like, "Way to go, Mom." I think he'll like you as well.'

'Even if I am not the bohemian he aspires to be.'

'You write. You've changed your life. You love his mother and make her supremely happy. Trust me, he'll be cool with all that.'

'You're so lucky having a son like that – talented, clearly sensitive and emotionally smart.'

I put my hand on his arm and squeezed it, saying:

'I know you're thinking about Billy right now.'

'I'm always thinking about Billy. The fact is, there is nothing I can do about Billy anymore. His future is in the hands of the state. He is now so thoroughly institutionalized – and so personally lost – that I can't see him rejoining his family, let alone society, for the foreseeable future. And yes, that tears away at me all the time. But I've also learned to accept that there are certain situations that cannot be put back together again, that are beyond redemption, let alone a happy ending. Like my marriage. And alas, like Billy.'

'You know you can count on me when it comes to helping you through anything. And you must always tell me everything when it comes to Billy or anything else in your life.'

'Just as you know, when it comes to Ben and Sally, I am always with you. And I certainly hope Ben manages to continue to lift himself out of that bad place he found himself in.'

'Curiously, I am coming to believe that his breakdown might mark the beginning of the makings of a much stronger, more independent young man. I think, like all of us, he had the illusion that someone else can fill in all the psychic gaps and holes within you. But what I sense is that, in the wake of his collapse, he's started to realize perhaps the toughest and most important lesson you have to learn as an adult is that no one but yourself is responsible for your happiness. Just as you are not ultimately responsible for anyone else's happiness.'

'And the other great truth behind what you've just said is that you have to want to be happy in order to be happy,' Richard said. 'I think, for years, I simply accepted my domestic unhappiness as my due – part of the infernal compromise I made. And now . . .'

'Now we can do this all differently. Now we can rewrite the rules of our respective lives.'

It did somewhat bemuse me, hearing myself say such things out loud. Just as I was so conscious of the hugely direct way Richard and I were expressing our love for each other. *'I have never made love like that before.'* Take it out of context and you think it's this side of treacly. But isn't that one of the great wonders of falling in love; the way you start articulating emotional truths in such an unabashed, un-self-censored way? My father once admitted to me after my mother died that he had always had great difficulties telling her, 'I love you'; that even though theirs was a good marriage, he rarely could bring himself to make that sweeping, crucial declaration on even an irregular basis. Dan was cut from the same reticent material. (Did I subconsciously choose him because he so mirrored my father's emotional distance?) That, in turn, made the impassioned articulation of feeling between myself and Richard so revelatory. Here was a man who wanted to tell me how much he loved me at every opportunity.

'"Life can change on a dime," as my grandfather used to say. Far too much, I should add. But still . . . how to explain all this?'

'Love . . . in all its manifest indisputability.'

'Now you are showing off,' I said, laughing. 'But I still like the sentiment. Especially as it is so true.'

Richard glanced at his watch.

'Just coming up to ten a.m.,' he said. 'I'm going to call the realtor and make the offer on our apartment.'

'You are amazing, Mr Copeland.'

'Not as amazing as you.'

He went into the bedroom to collect his cellphone. I used this opportunity to do something I was dreading: turning on my own phone and discovering what messages were awaiting me. I found my bag, dug out the phone, hit the power-on button, and listened while, in the next room, Richard was already speaking with the realtor. The price he would pay was two-forty-five. No negotiation. This offer was on the table for forty-eight hours, no more. His tone was perfectly pleasant throughout – but he was also making it very clear that he wanted to close this thing fast and with as little encumbrance as possible. What struck me so forcibly was the confidence in his voice, the sense of being reasonable, yet authoritative. Which also struck me as immensely attractive and reassuring.

There was another thought behind all this: *The man I love is buying an apartment for us.* Yesterday he talked about moving to Boston in 'the next life'. Today the next life has actually begun.

An apartment for us.

*Us.* What a lovely pronoun.

*Bing.* The telltale tone informing me I had text messages.

Actually just two messages. Both from Dan. The first time-marked 6:08 last night:

Sally's headed off with her friends to Portland. Thinking about tackling the railings on the front porch tomorrow. You're right, they really could use a paint job. Hope you're having an OK evening. D xxx

Did I feel a stab of guilt when I read this? Yes and no. Yes because, *yes,* I had stepped outside my marriage and had slept with another man. No because Dan's text was just another attempt to put a band-aid on what had been a slow, but steady, bleeding dry of any emotional connection between us. And it made me think: *A man I just met two days ago can't stop telling me that he loves me, and my husband of over twenty years can't ever bring himself to make that declaration. Because he truly doesn't feel that.*

The next text from Dan was marked 10:09 last night.

Hoped to hear from you before getting to bed early. Still trying to get my body clock adjusted for the four a.m. wake-up call on Monday. Why didn't you call/text tonight? Everything OK? D xxx

Is everything OK? Actually, falling in love has made everything beyond OK. It has changed the landscape of my existence. But if I indicated now that 'we need to have a serious talk' – a hint that things between us had, as far as I was concerned, reached the endgame phase – I knew that he might start bombarding me with calls or texts today. And I wanted this day with my love to be free of such interference. There would be seriously trying days ahead with Dan; a rite of painful passage I'd have to negotiate, and help him through as well (though I already sensed that his initial shock would be usurped by rage when he knew that I was in love with another man). But for now . . .

Hi there. Girls' night out yesterday evening with three radiologists. A little too much wine ingested. Am suffering bad head this morning. Remember my friend Sandy Nelson? Working at Mass General in Radiology. She's asked me over for dinner to her home in Somerville tonight.

In the recent past I would have read through even the most benign text to Dan several times over before dispatching it – because I had become so super-conscious of my husband's ability to find grievance in even the most seemingly straightforward of words. But this morning I just hit the 'send' button on my phone, while hearing Richard next door tell the realtor:

'So if you can get a yes from the seller today I can come in and see you at your Mass Ave office tomorrow at nine a.m. to sign the paperwork, and arrange my bank to transfer the deposit – a deposit that will be refundable if my surveyor finds something very wrong with the place. But that's not going to happen, right? OK, I'll keep my phone on this morning and afternoon. But tell the guy, the offer is non-negotiable. And as you know, I'm a cash buyer.'

*Bing.* A new text on my phone. As expected, from Dan:

Envy you the night out. And dinner with Sandy sounds like fun. Hope hospital will cover extra night at hotel.

Leave it to Dan to think about the extra cost. But I decided to put his mind to rest:

Sandy asked me to stay the night – so no cost involved. Hope you'll get a good sleep tonight – and that new job turns out better than you imagine. It's a good re-start, and will hopefully lead to better things. L xxx

As I dispatched this, a thought crossed my mind: might Dan somehow try to contact Sandy during the course of the evening? Then again, he hadn't seen Sandy in years – we'd first met when we were both doing the radiographic technicians course at Southern Maine Community College – and she dropped in to see us with her then new husband (whom she subsequently divorced) once thereafter in 2002. We'd kept in touch since then by email – and I knew she was now living with a new man in Somerville. But if Dan couldn't get through to me on my cellphone – that is, if he even tried to get through – would he call Information for Somerville and try to find Sandy's number? Maybe I should give her a call and ask her to cover for me just in case. But I'd then have to explain everything to a woman I consider more an acquaintance than a friend. Maybe I am being wildly over-cautious here. Maybe this is the reason why I am so glad that Richard and I have cut straight to the chase, and are starting a life immediately together. No months of sneaking around. No cavalcade of lies, or the need to invent scenarios to cover our tracks. Just the blunt truth: *I've fallen in love. Our marriage is over. I'm moving out.*

But in the meantime, there were certain essential immediate things to take care of. Such as . . .

A fast text to my colleague Gertie: could she cover my morning shift tomorrow?

*Bing.* Gertie texted me right back:

Let me cover your whole day tomorrow – if you are willing to do my all-day Saturday shift this weekend. Would love to get out of it.

Great news. This meant I wouldn't have to rush back early tomorrow morning. More time with Richard. I texted straight back:

You've got a deal. Can you please inform hospital admin today that we're trading shifts. You're a star. L xxx

And then there was a very important text I needed to send to Lucy:

Can't talk right now. But something rather momentous has arrived in my life – and I was wondering if I might be able to drop by tomorrow sometime? Is that apartment of yours over the garage still available?

Well, that was being all but direct. But Lucy was my best friend. And I needed a best friend to talk to before I dropped the bombshell on Dan.

*Bing.* My luck was holding when it came to instant responses.

Well now you have me more than curious! Am just working morning tomorrow at library, so drop by whenever after 1 p.m. Yes, the apartment is still empty. If you need it, it's there. And if you can talk, I'm around all day today. So want to know the story behind all this intrigue. Love – Lucy

Intrigue. How I wanted to text back: It's not intrigue. It's the love story of the century! Prudence stopped me from such rashness. Anyway, Lucy would know the entire saga tomorrow. So I just wrote:

All will be revealed when we meet. You're a great friend. *Bing.*

Oh God, Dan again.

Seems like you're doing your best to stay away from home as long as you can . . . and who can blame you, right? I mean, who would want to come home to me? But thanks for wishing me well in the new job. Really appreciated.

Now I did feel aggrieved. This was Dan's ongoing repertoire, his schtick. Having made reconciliatory gestures here he was again, being bad-tempered and small – and knowing so well that such behavior always disquieted me.

As I read this a coldness – one that I had always fought off in the past – took hold of me, letting me know: *This is truly finished.*

'Some bad news?' Richard asked. I looked up from my phone, trying to wipe the tension off my face, then telling myself: *Why don't you, from the outset of this new love, make a commitment towards communicating what is actually on your mind . . . rather than self-censoring and shoving all that you are thinking, feeling, under the proverbial carpet.* So:

'My husband is making me feel bad about spending an extra day to see an old friend in Boston. And he's also letting me know he already hates the job he'll be starting tomorrow.'

'He never really saw how wonderful you are, did he?'

I shut my eyes and felt tears.

'You lovely, lovely man,' I said.

He came over and put his arms around me.

'You are extraordinary,' he said.

246

'As are you. And I bet that's something *she's* never told you.'

He just shrugged. And said:

'Does that even matter anymore?'

I kissed him. Then said:

'You're right. All that matters is—'

'Us.'

We began to kiss again. Deeply this time, our hands slipping into each other's bathrobes.

*Bing.* It was Richard's cellphone. He ignored it, especially as we were both so quickly aroused. *Bing.* The tone again. And when it went ignored again, the actual phone then started to ring.

'Great timing,' Richard said under his breath.

'Whoever it is clearly wants to speak to you.'

'To hell with it.'

'Take it,' I said, thinking maybe it was some update on Billy, and he needed to be on the other end of the line.

Richard fished into his bathrobe pocket, squinted at the screen, then answered the call.

'Oh yeah, hi there,' he said to whoever was on the other end. 'I didn't expect to hear from you until . . . I see . . . that was fast . . . right . . . and? . . . really?. . . . just like that? . . . yeah, that makes sense . . . well then, there we are . . . that's right . . . see you then . . . and yeah, I remember this address . . . and a very good morning to you too.'

He ended the call, his lips pursed in a near smile.

'Good news?' I asked.

'Very good news.'

'Tell me.'

Now the part-smile became a full smile.

'The apartment is ours.'

# *Three*

WE GOT OUT of bed again around midday. This was such new
territory for me – the constant need to be making love, to have
my love deep inside me. Yes, I remember, all those years ago with
Eric, the way we were always falling into bed during those first
heady months of our romance. This was coupled with the discovery
of sex: the wide-eyed wonder at the pleasure of all that intimate
friction, of bodies electric; the sheer animalistic abandon that
accompanied the act itself. Even after this initial discovery period
– heightened with that overwhelming feeling of being truly in love
for the first time – there was still a desire that never abated. I
cannot remember a night when we didn't make love – and there
was always this infectious delight in having each other day in, day
out.

With Dan . . . well, the sex was just that. Sex. Pleasant.
Reasonable. Semi-engaged, but never infused with the sort of
passion that was ever transporting. I knew this from the outset
– and accepted it as cosmic payback for losing the man I so adored.
And then, when I got pregnant . . .

But I remember holding Ben for the first time after the delivery,
and crying as I saw my son, and knowing immediately that, even
if this child was not made in love, my love for him would be
absolute, unconditional. Just as I felt the same way when Sally
arrived two years later. So the passion I have for everything to do
with Ben and Sally has always counterbalanced the lack of passion
in the marriage.

Richard reported to me that his own marriage was even more
sexually moribund than mine; that he and his wife only 'coupled'
(her verb of choice, he told me) two or three times a year, and
that he had essentially closed down that part of his life.

And then we came together. And . . .

I am not very experienced in the wider world of sex. Even Lucy
was shocked to learn that Eric and Dan were the only two men

I had ever slept with. She herself could count eight lovers 'before, during and after my bad marriage . . . and the fact that I can count them all on less than two hands makes me think I really should have been having more sex with more men at that point when it wasn't so damn hard to meet the sort of men you want to be having sex with, rather than the nightmares who only seem to be on offer to middle-aged women living in small Maine towns'.

I had to laugh when she told me this. Just as it also fueled a larger encroaching despair I'd had for years about the lukewarm physical life I had with Dan. Until he lost his job we made love at least three nights a week. Even if it was, at best, thermal and adequate, at least it was there. But when he lost his job, his libido also went south.

Making love with Richard was nothing less than revelatory. In the three, four times we had fallen into bed since arriving here yesterday evening, the profundity of the act itself – the way it so expressed the overpowering love we had just discovered and now shared – seemed only to augment and grow every time we were entwined together. Feeling him move inside me didn't just trigger an eruption of sensuality so far beyond anything in my past experience; it was also so palpably intimate. What was even more extraordinary was the fact that this conjoining, this total fusion, was so immediate. From the very moment he first entered me.

'I never want to leave this bed,' I whispered as we clung to each other afterwards.

'Well, we can stay here all day then.'

'There is the little problem of all our things at our respective rooms back at the God-awful hotel. Sorry to raise this dreary practicality . . . but won't they want us checked out of there by midday . . . which is kind of now? And my car is still there.'

'Yes, that thought did cross my mind. But I use that place all the time and know all the duty managers there. So I'll give one of them a call in a few minutes, and see if I can negotiate a late checkout . . . or even offer to tip one of the maids twenty bucks if she'll pack up everything for us. Then we can run over there and pick everything up later this afternoon.'

'A change of clothes and a hairbrush would be welcome. But this suite is a fortune. And we certainly don't have to stay here tonight. In fact, we could—'

'We're staying here tonight,' Richard said. 'I've spent far too much of my life being cautious about money. And what has such frugality finally given me?'

'Well, it's given you the money to buy that apartment – and change your life.'

'True – but I should have been really living before this weekend. I've gone nowhere, seen so very little. Haven't been to a concert or a play in years.'

'But you have been reading.'

'The cheap escape route. It's like what Voltaire said about marriage – it's the only adventure available for the coward.'

'But the fact that you can quote Voltaire—'

'Big deal.'

'Tell me another insurance man from Bath, Maine – or anywhere else for that matter – who can do that. Anyway, now that we'll be here, in Boston, much of the time, there's a great orchestra here. There are great museums, good theatres. We can do all that. And here's another thing I was going to mention earlier – all right, I will probably use around two-thirds of my overdue vacation money from the hospital to help top up Ben and Sally's college tuitions next year. But that will still leave me maybe seven or eight thousand dollars. Why don't we go to Paris for six weeks on that?'

'Paris,' he said, mouthing the word as if it was almost proscribed; the reverie he'd never dared articulate. 'You serious?'

'Just last week, before you turned my life upside down in the most amazing way, I spent an evening at home, looking at short-term rentals in Paris. Traveling vicariously, so to speak. We could find a very nice studio in an area like the Marais for around five hundred dollars a week. Airfares – if we book well in advance – are around six hundred each. You can eat well and reasonably in Paris. And the studio will have a kitchen . . . so, yes, we could do a month and a half on seven thousand. I would negotiate with whatever hospital down here took me on to ensure that I'd either have six weeks' unpaid leave sometime during the first year – or, better yet, to push back my starting date until after Paris. In fact, if the apartment renovations might not be finished until early February we could go to France right after Christmas . . .'

'Paris,' he said again. 'Six weeks in Paris. I never thought that possible.'

'It's possible.'

'Let's do it then.'

I kissed him, then said:

'Well, that was quite a difficult negotiation.'

He laughed.

'Nothing with you is difficult,' he said.

'And nothing with *us* will ever be difficult. I know that sounds maybe like far too much wishful thinking. But the truth is we've both done difficult. We've both done circumscribed lives. And now . . .'

'The art of the possible.'

'Exactly. In fact, that must be our credo. Those five words. The art of the possible.'

'It's a good modus vivendi.'

'The best.'

*Bing*. A text message on my phone. I hesitated reaching for it, but Richard told me to take it. He needed to call the airport hotel and get our late checkout organized. As he disappeared into the other room with his phone, I picked up my cell and saw that Ben had written to me (spread out over four texts):

Hi Mom – still in Boston? Working flat out on new painting, and have run out of a certain azure blue I really need. Can't be found in Maine, so I get it from an art supply place in Boston. Would cost me mucho to get it here by Tuesday. If you could pick up today and drop at Portland Museum of Art on your way home, Trevor will be there tomorrow at noon and can collect it. Sorry to be a pain. Would be doing me huge favor. You're the best. Love – Ben

Immediately I called Ben.

'You're up early,' I said when he answered on the third ring.

'Very funny, Mom,' he said, his voice all amused irony. 'You evidently got my text.'

'I'm thrilled the new painting's coming together so brilliantly.'

'Don't use the word "brilliant", *please*. It might jinx it. But Trevor –' Trevor Lathrop, his visual art professor and all-purpose mentor at Farmington – 'is rather enthusiastic. For him that's big. Anyway, if you could get the paint . . .'

'I'm still in Boston, as I've decided to stay on and see an old friend tonight.'

'And miss Dad's middle-of-the-night send-off tomorrow to L.L.Bean's?' he said, his tone light, but clearly pointed.

'I do feel guilty about that.'

'Considering how you've been carrying the entire financial burden for the past two years . . .'

'It wasn't your father's fault that he was let go during a cutback.'

'But it was his decision to act like an ill-tempered grump all that time. Even now. I called him last night to say hello, make a gesture and all that, and the guy asked me standard-issue questions about school and stuff, "You feelin' OK?", that kind of "tick the boxes with your son" conversation . . . then when I asked him about the new job, he got all mealy-mouthed and sullen. All I could think was: *Who's the adolescent here?*'

'You're hardly an adolescent, Ben.'

'I'm only beginning to understand what you've been dealing with for years.'

'That's a conversation for another time. On which note . . . say I dropped by to see you sometime next weekend.'

'Here's a better idea. I get a lift down to Portland on Saturday and we hang out for the afternoon and evening. And you can take me to dinner at that groovy Italian place we both like.'

'It's a date.'

'You sound in a good place, Mom.'

'Actually I am.'

'Not that you've ever sounded like you're in a bad place. I mean, you could give lessons about "putting a good face on things". Still, nice to hear a hint of upbeat in your voice.'

Time to change the subject.

'So give me all the details about the paint you need, the shop, and all that.'

Ben told me that when I got to the art supply store, just opposite Boston University on the Fenway, I was to ask for a guy named Norm 'who's been running this place since the nineteenth century' and always mixed up the azure blue exactly the way Ben needed it.

'The thing about Norm – he will never mix the paint until he has cash in hand, or a credit card number that works. And he's only open until four p.m. today. But I'll call him and say you're coming . . . if you're sure that's not going to be too much hassle.'

'You're my son, Ben. It's no hassle. And I can drop the paints off at the Museum of Art in Portland tomorrow.'

'I'll also phone Trevor and tell him to meet you there at twelve noon if that works.'

'I've got the day off – so, yes, that works just fine. Give him my cell number and text me his. And I'll text you this afternoon when I have the paint.'

'You're a star, Mom.'

As I put down the phone I found myself beaming. Richard came in from the next room.

'So they've got a chambermaid at the other hotel, packing up both our rooms. I talked them into letting you leave your car there until tomorrow. And that phone call must have been a happy one, as you have the biggest smile imaginable on your face.'

I told him about the exchange with Ben, leaving out his comments about his father. I could see Richard again trying to get thoughts about his own son out of his head.

'He so obviously recognizes what an amazing mother you've been to him.'

'He's quite the amazing son. And I really think – if he can keep his nerve and not give in to all that self-doubt, and can also get out of Maine for a number of years and really keep upping his game – he's going to be important one day. Maybe even major.'

'With you behind him . . .'

'He still has to do it all himself.'

'Without you having to tell me anything I know that you're the parent who's been there for him.'

'All I know is this – I'm the parent who needs to pick up some special paints for him this afternoon.'

I explained all the details about the particular shade of blue that this particular art supply dealer mixes up near Fenway Park, and how I had to be there by around three p.m., as the shop closes an hour later, and my son's major new masterwork – *Hey, I'm his mother* – was awaiting completion.

'Well, you clearly need to be up there at three,' Richard said. 'So here's a plan . . .'

We decided that, after lunch, Richard would jump the T out to the airport and I'd head up to the other side of town and pick up Ben's paints, then we'd reconvene back here at the room around five.

But first we had a shower together, soaping each other up, kissing wildly under the cascading water, clinging to each other, promising to be always there for each other, repeating how much we loved each other, talking with an emotional freedom and openness that I had lost decades ago and never thought I would find again.

After dressing I sent a fast text to Sally:

Spending an extra day in Boston, playing hooky from the workaday world. How did the evening in Portland go? Love you – Mom

*Bing.* Back came the reply.

Concert was boring. Have an essay now to write on Edith Wharton. B-o-r-i-n-g. Dad says you have hangover. Cool.

My daughter the purveyor of a literary style that could best be described as 'sullen adolescent minimalist'. I dreaded to think the volcanic reaction that would follow my revelation to her about the major upheaval that was going to change the contours of our family life. But first . . . there was the rest of this wonderful weekend to get through.

Richard's phone *binged* a few times when we were dressing. He glanced in a cursory manner at the screen but chose to send no replies.

'Everything OK?' I asked.

'Just some business stuff,' he said. 'I've got this client – has about five hardware stores in the Lewiston/Auburn area – thinks he can call me day or night when he's got a claim on the go. The thing is, one of his warehouses burned down three weeks ago. A disgruntled employee lit the match. The guy's still on the run. My client suffered close to four hundred thousand dollars' worth of damage. Between ourselves, because he's had a couple of bad years, the insurance inspectors and the cops are wondering whether he might have talked the "disgruntled employee" into playing arsonist.'

'You are going to write this story, right?'

'Actually, it does have a nice James M. Cain feel to it . . .'

'Especially if you could add a *femme fatale* to it.'

'You amaze me,' he said.

'Because I know who James M. Cain is?'

'Because you're so insanely smart.'

I kissed him.

'Almost as smart as you.'

He kissed me.

'You're smarter,' he said.

I kissed him.

'You're being kind.'

He kissed me.

'Just accurate.'

'I so love you.'

'I so love you.'

On the way out of the hotel Richard stopped by the front desk to tell the woman there that we'd be staying in the suite another night. She checked its availability and said: 'No problem.'

The gods were, without question, with us. Especially as we stepped out into another dazzling autumn day. The sun incandescent. The sky devoid of clouds. A light wind cascading the fallen leaves. The city spread out before us, so welcoming, so freighted with the great possibilities. Richard took my hand as we crossed into the Common.

'Just yesterday . . .' I said.

'Just yesterday . . .'

He didn't have to complete the thought. Just yesterday the world was different. And today . . .

'Let's go back and look at the outside of the apartment,' I said.

'I'm for that.'

We walked hand in hand across the Common, talking, talking, talking. About getting down here the weekend after next to meet with Richard's contractor friend to discuss the renovations on the apartment. And also finding out who was conducting the Boston Symphony Orchestra that weekend, and trying to get seats. And yes, we would finally get to the Institute of Contemporary Arts that weekend. And we should also find out what's going on at one of the interesting professional theater companies around town.

'Leave all that to me,' I said. 'I'll play Cultural Event Organizer.'

'And I'll find us the hotel and arrange the appointment with my builder friend from Dorchester, Pat Laffan. Surprise, surprise, Pat is a retired Boston Irish cop turned builder. A rather plain-spoken guy, Pat, but reasonably honest . . . which is rare to find in a builder.'

'We could also start looking at furniture then . . . if that isn't rushing things.'

'I like the fact that we're rushing things. We're right to be rushing things.'

Ah, romantic discourse! How we both revelled in it – like two strangers who had separately thought: *I'll never master the French language*, and then woke up next to each other one morning to discover they were speaking it together with a fluency and a confidence that had seemed impossible before then. How we both wanted this love. How we both knew it was so right. I wanted to gush romantic. Just as I also wanted to tell myself that the shared will to make this wonderful was so immense that we were naturally going to cohabit beautifully and deal with the usual domestic stuff with an ease and a grace that comes out of knowing what a sad marriage is like on a year-in, year-out basis.

Again Richard seemed to be reading my thoughts as he stopped and took my hands and, looking directly at me, said:

'You know and I know we're still figuring each other out, still wondering if this can be actually happening, and if we can truly create this life together we so want. But the truth is, absolutely. I have no doubt about it. None at all.'

'Nor do I.'

And we kissed again.

Half an hour later we were in a restaurant on Newbury Street, having a late brunch, discussing how we would negotiate the next few complex days with our respective spouses.

'My desire is to simply tell Dan the truth when I get home tomorrow night,' I said. 'As I said earlier, I know it will hit him hard. I know he will be stunned by the news, then furious. I want to just get it over with – because I don't want to have to go through the motions of pretending that all is normal when I am longing all the time for you. But there is one major consideration here – the fact that he starts this new job tomorrow and will be exhausted from his first early-morning shift. Mind you, he will be working a four-day-on, three-day-off week, so—'

'So why don't you wait until Thursday evening – when he can absorb the news without having to then face work a few hours later?'

'It's the kinder option – not that there's anything kind at all about this. Still, given that I work until five-thirty Tuesday through Friday of this week, and he'll be going to bed around eight to get up at four a.m., we will be ships passing through the night for the next few days – which is a blessing. The few days means I can see my friend Lucy and start quietly moving some basic things into the apartment over her garage. So when I give him the news Friday after I come home from work I can sleep that night at Lucy's. It also means I can tell Sally that afternoon – and not have her reeling and having to go to school the next day. If she wants to come over with me that night to Lucy's, that's an option. But knowing her she'll run to her boyfriend. Which might not be a bad thing. Then I have to do the early shift on Saturday at the hospital, but plan to meet Ben late Saturday afternoon in Portland for dinner – which means I can then tell him directly. I'm pretty certain he'll take the news a lot better than his sister . . . and I'm really thinking out loud here, aren't I?'

Richard smiled and reached for my hand (we were always reaching for each other's hand, always there to reassure each other).

'It's huge what we're about to do,' he said. 'And it is going to hurt people with whom we've lived for years. So, of course you have to be considering how best to break the news in a way where it can be absorbed as best as possible. Part of me thinks that Muriel, even if she is privately knocked sideways by the news, will probably come on all cold and vindictive – which is, I'm afraid, her usual style. But that will be no bad thing. Better arctic chill than a wildfire. And if you plan to tell Dan on Friday I'll do it the same night.'

'Then maybe we should meet somewhere afterwards. I mean, the idea of not seeing you from tomorrow morning until Thursday . . .'

'Could you sneak away maybe Tuesday evening?'

'Actually, that would work fine. I could tell Dan I'm having dinner with Lucy, and could meet you . . .?'

'Could we meet at Lucy's apartment?'

'Absolutely.'

'And then, on Thursday . . .'

'Come straight up to Lucy's after you've broken the news.'

'Unless Sally wants to spend the evening with you there.'

'As I said before the chances of that happening—'

'Just in case I can always give Dwight a call. He knows how difficult things have been with Muriel, and his wife is also very sympathetic and kind, and they will let me stay in their guest room for a few days—'

'Anyway, we'll first be seeing each other on Tuesday night.'

'So there will just be a night apart.'

'Which is a night too long.'

'But as of Friday we will officially be a couple.'

'We're a couple already, my love.'

'That we are. That we are.'

Richard's phone *binged* several times during lunch. But he ignored it.

'I know who it is – that awful man in Lewiston who may have hired a proxy arsonist. And he can wait until after this lunch for me to return his damn calls.'

My phone *binged* once as well: a text from Ben, telling me he'd spoken to Norm at the art supply store, and he'd be expecting me at three p.m., but he told me that he needs thirty minutes to mix the paints, and won't begin mixing them until money has exchanged hands. So you really can't show up later than three-thirty. I so appreciate this, Mom. Hope your good mood is even better this afternoon.

While Richard headed off to use the washroom I texted back:

Tell Mr Norm I'm a prompt person – especially when it involves my son and his work. Will definitely be there in just under half an hour. (My watch read two-forty.) And yes, my good mood is augmenting by the moment right now. I'll text when I have the paints. Love – Mom.

As I hit the 'send' button Richard was back at the table.

'Everything OK?' he asked as I put my phone down. I explained the text from Ben and the fact that I really needed to get to the Fenway within the next fifteen minutes.

'I'll put you in a taxi,' he said.

'But Fenway Park is just seven or eight minutes away by foot.'

'Then I'll go with you.'

'And have to wait nearly an hour while this guy does his prestidigitation thing with his paints? You jump the T to the airport, my love, get our bags. I'll get my son his magic acrylics, then meet you back at the hotel by five at the latest, and promise to drag you back to bed.'

'That sounds like a plan,' he said, all smiles.

A few minutes later we were standing in front of the T-station at the intersection of Newbury Street and Mass Ave. I put my arms around Richard's neck.

'Now the idea of letting you go for two hours is not the most pleasing of prospects,' I said.

'Then let me come to the paint store.'

'The faster you get to the airport and get back with our bags the faster we can be making love again.'

We began to kiss. A long, intense kiss.

'I don't want to let you go,' he eventually whispered.

'Two hours tops and we're back in each other's arms.'

'Hurry back to me.'

'I will.'

We kissed again.

'How did we get so lucky?' he asked.

'We just did. And do you know what? We deserve it.'

One final long kiss, then I gently disentangled myself from his arms.

'I really want to get there in ten minutes. If the guy is as finicky as Ben makes him out to be . . .'

'OK then,' Richard said. 'Two hours. I love you.'

'I love you.'

He headed down the stairs of the T-station, turning back to blow me a kiss. For a moment – pulling up the collar of his brown leather Air Force jacket – he looked like a throwback to another era, and had suddenly lost around three and a half decades. He was a twenty-year-old, looking back with poignant wistfulness in his eyes at the woman he loved, as he was about to be shipped out somewhere potentially jeopardous. Then, with a sad smile, he was gone.

I headed out in the direction of Fenway Park, the sun beginning its afternoon slump towards the dark, but still bathing the street in a copper glow. The fall. A season whose peerless beauty – especially in New England – usually provoked a certain melancholy in me. Because after the kaleidoscopic crimson-and-gold hued wonders of the season, darkness then falls. With it the descent into the brumous shadow of winter, and the end of another year. Yet another twelve becalmed months behind me.

And then . . .

Just two days ago . . .

This entire extraordinary business underscored something I had not considered before: if allowed, life can also sidestep all its attendant mundanities and demonstrate its capacity to astonish; to remind you that you still have a capacity for the passionate. The thing is, you have to permit yourself to embrace such potential wonderment. If you have submerged your ability to marvel – to forget that you are truly worthy of love, and the benevolence it brings to you amidst all the middling concerns that crowd all our existences – fall after fall arrives with a metronomic regularity. You live a life of silent, ever-increasing longing for a bedazzlement that always seems tantalizingly close, yet so acutely out of reach.

I headed up the Fenway, leaving behind Newbury Street's atmosphere of elegant consumerism and moving into something a little more gritty, a lot less connected with shopping as a leisure activity. Norm's Art House was a nondescript shop on a nondescript corner of the Fenway. It was a small storefront, with one display window (in need of a cleaning), within which was a haphazard presentation of brushes, easels, tubes of paint. There was also a sign, in oversized stenciled letters, reading: '*WE DO ART*'.

This no-nonsense approach continued inside the shop. It was a cramped space, brimming with oils and acrylics and watercolors and every conceivable size of brush, and rolls of canvas waiting to be stretched, and wooden slats for frames.

'So you must be Benjamin the Brilliant's mother.'

The voice came from behind a series of overstocked, rather rusted metal shelves behind the sales counter.

'Are you Norm?'

'So he's briefed you. And you're here for the Tetron Azure Blue – the most lazuline of all modern blues.'

'*Lazuline*,' I said, trying the word out. 'Not bad,' I finally said.

'You have a better synonym, perhaps?'

'Cerulean?'

Silence. Then Norm emerged from the shadows of his shop's corroded shelves.

'Well, I'm impressed. And as it turns out, you're also beautiful.'

I tried hard not to blush. I failed. Norm was not what I expected. From his name to the way Ben hinted that he was crotchety, I had expected someone out of a Saul Bellow novel: an old-world merchant, avuncular, fussy, but with a knowledge of paints and artists that was as encyclopedic as it was passionate. But the real Norm was a tall stringbean of a man, around my age, with oversized, very hip black glasses and an equally hip goatee. You could easily imagine him lecturing on Abstract Expressionism at one of the colleges nearby – and being regarded by his students as benchmark cool.

'And you are the Norm?' I asked.

'I am indeed "the Norm". But not, I hope, *the norm . . .*'

A small smile crossed his thin lips. *Oh God, he's flirting with me.* Three days ago I would have been flattered. Today . . .

'I'm afraid I don't have much time,' I said, 'and I know you close at four.'

'And Benjamin the Brilliant probably told you that I only mix paint when paid.'

'Why do you call my son that?'

'You mean, Benjamin the Brilliant?'

'Yes, *that.*'

'Because he is that – brilliant.'

'Really?'

'Did my tone suggest irony?'

'Well, actually, it did.'

'A bad habit of mine, as my ex-wife never stopped telling me.' *And thank you for that little snippet of personal information.*

'But how do you know that my son is so . . .'

'You can say the word. *Brilliant.* How do I know that? He's been buying paints from me for around a year – and he's been dropping down here every five or six weeks, so we've started hanging out a bit. Quite an amazing cognizance of art, your son. Quite a lot of self-doubt in the mix as well. When he told me about getting that large-scale collage accepted at the Maine Artists show last year, I made a point of driving up to Portland for an afternoon and checking it out. And I have to tell you, Benjamin is brilliant.'

I felt a great frisson of maternal pride – and also immediately sensed that, like his tutor Trevor, this Norm character had assumed a mentor role in my son's life; the understanding, supportive paternal figure he'd never had.

'I couldn't agree more with you,' I said, 'but hearing you say it – someone who undoubtedly knows a lot of artists . . .'

'Your son's got it. And I was really pleased and, quite honestly, relieved to hear him on the phone yesterday, wanting to order paint, and talking about the big new canvas he's almost finished. I'd heard from one of his professors about his breakdown. I hope you don't mind me calling it that . . .'

'Why should I mind when it's entirely accurate?'

'Anyway, I had something similar when I was at the Rhode Island School of Art and Design, and I ended up drifting away from the ceramic stuff that was my specialty back then. Fell into this and that – teaching, art design at ad agencies, eventually this little shop which is, at least, my own. But I never got back to what I wanted to do . . . and I'm monologing, another of my bad habits. Anyway, it's great that Benjamin has found a way back to his work. And his need for my Tetron Azure Blue – that is, as they say in the San Fernando Valley, way cool. Because Tetron Azure Blue is, as you can gather, a highly rarefied color. Subtly, but significantly, different from other sky blues. But here I am, continuing to monolog as usual – too much time alone mixing paint – when you've obviously got better things to do.'

'You said you needed payment first before you mixed the color.'

'I'm afraid it's a strict rule of mine, having once been the sort of artist who stiffed many an art supply dealer, and having been far too indulgent when I started this business about offering credit. So I'm afraid I need one hundred and twenty-seven dollars from you before I work my alchemy in the backroom . . . which should take no more than thirty minutes.'

I tried not to blanch at the price. Norm could see my shock.

'I know, I know,' he said. '*Mucho dinero*. But if you want my Tetron Azure Blue, you pay a high price. But it's a price worth paying – as it has the most exceptional depth of coloration.'

I handed over my credit card. As Norm swiped it in the terminal attached to his cash register he said:

'I've got an espresso maker and a reasonably comfortable old Chesterfield chair in the back. So I'm happy to make you a good coffee and offer you more scintillating conversation while I mix the paint.'

I signed the credit card receipt.

'Since it's such a beautiful day . . .' I said.

'I hear you,' he said, trying to mask his disappointment. 'The river's two blocks over to your left. I will have all this ready to go by three-forty-five.'

I thanked him. Following his advice I walked the two blocks over to the Charles. It was the stretch of the river that ran, on this side, in front of the Boston University campus and gave you a perspective on Harvard imposing itself on the opposing Cambridge side. Two academic worlds – one ultra-elite, one several notches down the prestige food chain – staring out at each other. And separated by this river, along which a nascent colony was once constructed. From that early settlement emerged this city, this nation – and with it, so many hundreds of millions of stories of everyone who, in one way or another, did time here. Stories which largely vanished with those who lived them. An individual life is insignificant when considered against the metaphysics of an ever-flowing urban waterway. But one's own life should truly be lived otherwise. Because there is never anything insignificant about any of our stories – even if we ourselves consider the tale to be mundane. Every life is its own novel. And we dictate so much more about the way the story can progress and change – or remain middling – than we ever care to admit.

There were sculls on the river, being powered by half a dozen young men, slapping the water with oars, their unified downstrokes a miracle of timed synchronicity. There were the requisite joggers and parents with young children and a couple in their mid-twenties in the midst of a wild embrace on a park bench; an embrace that would have sparked a wave of unsettling jealousy a few days ago.

I stared out at the brownish waters of the Charles, my mind's eye full of my beloved, and how, in just over ninety minutes, we'd be naked together in bed, and he would, as before, be deep inside me, and we would tell each other again how this was the love of a lifetime, how we were no longer alone in the world.

My thoughts came back to that exchange with Norm. Clearly an interesting man. Clearly a lonely man. Clearly someone who wants to make a connection that might turn into *the connection* that changes the contours of his life.

He too was grappling with the fact that things had not turned out the way he wanted. *Don't give in to a bleak world view,* I felt like telling him. *Because life really can change on a dime.*

Back at his shop twenty minutes later he handed me a substantial shopping bag with two one-litre tins of the paint. He also had a small sample of the tint in a jar lid. Dipping a thin brush into its bluish hue, he quickly outlined a square on a piece of artist's paper, then (with several fast further dips of the brush) filled in the white space of the square so it was now all blue.

'Now there is the standard-issue sky blue you see everywhere. And then there is Tetron Azure Blue – which has such a crystalline density to it, such a pure ultramarine depth. Look deep into that square and what do you see?'

'Infinity. A very welcoming infinity. One with infinite possibilities.'

'Nice,' he said. 'More than nice. And may I ask you a personal question?'

'Yes, I'm married.'

'Happily?'

'Not at all.'

'I see.'

'But I am very much in love with somebody.'

His smile tightened into thin-lipped disappointment.

'Lucky man,' he finally said.

Forty minutes later – after deciding to walk all the way down Newbury Street and across the Common – I entered the hotel. My arm was a little stiff after lugging all that paint, but I didn't care. I was full of rising elation and manic-adjacent physical desire.

Taking the elevator up to the top floor I all but bounded down the hallway to the door of our suite, used my key card to pop the door open, and saw my suitcase just inside. Fantastic! He's here.

'Hello, my love,' I shouted, thinking he must be in the bedroom. But the only reply that came was silence.

'Richard?'

Silence.

I moved into the bedroom. Empty.

'Richard?'

Then I saw, on the bed, his new glasses folded atop his new jacket. Against a pillow there was a note. I reached for it. I read:

*Dearest Laura,*

*I love you more than anything. But I can't do this. I have to go home.*

*I am so sorry.*
*Richard*

*Four*


HAVE YOU EVER noticed how, when terrible news is landed in front of you, the world suddenly goes so quiet? It's as if the shock of the unbearable deadens all aural recognition of everything outside the reverberations of your extreme distress. I read the note once. I sat down on the bed. The same bed upon which we had consummated our love. The same bed to which we returned multiple times to lose ourselves in each other; to discover an intimacy that was hitherto a terra incognita for both of us.

*'I have never made love like that before,'* I whispered to him as we clung to each other after that first wondrous time.

*'Nor have I,'* he whispered back.

I read the note a second time. This time I tried to negotiate with it, attempting to unearth some sort of affirmative subtext in its language:

*I love you more than anything. But I can't do this. I have to go home.*

The fact that he declared his love for me so absolutely. The fact that this was the first thing he wrote. Surely that was the complete and utter truth; the veritable heart of the matter. All right, something had happened. Maybe he had to call his wife and *she* played some guilt card, which panicked him into thinking he had to go home. That's why he wrote: *'But I can't do this.'* Because she knew she was about to lose him, and had to reel him in. I wouldn't be surprised if she used their poor tragic son as a ploy. And my Richard – who's always been susceptible to familial pressure – felt stricken by this and decided he should simply get home and face the problem. But once he was back with the woman he described as arctic, removed, physically rejecting of him . . . surely he'd run for his car and find me. All would be restored between us. We'd be *us* again

I read the note a third time. And started to cry. Because I was replaying the absurd interpretation of his words that had just raced through my head. I realized that I was sounding like one of the many patients I have seen who – knowing that their cancer is probably Stage Four – still try to assure themselves they're going to beat the terminal diagnosis that is sure to follow.

*How can you sugarcoat the unbearable? It's impossible. Read the note again. It couldn't be more direct or to the point. Whatever about his declaration of love, the fact is that something has made him run off back home. And he is telling you: This is truly over.*

Yet, just three hours ago, in that restaurant on Newbury Street, everything had been so loving, so forward looking, so happy. We'd even agreed how we'd tell our respective spouses, how we'd move to Boston, how we'd spend six weeks in Paris, how we'd go to concerts and interesting plays and . . .

I started to cry again. The initial shock of it all had kept me muffled, constrained. Perhaps that was my way of not allowing the actual terrible reality of all this to be given credence. But all such efforts at restraint proved futile. The sobs were now something akin to keening. Me the original tight-lipped stoic – who, in recent time, was unnerved by even the slightest choked whimper emerging from my once ruthlessly rational self – was now weeping uncontrollably. I made no effort to bring it under control. Life is littered with disappointments. Life is strewn with setbacks. We all learn how to weather the small defeats, the nagging reversals of fortune, those interregnums where quiet desperation seems to be the ongoing order of the day. But even in these difficult passages, the majority of us still travel hopefully. Because hope is the one true commodity we all desire. But when hope is destroyed in such a way that it is not simply dashed, but actually murdered . . .

Outside of the death of a child, is there any death more terrible than the death of hope?

I sat on the edge of the bed, crying for a very long time. A moment came when I was so spent I felt like crawling under the covers and shutting out the world and telling myself that when I woke with the dawn this entire nightmarish tribulation would be behind me, and I would stir into consciousness to find Richard beside me and all would be right again with our life, with us.

*Us.*

I stood up, pacing the room, thinking, thinking. Telling myself that all I had to do was talk with him – a good long loving talk, in which I would reassure him that he could do this, that what we had was magical. As he said to me just a few hours ago: *'How often does this – us – happen in a lifetime?'*

He meant that. I know he meant that. Just as I know he adores me. Love at its most authentic, its most veritable, its most unquestionable.

Richard told me he loved me. That was no projection. That was the truth.

My hands shaking, I dug into my bag and found my phone. The quasi-rational side of my brain proclaimed:

*Don't you dare call him. He told you it's over. Why look for further desperate grief when you know there's no hope here.*

But another, seemingly logical, part of my psyche insisted that I make the call.

I hit Richard's number, and sat down again on the bed, my free hand reaching for one of the metal slats in the headboard: a way of steadying me, of keeping me somehow grounded.

The phone rang and rang and rang. Oh God, he's turned it off. To ensure there's no contact, no conversation, no chance of any reconsideration of his decision to flee. Please, please, please, give me a chance to—

Click. He came on the line.

'My love . . .' I said.

I could hear traffic noises in the background. And little else.

'My love, my love? Richard? You there?'

Finally:

'Yeah, I'm here.'

The voice was flat, denuded. There was a slight echo when he spoke. Coupled with all the ambient highway sounds it was clear he had me on speaker phone in his car.

'I love you,' I said. 'I so love you and I know how huge this all is, how having to end a marriage – even a hugely unhappy one – is such a vast—'

'Please, Laura. Stop.'

His tone chilled me. It was so emotionless, so vacant, with such a discernible sadness behind the void.

'If you just turn back and meet me somewhere, I know we could—'

He cut me off.

'I can't.'

'But you know that what we have is—'

'I know that. And I still can't . . .'

'But my love, after everything we said to each other . . .'

'Yes, I remember everything we said.'

'Was it all one big lie on your part?'

I could hear what I thought was a sob, and one choked back quickly.

'Hardly,' he finally said.

'Then you know that this, *us* . . .'

'Us,' he said, his voice so quiet, so toneless.

'*Us*. As we said, the most important pronoun . . .'

Silence.

'Richard, please . . .'

Silence. I said:

'Certainty. You talked about certainty.'

'I know.'

'Surely then you also know—'

'That I just can't . . .'

'But why, *why*, when you know how this sort of love only happens once, maybe twice?'

'I know all that. I know everything. But . . .'

Silence.

'Richard?'

'I've got to go.'

'Do you love me?'

'You know the answer to that.'

'Then please, *please*, turn around and come back here. We can—'

'We can't. Because I can't. That's all I can say.'

Silence. I could hear another choked sob. Then:

'Goodbye.'

And the line went dead.

I immediately hit 'redial'. And got a generic recorded voice:

'The person on the other line is not answering the phone right now. Please try back at a later time.'

I tried back one minute later, then five minutes later, then every five minutes after that until it was almost six p.m., and sunlight had been supplanted by the darkest night imaginable. During that hour when I relentlessly kept ringing him back – and kept getting that generic message (had he done something to turn off his voicemail, so I couldn't leave him a plea to reconsider?) – I kept running through our conversation, kept hearing the sob that choked his voice, kept trying to fathom why, when he all but declared his love for me, he had to keep saying: '*I can't.*'

But the answer to that question was already there. He couldn't start a new life with me because he just couldn't.

*I can't.*

There it was, in all its plain, unadorned truth.

*I can't.*

As that distressing hour drew to a close – and I finally stopped pacing the floor, and bursting into tears, and telling myself repeatedly that if he'd just turn his phone back on we could solve this (*solve* – as if this was a problem with a simple solution) – those two words kept tolling in my head like a funeral dirge.

*I can't.*

I so wanted answers, so wanted to know how he could, in just a few short hours, go from proclaiming I was the love of his life to '*I can't.*' But why look for answers when there is such a painfully evident one in front of you?

*I can't.*

No explanations, no entreaties for understanding, not even an attempt to offer me the slightest possibility of hope, a sliver of light behind this wall of resistance.

*I can't.*

The door had been slammed shut. Conclusively. Permanently. Try as I could to negotiate with this, the truth was non-negotiable.

271

*I can't.*

My head was reeling. So this is what it must have felt like when that truck slammed into Eric and he was sent into free-fall. The trauma of losing all control of your immediate destiny; of having everything you believed was solid, true, *there*, pulled away from you. With the result that you are now heading, with great velocity, towards the hardest surface you've ever encountered. Eric. My love. How I had wondered, in my darkest moments, if, in those terrible seconds between the initial impact and the landing that twisted his neck and flattened the entire left side of his head, he had the horrible nanosecond realization that he was going to die. That's the thing about free-fall. Even someone deliberately jumping out of a window must not think that there will be that horrendous impact. Until it actually happens.

I moved away from the hotel window – this jumble of free-fall thoughts spooking me.

But this was free-fall. And the landing would be a hard, despairing one: the return to my old life. The re-entry into a marriage that was lifeless, devoid of love.

The death of hope.

A living death. Based upon the recognition that the prospect of happiness had just been extinguished again.

Could I race to my car, race up to Bath, run to his front door, pound on it until he answered, fling myself in his arms, tell him we had to act upon all that we knew and felt for each other, fend off his angry wife, and convince him to drive off into the night with me?

*I can't.*

Now that was me talking.

*I can't.* I want to make a scene. I want to beg him to reconsider. *I can't.* Not just because I know it wouldn't change anything. But also because, quite simply, *I can't.*

With this realization came more tears. I had not cried like this since the police told me about Eric. But now the anguish was underscored by twenty years of life, in which real love had been absent.

The death of hope.

I moved over to the sofa, oblivious to the fact that there were no lights on in this room; that I was alone in the dark. I replayed everything that had happened since Friday. Every remembered conversation, every story we told each other, the first time he touched my arm, that moment in the Public Gardens when he first took my hand, the nervous delight he showed when he cast off the dull insurance-man clothes, my confession about Eric, his confession about Sarah, the dawning shared realization that we were falling in love, that extraordinary first kiss, the taxi ride to this hotel, the way he promised me to be mine forever when he first entered me, all the proclamations of love and excited future plans.

And then . . .

The death of hope.

*I can't.*

I wish I could dismiss it all as a fever, a virus, to which I briefly succumbed. But I knew it to be so concrete, so authentic, so rooted in reality. That made it even more unbearable. If it had been just some gushing, crazed romance . . . But this was it. The connection that I so privately longed for; the great love story I so wanted to have in the time remaining for me. To have been given a passionate glimpse of this new life – to have been told this was my future reality – and then to have had the whole magnificent edifice decimated only moments after it seemed so secure . . .

I now wanted to be furious, to turn my grief into pure undistilled rage. But I've never been able to do anger at such a vehement level. More tellingly, this was a man I was certain that I loved – and who'd shown me, in turn, the most extraordinary love. So there was just the most profound sense of loss. And of hurt.

The room seemed to grow darker. I felt completely immobile. The fact that he had also left his new jacket and glasses behind – he couldn't have been more absolute about divesting himself of the man he had decided to transform himself into, and return to the self and the life he didn't want. A stunned rationality had taken hold of me – which I knew would soon be overtaken by even more acute grief as the reality of what had just happened truly gained purchase.

*Bing.*

Oh my God. A text! He's texting me. Telling me he's made the mistake of his life, and is en route back to me right now.

I scrambled for the phone. There was a text. It was from Lucy. I felt myself get shaky again. Tears welling up in my eyes. A cry working its way up my throat. So much for that alleged moment of clinical calm. I wiped my eyes and peered at the screen.

**Just wanted to check in and get an update. You have me guessing! The apartment is yours when you want it. See you tomorrow. I am so envious. And that's from only surmising what your news is! Love – Lucy**

Before I could break down again I dialed her number. Lucy answered on the second ring.

'Hey there!' she said, her tone intimating that she knew romance – that commodity we both lacked – had come into my life. 'So can you tell all now?'

'I need a friend,' I said, my voice lifeless, flat.

'Oh God, I thought—'

'That the news was good? It was. But—'

I broke off, forcing myself not to break down.

'Oh, Laura . . .' she said, sounding so sad.

'I'm still in Boston. I have to go get my car, which is over by the airport. But I could be with you in about three and a half hours.'

'You get here whenever. I'll be up and waiting.'

I went into the bathroom and threw some water in my face, managing to avoid looking at myself in the mirror. Then I went into the bedroom and quickly folded up the leather jacket – dealing with it the way I had dealt with a leather jacket that belonged to Eric, which he'd bought in a Cambridge Army and Navy shop and which I had to fold up after he died. Though I gave away most of his other clothes I kept his jacket. Because he so loved it and wore it all seasons except for the sticky height of summer. Because it too was an old Air Force jacket. Like the one which I was now folding and stuffing into my little suitcase as quickly as I could. Then, pocketing his glasses, I pulled up the telescopic handle of my suitcase and headed to the door, not wanting to look back in case the tears were triggered again.

I headed out the hotel entrance and to the street. There were a couple of cabs outside. I asked one of the drivers how much it would cost to get me to the Fairfield Inn Airport Hotel. He said around thirty bucks, plus three-seventy-five for the tunnel and, of course, there was the tip. Forty dollars. I don't spend that sort of money on luxuries like taxis. So I crossed the street, entered Park Station, and at a cost of two dollars I made it to the airport half an hour later. Then I had to wait twenty minutes for the hotel courtesy coach – which stopped at all the terminals and didn't deposit me at the hotel until around seven-thirty p.m.

My car was in the lot, exactly where I parked it just two days ago. Loading my suitcase in the trunk I thought: *I am a different person than the one who got out of that vehicle just over forty-eight hours ago.* But another part of me simultaneously reasoned: *The only thing that has changed in your life is that you now have a huge sorrow to carry forth with you.*

The highway was clear all the way north. I blared the radio, trying to lose myself in that evening's NPR programing, to keep the anguish at bay, occasionally wiping tears from my eyes, keeping my foot down on the pedal, making it to Lucy's front door just before ten-thirty. All the way up to Maine, one supposition kept dogging and unnerving me: had I been more attune to the subtext of the moment – had I said to him, 'Yeah, let's do the art supply shop together, then get our suitcases at the airport' – would we be in bed at the hotel right now, telling each other yet again how lucky we were to have found such love at this juncture in life?

This question got raised around an hour after I arrived at Lucy's house. When I reached her door she took one look at me and put her arms around me, saying:

'You need a very large drink.'

She produced a bottle of something French and red. We sat down in the two overstuffed armchairs by her fireplace. The whole story was recounted by me in the sort of hushed, emotionless tone of someone who has just witnessed a terrible accident and is reiterating her account without realizing that the calmness she is displaying is a byproduct of the trauma suffered. When I finished, Lucy said nothing for a very long time. But I could see her trying to keep her own emotions in check. I looked at her, bemused.

'You're crying,' I said.

'Does that surprise you?'

'I'm . . .'

Words were suddenly beyond my reach. It was as if I had lost all my bearings, my way in the world. Whatever small reserves of equilibrium had gotten me through the past few hours had just run dry. I was truly lost.

That's when I found myself letting go again. As the crying escalated Lucy came over and held me for the many minutes it took me to subside, never once trying to soothe me with any kind words or the sort of specious bromides that well-meaning people often invoke when faced with someone in the throes of grief. Instead she just let me cling to her until I was cried out. Then I staggered off to her bathroom to wash my face and attempt to do something with makeup that would lose the terrible darkness that had formed around my eyes. When I returned she handed me my refilled glass of wine and the following smart observation:

'I won't say something stupid like, "You'll get over it." Because I don't think you will. But what I will say is this – that man has already realized he's made the mistake of his life. Though part of me despises him for his cowardice – and most especially for causing you such horrendous anguish – part of me pities the sad bastard. Because even if it will always hurt you in some way – as I know it probably will – the truth is you will find some sort of accommodation with this heartbreak. And as to your earlier question, would the two of you still be together if he hadn't gone off to fetch your suitcases—'

'If I hadn't been clueless to what he was actually telling me,' I said, cutting her off.

'Clueless? Oh, please. Even if you were together now, his doubts, panic, *whatever*, would have started the moment he was away from you.'

'But had we been together tonight, perhaps he would have—'

'What? Had the Pauline conversion that would have kept the two of you together?'

'It was love, Lucy. Real love.'

'From everything you reported, I believe you. And that's why he too will be broken by this. But still too frightened, too cowed, to get back in touch with you.'

Silence. Then Lucy said:

'Do you know why I cried earlier? In part, because of the hurt rendered on you. But also – and I hate to admit this – because of sheer, sad envy. How I have longed to feel what you've felt for the last few days. To be wanted that way by someone. To find actual love – even if it just lasted a weekend. To think: *I'm no longer alone in the world.*'

I shut my eyes and felt tears.

'You have your children, you have your friends,' Lucy said.

'And I'm still alone.'

Another silence.

'We're all alone,' she finally said.

We talked until well after midnight, finishing the bottle of wine. I managed to avoid another bout of tears. Then exhaustion hit. Lucy pointed me in the direction of her guest room, telling me that I should sleep as late as I wanted. If I woke and she was gone, I should make breakfast and coffee and loiter here as long as needed.

'And if you don't want to go home, the garage apartment is yours,' she said.

'I'm going home,' I said.

'I hope that's the right decision.'

'Whether it's right or wrongheadedly wrong, it's the decision I'm making.'

'Fine,' Lucy said, her tone lightly hinting at a disapproval she would never actually articulate, but which she clearly felt.

Lucy's guest room had a double bed with the sort of ancient

mattress that seemed to have caved in around the time of the first Kennedy assassination.

At three-thirty in the morning I admitted defeat when it came to surrendering to sleep. Getting up, getting dressed, I left a note on Lucy's kitchen counter:

*Going home. To what? Well, there's the rub. Thank you for being, as always, the best friend imaginable. And please know that you too are not alone.*

Ten minutes later, I pulled up in front of our house. Dan was sitting on the swing bench on our front porch, smoking a cigarette. As soon as I pulled up he tossed the cigarette away, his face all schoolboy guilt.

'Hey,' I said, getting out of the car.

'Hey,' he said back. 'Weren't you supposed to be staying in Boston tonight?'

'Couldn't sleep. Decided I should come home and be in time to see you off on your new job.'

He looked at me carefully.

'You really drove all the way back here in the middle of the night just to do that?'

There wasn't suspicion in his voice, just the usual quiet, world-weary disdain.

'How long have you been awake?' I asked.

'All night. You weren't the only person who couldn't sleep.'

'Dan, you don't have to do this job.'

'Yes, I do. And we both know why. But thank you for coming back in time to see me off to my new role as stockroom clerk.'

I blinked and felt tears.

'You're crying,' he said.

'Yes. You've made me cry.'

'And now I feel like an asshole.'

'I don't want an apology. I want love.'

Silence. He stood up, reaching for his car keys, clearly thrown by what I had just said.

'See you tonight,' he said.

Silence.

He headed off. Then, with a quick about-face, he turned back to me and gave me a fast kiss on the lips.

'I'm sorry,' he said. 'Sorry for so much.'

I searched high and low within me for a retort. But all that came to me was the loneliest of replies:

'Aren't we all.'

Dan got into his car and drove off to his new job. I sat rooted to the garden chair, staring up at that big black infinite sky, the limitless possibilities of the cosmos. Thinking one thought:

The death of hope.

# Thursday

SUNRISE. I USED to get up after it. Now I wake well before the dawn. A readjustment of my body clock that also arrived with my ability to again sleep through the night. Sunrise. I usually have had the second cup of coffee by the time those initial tentative shafts of light have found their way into my kitchen. On fine clear mornings – and there have been a string of them this week – the early-morning light, especially at this time of year, can be like copper filament; a luminous braiding that always seems to target the little counter where I sip the Italian roast that I make in a cafetière, and which I now get specially ground for me.

The interplay of the light, the heavy aromatics of the coffee, the fact that I have just woken up from a reasonable night's sleep without (for the past six weeks) the aid of medication. Significant small details to celebrate at the beginning of another day of life.

I have become a runner. Every morning, after a sunup breakfast, I put on a very lightweight pair of track shoes that Ben convinced me to buy (he too has gotten the running bug) and go out for a five-mile jog to the water. My route rarely changes. Houses, avenues, road, more houses (the initial stretch of neighborhood modest, the next expansive and expensive), a bridge, trees, open spaces, rolling green lawns, then that telltale white marine light announcing that I am close to the water's edge.

Running suits me. Solitary, singular, very much bound up in a daily negotiation with how far you're willing to push yourself; the frontiers of your endurance. At first, when I decided that, yes, I would force myself out for a daily run, I was a mess. I could not get myself further than a half-a-mile, and I would frequently find myself winded, or suffering the sort of physical agonies that beset neophytes to the jogging world. Then Ben – who'd become so smitten with the sport that he ended up on the university's cross-country team – told me I should come spend a Saturday with him at Farmington, during which he'd take his mother out and teach her a few tricks of the running trade. Actually my son bettered that promise, as he convinced his coach – a very nice young guy named Clancy Brown (very thoughtful and cool in his non rah-rah way, and clearly pleased to have a talented young painter as one of his star runners) – to spend an hour looking over my form. He helped me rid myself of all sorts of bad habits I had already picked up.

Since then, Ben and I run together whenever we see each other (which is about once a month – not bad considering that, when I was in college, I only went home at Thanksgiving, Christmas and Easter). My form has considerably improved. Five miles is now the quotidian target – but, as Clancy recommended, I do take one day off a week. I also pace myself with care, as I don't want to court serious injury or the sort of burnout I read about all the time in the running magazines to which I now subscribe. Now I can do the five-mile jog in around an hour – and I'm pleased with that. Like Ben, it is the ability to lose myself in the tangible physicality of running – coupled with the rising endorphins which brighten life's darker contours – that has made me such a convert.

And this morning – given the meeting I must attend in a few hours' time – an endorphin rush will be most welcome. The fact that the daybreak sunlight is so radiant certainly helps. So too does the fact that, at six-twelve a.m., which is when I started my run this morning (I now always regard the digital readout on the watch on my wrist before starting), the city of Portland is only just waking up. As such I can make it to and from my apartment on Park Street to the lighthouse in Cape Elizabeth before the bridge traffic begins to build up.

My apartment: a two-bedroom place in a reasonably well-preserved Federalist building on what I think is the city's nicest street. When I came to look at it around some months ago, my first thought was that the houses here are very like the sort you find on Commonwealth Avenue in Boston. Immediately I found myself having one of those moments of encroaching melancholy that became so predominant after that weekend, and which I finally took steps to curb (the jogging being one of the ways out of the darkness into which I fell for a time). But I still adored the street – and the apartment was, at $1,150 per month, not exactly a bargain. Just under one thousand square feet. A little homey, a little old-fashioned, a little bit scuffed up. But the owner told me (via the realtor) that he knew it needed a paint job and sanded floors and revarnished kitchen cabinets and a bunch of other home improvement details. So he was willing to knock off two-fifty per month from the rent for the first two years if I would undertake it. Again it was Ben who stepped in. We set a parts and labor budget of around $4,000 – absolutely all I could afford. In August he and two college friends literally moved in with air mattresses and sleeping bags. They did all the work in three weeks, pocketing $1,000 each. They left me a very clean and airy place of white walls and varnished floorboards. I then worked twenty hours a week overtime for the next two months – and through judicious shopping at several of the quirky secondhand stores around town, I managed to furnish it in a style that is largely rooted in mid-fifties Americana, and which Lucy deemed 'retro cool' when she first saw the apartment put together. Frankly that's a little generous on her part. It still feels very much as if it is a work in progress, just one step above basic. But there's a room for Ben or Sally when they come visit. And Ben surprised me with a gift of an original painting of his: a blurred series of blue geometric shapes, on a grayish-white background; very Maine marine light in its sensibility, very much using that Tetron Azure Blue I scored for him. I had to hold back my tears when my son showed up with the painting, telling me: 'Let this be your water view.'

He's right: the apartment itself doesn't have much of a view (it faces the rear alleyway behind my building and is on the ground floor). But outside of the occasional weekend revelers who stagger down the rear passageway late Saturday night, it is fantastically quiet. And it does get the most sensational early-dawn light. And it's been such an important bolthole for me.

Coffee and muesli finished, I washed up the dishes (I still don't have a dishwasher), then reached for my nylon running jacket on the back of the stool at the little kitchen counter-bar where I eat most of my meals. I am very conscious of the time this morning, as the meeting in question begins at eight-thirty, and is a ten-minute drive from here. I'll need to shower and wash my hair and put on the one suit I own beforehand – which means a good hour when I get back from my run. Which means I must leave now.

October again. The first Thursday in October. A year ago to the day, it was the eve of my leaving for Boston. And now . . .

Now I run.

Grabbing my keys I zipped up my jacket, locked my door behind me and hit the street. A perfect day. The sun gaining altitude, that bracing autumn chill underscoring the morning, the city still hushed, the elms and pines on my street truly golden. I turned right. Two jogging minutes later I was down by the port. Another right-hand turn, a hard uphill climb on the pedestrian pavement that accompanies the car ramp up to the bridge, then a spectacular run at suspended altitude across Casco Bay. Then a stretch of shopping centers. Then an extended neighborhood of middle-class modestness until I reached that stretch of grand homes fronting the water. The homes of the city's top lawyers and accountants and the few captains of industry that we have in the state. Homes that speak of discreet wealth. No ostentation. Just understated ocean-view reserve. Beyond this small enclave of serious money (and there are so few of those in Maine), there is a public park built around Portland's venerable lighthouse. It's a ravishing public green space; a hint of savage sea just a short distance from the city center. My run takes me right down to the water's edge, then up a path to the lighthouse: a white beacon standing in crisp silhouette against the angry majesty of the encroaching Atlantic. I read somewhere that Henry Wadsworth Longfellow – when resident in Portland – used to walk here every day. In my darker moments some months ago – when I had just moved into the apartment, when the gloom that had encircled me for so long like a particularly bad weather system was still refusing to blow off into the next county – I couldn't help but wonder if Longfellow had plotted out his most famous poem,

*Evangeline*, while following the same lighthouse route along which I jog almost every morning. And given that *Evangeline* is a sort of American *Orpheus and Eurydice* tale of separated lovers searching for each other amidst the continental vastness of this once-new world . . . well, life has its attendant ironies. Even when jogging.

This morning there were just two other runners out by the lighthouse, including a man of around seventy whom I seem to inevitably pass every morning. He's highly fit, his face as taut as piano wire, always dressed in the same gray sweat pants and a Harvard sweatshirt. As he jogged by me today he gave me his usual brief wave of the hand (which I always reciprocate with a smile). I have no idea who this man is. Nor have I made any attempt to find out, as he, in turn, has never chosen to discover my name and particulars. I sense that, like me, he prefers to keep it that way. Just as I also appreciate the fact that, for a few seconds every morning, I have this silent greeting with this individual about whom I know absolutely nothing. As he knows nothing about me. We are passing objects with no knowledge of each other's story; of the accumulated complexities of our respective lives; of whether we are with someone or alone; of the way we will individually negotiate the trajectory of the day ahead; of whether we think life is treating us well or harshly at this given moment in recorded time.

Or, in my case, the fact that, ninety minutes from now, I will be in a lawyer's office, signing the legal agreement that will trigger the end of my marriage.

* * *

*The legal agreement that will trigger the end of my marriage.*

Yes, it's legal – in that two lawyers have negotiated it, and once it is signed by both parties it will be legally binding. And the split of the shared assets we have has not been contentious. But the word 'agreement' hints at a reasonable parting of the ways. Sadly this has been anything but an amicable parting – as Dan, all these months later, still cannot get his head around the fact that I ended the marriage; that I left him because I was unhappy and felt our relationship was terminal, dead; that, as he put it during one of the many moments when he pleaded for a second chance, 'If you were actually leaving me for someone else at least I could understand. But to leave me because you just want to leave me . . .'

He never found out about how I was going to leave him for someone else, or how broken I was in the wake of all that suddenly not happening. The very fact that he never registered the emotional slide I had slipped into thereafter . . . well, that was our marriage. And one which I continued to accept in the initial months afterwards, largely because I was still carrying so much injurious sadness. Going through the motions of life, but coping with the most aching sort of loss.

My children, on the other hand, quickly registered the distress I was in. On the morning that I arrived back home before dawn to see Dan off to his new job – and found myself in tears at the realization, *I should not be back here with this man* – I was found three hours later by Sally, passed out in the porch chair in which I had parked myself; sleep overtaking me as I gazed upwards into the limitlessness of space.

'Mom, Mom?'

Sally nudged me back into consciousness. I woke, feeling stiff and unwell. When she asked me what I was doing out in the cold, all I could do was bury my head in my daughter's shoulder and tell her I loved her. Usually Sally would have reacted with adolescent horror at such a show of parental emotion – especially as I had to fight to maintain my composure when hugging her. But instead of displaying sixteen-year-old disdain, she put her arms around me and said:

'You OK?'

'Trying to be.'

'What's happened?'

'Nothing, nothing.'

'Then why are you out here in the cold?'

'That's a question I've been asking myself for years.'

Sally pulled back and looked at me long and hard, and finally asked:

'Are you going to leave him?'

'I didn't say that.'

'And I'm not stupid. Are you going to leave him?'

'I don't know.'

'Don't stay for me.'

Hugging me again tightly she then left for school.

An hour or so later I had to head back south to Portland and get Ben's paints into the hands of his professor. Heading south meant passing through the town of Bath. I still had Richard's business card, and had earlier unpacked his leather jacket from my suitcase and put it in the trunk of my car. I also still had his glasses in my shoulder bag. No, I wasn't going to do anything dramatic like drop them both off personally at his office. Though I also toyed with the idea of putting them both in a box and mailing it to him with a simple one-line note, '*I wish you well*', I instinctually knew that the best thing to do now was to do nothing. So I got to Portland and dropped the paints in with the receptionist at the Museum of Art, who assured me that she'd get them to Professor Lathrop. En route back to the car I texted Ben, telling him the Tetron Azure Blue had been delivered to the museum and should be with him tonight. Then I passed one of the many homeless men who always seem to line Congress Street in Portland and always ask for a handout so they can eat that day. The guy I saw just a few steps from the museum looked around fifty. Though he was unshaven and clearly downcast I could see from the soft way he asked if I could help him out that he was someone whom life had banged up badly. The morning had turned cold and gray. He was just wearing a light nylon jacket that wasn't providing much in the way of insulation. Walking on to my car, I retrieved the leather jacket from my trunk, then returned to where the man was crouching by a lamppost and handed it to him.

'This might keep you warmer,' I said.

He looked at me, bemused.

'You're giving me this?' he asked.

'Yes, I am.'

'But why?'

'Because you need it.'

He took the jacket, and immediately tried it on.

'Hey, it fits,' he said, even though it actually swam a bit on his lanky frame.

'Good luck,' I said.

'Any chance I could hit you for a couple of bucks as well?'

I reached into my bag and handed him a $10 bill.

'You're my angel of mercy,' he said.

'That's quite the compliment.'

'And you deserve it. Hope you get happier, ma'am.'

That comment gave me pause for thought all the way back home. Was I that transparent? Did I look that crushed? Though the man's observation got me anxious, it made me force myself to present a cheerful face to my hospital colleagues when I returned to work the next morning. By the end of the week Dr Harrild also discreetly asked if there was 'something wrong'.

'Have I done anything wrong?' I asked.

'Hardly, hardly,' he said, slightly taken aback by my tone. 'But you've seemed a bit preoccupied recently. And I'm just a little concerned.'

So was I, as I hadn't slept more than three hours a night since returning from Boston, and was beginning to feel the instability that accompanies several nights of insomnia. But I also understood the message behind Dr Harrild's voice of concern: *Whatever is going on in your life that is so clearly vexing you, you can't start letting it affect your work.*

I called my primary physician that evening – a local woman named Dr Jane Bancroft who is very much an old-school local doctor: straight talking, no nonsense. When I phoned her office and told her receptionist it was a matter of some urgency – and could she ring my cellphone, and not the land line – I got a message back five minutes later, saying the doctor could see me the next morning if that would work.

I changed plans and decided to drive over to Farmington and spend the day with Ben there. Texting my son and saying I would now arrive around one p.m., I made it to Dr Bancroft's office, as arranged, at nine a.m. – after another night where sleep only overtook me around five. Dr Bancroft – a woman of about sixty, petite, wiry, formidable – took one look at me and asked:

'So how long have you been depressed?'

I explained how the sleeplessness had arrived in my life only a few days ago.

'Smart of you to get in here fast then. But the insomnia is usually a sign of larger long-term difficulties. So I'll ask you again – how long have you been depressed?'

'Around five years,' I heard myself saying, then added: 'But it hasn't affected my work or anything else until now.'

'And why do you think the sleeplessness has arisen this week?'

'Because . . . something happened. Something which seems to have crystallized a sense that . . .'

I broke off, the words swimming before me but unable to find their way into my mouth. God, how I needed to sleep.

'Depression can be there for years,' Dr Bancroft said, 'and we can function with it for quite a long time. It becomes a bit like a dark shadow over us that we choose to simply live with, to see as part of us. Until the gloom begins to submerge us and it becomes unbearable.'

I left Dr Bancroft's office with a prescription for a sleeping pill that was also a 'mild' anti-depressant called Mirtazapine. One per day before bedtime, and she assured me it wouldn't leave me feeling groggy. She also gave me the name of a therapist in Brunswick named Lisa Schneider whom Dr Bancroft considered 'sound' (and that was high praise from her), and whose services would be covered by my health plan. I got the prescription filled at my local pharmacy. I drove the two hours to Farmington. I was relieved to see Ben looking far better than I had seen him in months. I viewed the work in progress. It was astonishing in its scale – a huge nine-foot-by-six-foot canvas – and in its ambition. Seen from afar it was boldly abstract: wave-like shapes, contrasting blue and white tonalities, with an energy and a ferocity to the brush strokes that called to mind the anger of the coastal waters which so defined Ben's childhood and also (I sensed) a reflection of so much of the turmoil that had characterized the last year of his life. Maybe it was my lack of sleep, my own personal turmoil, and seeing how Ben had articulated his own recent anguish into this clearly remarkable work (all right, I am his mother – but even given my natural maternal bias, this was such an impressive and daring painting), but I found myself fogging up again.

'You OK, Mom?' Ben asked.

'I'm just so impressed, overwhelmed.'

The tears now began to flow – despite my ferocious efforts to curb them and the sobs that suddenly accompanied them. To his immense credit, my son did not blanch in the face of such raw emotion. On the contrary, he put his arms around me and said nothing. I subsided quickly, apologizing profusely, telling him I hadn't slept well the past night or so, and I was just so incredibly proud of what he had achieved, how he had bounced back from such a difficult moment in his life.

Ben just nodded and said that I was the best mother imaginable. This set me off crying again, and I excused myself and found the bathroom off his studio. Gripping the sink I told myself that all would be better after a night's sleep.

Once I pulled myself together Ben and I went out to eat at a diner.

'We could have done something a little more fancy,' I told him as we slipped into a booth.

'Why drop money on restaurant food? Anyway, this is my hangout – and even though it's cheap I've yet to get food poisoning.'

A waitress came by. We ordered. As soon as she was out of sight Ben looked up at me and said:

'Sally called me the other day.'

'Really?' I said.

'You sound surprised.'

'Well, I just didn't think you guys were in much contact.'

'We speak at least twice a week.'

And why hadn't I figured this out? Or noticed their closeness?

'That's wonderful,' I said.

'And you sound a little amazed because you thought my cheerleader sister and her arty-farty brother could never be close.'

'I stand corrected.'

'She's a little worried about you, Mom. As am I. And she told me about the other night when you got back from Boston and she found you asleep on the porch. It's a little late in the year for that, isn't it?'

'I was having a bad night, that's all.'

'But you told me earlier that it was the only last night or so when you hadn't been able to sleep. Sunday was six nights ago – and judging from the rings under your eyes . . .'

'All right, I've been having a bad week.'

'Why?'

'Stuff.'

'Stuff with Dad?'

I nodded.

'Sally told me that too. Do you want to talk about it?'

Instinctively I shook my head. Then:

'I do . . . but I also don't think that's fair to you. Because it means you're hearing my side, not his side.'

'Not that Dad would ever dream of telling me his side of anything.'

'I know you have your problems with him.'

'Problems? That's polite. No communication whatsoever is more like it. The guy and I just don't connect. Haven't for years. I get the feeling he doesn't really like me.'

'He loves you very much. It's just that he's become so lost over the past few years. That's not making any excuses for him. I think he's genuinely, clinically depressed. Not that he would ever acknowledge that, or seek help.'

'And what are you?'

'Functionally depressed.'

'That's news to me.'

'And to me too. But this sleeplessness I've been having recently . . . my doctor feels that it's as if the depression, which I've kept so submerged for years, has finally found some sort of physiological outlet to let me know I am really not in a good place.'

'So you are getting help for it?'

I nodded.

'That's good,' Ben said, putting his hand on my arm and squeezing it, a gesture so sweet, so benevolent, so grown-up that I found myself choking back tears again.

'Sally also hinted that there was something which triggered all this.'

'I see,' I said, thinking: *My children really do discuss their parents when they are out of our field of vision.*

'Did something happen?' Ben asked.

I met my son's gaze and said:

'A disappointment.'

Ben held my gaze – and in his eyes I could see him registering this, considering its deliberate vagueness, its multiple possible meanings, its implications . . . and eventually deciding not to push the matter further.

'Sally told me you've been very much elsewhere all week – that she was cutting you a wide berth you seemed so withdrawn.'

'No sleep does that. But I have some pills to help me now. And I am determined to do what you did – get myself out of the dark wood.'

Some hours later, in the little motel room I had taken for the night (there was no way I was dealing with darkened Maine back roads on no sleep), I found myself crying again as I replayed my conversation with my wonderful son. I also made a mental note to call Sally first thing in the morning – which, for her on a Sunday morning, meant sometime after twelve noon.

Of course there was the little matter of sleep. Dr Bancroft had put me on a strong dose of Mirtazapine, 45 milligrams. And she told me that, if possible, I should take the first dose and not set the alarm clock: just let chemically aided sleep finally wash over me, and wake up when my body decided it wanted to resume consciousness. So I took the pill just after ten p.m., thinking: *If anything the drugs will take me away from this fifty-dollar-a-night motel's fifty-dollar-a-night decor.* Then I crawled into the somewhat mildewy bed with a copy of the book I'd brought with me: a collection of poems by Philip Larkin, whom Lucy had been raving about for a while. Shortly after that evening when I ran to her house after Boston, a package from our local independent bookshop in Damariscotta arrived on my doorstep. A new American edition of Larkin's *Complete Poems*, with a note from Lucy:

*From all accounts, he was the worst sort of Little Englander. But as a poet, the gent really knew how to cut to the heart of the matter and address all that big four-in-the-morning stuff we don't want to contemplate. If you don't mind a recommendation, start with 'Going' on page 28. Always know you have an escape hatch and a friend here. As you wrote me a few days ago, you're not alone. Courage and all that. Love – Lucy*

The book arrived on Thursday. Though hugely touched by the gesture, and the immense kindness of her note, given the nature of the week I didn't have the reserves of stamina to tackle anything so clearly close to the emotional bone. But I still packed it in my overnight bag before leaving today. Downing my prescribed dose of Mirtazapine I opened the volume. As suggested by Lucy I turned to page 28 and . . .

GOING

*There is an evening coming in*
*Across the fields, one never seen before*
*That lights no lamps.*

*Silken it seems at a distance, yet*
*When it is drawn up over the knees and breast*
*It brings no comfort.*

*Where has the tree gone, that locked*
*Earth to sky? What is under my hands*
*That I cannot feel?*

*What loads my hands down?*

I read the poem once. I read it again. I sat even further up in bed and went through it a third time. So that's where I've been for the past few years. The shroud of despair which I mistook for everyday vestments, and which I had pulled over myself, thinking it was my destiny to wear it. I had become convinced that sadness was a condition I simply had to bear. As much as I still ached for Richard – thinking back that, around this time last year, we were making love in that big hotel bed in Boston – I also knew, after reading that extraordinary Larkin poem, that Richard was very much someone who, given the prospect of happiness, decided the hair shirt of ongoing sorrow was one he simply had to wear. He broke both our hearts by making that choice. But what the Larkin poem told me – that the veil of sadness is always there to enshroud us, should we so choose it – was strangely comforting. Because it reminded me that, yes, I wasn't alone . . . even if I also knew that the wake of grief trailing me wouldn't dissipate for some time to come.

Then I felt the ether of grogginess drift over me. I switched off the light. With the blackout came, for the first time in days, that vanishing act from life's harder realities. Sleep.

* * *

The pills worked wonders. They knocked me out every night and ensured that I stayed knocked out for at least seven hours. The ongoing sleep – coupled with (what Dr Bancroft called) the mild anti-depressive properties of Mirtazapine – seemed to let me get through the day without falling victim to the deeper recesses of my sadness.

But I was still sad. I was still not getting over it. Around a week after I'd started taking the pills, Dan surprised me by making an amorous move in bed one night (his pre-dawn schedule and my silent melancholy had, until now, kept us even more on our respective sides of the bed). I didn't push him away. Pulling up my nightshirt, he began to make gruff, needy love to me. He was inside me within moments. He came around three minutes later. He rolled off me with a groan, then spread my legs and started trying to arouse me with his index finger. I closed my legs. I rolled over. I buried my head in the pillow.

'You OK?' he asked.

'Fine,' I whispered.

'We don't have to stop,' he said, kissing the back of my neck.

'I'm tired,' I said, shifting myself further away from him.

'OK,' he said quietly. 'Goodnight.'

And there we were, alone together again in bed.

The next evening he came on to me again – a little more tenderly this time, but still with that undercurrent of rushed gruffness that had characterized our lovemaking for years. I can't say that I was attempting to augment things – as I remained quietly detached throughout. I felt bad about my dispassionateness, because my husband was trying to re-establish a connection so long lost. All I could think about was love found, love lost – and how I was back treading domestic water with a man with whom there had been no love for years.

After our ten minutes of sex, Dan kissed me goodnight and promptly fell asleep. It was still early – around eleven p.m. – and tomorrow was Sunday. Sally was out for the evening. The house was quiet. Disquietingly so. This was the future sound of silence that would become quotidian when Sally left for college next year. The deep silence of an uneasy marriage now devoid of the necessary clamor of children, with the left-behind couple wondering how to fill the void between them.

I went down to the living room, poured a glass of red wine, and found myself reaching for *The Synonym Finder* – omnipresent on the small desk I had set up in a corner of the room. As I sipped the wine, I turned the pages until I came to the word I was looking for: *Unhappiness*. There were – and I counted them – over one hundred and twenty-two words listed to denote the dissatisfaction that is such an intrinsic part of the human condition. Flipping back to the listings under the letter *H* I noted that *Happiness* only contained eighty-one synonyms. Could it be that we search for more words to describe our pain in life rather than the pleasures we can also experience? Would I, a few years from now, on the cusp of my half-century, be sitting here late one Saturday night, flipping through the thesaurus yet again and wondering why I had forced myself to stay put?

I closed my book of synonyms. I opened the front door, I stepped out on the porch. We were now deeper into October. The mercury was on a downward curve. So I could only stand outside, covered just in a robe, for a minute or so. But in that time I resolved to end my marriage just after Sally finished school in June.

\* \* \*

I let only two people in on my plan. Lucy knew. And Lisa Schneider knew.

I called Dr Schneider the day after I made my decision to go. She'd already been contacted by Dr Bancroft, so she was expecting my call. Lisa – we were on a first-name basis onwards from our first session – was in her mid-fifties. A tall gangly woman who radiated quiet intelligence and decency. Though she had her clinical side, she was nonetheless always engaged in my story and the way I so wanted to change its depressing narrative. Her office was near the college. I began to see her once a week, every Wednesday at eight a.m., adjusting my work schedule to start at ten that morning in the hospital. As Dan was already at work by the time I drove off to Brunswick he never knew that I was now talking with a therapist about an exit strategy from our marriage – and about everything else that had been unsettling me for years.

'Why do you think you are one of the underlying reasons for your husband's emotional detachment?'

'Because the entire marriage started under the shadow of loss. My loss of Eric. Dan knew how broken I was by his death.'

'So Dan took on that part of you when he got involved with you. He understood instinctually that you did not have the same love for him that you had for Eric. Yet he wanted to be involved with you. Sounds like he made a decision to engage with your ambivalence towards him – an ambivalence that, as you've reported, was clearly there from the start.'

In a later session, when I described my ongoing lack of passion for my husband – and how I was going through the motions – Lisa said:

'But didn't you try to be passionate with him for years . . . despite the fact that you never really felt the love for Dan that you did for Eric?'

'That still makes me guilty of being with someone for two decades whom I never should have been with, and wasting his time as well.'

'So Dan never had the capacity to leave you, to register your diffidence towards him? To think, *I can do better.*'

'I could have been a better wife.'

'Did you ever reject him physically?'

'No. Whenever he wanted sex I never pushed him away.'

'Did you ever criticize him, make him feel small, insignificant?'

'I was always trying to keep him buoyed, especially after he was fired.'

'Did you ever, before a few weeks ago, sleep with another man during the course of your marriage?'

I shook my head.

'Given what you've reported to me – his isolation, his emotional distance, his anger towards you – do you really blame yourself for having an affair?'

I lowered my head and felt my eyes go all moist.

'I still love Richard.'

'Because he showed you love?'

'Because he was so right. And I lost him.'

' "Lost him" makes it sound as though it was your fault he went back to his wife. Whereas the truth is, having agreed together to leave your respective spouses he got a case of profoundly cold feet. So why was that your fault?'

'Because I feel it's always my fault.'

They call it 'the talking cure'. I don't know if it cured anything, as every time I drove through Bath I had a stab of sadness that would then linger for hours. There would be frequent moments while having sex with Dan – it was never 'making love' – when I would remember Richard's touch, his hardness, his absolute desire for me. There were times at the dinner table – especially on nights when Sally was at Brad's and Dan and I were alone – when I would get to talking about something I'd read in that week's *New York Times Book Review*, and Dan would try to show interest, and I would be reminded of the way Richard would be so engaged when it came to anything literary, and how animated the conversation always was between us.

Months passed. Winter edged into spring. I did my work. I spoke twice a week with Ben and saw him once a month – and helped him through a difficult patch when that amazing abstract painting he was working on was turned down for the big Maine Artists show that May; the reason given that he was the student artist selected last year, and they couldn't bestow the honor on him again. Though Ben understood this logic the rejection still bothered him. There were a few weeks where we were talking daily, as his self-doubt had become more vocal again, and he wondered aloud on several occasions whether he was good enough to really make it in the ultra-competitive art world.

'Of course you are,' I said. 'You know how your professors and the people at the Portland Museum of Art rate you.'

'They still rejected the painting.'

'It wasn't a rejection – and you know the rationale behind their decision. It's a fantastic piece of work. It will find a home somewhere.'

'And you are the eternal optimist.'

'I'm hardly that.'

'But you seem to be in a better place than a couple of months ago. Are things improved with Dad?'

I chose my next words carefully:

'Things are somewhat better with me.'

Because things were quietly progressing towards the big change I would institute shortly. I'd found a job – as a senior radiographic technician at the Maine Medical Center down in Portland. Besides being the most prestigious hospital in the state it had also attracted so much medical talent from Boston, New York and the other big East Coast cities, for all those 'lifestyle' reasons that local magazines trumpet. The radiography department was a significantly larger one than our modest operation in Damariscotta. There would clearly be far more patient traffic and professional pressures than I had been dealing with. I found the head radiologist – a woman named Dr Conrad – very curt and to the point. But during my interview it was evident that she was impressed. I had taken Dr Harrild into my confidence when it came to applying for this job (especially as a reference from him would be crucial). And Dr Conrad did say, after offering me the job, that I had received the most glowing recommendation from 'your boss' in Damariscotta. The job paid $66,000 a year – a $15,000 improvement on my current post. I found the apartment in Portland. Through Lucy I also found a lawyer in South Portland who told me that, as long as my husband didn't contest things, she could get the divorce through for around $2,000. Sally got accepted at the University of Maine, Orono, where she'll eventually major in business studies ('because I like the idea of making money'). She was surprisingly resilient when Brad dropped her the week after their graduation.

'I knew it was coming,' she said when she broke the news to me. 'And when you know someone's going to eventually dump you, hey . . . can you really sit there and cry when it happens?'

But when you don't know that someone's going to dump you . . .

A week after this conversation Sally took off for a summer job as a camp counselor in the Sebago Lake region in the west of the state. Ben, meanwhile, had received some truly good news – a year-long junior year fellowship at the Kunstakademie in Berlin. They only take two dozen American undergraduates a year. His new painting apparently clinched the deal for him. He was beyond dazzled by his acceptance, and was already immersed in learning everything imaginable about Berlin. To earn money for the year ahead he took a job at the summer school in Farmington, teaching painting. Meanwhile I found the apartment in Portland – and did the deal with the landlord about redecorating it myself in exchange for a lower rent.

'So when are you going to ask Ben if he and some friends would

301

like to do the work?' Lisa Schneider asked me in one of our sessions around that time.

'When I get the courage up to tell Dan I'm moving out.'

'And what's stopping you, especially now that Sally's finished school?'

'Fear.'

'Of what?' she asked.

'Of hurting him.'

'He may be hurt—'

'He *will* be hurt.'

'Nonetheless that will be his problem, not yours. My question to you is, do you want to go?'

'Absolutely.'

'Then have the conversation. It will be difficult. It will be painful. But once it is done, it will be behind you.'

I made final plans. On the week of June 15th I quietly moved a few things into Lucy's spare apartment, as the Portland place wouldn't be free until August 1st. Hoping I could convince Ben and friends to start work around August 10th (when his summer school duties were over) I figured I could take up residence there by Labor Day. I had two meetings with the lawyer in South Portland – who was primed and ready to put the divorce in motion. Then, on the day I decided I would break the news to Dan, I also gave notice at the hospital, knowing full well that word of my departure from my job would be around town the next morning. Which is why I timed my resignation to take place just an hour before I came home. After fixing dinner for us, I asked Dan if we could sit out on the front porch for a while and take in the reclining light of early evening.

Once settled there I came out with it. Told him that I'd been unhappy for a very long time; that I felt there was nowhere to go in the marriage; that I didn't think we were a good fit anymore; that, as hard as this was to do, I simply had to leave and start a life without him.

He said nothing as I explained all this. He said nothing as I told him about the job in Portland, and how I'd be moving into

Lucy's garage apartment before the place I found near Maine Medical was ready for occupancy. He said nothing when I explained that I had found a lawyer who was willing to do a no-fault divorce for us very reasonably, that I didn't want much, that he could take the house, but I did want the savings plan we had put money into over the years (and into which I did all of the contributing for the past two years), and which was worth about $85,000. Since the only other asset of ours was the house with a market value of about $165,000, he'd be coming out ahead. And—

Before I could continue he interrupted me, his face white with anger.

'I always knew this was going to happen – because I always knew you were so ambivalent about me.'

'I'm afraid that's the truth.'

'So who's the guy?'

'There is no "guy".'

'But there was a guy, right?'

'I am not leaving you for someone else.'

'You're dodging my question. Because I know that if there isn't someone now, there *was* someone. And I'm pretty damn certain you met him that weekend you were in Boston.'

Silence – during which I decided to drive the car straight off the cliff.

'That's right,' I said, meeting Dan's shocked gaze. 'There was someone. It just lasted the weekend. Then it ended. Then I came home, quietly hoping that things between us could improve. They didn't. And now I'm going.'

'Just like that.'

'You know we've been in a bad place for years.'

'Which is why you fucked some other guy.'

'That's right. If this marriage hadn't turned moribund, I would never have dreamed of—'

'"*Moribund*",' he said, repeating the word with contempt.

'Me and my big words again, right?'

'You're beneath contempt.'

'Thank you for such clarity. It makes this much easier.'

303

And I stood up and walked to my car and drove away.

Earlier that morning, after Dan had gone off to work, I had packed a final suitcase and dropped it off at Lucy's. During lunch I had returned home and cleared away my laptop, my favorite fountain pens and notebooks, and several key books, including, of course, *The Synonym Finder*. These items were already packed into the trunk of my car. When I got to Lucy's house and began to unload them I had a small private moment of grief. Lucy arrived home from the supermarket a few minutes later with food for our dinner that night. Seeing the red around my eyes she asked me:

'Was it that bad?'

'Actually, he was more angry than hurt – which was easier to deal with.'

'The hurt will come later.'

I drove over to Farmington the next day to see Ben, a date I'd arranged with him earlier in the week. When I got there he told me that his father had called him late last night and was crying down the line, telling him that I was leaving him.

'Did he say anything else?'

'He told me you'd been unfaithful to him.'

Oh God. I put my head in my hands.

'I wish he hadn't said that.'

'Well, I kind of knew that already, didn't I? Or, at least, worked it out after we had that talk following your Boston trip.'

'Your father still shouldn't have involved you.'

'I agree – but the guy is clearly so distressed by what's happened he's decided to lash out in all directions.'

'I'm so sorry. What happened – it was just a weekend thing. And the only reason it happened is because—'

'You don't have to explain, Mom. I might not like what I heard, but I am certainly not going to take his side in all this. And I'm pleased that you've moved out . . . as long as, wherever you are, there will always be a spare bedroom for me.'

'I promise you there will always be a room for you in whatever home I have for the rest of my life.'

Then I pitched him the idea of me hiring him and a couple of friends to do the renovations on the apartment in Portland. He was immediately enthusiastic, saying he'd talk to two fellow art students he knew who did a lot of part-time decorating.

'You've come to the right place for home improvements, ma'am,' he said, his voice arch and funny. But then:

'I do have to tell you something, Mom. After what went down with Dad last night I took it on myself to call Sally on her cell at the camp. And I told her what had happened, and what Dad had told me.'

Oh God . . . but this time to the power of ten.

'The way I figured it,' Ben continued, 'if I didn't tell her first Dad would have. And that would have really thrown her. Thrown her badly.'

'You did the right thing,' I said, thinking to myself: *Why is it that when people lash out in fury they do their best to entangle those closest to them in their web of harm?*

I had already arranged to drive down and see Sally at Camp Sebago the next morning. I was fully expecting her to call me a scarlet woman (or worse), and slam a metaphoric door in my face. To my surprise, however, she put her arms around me when I showed up and said:

'It's going to take me a long time to forgive my father for saying all that shit.'

We went out to lunch. I was as direct as possible with her about how her father and I had fallen out of love. I assured her that she could always count on me for everything, and that me moving to Portland wasn't me disappearing from her life.

'I kind of worked that one out already, Mom. I also worked out something else – you waited all this time to leave because you didn't want to mess up my last years of high school. And I am incredibly grateful to you for that.'

Life moved forward. My lawyer, Amanda Montgomery, counseled me not to say anything to Dan about his attempts to get Ben and Sally into his camp:

'Your children have already seen through that tactic – what we want to do now is get a deal in place without too much drama.'

Still, she had to send some very stern letters to the lawyer representing Dan, asking him to tell his client that if he made absurd demands – like wanting the house and half of the savings account and everything that I didn't take with me when I moved into that temporary apartment at Lucy's – we would now demand half the house etc. Did he really want to spend thousands in legal bills, especially when I was asking for so little and there was so little to actually divide?

Dan saw sense. The two lawyers met once and hammered out an agreement. Dan asked that it not be signed for a couple of months to give us both time to think about it; which was clearly his way of hoping against hope that I would change my mind. The curious thing was, once I had left the house he never phoned me – preferring to communicate by email, and only when he had something practical to discuss regarding the house or our children. According to Amanda – who gleaned this information from Dan's lawyer – my husband still wanted me to make the first move when it came to reconciliation, even though he had to understand that, as I was the one who'd left the marriage, that was never going to happen.

'People go truly strange in the wake of a long marriage detonating,' Amanda said. 'I sense that your husband simply can't face up to what's happening – and expects you to make it all right for him. Which, as I explained to his lawyer, was something you had repeatedly informed me was beyond the realm of possibility.'

'I feel sorry for him.'

'Not as sorry as he feels for himself.'

News of our impending divorce got around Damariscotta in the expected matter of nanoseconds. But the hospital still organized a goodbye drink for me; a little after-work soirée at the Newcastle Publick House in town. To my immense surprise, Sally showed up. And then, around an hour into the proceedings, in walked Ben.

'Surprise,' he said quietly, planting a kiss on my cheek.

Dr Harrild made a little speech, talking about how I knew more about things radiographic than he did, and how my 'professional rigor' was 'matched by an immense decency', and how the hospital would be a lesser place without me. I found myself blushing. I have never been totally at ease with praise. But when asked to speak, after thanking Dr Harrild and all my colleagues for such interesting years and such 'ongoing colleagiality', I then said this (having thought it through beforehand):

'If there's one thing I know about my work it's that it constantly reminds me of the enigmas we all live with. The discovery that what seems to be evident is frequently cloudy; that we are all so profoundly vulnerable, yet also so profoundly resilient; that, out of nowhere, our story can change. I'm always dealing with people *in extremis*, in real possible danger, and grappling so often with fear. Everyone I have ever scanned or X-rayed has a story – their story. But though my equipment peers behind the outer layer we all have, if all these years at the hospital have taught me anything it is that everyone is a mystery. Most especially to themselves.'

Three days later I awoke at five and headed south to Portland, reporting as agreed at an early hour to go through the usual employee registration process: being photographed and finger-printed, being issued an ID and parking sticker, doing all the paperwork to transfer me to the hospital's health scheme, being given a complete checkup by a staff doctor, then spending much of the day being taken around by a soon-to-be-retiring technologist named Ruth Redding – who, in her own quiet way, made it clear that this was the closest Maine came to a high-pressured urban hospital. Radiography operated day and night, 'and though we might not be Mass General, the pressure is always on. But, trust me, it's never less than interesting – and from what I saw in your file, you can handle the pressure.'

Pressurized it was, especially as we were very much an adjunct of the ER and seemed to be dealing with at least a dozen bad accidents per day. Then there was the booked-full stream of scheduled procedures – and the need to maintain time-management efficiency (in Damariscotta we might have an entire forty-five minutes twice a day when no patient was scheduled, and accident cases usually were rushed to the bigger hospital in Brunswick).

The head of radiology, Dr Conrad, was hyper-rigorous and exacting. But I had worked with this sort of boss in the past – and decided to show her, early on, that I would match her professionalism and clinical cool. Though she was notoriously closed-lipped when it came to praising others (as the other technologists in the department told me), she did turn to me after a few weeks on the job and say: 'Hiring you was a good call.'

End of praise. But it still touched me.

'So it's all right accepting praise from others?' Lisa Schneider asked during a session a few days later.

'I'll tell you something rather interesting – the crying fits that used to characterize so much of the last year have largely stopped. Yes, I can still get deeply affected by a patient. There was a sixteen-year-old girl in last week with what was clearly a major malignancy in her uterus – and that was a tough hour. But I didn't break down afterwards, as I had done so often last year.'

'And why do you think that is?'

I shrugged, then said:

'I don't know . . . maybe the fact that I am no longer in an unhappy marriage. I can't say I am in a happy place myself . . . but then again, as you keep telling me, this is a period of serious transition, so don't expect "inner peace" or zen-like calm.'

Lisa Schneider looked at me quizzically.

'Now I think you're putting words in my mouth.'

'Actually, those were Sally's words – when I settled her into her dorm room at U Maine last weekend. "You're looking a little happier, Mom. Don't tell me you've gone all inner peace and zen on me."'

'How did all that go with Sally?'

'It was a wrench, seeing my youngest child now starting college, for all the obvious reasons. Then again, having moved out of the house a few weeks before, there wasn't that terrible silence of coming home afterwards to the proverbial empty nest. Dan suffered that, however. We agreed by email that I would settle Sally in on Friday and Saturday, then leave Sunday morning – and he'd come up and see her then. Around ten o'clock that night, long after

Dan usually goes to bed, I got a call on my cellphone. It was my soon-to-be ex-husband. Sounding beyond sad. Saying that coming home to this empty house was beyond awful. Telling me how stupid he had been. How if he could turn back the clock . . .'

'And how did you reply to all this?'

'I was polite. I never once mentioned how he had talked about my affair with our children, and how monstrous I thought that all was. But when he asked if he could come over now and see me – that he really wanted to try and work things out – I was very definitive. I simply said no. That's when he started to cry.'

'How did you feel about that?'

'Sad, of course. But – and this was an interesting change – not guilty at all.'

'That is an interesting change,' she said.

'It's all interesting change, isn't it?'

'You tell me.'

'Something else happened a few days ago. During coffee break at the hospital I picked up the *Portland Press Herald* that is always left for us in the staff room every morning. Turned a page, saw a small-item in the "In State" columns – the suicide of a prisoner at the State Psychiatric Prison Hospital in Bangor. William Copeland, age twenty-six. Richard's son.'

'What terrible news,' she said with studied neutrality.

'I was very shaken by it.'

'Because?'

'Because . . . Billy would have been my stepson, had everything worked out as we – *I* – had hoped. Because I felt so sorry for Richard. Because I still feel so insanely confused about my feelings for him. Part of me still loves him. Part of me is finally somewhat angry about it all – which I know you will tell me is "good", because you think my inability to express anger has caused me to throw up these blockages that have stymied my life, right?'

'You tell me.'

Oh God, how she wielded that line all the time like a scalpel.

'I am still so incredibly hurt by what happened, and how his panic cost us both so much. Part of me thinks, *What a coward.*

309

Part of me also thinks, *What a sad man*. Part of me also thinks, *Thanks to Richard I was able to get out of my marriage*. Right now, I so feel for him. He loved Billy. His son's life was such a tragic one.'

I fell quiet for a few moments. Then:

'A day or so after reading the piece about Billy's suicide I sent Richard an email. Short. To the point. Telling him how what he was now going through was the worst thing that could befall a parent, and how I was thinking about him as he negotiated this very terrible period.'

'Did he reply?'

I shook my head.

'Did that bother you?'

'We can't script anything, can we? I mean, it's not a novel, where the writer can make happen anything *actually* happen. But, yes, there was a big part of me that wanted Richard to call me up, tell me he had never stopped loving me, that the loss of his son had finally freed him from any sense of ongoing emotional guilt when it came to the wife he'd never really loved, and – then – he shows up on my doorstep and, *voilà*, the happy ending that never really arrives in life.'

'But say that did happen? Would you open the door to him now?'

'Yes, I would. That doesn't mean I wouldn't be a little wary as well. But what we discovered in each other that weekend, what we shared . . . I am not going to diminish it by saying I spent those three days living a middle-aged romantic hallucination that had no bearing on actual reality. Better than anyone – because I have taken it apart so much with you – you know that, for me, this was so completely real. As I know it was for Richard as well. So I can say something really obvious like, "Life is sometimes so unfair." But the truth is, we are usually so unfair to ourselves.'

'And knowing that now . . .?'

I shrugged again.

'I still mourn what should have been. Just as I know that I can now do nothing about it. Maybe that's the hardest lesson here – realizing I can't fix things.'

310

'Or others?'

'That too. And now you're going to tell me, "But you can fix yourself." '

'Can you?'

'I don't know.'

'An honest answer.'

The only answer.

\* \* \*

I moved into the new apartment. All the furniture I'd ordered from assorted secondhand shops around Portland arrived over a forty-eight-hour period. Ben and his two friends – Charlie and Hayden (both stoners, but sweet) – chipped in and bought a bottle of champagne to mark the occasion. Charlie had a van. He kindly drove up to Damariscotta to collect all my clothes and books. I had arranged with Dan a time when I could return to the house and pack up my library – maybe four hundred volumes – and the things we had agreed in principal that I could take with me. Charlie then transported them down with me to the new place – where the three boys also insisted on lugging everything up the stairs for me. Then we opened the champagne and toasted the great job they had done (the place really did look airy and light). After paying them each $1,000 cash I insisted on taking them all out to a local pizza joint. When I slipped off to use the washroom at the end I came back to find the bill had been paid.

Walking back to the apartment afterwards with Ben – Charlie and Hayden had decided to head off to a late-night rock joint – he let me know that 'my friends think I have a cool mom'.

'I'm hardly cool.'

'That's your take. But I'm with Charlie and Hayden – you're cool. And the stuff you've chosen for the apartment – way cool. But hey, if you want to think otherwise . . .'

'Thank you.'

'Berlin in three days.'

'You excited?'

'Excited, terrified, worried, a little cowed by the idea of me at the art academy there.'

'"*Cowed*",' I repeated. 'Good word.'

'Like mother like son.'

'I am going to miss not having you down the road. But I also think this is going to be fantastic for you.'

'And I'm going to insist that you come spend a week with me over in Berlin.'

'I won't be able to ask for any time off until the New Year.'

'Easter then. The academy's closed for a week. I sent an email to them last week. They will rent out dorm rooms to family members of students for very little. If you book now you can find a Boston–Berlin airfare for around five hundred bucks.'

'You've really researched this, haven't you?'

'Because I know you, Mom. And I know that, though you would empty your bank account in a second for me and Sally, you hate spending a dime on yourself. And if allowed you'll talk yourself out of this trip.'

'You do know me too well, Ben.'

'I'll take that as a compliment.'

Four days later, Sally arrived down in Portland by bus. We went out for Japanese food – and she stayed the night at my new apartment, telling me:

'So you've been secretly reading design magazines for years, Mom.'

'It's hardly designer. Everything came from junk shops.'

'Which makes this all way cooler. My only question now to you is, why didn't we live this way when we were a family? Why didn't you do this for us?'

Did I feel a stab of guilt? Initially yes. But then another thought came to me; a thought which was, for me anyway, an articulation of a certain truth.

'Because I didn't realize we could live this way. Because I spent years stymieing my imagination, my horizons. I don't blame your father for that. It was me, myself and I who kept myself so hemmed in. And I feel bad about that.'

'Well, it's not like I'm going to blame you for the rest of my life. But when I finally get my own place I am going to demand payback . . . and get you to help me design it.'

The next morning we drove up to Farmington to collect Ben. He had just one duffel bag of clothes and one case full of art supplies for his year in Berlin. En route to Boston he announced that he wanted to stop by Norm's Art Supplies to pick up a half-litre of Tetron Azure Blue to pack along for Berlin.

'You mean,' Sally asked, 'you don't think they sell paints at that way-too-cool Berlin art school you're heading to?'

'I'm sure I can easily get an azure blue over there, but not Norm's. So indulge me here.'

'What do you think I've spent my life doing?' Sally asked.

'So speaks the refugee from cheerleading.'

'By the time you get back next summer I'll be a Goth with a shaved head and a biker boyfriend.'

'Is that a promise?' Ben asked.

Traffic into Boston was terrible. We only had a few minutes to spare by the time we reached Norm's. Ben had phoned ahead – and when he explained he was leaving for Berlin that night, Norm broke a rule and agreed to have the paint mixed and ready to go before getting paid for it.

I found parking outside his shop.

'You've got to see this place,' I told Sally, and we ducked inside.

'So I get to meet the whole family,' Norm said.

'Just about,' Ben said, and there was an awkward moment thereafter which Norman cleverly broke.

'Now I have to say that I am flattered to be having my own Tetron Azure Blue accompanying you to Berlin. And if you need a refill while there . . .?'

'I can always pay for it,' I said.

'You don't have to do that,' Ben said.

'Here's my email address,' I said, writing it down for Norm.

'And here's my card,' he said, all smiles. 'Drop in any time you're next in Boston.'

I smiled tightly.

Once back in the car, Ben noted:

'My mother has an admirer.'

To which Sally added:

'And even though the shop's a little too deliberately weird and I'd get rid of that goatee if I was him, he's kind of cool.'

'I'm not in the market,' I said.

'You will be,' Sally said.

'Oh, please,' I said.

'All right, live the life of a nun then,' Sally said. 'All pure and sad.'

'Haven't you noticed,' Ben said, 'Mom doesn't do sad much anymore.'

But an hour later I was very much alone. We got Ben to Logan just seventy minutes before his flight. As rushed as it was to get him checked in and over to the security checkpoint, one good thing about the lack of time was the fact that it made saying goodbye less tortured (for me anyway). Ben hugged his sister. He hugged me and promised to email as soon as he was settled in and online tomorrow. Seeing the tears in my eyes he hugged me again and said:

'I guess you could say this is a rite of passage for us all.'

Then he headed off, turning back once after he cleared the boarding-pass check to give us a fast wave. A moment later he headed into the security maze. Other passengers crowded in behind him. And I had to cope with the realization that I would not be seeing my son until Easter of next year.

Sally had prearranged to meet a group of friends that night in Boston. I'd offered to drop her off at the café on Newbury Street where she was due to hook up with them, but was relieved when she insisted on taking public transport into the city. Newbury Street still had too many shadows for me.

'You going to be OK?' she asked as we parted in front of the international terminal.

'I'll be fine,' I said. 'And anytime you want to escape Orono for the bright lights of Portland . . .'

'You'll be seeing me often, Mom. Especially because of your cool apartment.'

Then, with a final hug, she jumped the bus to the nearby T-station. She waved again as the vehicle headed out into the early-evening traffic. Then she too was gone.

A few hours later I walked back into my apartment. All the way north I was dreading the moment when I first stepped inside, shutting the door behind me, thinking: *I am very much by myself.* Though I had no desire whatsoever to be back in the place once called 'our house', returning to this empty apartment tonight was more than a little hard. Ben was correct: this was another rite of passage. And life is, verily, like this. The ties that bind are inevitably picked apart – by biology, by change, by disaffection, by the inexorable forward momentum within which we all travel. With the result that, at some juncture, you do come home to an empty home. And its silence is as huge as it is chilling.

\* \* \*

The next morning I awoke late (by which I mean nine a.m.) to a text from Ben:

I'm here. Jet-lagged and weirded out. Sharing a room with a crazy sculptor from Sarajevo. Hey, it's not Kansas, Toto. Love – Ben

There was also, surprisingly, an email from the famous Norm of Norm's Art Supplies; a rather witty missive in which he hoped I wouldn't consider him a stalker for dispatching this communiqué to me, and that he isn't in the habit of hitting on customers (let alone mothers of customers), but he was wondering out loud now if we might be able to meet up for dinner the next time I found myself in Boston. Or I could meet him somewhere between Portland and Boston like Portsmouth ('*the only non-fascist town in New Hampshire*'). He went on to explain that he was divorced with a sixteen-year-old daughter named Iris, and '*an ex-wife who married a mutual funds guy as a way of refuting all those bohemian years with yours truly*', and that he wasn't going to tell me that his favorite color was black, his favorite Beatle was John, the person in history he identified with wasn't Jackson Pollock ('*I don't drive drunk*'), and

315

this was the offer of a dinner, no more. '*Or maybe movie and a dinner, if there's something interesting playing at the Brattle Street . . . the last great revival house holdout.*'

I smiled a bit while reading the email. He did have a nice, self-deprecating comic touch. But the mention of the Brattle Street Cinema was like the mention of Newbury Street yesterday: a remembrance which triggered a flash of sadness that, though dissipated, still had, all these months later, the ability to unsettle me; to remind me that, as much as I felt myself ever freer from the bonds of despair, the grief could still reassert itself out of nowhere.

There was only one solution to such an unsettling moment: a run. I squinted out my window at the day outside. Overcast, dark, but the impending rain had yet to fall. Five minutes later I was in my running clothes and shoes, pounding the pavement, each stride an attempt to distance myself further from the heartache that, like a stubborn stain, simply would not wash clean.

When I returned home from my five-mile cascade I sent a brief note to Norm:

*I'm flattered . . . but am not in a place to even entertain the idea of a nice dinner with a clearly nice and interesting man. When and if that changes, I'll send you an email . . . though, by that time, some smart woman will have snapped you up.*

Was I flirting with him? Of course. But I also knew that, for the foreseeable, all I could do was keep running.

\* \* \*

I was running when I saw him. Running down a corridor of the radiography unit, having just X-rayed a fifty-nine-year-old construction worker whose left leg had been trapped under a falling steel beam (it was a mess). I had an ultrasound to do on a young mother (seventeen years old) with a suspected ectopic pregnancy. That was three minutes from now. Life in our unit is very much a time-and-motion study, an endless attempt to keep to the very tight schedule we work under, punctuated by emergency cases like the poor man who'd just arrived with a limb that had been virtually pulverized. But three minutes meant time for a much-needed coffee, though not enough time to run back to the staff room and use the very decent Nespresso machine that the six of us in radiography all chipped in $35 each to buy. So I stopped at the vending machine in the hallway that runs between the X-ray, ultrasound, and scanning suites. The public waiting room is also just off this corridor, which means you often run into patients and their families in front of the vending machines. Given how little time I had – and how slow that coffee machine was – I sighed an inward groan when I saw a man putting money in its slot. From a distance I could see he was in his fifties, gray-haired, old-style glasses, a zip-up golf jacket in a mid-blue fabric. Hearing my hurried footsteps he looked up. And that's when I caught sight of Richard Copeland.

He blanched at first sight of me. Looking beyond shocked. Mortified. I too was stopped in my tracks. I immediately took in just how much he had returned to looking like the man I first met that Friday at the hotel check-in. Only now the chatty charm he had displayed from the outset had been replaced by an aura of world-weariness, of resignation. As befits a man who had lost so much. Most especially his son. He met my stunned gaze for a moment, then turned away.

'Hello, Richard,' I said.

He said nothing.

'What brings you to my corner of the world?' I asked.

'My wife. She needs a scan. Some spinal thing. Nothing life threatening. More a curvature thing. They had a space here before Midcoast in Brunswick. So . . .'

I glanced down at the chart I held in my hand. A chart listing my next five appointments before lunch break. Muriel Copeland was not listed there. Sometimes there is a God.

Richard saw me check my chart.

'Don't worry,' he said, 'she's having the scan done now.'

'I hope she'll be OK. How are you?'

He gave me the most cursory of shrugs, then looked up at me again, taking me in this time.

'You look wonderful,' he finally said.

'Thank you,' I said. 'I was so horrified and saddened to hear about Billy.'

He bit down on his lower lip and bent his head again. Then, in a near whisper:

'Thank you.'

'I don't know how you cope with such a terrible—'

'I don't talk about that anymore.'

His tone was abrupt, like a door slammed shut.

'Sorry,' I said.

'I heard you're no longer living in Damariscotta.'

'And where did you hear that?'

'It's a small state.'

Silence. Then he said:

'I made a mistake. A big mistake.'

'So it goes.'

'I think about it all the time.'

'So do I.'

Silence.

His coffee finished dispensing. He let the cup sit there.

'So you live in Portland now?' he asked.

'That's right.'

'Are you happy?'

'Happier.'

Silence. I checked my watch. I said:

'My next patient awaits me. So . . .'

'I've never stopped—'

I held up my hand.

'That's the past tense.'

Silence. He hung his head.

'I wish you well, Richard.'

And I walked away.

* * *

I ran when I got home that night. I ran the next morning. I ran and ran and ran. Six days a week, five miles a day. Rarely heading out in the evening – unless the old distress was creeping in. Always up before dawn. Always heading across Casco Bay, careening my way through assorted neighborhoods, encircling the Portland lighthouse, saluting that septuagenarian fellow jogger with a quick wave, then pushing my way towards home.

Home.

The realtor called me last week, informing me the owners of the apartment – a retired couple who now live most of the time in Florida – needed to sell the place. And they needed a fast sale. As in, they would be willing to accept $190,000 if I was willing to close on the sale within two months.

'Let me think about that,' I said.

I called Lucy. She called a man named Russell Drake in Brunswick who organized mortgages. Money was cheap right now, he explained. Around $75 a month repayment per $1,000 borrowed. So if I was to borrow $150,000 dollars for a period of twenty-five years, I'd be paying $1,350 dollars a month . . . just a bit more than what I was paying right now for rent. And yes, the sum borrowed would be the equivalent of two and a half years of my salary at the hospital, so several banks would be most pleased to offer me a mortgage. 'You'll probably have a bunch of suitors – which means we can negotiate the finer points to your advantage. And yes, I think a two-month closing is perfectly doable. So shall we meet within the next day or so and get the ball rolling?'

I called the realtor back and said:

'One sixty-five is what I can pay. If the sellers accept that, we can close within the time frame they want.'

The offer was accepted the next morning.

Home.

The apartment no longer would be someone else's property in which I was loitering for a spell. It would be mine – and a place for Ben and Sally to return to in the years to come before it became theirs. The place you 'return to' inevitably becomes the place you 'come into'. As my father used to say, the farce of life is grounded in one terrible truth: we are all just passing through.

* * *

Home.

On the morning that I was to sign my divorce agreement I did my post-dawn run, then came home and showered and changed into a suit – the one suit I own. The black suit I wore at my father's funeral. The suit I should have augmented with another suit by now. But since I never wear suits . . .

There was absolutely no need to put on these funereal clothes – except that something within me told me I should mark the occasion formally. Even though my lawyer said that she could mail or courier the papers to me at home or work, I told her I would come by her office and sign them myself.

And if you are signing a legally binding document that is about to end a two-decade relationship – and one which has taken up half my life – dressing formally for the occasion seems only appropriate.

Amanda Montgomery's office was a ten-minute drive across Casco Bridge in an old warehouse building in South Portland. A quasi-funky, quasi-gentrified area. Amanda was a large, relentlessly cheerful woman around my age. She worked alone – only employing a receptionist who doubled as her bookkeeper, secretary and general major-domo. She made a point throughout the divorce of trying to keep the process as non-disputative as possible in order to keep the cost reasonable. She coolly stood down Dan's initial belligerence. Once he saw sense (and it was his lawyer who – according to Amanda – got him to lose his anger and realize that we were offering him a very good deal), it was simply a matter of 'the usual legal and state bureaucracy – and a considerable amount of tedious paperwork'.

Here I was today, on time for our prearranged morning meeting, being offered coffee by her assistant before being ushered into Amanda's office.

'My, you're dressed up,' she said as I came in. Her office had a big old-fashioned wooden desk. A big high-back swivel chair, also very much a throwback to the 1930s, a pair of overstuffed armchairs for clients. A small conference table, covered with documents. Amanda was dressed in a similarly somber suit, and explained she was due in court in an hour 'to try to stop my client from being eviscerated by his soon-to-be ex-wife. Your ex doesn't know how lucky he was that you were not interested in the sort of scorched-earth divorce I am trying to quell right now. Then again, did he ever know how lucky he was?'

'You'd have to ask him that,' I said quietly.

'Somehow I don't think that opportunity's ever going to arise. Anyway, you have a job to go to, and I have a courtroom fistfight to go to. So all we have to do now is sign the papers and they will get shipped back to the court for official judicial signature. Then they will go up to Augusta where the actual Final Decree is issued.'

I nodded, saying nothing. I could see Amanda studying me.

'You OK, Laura?'

'You mean, am I having second thoughts?'

'That has, in my experience, happened . . . though, most of the time, six months later, the client was back here again.'

'I've never had second thoughts from the moment I decided to end the marriage.'

'I always knew that. But I am still bound – not by law, but by my own set of rules – to ask that question before a client signs the papers and things are all but writ in stone.'

'I wish I had second thoughts.'

'It's a terrible moment, even if it's the right decision. The death of—'

'Hope,' I heard myself saying. 'The death of hope.'

I blinked and felt tears. Amanda said:

'I've sat here and seen the toughest businessmen in the state – real cutthroat bastards – sobbing their eyes out before signing the papers. One guy – I can't tell you who he is or what he does, because you'd know his name – old schoolfriend of mine which is how I got the case . . . he actually spent almost half an hour just staring at the document before I gently told him that his wife was categorical about the fact that the marriage was over. "I'm afraid you have to sign the papers." But he kept shaking his head, all disbelief. The death of hope. You got that one right. But when one hope dies—'

'It *really* dies,' I said, cutting her off before she could talk about new hopes, new dawns, buds sprouting from barren land, sunlight always following the darkest of nights.

'Sorry, did I say the wrong thing?' Amanda asked.

'No. I believe in hope as much as the next fool. I just know that disappointment is such an equal part of the equation.'

'Well, they're counterweights, aren't they? And you are, in essence, signing off on disappointment this morning.'

'And signing on for what?'

'Whatever you do or find next in your life. Which could be wonderful or terrible or just plain banal or a mixture of all of the above. But whatever arises, even if you make the worst decision or choice imaginable, it will all be driven by one basic thing – hope. Which is the one commodity we all desperately want to hang onto. And that's my sermon for the morning,' she said with a smile. 'Shall we get this done?'

She ushered me over to the conference table – and a legal document. I'd already read the draft some weeks ago and then the final fine-tuned version just last week.

'Nothing's changed in the interim,' she said. 'But if you'd like to read it through again . . .'

'No need.'

She proffered a pen. She flipped through the document to a signature page right at the end of it all. I looked down and saw that Dan had gotten there before me – as his tightly knotted signature adorned the line above his printed name.

'The other side did the deed yesterday afternoon. Then his lawyer dropped the papers in here yesterday evening on his way to a hockey game. Very Maine, eh?'

The pen was shaking in my hand. Why is it that your body so often tells you things that your mind is trying to dodge?

I steadied my hand. Signing the divorce agreement took two seconds. Then I pushed the document away. I wiped my eyes. I took a deep becalming breath. I sat there, knowing I had to move. Amanda put a hand on my shoulder.

'Are you all right?'

'Not really. But . . .'

'What are you going to do now?' she asked.

'What everyone else does. I'm going to go to work.'

\* \* \*

I saw the cancer immediately. It was right there in front of me. A cancer called despair.

The patient was a woman who was exactly my age. Born three months after me. A native Mainer, she told me. 'Not from away', but someone who went away to a 'pretty good college' in the Pacific northwest and 'an even better' law school in Boston, and was groomed for big things in a big 'white shoe' Beacon Hill law firm. She married a hotshot financial whizz kid and they lived far too well. 'Life in the fast lane.' Then he got caught on an insider trading scam, and his legal fees wiped them out, and she never made it beyond associate in that ultra-prestigious, ultra-WASP law firm (where she was just one of three lawyers without an Ivy League degree) because of her husband's conviction and seven years in a Club Fed sentence. After all that, she had nine months where she was out of work. Then a friend of her dad's found her a job in one of the bigger law firms here in Portland. Coming back to Maine wasn't what she really wanted. But having a soon-to-be ex-husband in prison for financial fraud wasn't helping her employment prospects, and it was a prestigious outfit 'as Maine firms go'. Even though she was finding a lot of the contractual work she'd been given to do this side of boring ('Hell, I'm a born litigator'), she was making enough to live in that condo development off the Old Port, and—

'By the way, my name is Caroline and I'm nervous as shit.'

I told her my name and explained, in my usual professionally calm voice, the scanning procedure and how, outside of the needle in her arm—

'I hate needles.'

'A small momentary prick and then it's done.'

'And I'm not ten years old and you don't have to promise me a lollipop at the end.'

'We do have them if you really want one.'

'That's your way of telling me I'm a bitch, right? Paul always says that. Says when I get into one of these manic moods I am fucking impossible.'

'A scan is always stressful.'

'And you are Miss Zen-o-rama.'

*If only you knew, if only you knew.*

'I know how worried you must be now,' I continued. 'But—'

'But *what?* I have a lump in my left breast, a very big lump near a very important lymph node. And though my doctor wanted me to have a mammogram I insisted on a CT scan – because with a CT scan you can see how seriously the cancer has metastasized. So you're now telling me *what?* To try to stay calm and focussed and centered and all that New Age shit? Did my doctor tell you I'm four months' pregnant?'

'It's there on your chart, yes.'

'But what she didn't tell you is that this is the first pregnancy that I have been able to carry beyond the initial trimester. I fell pregnant twice while married. Boom. Two miscarriages at eight and eleven weeks respectively. Now I'm pregnant again – at forty-three. An unmarried mother. Not that my firm knows anything about this yet. If I can hold onto the baby – if my body shows me a little grace this time – I am going to probably find myself professionally demoted. Especially if the father of the baby – who happens to be a partner in the same firm – leaves his wife for me. Which I don't think he'll do. Which is pulling him apart and pulling me apart. Because we love each other. Because we're so right for each other. And because I feel that, yet again, life has dealt me the shittiest hand imaginable, even though I know it was my choice to get involved with him, my choice to fall in love with him, my choice to get pregnant by him – a very deliberate choice, I should add, but you probably figured that out by now. And I bet all this is being taken down on a hidden microphone and is going to be used against me.'

'Fear not,' I said, helping her onto the bier and strapping her down. 'Anything you say here stays here.'

'So you're my father confessor, right?'

I swabbed her arm with an antiseptic wipe.

'Here comes the needle.'

Her entire body stiffened – always a sign in my professional experience of someone who expects the pain to be deservedly painful. The needle slipped in. I taped it down. I explained that the whole procedure would last ten, fifteen minutes at most.

'I know it's cancer,' she said. 'I've been on the Internet. Crawling all over the Mayo Clinic's website. From non-stop self-examination I know that it has all the telltale signs of a malignant tumor.'

'As I've often told so many people I see here, stay off the Internet when it comes to lumps and growths and blood being passed.'

'But you've got to understand – my entire adult life has been about things being taken away from me. My husband. Our home. Two wonderful babies. And now, given how the cards keep falling for me, at best I am going to lose a breast and probably the child when they put me on a huge course of chemotherapy. Given my age this will be the last time I ever get pregnant. And—'

'Aren't we getting a little ahead of ourselves here?'

'I'm going to die.'

'Did your doctor indicate that?'

'She did what all you people in the medical world do – commit to nothing until you have the actual death warrant in your hand.'

'And your boyfriend – Paul, right? What does he say about all this?'

'He came with me today.'

'That's good.'

'Before I came in here he told me how much he loved me.'

'That's even better.'

'The thing is, he'll never leave his wife. He's told me recently that, yes, he would move in with me when the pregnancy started to show. But he knows what that will do to his standing at the firm. And his wife is the niece of the senior partner.'

'But it is, nonetheless, love?'

I could see she was crying.

'Yes,' she said. 'It is love.'

'That, in itself, is wonderful.'

'I keep telling myself that. But . . .'

I wanted to say: *I know all about that 'but'.* Instead I squeezed her shoulder and said:

'Let's get this behind you.'

I left the scan room as quietly and quickly as I could, moving into the technical booth. As I programed in the necessary data I felt the usual moment of tension that still accompanies the start of each of these procedures. The realization that, from the moment I shoot 80 milligrams of high-contrast iodine into Caroline's veins, I will then have less than fifty seconds to start the scan. Begin the scan a few critical seconds ahead of the Venus phase – when all the veins are freshly enhanced with the iodine – and you will be scanning ahead of the contrast, which means you will not get the images that the radiologist needs to make a thorough and accurate diagnosis. Scan too late and the contrast might be too great.

Timing.

It really is everything.

I leaned in to the microphone on the control panel and flipped a switch.

'Caroline?'

My voice boomed out on the speaker within the scan room. She shifted her gaze to the technical booth window, her eyes flooded with fear. I followed the script I always use when it is clear a patient is terrified.

'Now I know this is all very spooky and strange. But I promise you that it will all be over in just a few minutes. OK?'

I hit the button that detonated the automatic injection system. As I did so a timer appeared on one of the screens. I turned my vision immediately to Caroline, her cheeks suddenly very red as the iodine contrast hit her bloodstream and raised her body temperature by two degrees. The scan program now kicked in, as the bed was mechanically raised upwards. Like almost every other patient Caroline shuddered. I grabbed the microphone:

'Nothing to worry about, Caroline. Just please keep very still.'

To my immense relief she did absolutely as instructed. The bed reached a level position with the circular hoop. Twenty-eight seconds had elapsed. The bed began to shift backwards into the hoop. Thirty-six seconds when it halted, the hoop encircling her head. Forty-four seconds. Forty-six. My finger was on the scan button. I noticed it trembling. Forty-nine. And . . .

I hit the plunger. The scan had started. There was no accompanying noise. As always I shut my eyes, then opened them immediately as the first images appeared on the two screens in front of me, showing both mammary glands. Again I snapped my eyes shut, thinking about how her doctor would break the news to her if the growth was malignant.

But professionalism trumped fear. My eyes sprang open. And what I saw was . . .

A fibroadenoma. I'd seen so many of them over the years I could spot them immediately – and I'd yet to misjudge one. Without question, Caroline was harboring a fibroadenoma: a solid, round, rubbery lump that moves freely in the breast when pushed and is usually painless.

They are also benign. Always benign.

I now began to scrutinize the scan with care – my eye following every contour and hidden crevasse around the two mammary glands, like a cop scouring all corners of a crime scene, looking for some hidden piece of evidence that might change the forensic picture entirely. I searched the areolas, the nipples, the ducts, the lobules, the fat deposits, not to mention the adjoining ribs, the sternum and the surrounding muscles.

Nothing.

I went over the scan a third time, just to cover my tracks, making certain I hadn't overlooked anything, simultaneously ensuring that the contrast was the correct level, while the imaging was of the standard that Dr Conrad required.

Nothing.

I sat back in my chair and found myself smiling. Good news. But news that I myself could not impart, though I would find Dr Conrad in a few minutes and hope that – after hearing about the patient's pregnancy, her previous miscarriages, and her great understandable fears – she'd show the humanity I'd occasionally seen lurking behind the granitic exterior and speed through a diagnosis to Caroline's doctor.

I peered out again at this anguished, frightened woman. My contemporary. And so much a fellow sufferer. In a moment I would reach for the microphone and tell her that the scan was over and compliment her on her bravery and brace myself for an onslaught of questions – *What did you see? You've got to tell me, is it malignant? Is it benign? What did you see?* – as soon as I walked back in to release her from the bier.

Were this my world – and it's nobody's world – what would I actually say, besides the fact that the lump is benign? What piece of counsel might I impart to her? Not wisdom – because one person's wisdom is another person's clichés. And as there are absolutely no answers to life's larger conundrums, it might be something as simple and blunt as this:

Amidst all the fear, the doubt, the longing, the setbacks, the hope for something better, the sense that you have boxed yourself in . . .

Amidst all the infernal struggles you will always have with yourself, and the realization that everything is so profoundly temporal, there is what the screen in front of me tells me: *That growth within you will not kill you.*

And even if, from this moment on, you continue to block yourself, disappoint yourself, lock yourself into an existence you know you don't want, the screen still says: *All clear.* There is a chance now. But if, in the end, you can't convert that chance into change, there is still one great consolation . . . if you choose to see it:

You're going to live.